Migration and Literature

Migration and Literature

Günter Grass, Milan Kundera, Salman Rushdie, and Jan Kjærstad

Søren Frank

palgrave
macmillan

MIGRATION AND LITERATURE
Copyright © Søren Frank, 2008.

An earlier version of the "Territories and Histories" section in the chapter on Günter Grass originally appeared in the Belfast-located journal *Quest* (vol. 2, 2006) under the title "Territories and Histories. Transgressive 'Space Travels' and 'Time Travels' in Grass's *Dog Years*."

First published in 2008 by PALGRAVE MACMILLAN® in the US - a division of St. Martin's Press LLC, 175 Fifth Avenue, New York, NY 10010.

Where this book is distributed in the UK, Europe and the rest of the world, this is by Palgrave Macmillan, a division of Macmillan Publishers Limited, registered in England, company number 785998, of Houndmills, Basingstoke, Hampshire RG21 6XS.

Palgrave Macmillan is the global academic imprint of the above companies and has companies and representatives throughout the world.

Palgrave® and Macmillan® are registered trademarks in the United States, the United Kingdom, Europe and other countries.

ISBN-13: 978-0-230-60828-3
ISBN-10: 0-230-60828-0

Library of Congress Cataloging-in-Publication Data

Frank, Søren.
    Migration and literature : Günter Grass, Milan Kundera, Salman Rushdie, and Jan Kjærstad/by Søren Frank.
        p. cm.
    Includes bibliographical references.
    ISBN 0-230-60828-0 (alk. paper)
1. European fiction—20th century—History and criticism. 2. Emigration and immigration in literature. 3. Grass, Günter, 1927—Criticism and interpretation. 4. Kundera, Milan—Criticism and interpretation. 5. Rushdie, Salman—Criticism and interpretation. 6. Kjærstad, Jan, 1953—Criticism and interpretation. I. Title.

PN3352.E45F73 2008
    809'.933552—dc22

                                                                2008007260

A catalogue record of the book is available from the British Library.

Design by Macmillan India Ltd.

First edition: October 2008

10 9 8 7 6 5 4 3 2 1

Printed in the United States of America.

for Sofie,
who in her movements knows nothing about
the inertia of matter

Contents

Acknowledgments

I am grateful to the many colleagues and friends who have been so generous as to let their ideas flow into this book. At the University of Southern Denmark, I want to thank Sten Pultz Moslund, "the phantom walking this text," for his academic composure and for his limitless faith in my abilities; Jørgen Dines Johansen, for never allowing me to choose the easy solution; Lars Ole Sauerberg, for believing in me in the first place and for his unlimited "office hospitality"; Henning Goldbæk, for being an "archive" of cultural history with a predilection for the exilic temperament; Lars Kiilerich Laustsen, for many inspiring and humorous conversations; Annelise Ballegaard Petersen, for sharing her immense knowledge of Grass with me; Thomas Illum Hansen and Benjamin Boysen, for stimulating talks; Hanne Lange, for always being there when needed; and Per Krogh Hansen, for his "narratological" gifts. At the University of Aarhus, I wish to thank Mads Rosendahl Thomsen for his intellectual sharpness and for setting up the "Palo Alto Connection." At Stanford University, my thanks go to Sepp Gumbrecht for his ability to constantly trigger my motivation and for encouraging me to stick with my original idea (and for sharing the passion of Fussball and Diet Coke with me); to Karl Heinz Bohrer, for his immense generosity and for motivating conversations; and to Jessie Labov, Franco Moretti, and Russell Berman, for inspiring talks. At the University of Copenhagen, I want to thank Anders Fogh Jensen for keeping me intellectually alert and for exemplifying in all his being just how much the matter of language matters; and Frederik Tygstrup, for his Deleuzian mind and for his encouragement during the early days of conceiving the whole project. Finally, I am indebted to everyone at Palgrave Macmillan involved in this book for their kindness and professionalism.

Abbreviations

Günter Grass:

TD: *The Tin Drum*
DY: *Dog Years*

Milan Kundera:

BLF: *The Book of Laughter and Forgetting*
ULB: *The Unbearable Lightness of Being*
Ig: *Ignorance*
AN: *The Art of the Novel*
TB: *Testaments Betrayed*
Cu: *The Curtain*

Salman Rushdie:

MC: *Midnight's Children*
Sh: *Shame*
SV: *The Satanic Verses*
IH: *Imaginary Homelands*
SATL: *Step Across This Line*

Jan Kjærstad:

Se: *The Seducer*
Co: *The Conqueror*
Di: *The Discoverer*

Prolegomena: Toward a Literature of Migration

For your *Bildung* you should choose the most difficult and splendid problem, but as subject for a dissertation choose no more than a very limited and remote corner.

—Nietzsche: Letter to Paul Deussen, 22 June 1868

During the twentieth century, we witnessed the revenge of a new nomadic life form over the hitherto hegemonic settler life-form. Today, Daedalus has once again put on his wings in order to challenge the force of gravity and soften the roots of belonging, whereas Odysseus's homecoming (a return to and of the same order) no longer seems possible in our contemporary world of rapid transformations. And yet, one of the defining myths of Western culture is that rather than with the feet on which we move, we imagine ourselves equipped with roots intended to keep us in place. However, the main protagonist in the twentieth century turned out to be the migrant. No longer to be looked upon as anomalous, migration has actually become the norm and has resulted in a profound renegotiation of the concepts of identity, belonging, and home.

Is this a good thing? It probably depends on who you are, but it seems pointless to dispute the fact that the twentieth century was an age of migration. Events such as the two world wars, the countless number of regional wars, the process of decolonization, and the emergence of totalitarian regimes played a major role in bringing about the waves of migrants, refugees, and exiles that crisscrossed the globe during the twentieth century. In addition, technological developments from the late nineteenth century until today (e.g., Greenwich mean time [GMT], telegraph, telephone, railway, automobile, airplane, radio, television, internet, etc.) have made traveling and communication possible on a scale previously unimaginable. The consequences are there for everyone to see: the world is accelerating and contracting at one and the same time; material and immaterial borders are blurring and becoming permeable; the old nation-states are imploding while new ones are emerging; the global permeates the local, while the local dissipates into the global; and the production of human identity is informed by new coordinates. It is a time of the redrawing of maps, of intense deterritorializations and reterritorializations: people are passing borders, but borders are also passing people.

Besides the immense consequences for society and humanity in general, these technological developments and world-scale events have also had a deep impact on literary history in that we can trace an increase in the number of migrant authors within "the world republic of letters." By choosing to split up the post–World War II period into two volumes—one dealing exclusively with migrant authors, entitled *1948–2000: The Internationalization of English Literature,* and one dealing primarily with "core English" authors, entitled *1960–2000: The Last of England?—The Oxford English Literary History* not only confirms the numerical escalation of migrant authors, but also testifies to their growing literary, sociological, and phenomenological importance. Besides leading to a problematization of the way in which literary studies and literary historiography are traditionally organized in accordance with nationally based curricula, the growing number of authors belonging to two or more countries imposes upon us the task of clarifying the thematic and formal distinctiveness of migrant literature vis-à-vis nonmigrant literature, which is precisely one of the primary ambitions of this book.

I will also argue that a general transformation is taking place in the way much literature is written, both as a result of the influence migrant authors exert on nonmigrant authors and as a consequence of the intensified mobility and extraterritoriality in our globalized world. As Rebecca Walkowitz claims, it is the literary system as a whole that is influenced by the political and social processes of migration and not merely the part of the system that involves books written by migrants.[1] Consequently, "migration literature" refers to all literary works that are written in an age of migration—or at least to those works that can be said to reflect upon migration. The point is that whether we favor social context or literary content/form, the distinction between migrant and nonmigrant writers becomes increasingly difficult to uphold: "The literature of migration is not written by migrants alone," Leslie Adelson states simply.[2]

So, using as a starting point the assertions that the twentieth century was an age of migration and an era during which more and more authors had migrant backgrounds, this book seeks to examine the *distinctiveness* of literature written by migrants; in addition, it claims as one of its main theses that there is a *tendency* in nonmigrant literature to reflect themes and employ discursive strategies often thought of as typical of migrant literature. This book therefore proposes a shift in terminology from "migrant literature" to "migration literature"—that is, a move away from authorial biography as the decisive parameter, emphasizing instead intratextual features such as content and form as well as extratextual forces such as social processes.

* * *

Before proceeding any further, I would like to present a "reader's guide" to what follows in this introduction as well as in the book as a whole. In the following I explain migration as my chosen conceptual point of departure and discuss the methodological implications that such an approach entails. Subsequently, I touch upon some theoretical reflections on the relationship between aesthetics and sociology in order to establish migration as a concept of both aesthetic and sociological relevance before briefly introducing the material to be analyzed to support the theses of this study. The next step entails a discussion of the concept of migration, and this is followed by reflections on the principles of selection with regard to my choice of material. After that I will briefly introduce scholars who have worked on the relationship between literature and migration, but at the same time I will point out in what way my understanding of migration differs from traditional understanding. This is followed by a discussion of methodological considerations in which I attempt to outline my reading strategies for the analytical chapters to come. Then follows a more precise definition of the concept of migration as employed in this book.

I move on from there to propose five thematic and three stylistic subcategories that are significant for determining the distinctiveness of migration literature. What is more, in relation to each of the subcategories, I explain the criteria and qualities required if we are to speak of migration literature. This delineation of constitutive elements and qualities functions as a framework for the subsequent analysis of the novels. In the last part of the introduction, I will introduce the theoretical positions of Georg Lukács and Gilles Deleuze, especially some of their aesthetic concepts and thoughts on novelistic form that I find relevant for developing a more thorough definition of the migration novel and that will inform my reading of the novels.

After the introduction I will move on to the core of the study, which is the analysis of four contemporary novelists, Günter Grass, Milan Kundera,

Salman Rushdie, and Jan Kjærstad. I have chosen to devote a chapter to each author, and I present them in chronological order—that is, Grass is followed by Kundera, Rushdie, and, finally, Kjærstad. I will focus on two or three novels by each author, and, in the course of my analysis, I will bring in theoretical reflections of a more specific nature when it seems relevant and productive. This means that the theoretical problems discussed or only briefly touched upon in this introduction will be elaborated, illustrated, and supplemented throughout the book. Finally, in addition to summarizing some of the main analytical "results," the book concludes with a brief discussion of the role and method of comparative literature and literary studies in general in an age of globalization and hypercanonization.

*   *   *

In his seminal essay "Philology and *Weltliteratur*" (1951), Erich Auerbach outlines a methodology for the future of literary scholarship in which the key notion is *Ansatzpunkt*. The *Ansatzpunkt,* or the "point of departure," is like the striking of a chord, a preliminary note, which determines what follows. The point of departure represents a distinct angle and an innovative grip that provides the literary scholar with a principle of selection.[3] To Auerbach, the original point of departure is of great importance in twentieth-century literary studies, primarily because the amount of accessible material constantly increases in the globalized world market of literature, making it impossible for the literary scholar to survey the totality of material at his or her disposal. But from this problem of quantity follows a problem of epistemology: it becomes increasingly difficult for the literary scholar to locate patterns of order in the unmanageable body of material.

Implied in Auerbach's description is that the *Ansatzpunkt* functions as a prism with the necessary ability to link authors or works hitherto not seen in relation to one another. In addition, it enables the critic to shed new light on these authors or works precisely because of the affiliations made possible through the *Ansatz*. The question of *linkage* relates to the problem of synthesis, of establishing a pattern within a chaotic system, and here Auerbach evokes a twofold method consisting of intuition and personal commitment grounded in historical experience. The question of *illumination* relates to the problem of quality and relevance, and here Auerbach speaks of the *Strahlkraft* of the good point of departure. In order to possess this illuminating power, the point of departure must be both dynamic and rooted in concrete material—that is, it should not spring from some theory or historical period, because that would be a case of the abstract-general subsuming the specific. Furthermore, the point of departure must be selected from a confined and attainable body of material, and the analysis of this material must be able to organize and shed new light on a larger body of material. That is, a good point of departure must be both precise and intrinsically related to its object; it cannot be abstract in itself; and it should nonetheless point to general perspectives. To sum up: The problem posed by the immensity of material is solved by the good point of departure because it is capable of both synthesis and radiance.

The *Ansatzpunkt* for this book is migration, a concept that had come to play an increasingly significant role in the twentieth century and the beginning of the twenty-first century in relation to politics, economics, geography, culture in general, and literature in particular. I will argue that migration is capable of acting as a "synthesizer" (which differs from a "totalizer") in the bringing together of four otherwise distinct novelists. What is more, migration as *Ansatspunkt* enables me—by the sheer fact of bringing these canonized authors together—to illuminate them in new ways just as it makes it possible to shed light on much of contemporary literature as it arguably bears traces of migratory thematics and stylistics.

To paraphrase Georg Lukács in his foreword to *Entwicklungsgeschichte des modernen Dramas* (1911), I would say that the fundamental questions posed in this book are the following: Does a modern novel of migration exist, and, if so, what style does it have? However, in Lukács's historical-philosophical approach, style is from the outset intrinsically related to the social sphere. Each epoch has its own aesthetic form, so to speak: "But in literature what is truly social is form. [. . .] Form is social reality, it participates vivaciously in the life of the spirit, and therefore it does not operate merely as a factor acting upon life and molding experiences, but also as a factor that is in its turn molded by life."[4] What is expressed here is a belief in the mutual dependence of worldview and form. In "Zur Theorie der Literaturgeschichte" (1910), he says, "Every form is an evaluation of and a judgment on life, and it draws this power and strength from the fact that in its deepest foundations form is always an ideology. [. . .] The worldview is the formal postulate of every form."[5] In the present study, I argue specifically that the concept of migration functions as a bridge linking aesthetics and sociology, as migration relates to both theme and form.

A few pages further on in "Zur Theorie der Literaturgeschichte," Lukács actually formulates the exact opposite view when he describes form as the petrification of a moving life. That is, form is not considered the "truly social," rather, form and aesthetics are autonomous phenomena characterized by their insularity. In his discussion of Lukács's text, Franco Moretti claims that Lukács actually radicalized this second version of his concept of form in the years between publication of *The Soul and the*

Forms (1910) and *The Theory of the Novel* (1916/1920). I am not sure, though, that I can follow all of Moretti's conclusions in his elaborations on Lukács's idea of form:

> In *Theory of the Novel* the *historicity* which is consubstantial with the novel means that the formal accomplishment of a novel is always and only "problematic": a "yearning" for form rather than its attainment. Between Life and Form, history and forms, the young Lukács digs an ever-deepening trench. Life is "movement," form "closure." Life is "concreteness" and "multiplicity," form "abstraction" and "simplification." Form is, in a summarizing metaphor, petrified and petrifying: life is fluid, ductile, "alive."[6]

Here, Moretti actually points to Lukács's idea of the unattainability of formal perfection in *The Theory of the Novel,* only to argue that this means a deepening trench between life and form. However, as I see it, Lukács sticks with his idea of the interdependence between sociology and aesthetics when in *The Theory of the Novel* he speaks of the novelistic form as "something in process of becoming [etwas Werdendes, als ein Prozeβ]."[7] The restless and migratory form of the novel is thus an aesthetic attempt to answer the questions posed by the new social and cultural condition characterized as the age of migration.

Moretti himself is clearly influenced by Lukács's idea of the interdependence of sociology and aesthetics, and in his own work he attempts to practice what he calls "sociological formalism." To practice sociological formalism most productively means turning one's attention toward the study of the temporary structures that usually go by the name of genres (i.e., cycles situated between the flow of events and the structure of the *longue durée*). Here, literary texts are seen as historical products organized according to rhetorical criteria—that is, according to Moretti, a Darwinian combination of random variation and necessary selection: "In our case: *rhetorical innovations,* which are the result of chance; and a *social selection,* which by contrast is the daughter of necessity."[8] Performing literary criticism understood as a historical discipline thus calls for concepts that are both historiographical and rhetorical: "These would enable one to perform a dual operation: to slice into segments the diachronic continuum constituted by the whole set of literary texts (the strictly historical task), but to slice it according to formal criteria pertaining to *that* continuum and not others (the strictly rhetorical task)."[9]

If we turn our attention toward the present study, it seems legitimate to characterize it as a study of a special (sub)genre or cycle—that is, the migration novel. As George Steiner argues in *Extraterritorial* (1971), it is indeed plausible to speak of a whole genre of twentieth-century Western literature as extraterritorial—that is, a literature about exiles and migrants written by "poets unhoused and wanderers across language."[10] Furthermore, this book specifically attempts to combine a definition of the genre's internal laws (the formal criteria) and its historical range (the segment of a continuum)—that is, it attempts to combine the questions of "how" (the formalist) and "why" (the sociologist). Moretti states:

> But will they agree, the formalist and the sociologist? Yes, if the sociologist accepts the idea that the social aspect of literature resides *in its form,* and that the form develops according to its own laws; and if the formalist, for his part, accepts the idea that literature *follows* great social changes—that it always "comes after." To come after, however, does not mean to repeat ("reflect") what already exists, but the exact opposite: to *resolve* problems set by history.[11]

This passage sums up Moretti's idea of sociological formalism. On the one hand, Moretti ascribes a formal autonomy to literature, admitting that it develops in accordance with its own immanent laws. On the other hand, he upholds the interdependence between aesthetics and sociology in that literary form in a way reacts to historical transformations, not by a delayed reflection of history but by attempting to resolve (by formal-technical means) the problems that history produces. "Shaped from without, as well as from within . . ."[12] *Through its form* the migration novel specifically sets out to *express* the content of our experiences of interculturalism and globalization (i.e., "shaped from without") and to *resolve* the problems posed by these same experiences (i.e., "shaped from within"). So, its form "reveals the direct, almost tangible relationship between social conflict and literary form. Reveals form as a diagram of forces; or perhaps, even, as *nothing but force.*"[13]

* * *

This book sets out to explore migration and the concept's explanatory power in relation to four contemporary novelists. One of its working theses is that migration is exactly what is *both social and formal* in their novels. As Azade Seyhan remarks, descriptions referring to authorial background "such as *exilic, ethnic, migrant,* or *diaspora* cannot do justice to the nuances of writing between histories, geographies, and cultural practices."[14] Hence, migration is not only to be understood in relation to authorial biography. Rather, the concept of migration is able to encapsulate the overall thematic and stylistic elements of the novels, as when Edward Said speaks of "a particular sort of nomadic, migratory, and anti-narrative energy."[15] This "migratory energy" has two interdependent aspects in that it functions both as a mimesis of the contemporary world (sociology, "why") and as an immanent formal feature (aesthetics, "how").

The four novelists are Günter Grass, born in Danzig (now Gdańsk, Poland) in 1927, emigrated to Düsseldorf, Germany, in the Western occupied zone in 1945, lived in West Berlin for several years, but is now living in northern Germany; Milan Kundera, born in Brno, Czechoslovakia, in 1929, emigrated to Rennes, France, in 1975, and has been living in Paris since 1978; Salman Rushdie, born in Bombay (Mumbai), India, in 1947, emigrated to London, England, in 1961, went into hiding in 1989 because of the death sentence issued by Ayatollah Ruhollah Khomeini, and is currently living in New York; and Jan Kjærstad, born in Oslo, Norway, in 1953, where he still lives. In my analysis I will focus on *The Tin Drum* (1959) and *Dog Years* (1963) by Grass; on *The Book of Laughter and Forgetting* (1979), *The Unbearable Lightness of Being* (1984), and *Ignorance* (2000) by Kundera; on *Midnight's Children* (1981), *Shame* (1983), and *The Satanic Verses* (1988) by Rushdie; and on *The Seducer* (1993), *The Conqueror* (1996), and *Oppdageren* (*The Discoverer*) (1999) by Kjærstad.

It was during my work on *Salman Rushdies kartografi* (2003) that I came upon the idea of examining the contemporary novel in relation to migration. An inspirational impulse for the present study is Rushdie's essay on Grass from 1984 in which he describes Grass as one of the principal exponents of a so-called literature of migration.[16] Rushdie promotes a conception of migration that is more inclusive than the usual understanding of migration as a person moving from one (fixed and determinable) place to another. Instead, migration refers to both an author's and a character's spatial as well as temporal movements, just as it is used to describe the dynamic textual strategies and thematic focal points of the literary work. Following much the same line of thought, Kjærstad argues in his essay "Fram for det urene" ("Bring on the Impure") that the twentieth century sees the development of an "impure" novel in which religions, cultures, genres, and languages mix as a result of the world's spatial contraction and temporal discontinuity.

In its traditional use, migration refers to very specific events—for example, the seasonal migration of birds or the (voluntary or involuntary) geographical uprooting of people. However, etymologically the concept of migration originates from the Latin *migrare,* meaning simply "to wander" or "to move"—that is, movement per se. Migration as employed in this study thus signals *oscillatory and inconclusive processes* that manifest themselves on different levels in the literary work—for example, in relation to personal, national, and cultural identity, language, narrative form, and enunciation.

With Auerbach to provide me with the idea of a principle of selection, I use migration as my distinct angle. As for the more specific reasons behind the choice of Grass, Kundera, Rushdie, and Kjærstad: Grass is chosen because the role of migration and intercultural negotiations in his novels has been somewhat neglected. The role of emigration and exile in Kundera's novels may have received a fair amount of critical notice, but it is my intention to draw attention to and discuss a number of seemingly internal paradoxes in Kundera's writings in order to provide nuance to the understanding of the complex roles of emigration and exile in his work. Rushdie represents the self-evident choice, as he quite simply epitomizes the migrant author: not only does he constantly portray migrants in his novels, but he also reflects theoretically upon the migrant condition in essays and thus offers a range of elaborated concepts and useful insights. It is my intention, however, to challenge those readings of Rushdie that tend to focus too unequivocally on the fictional characters and their rootlessness, and instead to emphasize the significance of novelistic form and Rushdie's renegotiations of being rooted. As for Kjærstad, on the one hand he exemplifies the phenomenon of, and fascination with, migration permeating the contemporary literary system as a whole—hence he can and should be read as an author writing transnational literature from *within* the nation; on the other hand, Kjærstad is a unique phenomenon in Scandinavia, as no other (widely read) author from that part of the world has attempted so thoroughly to thematize the modern nomad identity and the glocalization of the nation and so radically to revolutionize the form of the novel.

I will also argue that my "circumscribed and comprehensible" body of material has the ability to illuminate the larger corpus of migration literature, because, among other things, of the constellation's multicontextual rootings and each author's accredited status on the literary world stage. Moreover, I believe that when brought together in a comparative study, the four authors' different (multi)national backgrounds might trigger some interesting transversal communications, thereby offering a complex image of "Europeanness." This image, as we shall see, portrays the European territory as a sort of "beyond of" space or space as process. The European territory is thus considered an unfinished potentiality, and partly because of this spatial incompleteness, the identity of Europe should be regarded as a Sisyphean work that is always in the making.

According to Auerbach, a historical period should not in itself form the *Ansatz*. I would argue that the same holds true here as well. It has not been the period that has deductively determined the concept of migration and the selection of novelists. Rather, it has been the particular novels of Grass, Kundera, Rushdie, and Kjærstad that have inductively provoked the idea of migration's important role. This being said, it cannot (and should not) be denied that migration is to some degree an epochal concept (determining a segment of the continuum of all literary texts); but this is not the same as asserting that it had not played a role before the twentieth century. Migration is indeed both a *historical* and a *transhistorical* concept: historical in that the twentieth century and beyond can be described as "the age of migration," and transhistorical in that mankind and literature have always migrated. Edward Said, considering the role of migration and exile in history, thus speaks quite rightly of a question of "scale."[17] The acceleration of the phenomenon implies a shift from individual cases (Ovid, Dante, Voltaire) to collective waves, the latter certainly applying to the post–World War II situation of decolonization and globalization.

Finally, one might feel inclined to ask, Why only novels? Why not poetry or drama? Two answers: The first would readily accept the relevance of examining and including poetry and drama, but would then conclude that a selection had to be made, and that hopefully the selection of these four novelists would prove its worth in the course of the book. The second would be slightly more provocative as it would claim, as Christopher Prendergast does, that the novel is "the most buoyantly migratory" genre— that is, the genre most adept at incorporating migratory elements into its form (but also the genre that most easily crosses national borders).[18]

* * *

While I have found methodological inspiration of a more general character in Auerbach and his idea of the necessity of an intuitively grasped and innovative *Ansatz* with the ability to illuminate and synthesize without totalizing, another great critic from his generation has provided me with support of a more specific kind—that is, regarding the relationship between literature, migration, and exile. I am referring to Harry Levin and his 1959 essay "Literature and Exile," in which he ascribes to writers in exile a privileged position as witnesses to human experience. Furthermore, Levin backs the idea of epochality when he speaks of the accumulation of exilic writing on such a scale that "it speaks with the voice of our time."[19] Finally, Levin also touches upon the role of the literary scholar in an era in which the corpus of accessible literature not only increases but also undergoes extensive transformation, meaning that the accumulation of migration literature not only calls for a redrawing of the map of literary history but also challenges the way literary studies is often organized in nationally separated contexts.

Levin claims that, apart from Georg Brandes's *Main Currents in Nineteenth Century Literature* (1872–90), hardly any attempt has been made to grasp the collective significance of migration literature. In the introduction to *The Emigrant Literature* (1872), the first volume of *Main Currents*, Brandes characterizes the comparative approach in the following way: "The comparative view possesses the double advantage of bringing foreign literature so near to us that we can assimilate it, and of removing our own until we are enabled to see it in its true perspective."[20] Brandes's description of the literary comparatist is remarkably close to that of the dual role of the migrant author who offers a foreign voice to a local material just as he or she makes a foreign material more familiar to his or her new local environment. Levin concludes: "It will take many such volumes, probably written by many collaborators, to chronicle the literary migrations of the twentieth century on a scale commensurate with their importance in our lives."[21] This book should be regarded as a modest attempt to rise to Levin's challenge.

Since Levin made his appeal, many scholars—among whom Edward Said and Homi Bhabha are among the most prominent—seem to have heeded his challenge. A vast amount of scholarly literature on the role of migration and exile in literary history has thus been written within the past fifty years or so. Characteristic of this literature, however, is that it deals primarily with colonialism/postcolonialism, which means that migration is regarded as a phenomenon strongly related to people who were formerly colonized, most notably by the British Empire. Postcolonialism is, admittedly, an important element of the overall image of the twentieth century as the age of wandering, but it is, I will argue, not the only context relevant to literature and migration.

Two problems arise from the tendency to regard migration more or less exclusively in relation to postcolonialism. The first problem concerns migration literature written in English (or any other colonial language) but which cannot be analyzed in any meaningful way with the aid of the "old" vocabulary of postcolonialism. As Roy Sommer has shown in his exemplary *Fictions of Migration* (2001), this is the case with much contemporary "ethnic" literature in Britain that has been written by second- or third-generation immigrants for whom dichotomies such as center-periphery and foreigner-native are no longer valid (the same obviously applies to the current situation of, for example, the "Maghreb" writers in France and the "Turkish" writers in Germany). Hence, Sommer develops new analytical tools for this kind of literature in the British context and operates with two general subcategories of the intercultural "fiction of migration": the multicultural novel informed by pluralistic ethnocentrism and the transcultural novel informed by cosmopolitan universalism.

The second problem concerns literature written outside the sphere of postcolonialism and either outside or on the borderlines of the traditional

British, French, or German contexts—that is, the kind of *Weltliteratur* the ageing Goethe spoke to Eckermann about in 1827. Goethe's (partly Eurocentric) idea of world literature as a phenomenon related to both quality (universal appeal/value, masterpiece) and sociology (internationalization of market, importance of translation) is evidently of relevance to this book, whose aim is to present a comparative study that includes such different trajectories and contexts as India-England-United States (postcolonialism), Czechoslovakia-France (Communism), Poland-Germany (Nazism), and Norway-World (globalization in general), with all the complexities of divergent, clashing, and merging languages, cultures, territories, and histories that this amounts to between and within each author's artistic profile. As Auerbach reminds us, "our philological home is the earth: it can no longer be the nation."[22] I find these words highly appropriate for the task that lies ahead of us, not merely in this study but also in literary studies in general.

Hence, it has been fully intentional on my part to link authors from entirely different contexts in terms of both geography, culture, and language in the belief that migration provides the grip that can hold the diverse parts together in a hopefully meaningful and prolific pattern. This multicultural and multicontextual commitment is strongly related to my belief in the necessity of reading literature outside the confines of the national context (but without discarding the local specificity). This being said, it requires a sensitive balancing act not to fall into the universalist trap on the one side—in which migration comes to mean exactly the same regardless of the context (as in a Morettian global wave that is dependent on geographical continuity)—or the nationalist trap on the other side, in which migration is viewed exclusively as bound up within a local context, thus ignoring the impulses and tendencies that constantly travel across national borders (as in a Morettian local tree that is dependent on geographical discontinuity). In short, my aim is to show, on the one hand, that certain uniformities in terms of style and theme apply to the four novelists as a result of wavelike interbreeding (caused by fellow authors as well as post–World War II society in general) and, on the other hand, that there are diversities that can be traced back to the local specificites of their respective contexts.

I will attempt to practice what Said calls a "global, contrapuntal analysis"—that is, an integrative analysis (on a global scale) that is not modeled on a "symphony" but on an "atonal ensemble."[23] We are not talking about the old comparative and binary approach of retrieving identities (influences) and highlighting differences (nativist essences). Instead, this multicontextual approach is characterized by its alertness toward a multiplicity of simultaneous dimensions. This means that it takes into account historical, geographical, and rhetorical "strategies," thereby revealing a complex and uneven territory—not merely between the authors but also within each author's literary design. The atonality is an effect of the interdependence and overlapping of locally inflected literary experiences across national borders, just as it is an effect of the migrant author's impurity of double belonging, a configuration that additionally transforms history and geography into new cartographies that are far less stable than before and where new transversal connections intensify: "The very concepts of homogeneous national cultures, the consensual or contiguous transmission of historical traditions, or 'organic' ethnic communities—*as the grounds of cultural comparativism*—are in a profound process of redefinition," argues Bhabha.[24] What is needed is a comparative method corresponding to the migratory and "unhomely" condition of the modern world. The method of combining the migratory (and thus the interconnected and translocally mobile) with the comparative (and thus the divergent and locally inflected) not only allows me to trace the influences that travel across national borders, but also alerts me to each author's relative (i.e., relational) position within the fourfold constellation, as well as to the continuities and discontinuities between and within the authors. The multicontextual configuration of connections and discontinuities proposes an enhanced awareness of each author's singular profile in that it allows them to be reflected through one another.

According to Bhabha, the concept of world literature does not signify so much a specific corpus of texts as it does a method of approach:

> The study of world literature might be the study of the way in which cultures recognize themselves through their projections of "otherness." Where, once, the transmission of national traditions was the major theme of a world literature, perhaps we can now suggest that transnational histories of migrants, the colonized, or political refugees—these border and frontier conditions—may be the terrains of world literature.[25]

Although he is less oriented towards the migrant's role in world literature, David Damrosch nevertheless agrees with Bhabha when he emphasizes the play and exchange between host and source cultures and the resulting relativization of essentialized images of cultures. Damrosch says of world literature that it is "a double refraction, one that can be described through the figure of the ellipse, with the source and host cultures providing the two foci that generate the elliptical space within which a work lives as world literature, connected to both cultures, circumscribed by neither alone."[26] In addition, Damrosch ascribes to world literature a (semantic) "variability"— that is, the quality that makes it possible for the work to travel between cultures. In fact, if world literature can be described as "locally inflected and translocally mobile,"[27] a phrase coined by Vilashini Cooppan that precisely captures the double refraction and variability of world literature, it may be argued that migration literature more or less automatically qualifies as world literature. But that is not all: migration literature is not merely inflected in a single locality; rather, it is inflected in a double locality because of its position between two (source) cultures. In that sense, its potential for translocal mobility is also already intensified.

If my methodological conviction complies with a "philology of world literature"—that is, a global, contrapuntal analysis with an eye for both trees and waves, thus prompting me to make a comparative study across linguistic, geographic, and cultural boundaries—it is also my intention to make the specific concept of migration relevant within other fields or contexts rather than merely the postcolonial. The concept of migration seems indeed to be strongly linked with decolonization (within the British Empire, more or less), but one of my aims in this book is to show its more global and transcultural relevance. Another intention of mine, and this offers another reasoning behind my choice of authors, has been to take the concept of Europe and what one might call "European literature in the age of globalization" into account. Europe is traditionally looked upon as a compartmental space of sovereign nation-states, but by focusing on Europe's recent histories of migration, the concepts of Europe and European literature are transformed into vectorial spaces of movements.

So, by considering European literature in the age of globalization, I attempt to liberate the concept of migration from its entrapment in postcolonial studies. Grass, Kundera, and Kjærstad have had very little to do with decolonization within the British Empire; hence, they illuminate the question of migration's role from a different perspective (Nazi and Communist totalitarianism, globalization and "dissemination" in general). But, alternatively, my orientation towards the European novel in the age of globalization is not an attempt to close off the impulses coming from outside the geographical entity referred to as Europe—if anything, it is the exact opposite. I fully agree with Said when he claims that without the (British) Empire, the European novel as we know it would not exist at all.[28] In this sense, the more traditional understanding of migrant literature and the developments within postcolonial studies help to shed new light on Grass, Kundera, and Kjærstad. The old European "center" is thus being revalued and renegotiated as it is plugged into the network of a literary world system in which the former "peripheries" are conquering territory and gaining access to the megaphones.

* * *

As previously indicated, the concept of migration is employed in a broad sense in this book. It is usually associated with a person's physical and spatial movement from one country to another or, alternatively, from a rural to an urban setting. It is in this demographic sense of the word that we speak of the twentieth century as the age of migration. Without question the twentieth century was a period of mass migrations on a scale previously unseen; it was an era during which people both voluntarily and involuntarily left their places of birth, either to escape persecution, war, or starvation, or "simply" to seek opportunities for a better life. As both Levin and Said have asserted, this development has had a deep impact on twentieth-century literary history. When Levin and Said speak of migration literature, they do so primarily in relation to authorial biography. However, this book asks the following questions: Is it not possible to speak of migration literature without reference to the author's life, instead focusing on the work's stylistic and thematic design? Can we make a distinction between *migrant literature* and *migration literature,* the former referring to the person behind the work, the latter referring to intratextual concerns? These questions lead to another: Does literature written by a migrant automatically qualify as migration literature?

Jan Kjærstad, not a migrant in the traditional sense of the word, is included in this book in order to provide answers to these questions. He is the book's experiment, so to speak. My intention is not to disregard the tormenting experiences of forced exclusion and displacement in the lives of Grass, Kundera, and Rushdie. I do believe that the life of the author, to some extent, colors his or her work. The experiment with Kjærstad should therefore not be regarded as an attempt to completely erase the differences between migrants and nonmigrants. Instead, it should be regarded as an attempt to see how and to what degree migrant authors and twentieth-century post–World War II globalization influence literature written by nonmigrants. I will argue that Kjærstad represents a new type of literature that both formally and thematically interbreeds with the increasing number of migrant authors just as his work is clearly shaped by and answers to the new social processes of globalization.

Hence, in this book migration refers not only to the life of the author, but also to the lives of the fictional characters and to the overall thematic framework and the discursive strategies of the novels. As mentioned earlier, migration concerns inconclusive processes, an idea supported by Iain Chambers in his *Migrancy, Culture, Identity* (1994) when he distinguishes between travel and migrancy (and, implicitly, between travel literature and migration literature). Travel involves a movement between stable positions, a point of departure and a point of arrival; furthermore, it implies the knowledge of an itinerary and operates with an idea of a potential home-coming, whereas migrancy "involves a movement in which neither the points of departure nor those of arrival are immutable or certain. It calls for a dwelling in language, in histories, in identities that are subject to constant mutation. Always in transit, the promise of a homecoming—completing the story, domesticating the detour—becomes an impossibility."[29] Roy Sommer's *Fictions of Migration* is another work in which migration is understood not merely in relation to the biography of the author or to the literal meaning of a spatial movement; "rather, it generally refers to the oscillation between two opposite cultural poles [. . .]. This broadly con-ceived concept of migration relates to different levels and forms of the liter-ary staging of cultural alterity and serves thereby as a metaphor for any inconclusive process."[30]

What is highly relevant for our purposes is that both Chambers and Sommer speak of migration as an oscillation and as something inconslusive. Furthermore, they support the idea of migration being applicable on dif-ferent levels of the literary work, such as language, history, identity, culture, and narrative form. Sommer thus places Zadie Smith's novel *White Teeth* (2001) in the same category as Rushdie's *The Satanic Verses*—that is, in the category of the transcultural hybrid novel. The point is that Smith is not a migrant in the traditional sense; she is a second-generation immigrant born and still living in London, meaning that she has not experienced uprooting in the proper sense. Her example thus illustrates the need for a work-oriented rather than an author-oriented way of reading and categorizing migration literature. In France the case of Paul Smaïl adds another dimen-sion to the problem of categorization, but, ultimately, Smaïl's case merely supports my thesis. Smaïl has published four novels dealing with issues typical of migrant or intercultural literature, all of which have been read as migrant literature. The name Smaïl points to an Arab background and the books' covers underline the "ethnic" character of the novels by displaying persons with dark skin. However, the name Paul Smaïl turned out to be a pseudonym for Jack-Alain Léger (itself a pseudonym for Daniel Théron), a French novelist and musician. So, "the Smaïl case" indicates that paratextuality—for example, "signs" of authorial biography—guides our reading, but, ultimately, it also proves that authors with no history of actual migration are able to write migration literature.

* * *

In the following, I will attempt to outline more precisely the different "func-tions" of migration in a novel. What I will present here is a list of eight subcategories—five related to theme, three to style—that are of relevance to migration literature. Furthermore, to each of these subcategories belong certain criteria or qualities that determine what distinguishes migration literature from other kinds of literature. Some of the criteria apply more directly to the specificity of migration literature, whereas others can be seen as part of a more general development in literature; but together they form a unique constellation of characteristics.

The thematic or social level is characterized by a mimetic logic, in that the novel creatively reflects an extratextual and migratory world. On the other hand, the stylistic or formal level is characterized by a constructivistic logic, in that the novel's form not only reflects but also *performs* intratextual migratory tendencies just as it offers formal "solutions" to the problems set by history. It goes without saying that the separation between theme and style and between the eight subcategories is, to some extent, an artificial separation. There are, of course, many overlappings between the subcategories, just as the general levels of theme and style will always be intrinsically related. I will argue, however, that the list of eight subcategories is a necessary step toward an operational method of analysis.

On the social level, the first subcategory is the most obvious, but not necessarily the most important for the overall determination of the novel as migration literature. I am referring to authorial biography. As Rebecca Walkowitz has argued, and as "the Smaïl case" shows in its own inverted logic, "literary classification might depend more on a book's future than on a writer's past. What has happened to the writer is less important, in these accounts, than what happens in the writing and in the reading, though the biography of the writer may influence the way that books are written and received."[31]

In this book I use migration in a broad sense, and this entails, among other things, that the term *migrant* is an umbrella concept that is able to include related concepts such as the exile, the expatriate, the refugee, the nomad, the homeless, the wanderer, and the explorer. This is not to say that these concepts all imply similar literary outcomes or personal experiences, but that by using migrant/migration as *Ansatzpunkt*, it becomes possible to outline a typology of subcategories, each representing different degrees of a migrant intensity. Speaking of the migrant, other distinctions such as voluntary-involuntary and temporary-continuous arise. Ovid and Dante were both involuntary exiles, and in much the same way as Boris Pasternak did, they lamented the loss of their home city or home country and thus longed for the termination of their banishment. Voltaire, on the other hand, chose exile instead of imprisonment, as he considered the displacement liberating for his intellectual development. With James Joyce we normally speak of a voluntary exile, a self-chosen physical as well as spiritual distancing that was very much a premise for his artistic success. An author such as Bruce Chatwin describes himself as a voluntary nomad.

The second subcategory consists of the novel's characters and runs parallel to the previous one. The difference is that we have now moved inside the work of art, thereby finding ourselves in more direct contact with the theme of the novel. What is of interest in these first two subcategories is the way the author and the characters cope with migration. Do they regard it as destructive, agonizing, and painful, or do they consider it to be productive, fascinating, and appealing? Is migration somehow a rupture of the "natural" order, or is it part of human "nature" and, additionally, an inescapable condition in the contemporary world of globalization? A novel dealing thematically with migration can portray it both positively and negatively (and as both at the same time, of course), and in both cases the novel qualifies as migration literature.

The third subcategory deals with questions of nation and nationalism that are also themes of great importance in the literature of migration. What does the nation mean to a person who does not belong to one, but to several nations, to a person who, in some cases, has been banished by his or her native country? How does the experience of migration and double belonging affect the authors' views on nationalism, internationalism, and postnationalism? And what are the differences between nationalism and national consciousness? Closely related to the question of the nation's role is the meaning of Europe, but also of European literature and the novel as a European genre, which forms the fourth subcategory. How should Europeanness be defined? In political terms, cultural terms, or geographical terms? How should literature of migration be defined geographically? In terms of place of production, language employed, the writer's country of birth, or the writer's adoptive country?

The fifth subcategory, globalization, is also a significant theme. Not always explicitly referred to by the authors, it nevertheless makes itself felt as an underlying subtext in the novels' reflections on and mirroring of the wide-ranging transformations of contemporary everyday life. Grass, Kundera, Rushdie, and Kjærstad are all very much concerned with what goes on in the world that surrounds them, and this engagement with worldly matters informs their novels, all of which have a strong mimetic element. The general developments and transformations in society are therefore a constant presence in their works. As for globalization, it is difficult to generalize their attitudes toward it, but they do seem to be preoccupied with pointing out the paradoxes and ambivalences inherent in globalization. As Zygmunt Bauman has said, globalization is valued both positively and negatively, but it is definitely "the intractable fate of the world, an irreversible process. [. . .] *We are on the move even if, physically, we stay put:* immobility is not a realistic option in a world of permanent change. And yet the effects of that new condition are radically unequal."[32] How does it affect people? How do people respond to this inevitable process? It is precisely the diversity and inequality of globalization's human consequences that form an essential part of the thematic framework in migration literature.

The themes of human identity, nation, nationalism, Europe, European literature, and globalization can be summed up as questions concerning personal, national, and cultural identity. History and geography become fundamental components in the rewriting of identities in order to evoke their impure and heterogeneous character. As I will show in my analyses, the authors invoke displacements of time and space in their efforts to rewrite and reinvent identities. Time and space are regarded as reservoirs of hidden or forgotten complexities and impurities thereby becoming deterritorializing and deterritorialized elements with regard to human, national, and cultural identities.

If the social level can be said to reflect an extraterritorial migratory world primarily through a mimetic mode, the level of style not only reflects but also helps create an intratextual migratory world primarily through a formal-constructivistic mode. The first stylistic subcategory is enunciation. The enunciatory strategies of the novels reveal a complex play with multi-perspectivism, wandering consciousnesses, and narratorial authority, as well as intratextual border crossings between story and discourse. What is more, the novels are often narrated through a migrant perspective that is characterized by an "unstable equilibrium" of familiarity and foreignness as it is positioned between cultures. As Gilles Deleuze and Félix Guattari point out, in-betweenness does not refer to a back-and-forth movement between fixed positions; rather, it implies the destabilization of each position as well as a movement into a completely new dimension.[33] The main question in regard to the enunciatory strategies concerns their ability to uphold a movement of oscillation and transformation that does not terminate in any stable axiomatic and semantic "compression" of the novels, but instead pursues new dimensions.

The second stylistic subcategory is composition or narrative form. How are the novels composed? What are their relationships to chronology, to causality, and to beginning, middle, and end? Are the novels determined and driven primarily by the actions of their characters, thus unfolding their plots through a "senso-motoric" model of actions and reactions? Or are there other explanatory modes, other discourses, employed in the overall architecture of the novels thus pointing to a multidimensional composition? In short, how are the elements of the novels linked? In addition to the pluralistic cultural impulses, the impurity of migration literature is due to the mixing of different "discursive tracks," a technique in which the novel as an art form excels. It is a common trait in Grass, Kundera, Rushdie, and Kjærstad that a variety of discourses and styles are combined into highly complex compositions. Such combinations imply that discursive borders are constantly relativized and transgressed, thereby intensifying the work's migratory character. The plurality of discursive tracks undermines the linearity of story and plot and, instead, an alternative chronotope evolves that can be described through concepts such as network, variation, and transversalism. Following are just a few examples of stylistic hybridity: Grass often incorporates lyrics as well as sections written in the style of absurd theater into his novels; Kundera mixes the level of story with dream sequences, essayistic reflections, and autobiographical elements; Rushdie frequently employs dream sequences and lyrics, too, and he also combines religious and film discourses with elements of slum naturalism; and Kjærstad plays with the biographical genre and the detective genre in order to question the borders between fact and fiction.

The third subcategory of style is language. Migration literature is extremely preoccupied with the role and status of language. This is partly due to the migrant's background in several languages: in Rushdie's case, Urdu and English; in Kundera's case, Czech and French; and in Grass's case, German, Polish, and Cassubian. Migration literature is thus characterized by a Bakhtinian heteroglossia, an acute sensibility toward language and an awareness of the world's high degree of constructedness (bilingualism makes an author more aware of the shortcomings of each language to describe reality, but also more aware of the ability of languages to complement one another and describe the world in new ways; inherent in each language is an entire worldview). In Grass and Rushdie we come upon an impurity of language as a result of their mixing of several languages, just as they both excel in portraying the different idioms and dialects of their characters. Kundera, on the other hand, uses language in a different way, as his characters and narrators speak in a very clear and eloquent manner that is much inspired by the literature and ideals of the Enlightenment. The impurity of language in Kundera shows instead in the narrator's metareflective meditations on the etymology or personal understandings of certain keywords. In general, language is thus used to destabilize doxa as it is constantly set in motion, varied, and impurified through the double awareness of two or more languages.

The above mentioned levels, subcategories, and criteria can be summarized in the following manner:

Social level (theme, mimetic, extratextual):
—Biography of the author (migrant, exile; loss/gain, temporary/perpetual)
—Biography of the characters (migrant, exile; loss/gain, temporary/perpetual)
—Nation and nationalism (hybrid national identity)
—Europe and European literature (secularism, migrants, and world literature)
—Globalization (mobility, inherent paradoxes)

Stylistic level (form, constructivistic, intratextual):
—Enunciation (vagabonding perspectives, foreignness of voice, self-correction)
—Composition and narrative form (inconclusive, rhizomatic, multidimensional)
—Language (heteroglossia, impurity, in-betweenness)

My analysis of the novels will evolve around these thematic focal points and textual strategies. In order to characterize a specific novel as migration literature, some of the abovementioned subcategories must support the classification. It will be the *combination* of the characteristics that in each case determines the character of the novel, and thereby I want to emphasize that migration literature does not require the presence of all of the subcategories and the specific criteria mentioned above. "Migration literature" is thus a term that does not entail a totalizing and complete definition; instead, it must be imagined as having blurred edges and no absolute lines of demarcation.

* * *

In the remaining part of this introduction, I will present the general theoretical and conceptual frameworks employed in this study. My aim here is to elaborate on the significance of the novelistic form in general, but more specifically in relation to the migration novel in particular. One of the most influential books in the history of literary theory is undeniably Lukács's *The Theory of the Novel* (1916/1920). The book's main idea is that the novel is "the literary form of the transcendental homelessness of the idea."[34] So, at the very level of form, the novel is characterized as migratory, unable to find rest in any transcendental home (e.g., beauty, goodness, nation, love, God, family). For Lukács, a transcendental point of convergence between the individual and the world no longer exists, and this prompts him to describe the novel's abstract form in the following formula: "The contingent world and the problematic individual are realities which mutually determine one another."[35]

Lukács considers the novel to be modernity's genre par excellence, as it is the form that most adequately answers to and expresses the contemporary world. This is, among other things, due to its capacity to incorporate "the fragmentary nature of the world's structure into the world of forms. [. . .] All the fissures and rents which are inherent in the historical situation must be drawn into the form-giving process and cannot nor should be disguised by compositional means."[36] As I read this passage, form and life are, contrary to Moretti's assertion, intrinsically linked in *The Theory of the Novel*. The overall idea of Lukács's penetrating essay is precisely that the novel—through its migratory form—is the most emblematic genre of contemporaneity. Form (migratory, fragmentary) is truly social (age of migration and fragmentation).

In the following, I will explain why I believe migration to be not merely a spatial but also a temporal concept. As a prelude to his analysis of Gustave Flaubert's *Sentimental Education* (1869), Lukács evokes Henri Bergson and his concept of *durée* (duration) in which time, in Bergson's own words, is understood as "invention, the creation of forms, the continual elaboration of the absolutely new."[37] Lukács precisely sees this Bergsonian temporality as a constitutive feature in the novel in general:

> The greatest discrepancy between idea and reality is time: the process of time as duration. The most profound and most humiliating impotence of subjectivity consists [. . .] in the fact that it cannot resist the sluggish, yet constant progress of time; [. . .] that time [. . .] gradually robs subjectivity of all its possessions and imperceptibly forces alien contents into it. That is why only the novel, the literary form of the transcendental homelessness of the idea, includes real time—Bergson's *durée*—among its constitutive principles.[38]

According to Lukács, Flaubert's novel introduces an important alteration in the way time and plot interact. Time usually assembles the different parts of a novel into a coherent whole, but in *Sentimental Education* the different parts of the novel never amalgamate into any coherent whole; rather, they are left to their own singularity and autonomy: "Of all great works of this type, *L'Education sentimentale* appears to be the least composed, no attempt is made here to counteract the disintegration of outside reality into heterogeneous, brittle and fragmentary parts by some process of unification [. . .]: the separate fragments of reality lie before us in all their hardness, brokenness and isolation."[39] The heterogeneity of the parts as they surface and then disappear in Flaubert's masterpiece may seem without any inner logic. For Lukács, an "overcoming" of the fragmentation of reality is nonetheless made possible, not through any ordinary unifying process (God, author, nation) but precisely through time understood as flow. The unity, however, is not an a priori but a unity that always comes *after*—an effect, not a cause.

So, why is it that every potential concordance with the transcendental home becomes impossible? Because *time has become constitutive;* it is now a transformative and innovative power in the overall architecture of the novel: on the one hand, the novel is subsumed time as a force that obliterates; on the other hand, the novel, as a result of time's eradicating powers, opens up the past, the present, and the future as virtual spaces in which new meanings can be inscribed. According to Lukács, "Only in the novel, whose very matter is seeking and failing to find the essence, is time posited together with the form: time is [. . .] the will of life to remain within its completely enclosed immanence. [. . .] In the novel, meaning is separated from life, and hence the essential from the temporal; we might almost say that the entire inner action of the novel is nothing but a struggle against the power of time."[40]

It is actually much the same line of reasoning we come upon in Deleuze's influential book on Marcel Proust, *Proust and Signs* (1964/1973). In the opening line of the book, he addresses the problem of unity in *In Search of Lost Time* (1913–27). Deleuze's polemic answer is that Proust's work is not to be regarded as a procession of involuntary memories but rather as a formative learning process. Deleuze thus denies that Proust's work is a retrospective search of the past where the unity of the work relates to the involuntary memories. Deleuze turns everything upside down by insisting on Marcel's "progressive" learning process (the process, though, is not a linear development; rather, its rhythm is one of disappointment and joy, inertness and ecstasy), thereby claiming that the whole work is oriented more toward the future than to the past.

Characteristic of Marcel's (and Frédéric Moreau's) semiotic education is that it never merges into any stable and accomplished end goal (as it can be said of Wilhelm Meister's and Elizabeth Bennet's education, for example). The novel's different parts are like pieces in a puzzle, but instead of fitting nicely together, they stick out in many different directions: "We have given up seeking a unity that would unify the parts, a whole that would totalize the fragments. For it is the character and the nature of the parts or fragments to exclude the Logos both as logical unity and as organic totality."[41] Deleuze's words remind us of Lukács's when he says of the modern work of art that it does not possess "a true-born organic relationship"; instead, it is to be considered a produced totality haunted by irony (i.e., an awareness of being produced).[42] Unity in Proust cannot be considered a principle; instead, it is to be regarded as an effect of a multiplicity excluding any possibility of a balanced organic whole. And just as unity is not a result of an original, transcendent matrix, meaning is not something to be discovered, but rather something to be produced.

In Search is a work in progress, not a dialectic composition planned in every detail beforehand in which the parts converge into a whole and the whole casts its unifying light back upon the parts. Deleuze's positive answer to the question of unity in *In Search* is "the transversal." The transversal is a line of communication that constantly arises between the otherwise non-communicating or incommensurable parts. However, transversal communication is never able to totalize the content of the parts into stable semantic unity. The transversal allows the individual parts to remain in their own incommensurable dimensions, but it unites them in the transversal dimension, thereby creating third spaces of new intensities and resonances. In this distinctive unifying dimension, totality cannot be traced back to any previous unity in which the parts can be nicely integrated; on the contrary, unity arises afterward as an effect of the individual fragments' resonating configuration whose premise is nothing but the transversal.

In the words of Moretti, we are dealing with a "whole that is formed *in* extreme contrasts, rather than in their resolution."[43] Moretti is here referring to what he calls the "modern epic"—that is, a flawed masterpiece of modernity. The modern epic combines the totalizing will of the epic with the subdivided, fragmentary reality of the modern world, and its imperfection is due to its living *in* history (duration). Characteristic of the modern epic is its indecisive endings and its ability to begin all over again. Rather than the linearity of the premodern plot, it employs "digressions of exploration" in an attempt to fit the whole world inside a single text. Hence, the modern epic may be unified, but it is never closed, and it is both formally and semantically monstrous.

Bergson's philosophy of time constitutes the foundation for both Lukács and Deleuze. Like them, Bergson is also deeply engaged in the relationship between life and form. If Bergson's idea of time as eternal flow somehow coincides with the understanding of time in the age of migration, one might ask what role form plays in this scenario. Is form not the opposite of flow, something that punctuates flow? Or can form somehow reflect or perhaps even generate flow? When I choose to devote a couple of paragraphs to Bergson's vitalism here, it is not because he will feature explicitly in the analysis later on. However, by briefly introducing his concept of form, I believe that we will be better equipped theoretically to perform the analytical task ahead. Bergson's work can be said to provide the abstract philosophical legitimization of my idea of the novelistic form as migratory.

The problem of life versus form occupies Bergson throughout his entire work. On the one hand, he acknowledges that forms exist; on the other hand, he rejects them as false interruptions. Here is what he said in 1907:

> Now, life is an evolution. We concentrate a period of this evolution in a stable view which we call a form, and, when the change has become considerable enough to overcome the fortunate inertia of our perception, we say that the body has changed its form. But in reality the body is changing form at every moment; or rather, there is no form, since form is immobile and the reality is movement. What is real is the continual *change of* form: *form is only a snapshot view of a transition.*[44]

So, forms do exist, but they are always already becoming different. However, this differentiation is partly due to matter (which manifests itself in forms), and this is very interesting for our particular purpose. On the one hand, the differentiation of life is first and foremost a result of an explosive force triggered by an unstable equilibrium of tendencies within life itself (the *élan vital* understood as the differentiation of difference). On the other hand, the differentiation is also a result of the collision between life and brute matter.[45] Matter represents an obstacle for life's otherwise smooth proliferation, but this obstacle must be acknowledged as part of life's differentiation (in individuals and species, i.e., forms). Matter and form are thus granted a certain *performative* potential as they help life to express itself in new ways. In other words, form itself is a constitutive element in life's continuous differentiation (migration).

Bergson's relationship to forms is thus ambivalent: on the one hand, forms represent a deceptive punctuation of the flow of life (e.g., everyday language); on the other hand, forms are necessary ingredients in life because they provide the medium in which life becomes capable of expressing itself in its continual variations, and, in addition, forms themselves are bestowed with the capacity to generate flow (e.g., poetic language). Hence, life always surpasses form, as form is a stylization of life, but form is also life-generating in relation to an otherwise formless life.

The negative side of form and language is that they usually prevent the proliferation of life's creative forces. Whenever form and language try to captivate a sensation, an impression, or a perception, these qualities have already vanished. Because language distorts by transforming elusive qualities into stable quantities, Bergson ultimately speaks of the incommensurability of life, thought, language, and matter. However, Bergson does acknowledge the necessity of this solidification caused in and by language in that it helps people function in the practical sphere of everyday life: "But this belief is natural to the human intellect, always engaged as it is in determining under what former heading it shall catalogue any new object; and it may be said that, in a certain sense, we are all born Platonists."[46] We are all born Platonists: this is for Bergson an incontestable truth, but at the same time he wants us to let singular events act upon us without our subsuming them under the logic of identity and recognition.

This brings us back to the question of novelistic form and the specificity of the migration novel. Is the novelistic form a "dead" form, a grid spread out over an otherwise chaotic matter induced by the explosive force of an *élan vital*? As already emphasized, Bergson seems to recognize the creative potentials of form itself; for example, when admitting to the singularity of every single expression in true poetic language. Bergson thus remarks about the novelist: "he has made us reflect by giving outward expression to something of that contradiction, that interpenetration, which is the very essence of the elements expressed."[47] That is, through the expression, through form understood as an unstable equilibrium of tendencies or as a contradictory constellation, the novelist can succeed in liberating life, in expanding it through an actualization of the virtual.

What I have so far presented of Bergson indicates why Lukács evokes the Bergsonian *durée* in his description of the novel's form as an expression of the transcendental homelessness of the idea. It must be mentioned, though, that Lukács actually sets up limits for the formal homelessness by speaking of the novel as primarily a biographical form. In that sense, Lukács acknowledges the necessity of a more or less stable, or at least contingent, form in order to tame an otherwise chaotic and endless material. The protagonist's life thread becomes the (contingent) prism through which the unfolding of a whole world proceeds. However, there is no contradiction between the idea of formal instability in the sense of transcendental homelessness and the idea of a biographical form, because the latter can easily be incorporated into the former. Frédéric Moreau, "die Zentralgestalt" as Lukács calls him, is not significant because the number of characters that surround him is limited; neither is his significance a result of a stringent composition centered on a subject; nor is it caused by an accentuation of Frédéric's personality on behalf of the other characters; rather, Frédéric's inner life is precisely as fragmented as the outer world, and this is why he is *zentral*. This shows that neither the biographical form (as abstract form) nor the modern hero (as an embodiment of the abstract form) excludes the general transcendental homelessness of the novel's form. On the contrary, they seem to complement each other very well. The heroes of the novel are, after all, "seekers."[48]

Deleuze's philosophy is characterized by its creation of concepts capable of formalizing concrete aesthetic processes of becoming. Hence, Deleuze's work offers a conceptual toolbox that is particularly suitable for examining the metamorphic processes characteristic of migration literature. Deleuze is in accord with Lukács's main idea of the novel as a migratory and homeless form. Instead of a set of binary and essentialized oppositions (points), Deleuze argues that the novel consists of both territorializations (segmentations, strata, punctuations), deterritorializations (lines of flight, destratifications, flows), and reterritorializations. A "territory" is not a space in the Euclidian or Kantian sense with geometrical coordinates; rather, it is a qualitative space in which a certain life-form exists, as when we speak of a bird's territory in zoology. To territorialize a given space is to make it "homely" (as when the child, alone in his or her room on a dark evening, starts humming and singing—that is, sending out sounds to striate space and to resonate with it in order to feel more comfortable). Deterritorialization refers to the transformation of the "coordinates" structuring a given space and its life form (the migrant, by embodying a difference within, instigates a deterritorializing movement). Reterritorialization refers to the stabilizing movement that occurs when a new territoriality (space and life form) sediments into a (provisional) stabile structure or system.

Deleuze's principal inspirational source, apart from Nietzsche, is undoubtedly Bergson and his vitalism. Deleuze regards the novel form as vitalistic, which is most evidently expressed in his concept of *effondement*, the oxymoronic combination of *fondement* (foundation) and *effondrement* (collapse), developed in "The Simulacrum and Ancient Philosophy" in *Logic of Sense,* and in his elaborations with Guattari on the rhizome, most notably in their book on Kafka and in "Rhizome," the introductory chapter of *A Thousand Plateaus.*

The root book, or the copy, represents a metaphysical world by way of resemblance. This type of book is characterized by convergence, circularity, and harmony in much the same way as Lukács (and Bakhtin) describes the epic. The root book is an integrated part of logos as it is a representation or a copy of the eternal ideas and models. Its formal interiority is not a produced totality but rather an a priori inner organicity. However, the root book is not capable of capturing or representing the fluidity of modernity. The human condition in modernity is the *terra infirma* where the ground constantly trembles beneath our feet. In modernity, art has become detached from any kind of cosmic integration; it has become autonomous and is no longer a representation of eternal values. Claiming that art has become autonomous is not the same as asserting its insularity, its complete severance from life. Art is still very much entangled in the world, and vice versa, but the common ground that everybody can agree upon has disappeared. Instead of being formed as a copy pretending to resemble a model, art is now produced as a simulacrum, with no pretence of imitating any model. Art no longer confirms logos (*mimesis*); it constructs antilogos (*creatio*). This is particularly true of migration literature, which is characterized by its homelessness in regard to both form and ideas.

According to Deleuze, the simulacrum is to be regarded as an *effondement*. Simulacrum is thus both foundation and the collapse of this foundation. It is to be understood as a symbolic cartography that is constantly modifying, transforming, and reconstructing itself as a consequence of the disappearance of any eternal space containing essences to be copied. With the concept of simulacrum, Deleuze strives to maintain an adequate concept of form in relation to contemporary literature. With his oxymoronic *effondement*, Deleuze insists upon duplicity of formalistic articulation and vitalistic becoming in literature, and this idea of art as both earth and earthquake opens up a conception of modern literature as instability between form and vitalism; that is, as *vitalistic form*. Simulacrum literature is described as continually transforming itself just as it cannot be said to have any stable center or central point of view.

Besides emphasizing process and artistic constructivism, Deleuze also highlights the fact that simulacrum literature incorporates heterogeneous lines, series, or perspectives that coexist simultaneously. As a result, concepts such as cosmos, logos, and convergence are replaced by chaos, antilogos, and divergence. This makes perspectivism a central concept in Deleuze's aesthetics, and he draws primarily on two sources: Leibniz and Nietzsche. In Leibniz's monadology it is the "pre-established harmony" guaranteed by God that ensures that the individual monads, despite their closed doors and windows, express the same world. Between their singular expressions, there is only a difference in degree. The relationship between the world understood as cosmos and the monad understood as a point of view on the world is the relationship between a macrocosmos and a microcosmos—that is, a synecdochic relation. It may be that the monad expresses only a part of the world, but that part converges with the cosmic world picture. The relationship between God $(\frac{\infty}{1})$ and monad $(\frac{1}{\infty})$ is thus a reciprocal relationship.

With Nietzsche, the Leibnizian "incompossible" has become the means of communication that guarantees becoming, says Deleuze: "Nietzsche's perspective—his perspectivism—is a much more profound art than Leibniz's point of view; for divergence is no longer a principle of exclusion, and disjunction no longer a means of separation. Incompossibility is now a means of communication."[49] Whereas Leibniz attempts to dissolve incompossibility and chaos into a higher level of harmony and compossibility by way of a filtration guided by the principle of the best of all possibles, Nietzsche includes heterogeneity and incompossibility as positive conditions in their own right.

No pre-established harmony exists in the Nietzschean universe, and no degree of cosmos is inherent in the singular perspectives on the world to make sure that the series of perspectives are compossible. In Nietzsche the world is bereaved of the guardian who guarantees that the world is One. Every perspective is an interpretation establishing its own value. As a result, we are dealing with a more radical perspectivism, holding no promise of convergence between the series. A perspective constructs its own unique (version/interpretation of the) world in the same way that a work of art constructs a unique and inimitable (version/interpretation of the) world. This is not to say that every version is as true as any other, but it implies that the world cannot be reduced to One.

Deleuze and Guattari find this radical perspectivism and aesthetics of complementarity unfolded in the rhizomatic novel. The rhizome consists of complementary universes that cannot be referred back to an a priori harmony and totality. Not only can the rhizome be read in mutually incompatible ways (as in Einstein's theory of relativity and Eco's "open work"), but the rhizome itself reads and constructs the world in complementary ways (as in Bohr's theory of quantum mechanics and his principle of complementarity). The rhizome is like a network that disseminates itself horizontally without any pure origin and teleological ending, but that is always situated in the middle making new alliances (like the migrant): "The tree is filiation, but the rhizome is alliance, uniquely alliance. The tree imposes the verb 'to be,' but the fabric of the rhizome is the conjunction, 'and . . . and . . . and . . . ' This conjunction carries enough force to shake and uproot the verb 'to be.'"[50] Consequently, like the World Wide Web the rhizomatic work consists of multiple entryways and exits, and every part is connected to every other part. The rhizome is the poetics of the fluid work that is constantly migrating and proliferating. When analyzing a rhizome, one should therefore not arrest its processes in a binary and static structure; rather, one should ask how it functions and of which lines it is composed:

> Unlike a structure, which is defined by a set of points and positions, with binary relations between the points and biunivocal relationships between the positions, the rhizome is made only of lines: lines of segmentarity and stratification as its dimensions, and the line of flight or deterritorialization as the maximum dimension after which the multiplicity undergoes metamorphosis, changes in nature.[51]

Although it consists of lines instead of points, one would nevertheless be wrong to perceive the rhizome as pure chaos or pure dissolution; instead, the lines of the rhizome assume different kinds of qualities. On the one hand, the rhizome is determined by lines whose directions point toward a stratification or a segmentation (a becoming-point); but on the other hand, the rhizome is also determined by lines that decompose or dissolve the formations that are inclined to become points (a becoming-dissolved). Either way, it is the processual element that is emphasized in the rhizomatic structure. As we will see in the following chapters, the rhizome proves to be a relevant structural concept in the analysis of the novels of Grass, Kundera, Rushdie, and Kjærstad.

CHAPTER 1

Günter Grass

Émigrés: Earned their livelihood by giving guitar lessons and mixing salads.
—Gustave Flaubert, *The Dictionary of Received Ideas*

As mentioned in the Prolegomena, Salman Rushdie describes Günter Grass as a writer of vital significance in the literature of migration. In addition to characterizing Grass as a migrant and his work as migration literature, Rushdie suggests that the migrant should be considered one of the defining figures of the twentieth century. Besides Grass, Rushdie mentions Kundera and Joyce as examples of migrants who have lost a city and subsequently rediscovered it through their writing.

Günter Grass was born in Danzig (now Gdańsk, Poland) on October 16, 1927, when it was a free city under the League of Nations. In a speech during the 1966 Bavarian election campaign, in which he tries to dissuade young Germans from voting for the NPD (National Democratic Party of Germany), Grass sums up his background as follows:

> At the age of ten I was a member of the Hitler Cubs. When I was fourteen I was enrolled in the Hitler Youth. At fifteen I called myself an Air Force auxiliary. At seventeen I was in the armored infantry. At the age of eighteen I was discharged from an American POW [prisoner of war] camp: it was only then that I became an adult—or rather that I gradually began to realize what, behind a smoke screen of martial music and irredentist bilge, *they* had done to my youth. It was only then that I began to find out—the full horror was not revealed to me until years later—what unthinkable crimes had been committed in the name of the future of my generation. When I was nineteen, I began to have an inkling of the guilt our people had knowingly and unknowingly accumulated, of the burden of responsibility which my generation and the next would have to bear. I began to work, to study and to sharpen my distrust of a *petit bourgeois* society which was once again assuming such an air of innocence.[1]

This passage gives us an impression of the unsentimentality with which Grass looks back upon his youth. However, it also indicates the mental upheaval Grass underwent as he realized the horrors of Nazism and the burden and responsibility passed on by the older generation to his own, which was still too young to be blamed for anything.

In 1927 Danzig was a multiethnic and multireligious city inhabited by Germans, Poles, Cassubians, Lithuanians, Jews, Protestants, and Catholics. Grass's parents owned a grocery store and belonged to the petty bourgeoisie, his father being a German Protestant, his mother a Cassubian Catholic. Grass grew up with German as his mother tongue, and he was raised as a Catholic but proclaims to be an atheist today. Grass's ethnic, linguistic, religious, and cultural in-betweenness is thus affected by both city and family and informs his entire work. Danzig had been part of the German Empire before and during World War I, and the majority of the city's population were Germans. They saw Hitler's idea of a new Great German Empire as a long-awaited opportunity to be once again "heim ins Reich," (home in the country) and this is why Danzig was one of the places where National Socialism found its most fertile soil. Hence, Grass's father was a member of the Nazi Party, and Grass himself was a member of Jungvolk (German Youth) and Hitlerjugend (Hitler Youth).

After the war nearly all of the German Danzigers were recognized as enemy aliens, and the Poles widely accused them of complicity in World War II. Consequently, most of the prewar German citizens of Danzig fled to Germany, just as many thousands of Germans were being forced to emigrate from Poland, Czechoslovakia, Austria, and Hungary. After Grass's release from the American POW camp in 1946, he roamed around in the Western occupational zone for a couple of years, living hand to mouth. Among other things, he worked in a potash mine in Hildesheim before moving to Düsseldorf in 1947, where he began his apprenticeship as a stonecutter.[2] Subsequently, he studied at the Academy of Art in Düsseldorf from 1948 to 1952. In January 1953 he moved to Berlin where he studied at the Academies of Fine Arts and became a sculptor and lithographic artist. Grass made his debut as a writer in 1956 with a collection of poems called *Die Vorzüge der Windhühner* (The Advantages of Windfowl). That same year he moved to Paris with his Swiss wife, the dancer Anna Margaretha Schwarz.

Accordingly, Grass lost his hometown at the age of seventeen, and since the war he has lived in Düsseldorf and Berlin, in Paris, in Lübeck, and in Schleswig-Holstein. On the fiftieth anniversary of the outbreak of the war, Grass reflected on his migrant destiny: "In 1945 I, too, lost an irreplaceable part of my origin: my hometown, Danzig. I, too, took the loss hard. Time and again I had to remind myself of the reasons for it." He continued:

"Siegfried Lenz and I were there when a document valid under international law sealed the loss of our homeland. We had long since accepted this loss; we had learned to live with it. Many of our books dealt with it and its causes."[3] Grass admits the loss was a hard blow, but at the same time he indicates that his loss is a (irrevocable) thing of the past with which he has learned to live, for example, through his artistic reworking of the past. The rationale behind the statement was the main purpose of the article—namely, to provide a critique of the thriving nationalistic bacillus in Poland, Germany, and France, but especially of those Germans who were still clinging to a nostalgic dream of returning to the former eastern areas and who refused to acknowledge the western border of Poland. "If sides must be drawn," he says in another speech dealing with German nationalism and unification, "let me be numbered among the rootless cosmopolitans."[4] We find a similar critique of nationalism in the national election speech from 1966, but here Grass also points to the difference between nationalism and national consciousness, the latter of which he finds fully legitimate and natural: "When will we learn to distinguish between national consciousness, a self-evident phenomenon grounded in reason, and the substitute for it that is being offered for sale, the hybris of nationalism?"[5]

Rushdie's characterization of the migrant as a person who has been uprooted from language, place, and culture seems at first only partly valid in regard to Grass. German has always been Grass's vernacular and working language, and he belongs primarily to a German cultural tradition. Apparently, Grass is only one-third migrant. It is Rushdie's belief, nevertheless, that Grass has not only crossed a border in a spatial-geographical sense, but that he is also a trans(p)la(n)ted person in a temporal-historical sense:

> Günter Grass is a migrant from his past, and now I am no longer talking about Danzig. He grew up [. . .] in a house and a milieu in which the Nazi view of the world was treated quite simply as objective reality. Only when the Americans came at the war's end and the young Grass began to hear how things had really been in Germany did he understand that the lies and distortions of the Nazis were not the plain truth. What an experience: to discover that one's entire picture of the world is false, and not only false, but based upon a monstrosity. What a task for any individual: the recon-struction of reality from rubble.[6]

So Grass is a migrant in both a geographical and a cultural sense because the passage from a Nazi-infected childhood and adolescence through a period of gradual denazification to an adult life of active participation in the German democracy is comparable to a mental and cultural revolution.

And according to Rushdie, Grass can also be described as a migrant on the level of language, as one of the major tasks for the postwar German writers was to rebuild the German language from scratch after the Nazis' destructive simplification. In a famous paragraph in *Minima Moralia: Reflections on a Damaged Life* (1951), Theodor W. Adorno reflects on the relationship between the emigrated writer and language and indicates that writing is the only home available for the migrant writer. However, the home of which Adorno speaks can only be provisional: "In the end, the writer is not even allowed to live [wohnen] in his writing."[7] As we shall see, Grass's novels are expressions of this idea of the migrant's linguistic homelessness, as they constantly seek to liquefy what is otherwise a solidified language.

Rushdie concludes his essay by stating that Grass can be considered a double migrant: "a traveller across borders in the self, and in Time. And the vision underlying his writing, both fiction and nonfiction, is, I believe, in many ways a migrant's vision."[8] It is precisely this "migrant's vision" in its manifold manifestations that I will examine in the present chapter, primarily in a reading of *The Tin Drum* and *Dog Years*. In what immediately follows, I will sketch out some of the artistic "migrations" that Grass underwent during the years leading up to the publication of *The Tin Drum*. This will be followed by an analysis of the novels' protagonists and an examination of the spatial and temporal configuration in the novels. Subsequently, I will look into the role of language, and, finally, I will examine the enunciatory strategies in the novels.

The Birth of the Trilogy

Yet it is no exaggeration to say that liberation as an intellectual mission [. . .] has now shifted from the settled, established, and domesticated dynamics of culture to its unhoused, decentred, and exilic energies, energies whose incarnation today is the migrant, and whose consciousness is that of the intellectual and artist in exile, the political figure between domains, between forms, between homes, and between languages. From this perspective then all things are indeed counter, original, spare, strange.

—Edward Said, *Culture and Imperialism*

A lot has been said about Adorno's famous 1949 dictum: "To write poetry after Auschwitz is barbaric. And this corrodes even the knowledge of why it has become impossible to write poetry today."[9] In regard to Grass, it is evident that the "damaged life" is a decisive incentive behind his early work. In a renowned speech entitled "Writing after Auschwitz" and in his 1999

Nobel Prize lecture "To Be Continued . . . ," we gain insight into the themes and poetological thoughts that occupied Grass during the formative years of his career as a writer. Grass admits that Adorno, and *Minima Moralia* in particular, exerted an enormous influence on his work. According to Grass, it was the first time that Auschwitz was seen as "an irreparable tear in the history of civilization."[10] As a result of the emergence of the concentration camp photos showing heaps of shoes, glasses, hair, and corpses, the young Grass was inevitably confronted with the question, How is it possible to write after Auschwitz? At first it seemed impossible to give a positive answer to this question—and for Grass, Adorno's imperative only sustained his own initial feeling of absurdity.

However, Adorno's apparent prohibition irritated Grass. After all, life had to go on . . . After a while, Grass realized that Adorno's imperative was not a prohibition, but rather a standard to be met. The imperative thus imposed an enormous responsibility on the writer, but Grass actually took encouragement from the dictum, as it provided the author with a unique opportunity to work seriously under the most demanding circumstances: "In Berlin there was no patience for flirting with the unspeakable. My last imitative finger exercises were corrected by a stern rubber eraser. Here, things wanted to be called by name."[11] To Grass, the restrictive poetics, which included key concepts such as askesis, grayness, and frugality, was a positive way of meeting Adorno's standard.

We find this early poetics unfolded in the programmatic poem "Askese" from *Gleisdreieck* (Railway Triangle, 1960). "Askese" explicitly thematizes the mood of grayness that has continued to infuse the works of Grass, and the atmosphere is characterized by frugality, hopelessness, and askesis. The formal strategies of the poem also point to abstinence and self-denial—for instance, through the structure of repetition, which encloses the poem in a rigid, almost introverted form. According to Grass, "Askese" indirectly answers Adorno's imperative "by setting limits to its own undertaking, in the form of a circumscribing reflex."[12] Hence, the poem seeks, on the one hand, to comply with Adorno, since it recognizes the historical caesura, but, on the other hand, it transgresses Adorno's dictum simply by being written. And writing had to be done, but within certain limitations. The poem thus renounces extravagance, colorfulness, and psychological introspection; instead, it is oriented toward concrete physical objects, and by praising the color gray, it points to a third space in between absolute opposites such as black and white.

However, in "Writing after Auschwitz" Grass asks if the imperative for askesis had to be expressed in such an "anorexic form." What happens between the writing of "Askese" and the writing of *The Tin Drum?* What lives on, and what "dies"? According to Grass, an important prerequisite for his change from the rigid and restrictive form of askesis to a fabulating and inclusive form of writing was his distance from Germany that resulted from his emigration to Paris. It was only with this distance—geographical as well as temporal, physical as well as spiritual—that he found a language and a breath capable of embracing such a volcanic rupture as the trilogy turned out to be. With *The Tin Drum* Grass distanced himself from some of the implications inherent in his former poetics of askesis: the self-enclosed anorectic form was replaced by a linguistic diarrhea, resulting in a monstrous form pointing in all directions; without renouncing the color gray as the principle of shading and as an alternative to binary thinking, the material is now exposed in full Technicolor. Out of the ashes and the askesis arises a plethora of stories characterized by their enormous epic scope, stories about the past, loss, origins, and guilt. Hence Grass furnishes his earlier "bare skeletons" with "flesh," so to speak. However, this is not to say that he abandons his ascetic attitude. His point of departure is still the damaged life, and his driving force is to keep the wound of history open. Furthermore, the transformation in Grass's poetics can also be described as a "return of the narrative," but it is a narrative that incorporates avant-garde and modernist techniques. And the themes that had been previously touched upon with a tentative, although sharp, pen are now painted with broad strokes of the brush, in many shades and hues, and with great depth in the coloring. Whereas Grass had previously worked with an evocative approach to objects in their objectness, objects are no longer isolated as poetical motifs but are now placed in a contextual and narrative configuration of meaning in which they are repeatedly modified and viewed in new ways.

But what provoked Grass into this project of megalomania besides his voluntary exile in Paris? In "Writing after Auschwitz" Grass mentions the demonization of the Nazi period as one important reason; another motivational factor was the walks he took in the Parisian parks with Paul Celan. Celan, who became more and more stingy with his own words, as in his famous poem "Engführung" (Stretta/Straightening) in a paradoxical manner encouraged Grass to pursue his own epic endeavor and was the first person to realize that *The Tin Drum* did not exhaust Grass's vastness of material. Both *The Tin Drum* and *Dog Years* embody an idea of art that is to some extent hostile toward formal patterning, at least if one understands formal patterning to mean the creation of a balanced, organic whole. The inexhaustibility of the Danzig material means that the formal design of the novels is capable of absorbing contrasts in order to "reflect" reality as tangled and incomplete.

We are also offered an insight into the birth of *The Tin Drum* in the essay "*The Tin Drum* in Retrospect or the Author as Dubious Witness" (1973). Here Grass admits that one of the main driving forces behind his work on *The Tin Drum* was his petty bourgeois background and the fact that he never finished his schooling. What is of interest as well is that Grass speaks of (aesthetic) distance as a very important prerequisite for the success of the whole project. Whereas the earlier poetics of askesis had emphasized a more direct approach to the objectness of the objects, Grass now emphasizes distance and playfulness, and this distance is to be understood as a biographical distance in both space and time, but also as a distance in style embodied in the use of irony as a poetic device.

The seeds for *The Tin Drum* can be found in a long, but unsuccessful poem that was written in 1952 during Grass's stay in France, in which Oskar Matzerath (before he actually became Oskar) is featured as a stylite. The poem is of generic importance to the novel because it represents the first step toward Grass's creation of a displaced perspective. The poem was about a young existentialist bricklayer who became disillusioned with worldly developments. His reaction was to build a pillar in the center of his small town, subsequently chaining himself to the top of the pillar. With this idea, Grass established a distance in perspective, but the elevated perspective was also too static.

On his way home from France, Grass passed through Switzerland, where he met Anna for the first time. The event that comes to play a major literary role in the creation of *The Tin Drum,* however, occurs when Grass, among coffee-drinking adults, spots a three-year-old boy with a tin drum: "What struck me and stayed with me was the three-year-old's self-forgetful concentration on his instrument, his disregard of the world around him."[13] The episode remains buried in Grass's memory for three years, though. Meanwhile, he still practices his primary line of work—that is, graphics and sculpturing—and he also starts writing poetry, a few one-acters, and librettos for the ballet. Some of the material from these "rehearsals" was later to be incorporated into *The Tin Drum* and *Dog Years*.

Having moved to Paris in 1956, Grass began working on the novel that eventually became *The Tin Drum*. Three versions ended up in the stove, however, just as Grass oscillated between different working titles such as "The Drummer," "The Tin Drum," and "Oskar, the Drummer." The birth of the novel, and the trilogy as a whole, was evidently preceded by a protracted labor consisting of a series of heterogeneous attempts, recovered fragments, impulses of both inner and outer character, and often accidental sources of inspiration. The displaced perspective of the stylite had materialized as the perspective of the boy drummer. As such, the elevated, aloof young bricklayer was replaced by the small child, whose perspective was distanced all the same, but now from below, and no longer static but mobile. Grass had thus found the proper perspective, but it was not until he had formulated the novel's opening sentence that his work on the final version of the novel progressed in a satisfying manner: "With the first sentence—'Granted: I am an inmate of a mental hospital . . . '—my block was gone, words pressed in on me, memory, imagination, playfulness, and obsession with detail gave themselves free rein, chapter engendered chapter. When a gap broke the flow of my story, I hopped over it; history came to my help with local offerings; little jars sprang open, releasing smells."[14] Gone is the linguistic scarcity, replaced by a linguistic diarrhea; gone is the anorectic form, replaced by a monstrous form; gone is the "Engführung," replaced by fabulation; gone is the burdensome seriousness, replaced by irony. In short, Grass had become a novelist. Before Grass moved back to Berlin, he was already working on *Dog Years,* whose working title was "Potato Peels," but once again he experienced creative setbacks along the way. It took the writing of the novella *Cat and Mouse* to get *Dog Years* back on track.

Heroes against Absurdity

> Outside the world, outside the past, outside myself: freedom is exile, and I am condemned to be free.
>
> —Jean-Paul Sartre, *The Reprieve*

We have to ask ourselves by which categories we should approach the heroes of Grass's novels and of migration literature in general. First of all, I have already argued that Lukács's idea of the novel's abstract form is a fruitful starting point. This means that our reading should be informed by the constellation of problematical subject, contingent world, and the (im)possibility of their reconciliation. Second, we need to examine the migratory status of the characters and ask how it relates to the problematical subject and the (im)possibility of reconciliation. This means that our reading will focus on the invigorating and affirmative powers of migration, as well as on its agonizing and destructive consequences. In the following, I will thus analyze the characters of Oskar Matzerath, Eduard Amsel, and Walter Matern in order to illuminate part of the multilayered role of migration in *The Tin Drum* and *Dog Years.*

For Grass the loss of his hometown was a painful experience. However, in his artistic enterprise, Grass is not only occupied with rendering this kind of loss, but as a consequence of his stoic approach, he is also extremely concerned with the insights that can be gained through loss. The relationship between epistemology and exile is precisely Said's point of departure in his classic essay "Reflections on Exile" (1984). Said is, in fact, rather ambivalent in his assessment of exile and its consequences. On the one hand, he refuses to see exile as a privileged access to a certain "humanism," because such an approach ignores the paralyzing sufferings of estrangement. On the other hand, the following question begs for an answer: "But if true exile is a condition of terminal loss, why has it been transformed so easily into a potent, even enriching, motif of modern culture?"[15] Are there any insights to be gained in spite of, or maybe even because of, the loss of home, traditions, family, and language? If Said, because of the sorrows and losses, expresses a certain cautiousness in regard to exile being understood as a privilege, he nonetheless considers the exile's dislocated perspective a privileged point of view through which the exile becomes capable of producing alternative versions of the "administered" modern world.

Oskar embodies this exilic position and perspective as described by Said. His physical appearance and his mental disposition consign him to the periphery of society and its institutional frameworks. Oskar's craving for isolation is underlined several times throughout the novel. At one point he says about his bed in the mental asylum that it "is a goal attained at last" (*TD*, 2). This and the following example reflect Oskar's urge to step outside the world and himself because he does not wish for the kind of freedom to which life condemns him, a freedom based on contingency: "Lonely and misunderstood, [. . .] and figuring that things would go on like this for some sixty or seventy years, [. . .] he lost his enthusiasm even before this life beneath the light bulbs had begun. It was only the prospect of the drum that prevented me then from expressing more forcefully my desire to return to the womb" (*TD*, 34–35). Oskar is portrayed here as an existentialist hero thrown into a contingent and absurd world in which the passage of time brings nothing but meaninglessness. The tin drum becomes an existential necessity for Oskar because it enables him to resist the absurd passage of time. The future promises no comfort and leaves no hope of reconciliation between Oskar and the world, however. Oskar's decision to stop growing and the isolation that follows indicate his rebellious attitude toward a contingent world without meaning. There is an element of (noncontingent) freedom in his choice of isolation that to some extent allows him to evade the deterministic forces of society.

One of those deterministic forces is family expectations. Oskar is supposed to take over his family's grocery store, but he immediately rejects the route planned for him by Alfred Matzerath. This is only the first of many examples where Oskar transgresses the pre-fabricated forms of society.

By rejecting his father's proposition, Oskar initiates an outward movement from the traditional structures of family and local community. In this way Oskar exemplifies how the mobility of the industrial age is replacing the more inflexible stratification of the old agrarian society.

Even if Oskar's refusal to be integrated into the petty bourgeois life-form indicates a new industrial mobility, his transgression of the petty bourgeois circles does not lead to his integration into industrial society. He remains a figure on the margins all his life. In the industrial age, the state relies on the education of its citizens, who must qualify themselves for the increasing complexity of the job market. The state is the only organization large enough to control and fund such a large-scale educational enterprise. Integration into industrial society thus seems to require the conventional education offered by state institutions. How does Oskar fit into this picture? In "The Schedule" chapter, Oskar tells us how on his first day at school, he upsets his classmates, along with their horrified mothers and not least Fraülein Spollenhauer, the teacher, when he starts beating his drum and refuses to stop. When Fraülein Spollenhauer tries to take the drum away from Oskar, he uses his voice to shatter her glasses:

> In other words, I composed a double cry which literally pulverized both lenses of la Spollenhauer's spectacles. Slightly bleeding at the eyebrows, squinting through the empty frames, she groped her way backward, and finally began to blubber repulsively, with a lack of self-control quite unbefitting an educator, while the rabble behind me fell into a terrified silence, some sitting there with chattering teeth, others vanishing beneath their desks. A few of them slid from desk to desk in the direction of the mothers.
>
> (*TD*, 68).

Apart from revealing Oskar's destructive powers, this passage also tells us of Oskar's isolation and his contempt for his classmates and for persons who lack self-control.

The consequence of Oskar's behavior is that his first day at school is also his last. He takes control of his own education, which, at this stage, takes place primarily in his own neighborhood. In Gretchen Scheffler's apartment, Oskar discovers Goethe's *Elective Affinities* and a pornographic book on Rasputin. The Rasputin book inspires Gretchen and Agnes to engage in sexual escapades, just as Gretchen allows Oskar and his "third stick" a taste of female flesh (as does Lina Greff, another neglected petty bourgeois housewife from the neighborhood): "But since on this planet nothing lasts forever, it was Oskar who left his bedridden teacher the moment it seemed to him that his studies were complete" (*TD*, 288). Although some affinities exist, we are indeed light-years away from the bourgeois *Bildung* (formation) of Wilhelm Meister and Elizabeth Bennet. By rejecting the family trade and school, Oscar has attained the status of an "alternative" to the mass institutions and ready-made forms of modern life, a status that is also confirmed by his disruption of the Nazi rally at the Maiwiese, his vandalization of the Church of the Sacred Heart, and his shattering of the windows in the Municipal Theater, three "institutions" of great symbolic value and with actual political, religious, and cultural power.

In Oskar's unconventional formation, Bebra is the one who activates and confirms his cosmopolitan and artistic potential. Their first meeting in 1934 turns out to be crucial, as Bebra encourages Oskar to seek a position on the podium instead of in front of it. At their second meeting, in 1938, Oskar falls in love with Roswitha. When he meets Bebra and Roswitha again in 1942, he decides to join Bebra's front theater, and in so doing he sets out on his first journey away from Danzig. His mobility continues after the war: on June 12, 1945, Oskar emigrates to Germany, where he arrives in Lüneburg, moves on to Hannover, and eventually settles in Düsseldorf. In Düsseldorf Oskar proceeds with his idiosyncratic *Bildung* in that he works as a stonemason apprentice, gets involved with the artists at the Academy of Art, and plays the drums in a jazz band. All of this—Oskar's isolation, his dismissal of the adult world, his decision to stop growing, his destruction or rejection of the institutions of organized society—adds up to a model for an unconventional life on the margins.

Apart from the mobility that characterizes Oskar as he disrupts one institutional frame after another, the most important feature of his character is his detachment. How does Oskar's regressive yearning for his mother's womb or for his bed in the asylum conform to the image of a migratory character? Is stasis not what he seeks? Indeed it is, but it is not what he gets. It is precisely his wish for isolation that makes him a detached person, and detachment prevents his integration into society, which then compels him to keep migrating from one role to another, from one institution to another, from one city to another, from one type of employment to another: "In contrast to almost every character in the novel, Oskar *chooses* his social roles according to expediency: he is [. . .] a virtuoso exponent of multiple, complex personae," Hollington observes.[16] In addition, the dualisms in his life emphasize the oscillatory nature of his character. The most significant is that of Goethe and Rasputin: "The conflicting harmony between these two was to shape or influence my whole life [. . .]. To this very day [. . .] I [. . .] fluctuate between Rasputin and Goethe, between the faith healer and the man of the Enlightenment, between the dark spirit who casts a spell on women and the luminous poet prince who was so fond of letting women cast a spell on him" (*TD*, 76). The opposition between Goethe and Rasputin indicates Oskar's oscillation between a light Apollonian persona of order and a dark Dionysian persona of chaos. Other dualisms that indicate his restlessness and in-betweenness are the ones between Hitler and Beethoven, Germany and Poland, Alfred and Jan, and Catholicism and atheism. However, Oskar both oscillates between them and transgresses them: "Paradox [Zwiespältig], I have said. The cleavage was lasting; I have never been able to heal it, and it is still with me today, though today I am at home neither in the sacred nor the profane but dwell on the fringes, in a mental hospital" (*TD*, 131).

Said claims that the exile compensates for his disorientation by creating a new world to rule: "Willfullness, exaggeration, overstatement: these are the characteristic styles of being an exile, methods for compelling the world to accept your vision."[17] This is true of Oskar, who can be considered a demiurge attempting to impose his own fictional version of the world on the reader. The epistemological point is that Oskar's version, no matter how unnatural, exaggerated, and fictional it may seem, offers the reader an alternative version of a world that is otherwise trapped in ready-made forms.

In the above, we have focused on Oskar's isolation as an important trait of his character. Said speaks in this regard about a "narcissistic masochism that resists all efforts at amelioration, acculturation, and community. At this extreme the exile can make a fetish of exile, a practice that distances him or her from all connections and commitments."[18] It is appropriate in the case of Oskar to talk of a fetish of exile, as he consciously and strategically chooses to live his life on the margins; Oskar takes pride in his detachment. The exilic position and his perspective from below make Oskar a *picaro*—that is, "an inveterate vagabond."[19] The picaro detaches himself through an ironic stance from the social order and puts his trust in himself as the only valid center of the world, because he sees what others do not see—that is, the disintegration of a whole society.

However, Oskar's detachment and irony are supplemented by opposite traits, those of involvement and affectivity: "there is a relationship marked by skepticism, detachment, independence, superiority, the operation of mind; and there is a relationship marked by involvement, dependence, vulnerability and impotence, the operation of feeling," John Reddick claims.[20] In other words, the picaresque mode alone is insufficient in articulating an adequate sense of uprooting because it operates by detached reflection. In order to capture the full extent of the processes and consequences of dislocation—and according to Reddick, dislocation can be seen as the trilogy's paramount principle of existence—it is necessary that Oskar also suffers reality:

> So long as Oskar is a complete, self-sufficient, static being, so long as he genuinely needs nothing from those he so peremptorily rejects [. . .] and so long as his inner activity does not go beyond the operation of eye and mind, he is in a supreme position. As soon as he *feels* and *wants*, thus joining after all in the normal order of existence, then the fact that he is a lone outsider with no links to his family works radically to his disadvantage.[21]

Reddick speaks here of Oskar's detachment as a mode of stasis, whereas I have claimed that Oskar may be regarded as a migrant. Robert Alter seems to support my claim, though, when he speaks of the picaro as a vagabond, and Grass himself has pointed to Oskar's mobility vis-à-vis the original conception of the stylite. How are we to respond to this seeming inconsistency? The solution, I believe, lies in distinguishing between Oskar's perspective and his personal identity. When Oskar acts in the picaresque mode, mobility relates primarily to his point of view and to his vagabonding through society, which gives the reader the impression of shifts and movement, whereas his inner self is left partly unaffected. Oskar's inner self is then the preserve of his vulnerable mode in which he suffers mental dislocations and disruptions. Hence, we have *self-chosen exile and sovereign picaro* on the one side, and *forced migration and wretched victimhood* on the other, a paradoxical structure that assures an inconslusive and oscillatory movement between poles.

Reddick points to the episode in which Oskar resumes his growth (in concurrence with his actual emigration) as the most obvious example of a shift from the picaresque to the affective mode. Oskar's superiority is undermined on several occasions in the novel, though. The affective mode is clearly felt in his relationship with both Agnes and Maria, the latter provoking the stiffening of Oskar's "watering can," thus indicating his vulnerability and lack of self-control. His feeling of guilt in connection with the deaths of Agnes, Alfred, and Jan are examples of his ethical awareness and compassion, which at times lead him to self-examination whereby he no longer occupies the role of (superior) subject but rather that of (suffering) object.

Oskar's superiority unmistakably shows in the episode in which he causes Fräulein Spollenhauer's breakdown. He leaves the school without showing any signs of regret for the lost prospects of a conventional education. However, shortly after his first and last day in school, Oskar actually reveals an affective trait when he sees other children carrying books on their way to school: "A suspicion of envy, I have said, and that is all it was" (*TD*, 73).

Oskar admits his envy of the other children, even though he tries to dismiss it as commonplace. Furthermore, Oskar's relationships with Bebra, Roswitha, Sigismund Markus, and Herbert Truczinski are all marked by the affective mode of the vulnerable Oskar. The death of Herbert thus leads up to and colors the disheartening and moving chapter on the Crystal Night, in which Sigismund also dies. That chapter, together with the chapter on the emigration in the goods wagon, is emotionally the strongest chapter in the book. Yet another turning point expressing the shift between the detached and affective modes occurs when Oskar, during a game of skat with Kobyella and the delirious Jan shortly before the latter's death, suddenly drops all disguises. The reason for this is Oskar's "never before experienced [. . .] feeling of responsibility" (*TD*, 222).

After his emigration, Oskar's sense of responsibility actually leads him to wish for his integration into society. He thus speaks of "the desire to become an honest citizen" by becoming "a businessman, a family man, a respected member of society," but this desire cannot be fulfilled: "Maria turned me down" (*TD*, 438–39). Instead, and this must be underlined, he remains an outsider of bourgeois society. At the end of the novel, after being arrested for a murder he did not commit, he just wants to stay in bed in the asylum. He is terrified of being released, just as he is terrified of the Black Witch, a symbol of the hostile forces that overwhelm him in his affective mode. And the fact that Oskar resorts to symbolism in order to express what he cannot understand is in itself a sign of his impotence: to Grass, symbolism is a reductive abstraction of a complex reality.

* * *

If Oskar oscillates between detachment, irony, and self-chosen exile on the one side, and involvement, vulnerability, and forced migration on the other, Eduard Amsel in *Dog Years* seems to have inherited only the superiority that followed from Oskar's ironic detachment. Amsel is practically invulnerable and fears no Black Witch; the persecution he suffers is unequivocally transformed into artistic strength. If Oskar at the end of *The Tin Drum* is afraid that the true murderer will be found, as this would cause his release from the mental asylum, Amsel at the end of *Dog Years* is the owner of a mine in which he produces scarecrows on capitalist terms. To speak of integration in Amsel's case thus seems legitimate, but only to a certain degree because integration is counterweighted by his unsettling scarecrow production, which should be interpreted as a bleak and grotesque vision of the world and a constant reminder of Germany's guilt-ridden past.

Amsel is a reddish, corpulent half-Jew, and this situates him, like Oskar, on the periphery of society. In the beginning of the novel, though, confusion prevails in regard to Amsel's paternal lineage. Eduard has never known his father, who died in World War I shortly before Eduard was born in 1917. Eduard is raised as a Protestant, and it is only when people around him insinuate his Jewish inheritance that he becomes aware of his father's roots. And when he confronts his mother, she replies in her own characteristic dialect (which the English translation unfortunately fails to transmit): "Ah, son. Forgive your poor mother. Amsel, you never knew him but he was your very own father, was one of the circumcised as they say. I only hope they don't catch you now the laws are so strict." ("Och Jonkchen. Väzaih dain arme Modder. Dä Amsel, dem de nech kennst, waas abä laibhaftich dain Vadder waar jewesen, daas warren Beschnittner, wie man so secht. Wennse dir nur nech mechten äwischen, wose doch jätz so scharf sind midde Jesätze.") (*DY,* 37)

So, Eduard Amsel is a half-Jew, and this does make him a victim of persecution during his childhood years. But as I said earlier, Amsel cannot help transforming his sufferings into artistic strength: "but through the tears which, as everyone knows, confer a blurred but uncommonly precise vision, his greenish-gray, fat-encased little eyes never ceased to observe, to appraise, and to analyze typical movements" (*DY,* 41). As a child he builds scarecrows famous for their effectiveness, and together with his artistic endeavors, he shows great talent for trading when he sells the scarecrows to local farmers. Socially, he is thus more integrated than Oskar, but his integration into society is combined with a detachment relating to his artistic practice. As opposed to Oskar, who is superior in one mode but vulnerable in another, Amsel is superior both as an artist and as a businessman.

Walter Matern, the other protagonist in *Dog Years,* acts as Amsel's protector during their school years. Roughly speaking, he provides the muscle, whereas Amsel provides the brain. Matern becomes dependent on Amsel, and his occasional attempts to break free from Amsel are always unsuccessful. Like God and Satan, they are opposites, yet inseparable, and in this sense they bear structural similarity to Fonty and Hoftaller in *Too Far Afield* (1995) and to Gibreel and Salahuddin in Rushdie's *The Satanic Verses.* One of the reasons why Matern is playing second fiddle to Amsel is his inability to cope with moral ambiguity and the pluralist complexity of reality. "He simplifies labyrinths into straight broad highways" (*DY,* 482), it thus says of Matern's reaction to a world that appears like a "net-like pattern" (*DY,* 38), whereas Amsel is praised for his "keen sense of reality in all its innumerable forms" (*DY,* 39).

Another reaction of Matern when he is overpowered by the inevitable and inexplicable forces of the world and life's evanescence—in this case the fact of death—is to grind his teeth: "Whenever he sees anything dead: a drowned cat, rats he has slain with his own hand, gulls slit open with a throw of his knife, when he sees a bloated fish rolled in the sand by the lapping of the waves, or when he sees a skeleton which Amsel wants to deprive of its skull, his teeth start in from left to right" (DY, 89). This reminds us of Oskar's behavior when he is confonted by the Black Witch or the incomprehensible forces behind this symbol. Both Oskar and Matern either withdraw into themselves or explode in a rage against the world when they feel overpowered by forces they do not understand or by memento mori [reminder of mortality] motifs: Oskar withdraws to his bed, to his closet, or under the skirts of his grandmother; or he destroys things by using his voice, as when he shatters the windows of the Municipal Theater because Agnes has abandoned him for half an hour in order to be with Jan. Matern retreats into an inner feeling of mental impotence that assumes the expression of toothgrinding; or he reacts violently, as when he hits Amsel because of the latter's insistence on taking a closer look at a skull.

Both Amsel and Matern are mobile identities, but they experience movement and instability differently. Matern's instability is emphasized by his work as an actor, by his moving from Danzig to Schwerin to Düsseldorf to the battlefront and back to Danzig, and by his jumping from one job to another and from one ideology to another—from Marxism to Nazism, for instance. In Matern's case, however, everything seems to be disguises that he merely tries on, and he clearly suffers "because of the troubled, masterless times" (DY, 398). His postwar odyssey, where he visits his old friends from the Nazi Party in order to avenge their past wrongdoings, is thus both fallacious and fruitless, as it is founded on Matern's conviction that he is different from his victims. However, he is guilty of the exact same atrocities, only he has repressed them. His whole existence thus reflects the German postwar propensity to forget the past. Matern's postwar wanderings merely underline his instability, and it is highly indicative that a lavatory at the Cologne station, a space characterized by movement and flux, functions as the symbolic center of his existence during this odyssey. This reminds us of Oskar's assertion at the end of The Tin Drum: "I felt quite at home on that escalator" (TD, 563). Escalator and station lavatory are both signs of Oskar's and Matern's deeply ironical sense of belonging.

In Matern's case, instability results in a complete lack of identity. His different roles are never absorbed into any whole, not even a whole that "comes after" as an effect or a provisional one: "Then Matern speaks bit by bit. He sets building blocks one on another" (DY, 419). The bricks, however, lack the cement necessary for joining them together. Hence his life is without continuity and memory. Matern himself admits: "Since then a lot of things have broken inside me incurably: dissonance, ostracism, shards, fragments of myself, that can never be put together again" (*DY,* 420). Matern is incapable of transforming the potential inherent in his disorientation into anything positive.

As Reddick correctly observes with regard to the crucial metamorphosis episodes where Amsel and Jenny Brunies are harassed by Tulla and the nine Stormtroopers (SA) men, including Matern: "Amsel, Jenny, Matern, and to a certain extent Tulla, are all metamorphosed by the two critical acts of persecution—but it is the would-be victims who are beneficially metamorphosed in Grass's fiction, while the persecutors paradoxically suffer, albeit in a nonphysical sense."[22] Whereas Matern and Tulla both suffer psychologically because of their guilt and their difficulty in coming to terms with their destructive deeds, but also because of their difficulty in coming to terms with the reasons behind their deeds—that is, their inability to cope with a complex and morally ambiguous reality—Jenny and Amsel actually benefit from the persecutions. Jenny, the plump gypsy, is transformed into an ideal ballet body, which makes it possible for her to pursue her, hitherto ridiculous, dream of becoming a ballet dancer. The corpulent Amsel is transformed into a lean, chain-smoking Haseloff, one of his many identities in the novel. Both of them, Haseloff immediately and Jenny a few years later, travel to Berlin and become successful artists.

Like Matern, Amsel deliberately assumes a long line of different roles. But all of these roles are linked to his artistic development and are therefore part of a continuous and absorbing whole. As Hollington remarks, "The flexibility and prolixity of personalities in Amsel is a conscious response to the 'absurdity' of history; what ties them together is a keen responsiveness to the pluralist complexity of reality."[23] If Amsel's plural identity is a conscious artistic strategy that enables him to respond to a complex world, Matern's plural identity is a consequence of his incapacity to endure a world of transcendental homelessness—that is, a world in which meaning is never "simply there" but has to be produced. What further separates Amsel from Matern is his ironic detachment from reality. Matern desperately searches for meaning in an absurd world; he takes the world much too seriously, whereas Amsel has come to terms with the world's absurdity. And Amsel does not suffer reality in the same way that Oskar does; he transforms every experience into powerful artistic expressions. The plurality of his identity is never a problem because he, as Reddick asserts, "has an unchallenged sense both of his own identity and of the true reality of the world around him, and as a result is able—thanks to his crucially characteristic *irony,* and notwithstanding certain temporary setbacks—to preserve himself in a position that is always viable, if only just."[24]

Dog Years thus offers a slightly less bleak vision of the world than *The Tin Drum* does, primarily because of Amsel's superiority and success as a businessman and artist. *The Tin Drum* ends with Oskar's vulnerability and fears in relation to a frightening world; *Dog Years* ends in Amsel's underground pandemonium, itself a frightening construction, but precisely because it is a construction, it is also mastered by its creator. Even though Oskar is a demiurge, a creator of the novel's fictional universe, he has not learned to master the world to the same degree that Amsel has: Amsel upholds his detachment, scrupulous honesty, and ironic stance throughout the novel. As to the question of reconciliation, in *Dog Years* it can be answered more affirmatively than in the case of *The Tin Drum*, but it is necessary to emphasize Amsel's role as a severe critic of the society in which he functions well nonetheless. And if Amsel's underground pandemonium is meant to serve as a modern journey of *Bildung* for the spectator, the final words of the novel nevertheless indicate that Amsel and Matern, though inseparable, remain unreconciled and separated: "He and I strip off our mine outfits. For me and him bathtubs have been filled. I hear Eddi splashing next door. Now I too step into my bath. The water soaks me clean. Eddi whistles something indeterminate. I try to whistle something similar. But it's difficult. We're both naked. Each of us bathes by himself" (*DY,* 610). Even though they are stripped naked, thus partly without their individuality, thereby underlining what unites them, the novel ends on a gloomy note as they still bathe separately. In fact, all of Book Three can be seen as a pessimistic view of a contemporary Germany "full of the forgetfulness which is pleasing to God" (*DY,* 579).

As different as Oskar, Eduard, and Walter may be, we are nevertheless left with three heroes battling absurdity, and as Harry Liebenau, the third narrator in *Dog Years,* says in a passage that might stand as a motto for Grass's work, the very battle may be reason enough: "Keep going! As long as we're telling stories, we're alive. As long as stories keep coming, with or without a point, dog stories, eel stories, scarecrow stories, rat stories, flood stories, recipe stories, stories full of lies and schoolbook stories, as long as stories have power to entertain us, no hell can take us in" (*DY,* 575).

Territories and Histories

Where a chain of events appears before *us, he* sees one single catastrophe, which keeps piling wreckage upon wreckage and hurls it at his feet.
—Walter Benjamin, "On the Concept of History"

All three works of *The Danzig Trilogy* are set in the unique cultural setting of Danzig and the delta of the Vistula River, and they are part of the artistic "movement" usually referred to as "Vergangenheitsbewältigung" ("a coming to terms with the past"), as they deal with the rise of Nazism, the war experience, and the postwar era of the German "Wirtschaftswunder" (Economic Miracle). In what follows I seek to examine what I choose to call "space travels" and "time travels" and the way in which they are interrelated in *The Tin Drum* and *Dog Years*. The narrators-protagonists have lost their hometown as a result of their emigration from Danzig to West Germany after the war. In other words, their emigration to the West implies the loss of the East—but also the loss of the past. In this sense their forced migration to the West causes the narrators to travel back in time in order to preserve the memory of the past and the East, but also in order to understand the present: the space travel in the present necessitates a time travel into the past.

The Tin Drum and *Dog Years* are usually associated with the city of Danzig and the petty bourgeois world, just as the era of the Third Reich is generally considered the historical period in which the action of the novels unfolds. However, I will argue that both these points call for reconsideration. As to the spatial configuration, I will show that Danzig is more than just a petty bourgeois world and that the city is only one spatial setting among others, although, admittedly, it occupies a central role. The impurity of the Danzig territory is not hightlighted enough in much literature on Grass, but my reading reconsiders the Grassian space and thereby "discovers" a more heterogeneous space. As for the temporal configuration, I will show that Grass does not limit himself to the years of National Socialism, although the narrated time concerns primarily this period. In the novels, time can instead be understood as a boundless reservoir, a virtuality bestowed with the power to constantly remodel the "official" version of history and the present. In this way time becomes a destabilizing factor in the novels. The complex constellation of time and space can thus be described in Bhabha's words as a "non-synchronous temporality of local and global cultures" that opens up a cultural third space in which "the negotiation of incommensurable differences creates a tension peculiar to borderline existences."[25]

Danzig and the suburb of Langfuhr may rightly be regarded as a microcosm with an exceptionally representative potential in Grass's work. The often quoted passage in *Dog Years* reads thus: "There was once a city—in addition to the suburbs of Ohra, Schidlitz, Oliva, Emmaus, Praust, Sankt Albrecht, Schellmühl, and the seaport suburb of Neufahrwasser, it had a suburb named Langfuhr. Langfuhr was so big and so little that whatever happens or could happen in this world, also happened or could have happened in Langfuhr" (*DY,* 337). With passages like this, it comes as no surprise that Grass's work is considered to be about Danzig-Langfuhr.

Hanspeter Brode thus speaks of Langfuhr "as a mirror of the world, as the-
atrum mundi [the world as stage], not in the sense of timeless allegory, but
rather as a sign of the Grassian setting as a focal point and its epochal significance," and Danzig is "for the period of time depicted by Grass a centre
of universal historical importance."[26] Brode's distinction between "timeless
allegory" and "epochal significance" is important because it implies that
Danzig must be "read" as a concrete historicity. But what does Brode mean
by "universal historical importance"?

In his book on the *Bildungsroman,* Franco Moretti discusses the novel's
relationship to universal history and everyday life. Moretti sees a polarized
relationship between these two spheres of life, in that universal history seems
to deal with major historical crises and acquisitions, whereas the sphere of
everyday life concerns the mundane and the ordinary. In the specific case of
the *Bildungsroman,* it is everyday life that serves as the background of what
Moretti sees as this genre's main characteristic—namely, the happiness of the
protagonist secured by an organic integration into society. So, in relation to
the *Bildungsroman* (where universal history would imply a "critique" of
everyday life, thereby preventing happiness and organic integration), but
also to the novel in general, Moretti argues that universal history is never
the viewpoint taken by the novel. How does this correspond with Brode's
assertion of the universal role of Danzig history in the works of Grass?
Moretti provides the answer himself: "Not blind to the progress of universal
history, novelistic form nevertheless 'reshapes' it as it is perceived from the
viewpoint of everyday life. Furthermore, the novel 'funnels' universal history
into this mode of existence in order to amplify and enrich the life of the
'particularity.'"[27] On the one hand, universal history is refracted by a viewpoint of everyday life; on the other hand, everyday life is enriched by the
impulses of universal history. In Grass, universal history is always refracted
through the eyes of a narrator situated very much in the sphere of everyday
life, but the narrator always embodies a certain eccentric perspective, too,
thus making the refraction even more "particular." As to Moretti's other
assertion, that of the enrichment of everyday life through the evocation of
the past and "universal" history, I will come back to it later on.

With regard to the emblematic role of Danzig-Langfuhr and its surrounding area, it is my belief that this role can be divided into two, in many
ways, opposing poles. First, and this is what Brode refers to and what the
critics usually agree upon, Danzig-Langfuhr contains the seeds of what
turned out to be world history—that is, the era of Hitler and National
Socialism. In this regard, Brode speaks of "Danzig in the forefront of world-
transformative processes."[28] This negative quality is closely related to the
German petty bourgeois society of Danzig. Second, and this is not always

sufficiently appreciated in the reception of Grass, but it is an important point for my overall argument, Grass's Danzig area also possesses a multi-ethnic, positive quality that makes it a territory with a certain international ambience. Thus, regionalism in Grass points in two directions: provincialism and cosmopolitanism.

As for the first pole, there is an example in *The Tin Drum* of Danzig-Langfuhr's role in world history when we are told about Alfred Matzerath's "prophetic shopkeeper's exterior [zukunftsträgtiches Kleinbürgertum]" (*TD*, 70). Here the petty bourgeoisie is characterized as an organism ripe with future developments. The petty bourgeoisie of Danzig is thus widely regarded as one of the premises for the invasion: "Their 'plight' was to be the pretext of Hitler's invasion of Poland in 1939," Michael Hollington points out. And in relation to Danzig-Langfuhr, Hollington also observes: "It is evidently provincial, philistine, materialistic, ugly. Its petit-bourgeois inhabitants, struggling to survive as the depression hit Germany, were prime targets for Hitler."[29] It is in this sense that Danzig can be viewed as a microcosm of what I choose to call the negative impulses of the period.

Grass's attitude toward the petty bourgeoisie is indisputably ambivalent: at times he depicts it with affection, but more often he portrays it with ruthless cynicism and "scrupulous honesty."[30] If one is to talk about a nostalgic tone—and nostalgia is a recurring theme in the literature of migration and exile (e.g., in Kundera and W. G. Sebald)—it is rarely to be found in Grass's depictions of the petty bourgeois world, but rather in his conjuring up of a more general Danzig atmosphere, invoked by descriptions of architecture, street life, beaches, trams, and the constant invocation of place names. W. G. Cunliffe recognizes this paradoxical oscillation of the exile's memory between nostalgia and ruthless honesty: "The accuracy of the background springs from the fact that the exile remembers his lost home with barely-suppressed nostalgia for its speech, customs, and place-names. Yet the same accuracy forces the narrator to include, for example, the concentration camp of Stutthof, near Danzig, which duly appears in Grass' picture of the region. Reality precludes the attitude of nostalgia."[31] Hence it is very difficult for nostalgia to sustain any significant role in Grass's technique simply because the harsh reality of his past prevents a nostalgic tone.

The trilogy contains numerous examples of cynicism toward the petty bourgeoisie and of the demasking of its empty ideals and hypocrisy. Oskar's birthday party, which turns into a German petty bourgeois version of Sodom and Gomorrah, is unveiled to the reader through the "innocent" eyes of the little drummer, thereby revealing the artificiality and double standards of the grown-up world; Fräulein Spollenhauer's attempt to turn all the schoolboys into a homogenous group of devoted sons of the fatherland is ruined by Oskar, who sees right through her insecure and barren character. In *Dog Years*, the stories about cynology and the recurring episodes concerning the genealogy of the dogs are ironic commentaries about the obsession of the petty bourgeoisie and the Nazis with genealogy and purity:

> The organ of the German Shepherd Dog Association sent a cynologist, whom my father was obliged to turn out of the house. For this dog expert began at once to carp at our Harras's pedigree. The names, he declared, were revolting and alien to the breed; there were no data about the bitch that had whelped Senta; the animal itself was not bad, but it would be his duty to inveigh against such methods of dog raising; precisely because this was a historical dog, a sense of responsibility was in order.
>
> (*DY*, 171)

The irony is unmistakable and the novel's frequent references to dogs and their pedigrees parody the idea of mythical Aryan origins that Hitler and his racist pseudo-authorities claimed for the German people. What is more, the irony is emphasized by the fact that Hitler's own dog, Prinz, is said to have impure origins, and this example is only one of many in which the illusions of national and racial purity are deconstructed from within through inevitable differences and impurities.

Another example of antisentimentality toward the petit bourgeoisie concerns Stutthof, whose name is invoked (according to Cunliffe) as a consequence of Grass's exilic, and thereby accurate, memory. In one of Harry's "love letters" to his cousin Tulla Pokriefke, he says,

> Stutthof: on your account!
>   That little word took on more and more meaning. "Hey, you! You got a yen for Stutthof?"—"If you don't keep that trap of yours shut, you'll end up in Stutthof." A sinister word had moved into apartment houses, went upstairs and downstairs, sat at kitchen tables, was supposed to be a joke, and some actually laughed: "They're making soap in Stutthof now, it makes you want to stop washing.
>
> (*DY*, 294)

First, this letter provides an example of what Reddick has described as an "ironic contrast" between style, language, tone, or genre (love letters) and the actual content (concentration camps). According to Reddick, this contrastive style of irony, detachment, and distance results in "a radical unsentimentality" in Grass.[32] The contrasting technique is a way of incorporating what Lukács called "the fragmentary nature of the world's structure into the world of forms." Second, Grass shows us how the word "Stutthof" is slowly absorbed into everyday conversation in a supposedly innocent way. The quotation suggests the complicity of the members of the petty bourgeois society who are laughing even though they have a pretty good idea of what is going on there. What Grass illustrates in a masterly way is the mechanisms of collective repression formally articulated through slogans that both conceal and reveal reality. Finally, there is the theme of purity, which was also present in the parody of cynology. As one of the expressions implies, what is usually a symbol of purity—that is, soap—is no longer pure, as it is made of "them," the "impure" Jews.

* * *

Danzig-Langfuhr and the novels as such are not inhabited by the petty bourgeoisie alone, though. This fact is not always properly recognized by the critics, who tend to focus exclusively on this milieu: "The 'Danzig Trilogy' confines itself to the world of the petit bourgeoisie," Volker Neuhaus claims.[33] As I will hopefully make clear in what follows, *The Tin Drum* and *Dog Years* also incorporate other "worlds." It is true that the petty bourgeois circle dominates the Grassian canvas, providing the prevailing gray color so precious to Grass. However, what really distinguishes the work of Grass are the small, yet intensive and colorful spots that protrude from the general grayness of the universe. Oskar Matzerath, Bebra, Oswald Brunies, Jenny Brunies, and Eduard Amsel are examples of colorful outsiders who transgress the otherwise closed provincial circle of the petty bourgeoisie. And as readers, we are led to sympathize with these transgressive and impure characters because they represent positive counterimages to provincialism.

One example that is explicitly indicative of *Dog Years*'s high estimation of Oswald Brunies is Brauxel/Eduard's admission that the whole novel is actually a tribute to Oswald: "the authors' consortium is planning to build him a monument" (*DY*, 102). However, as always in Grass's work, there are no simple black-and-white divisions. Even though Eduard and Jenny, together with Oswald, may pass for the novel's positive artistic-cosmopolitan protagonists, they are involved with the "Wehrmacht" (Armed Forces) during the war, as they work as Hitler's employees at the German Ballet in Berlin (the same is true of Oskar when he travels with Bebra's Theater at the Front). However, this somewhat dubious involvement with the Nazis cannot hide the fact that Jenny and, especially, Eduard are the true heroes of *Dog Years*. Both have been victims of persecution throughout their childhoods—one for being a gypsy and too fat; the other for being a Jew and too fat. One of the key episodes in the novel is the depiction of their simultaneous (literal) metamorphoses—both transformations triggered by

Tulla's and Walter's violent persecutions—into thin artistic figures: Eduard is transformed into the chain-smoking Haseloff, later to become master of the Berlin Ballet, and Jenny is transformed into the perfect ballet body, who eventually joins Haseloff in Berlin and becomes his star performer.

What is more, the following statement by Oskar also supports the idea of a transgression of provincialism:

> You will say: how limited the world to which this young man was reduced for his education! A grocery store, a bakery, and a vegetable shop circum-scribed the field in which he was obliged to piece together his equipment for adult life. Yes, I must admit that Oskar gathered his first, all-important impressions in very musty *petit-bourgeois* surroundings. However, I had a third teacher. It was he who would open up the world to Oskar and make him what he is today, a person whom, for want of a better epithet, I can only term cosmopolitan.
>
> (*TD*, 288)

In this passage, which deliberately plays with the conventions of the *Bildungsroman*, we are introduced to the otherness of the petty bourgeoisie, in this case an otherness embodied by Bebra. If the petty bourgeoisie is an indispensable part of Danzig, the city also has a more positive side to it nonetheless—that of cosmopolitanism and multiethnicity.

It must be acknowledged, however, that multiethnicity is in fact a char-acteristic of the petty bourgeoisie itself. Oskar's family is a prominent example, being a mixture of German, Polish, and Cassubian, as well as of Protestant and Catholic. Nevertheless, Oskar's statement above indicates that the world of the petty bourgeoisie is a somewhat claustrophobic and self-contained one. Although the petty bourgeois circle may encompass multiethnicity or hybridity in some cases, these qualities are always regarded as a problem in this society, never as a source of strength or creativity. Helen Croft thus speaks of "a society unable to channel its creative impulses posi-tively."[34] If the petty bourgeoisie does not possess the capacity to include impure and eccentric characters within its midst, the novels pay tribute to these characters all the same. What defines them is that they all originate in the petty bourgeoisie but end up transgressing its borders. The impurity and hybridity of Grass's universe is recognized by Brode:

> The Danzig milieu, this mixing of different peoples and cultures—German, Polish, Cassubian—a Catholicism mixed with pagan elements, the mysteri-ous widths of the Vistula landscape, Prussian mythology, and the gypsies in the woods near the former German-Polish border (e.g. in *Dog Years*), the

atmosphere of sea-port with far-reaching connections to all the other neighboring states in the Baltic Sea and beyond, and furthermore a dimension blurred in prehistory (in *The Flounder*)—an exotic flair radiates from the Grassian fantasy world, also when it is rooted in history. A literary cartography of the bygone Eastern Germany has since been attempted by other authors; however, no one has achieved the Grassian model.[35]

Brode makes it very clear that "the Grassian model" does not merely contain the petty bourgeois world; on the contrary, it is a model consisting of hybrid and bastard qualities in terms of people, religion, territory, and history. Grass's literary cartography is therefore one of heterogeneities, impurities, and transgressions.

There are constant reminders of transgressions of borders and clashes between segments in Grass's novels. The Danzig setting as a cross-cultural border territory is emphasized in the episode in which Oskar's cousin Stefan is beaten up by a kindergarten classmate because he is a "Polack": "'Polack!,' he hissed between blows. 'Polack!'" Stefan's teacher is of no help as she explains to the German children that being a Pole is not really Stephan's own fault: "He can't help it if he's a little Pole" (*DY*, 60–61). Besides revealing the perversion of childhood and the intercultural tensions of the area, this episode also reveals the degradation of the German language: "Gradually, words lost their original meaning and acquired nightmarish definitions. *Jude, Pole, Russe* came to mean two-legged lice, putrid vermin which good Aryans must squash," George Steiner remarks.[36]

The Polish-German dilemma is also brought forward by Sigismund Markus: When he realizes that he cannot persuade Agnes to follow him to London, he urges her to stick with the Germans (Matzerath) and give up her Polish adventures (Bronski) as the two sides are about to clash in what will inevitably lead to the victory of the Germans. Another example: When the gypsy Bibandengero in *Dog Years* hands over the bundle that contains Jenny Brunies, we are told that "Amsel isn't sure whether or not this is Polish territory. [. . .] Neither of them sees the border" (*DY*, 122). Incidents like these are constant reminders of the territorializations and deterritorializations that take place on this geopolitical level in the novels. What is more, the handover of Jenny at the border underlines her own status as a "Grenzgänger" (border crosser). And as Roger Bromley has pointed out in regard to migrant narratives in general, "Each deterritorialisation (of people, identity, form, or genre) constitutes and extends the territory itself; it is a way to keep on opening up meanings. We are talking about radical refiguration: against boundary, limit and demarcation."[37] Following Bromley, in Grass we come upon an extension of meaning, the opening up of a third space, as a result of the nonsynchronous temporality of divergent cultural spaces. Grass achieves this, as we shall see below, by activating or actualizing the inherent potentialities of a given space.

The inclusion of the Cassubians and their landscape also adds diversity to the fictional universe, introducing a completely different reality from that of the petty bourgeoisie in the city of Danzig. The Cassubian reality is rural and austere and more oriented toward the past than the future. As Hollington says, "They are a peasant race with a culture that still manages to cling on to survival, pious, thrifty, superstitious. Their folklore is not concerned with heroic exploits but rather with the dealings of trickster figures with a capacity for survival."[38] They are often portrayed with affection in Grass's work, but any form of nostalgia that might sneak into the discourse is always counterweighted with parody and irony. One example is the unforgettable scene of Agnes's supposed conception under Anna's wide skirts in the Cassubian potato field in the first chapter of *The Tin Drum*, which

> exorcises Grass's fifteen-year-old attempts to romanticize Cassubia for the consumption of Nazi schools. It contains the standard props of the Nazi rural idyll—the earth-mother, the emphasis on being rooted to the land, in the race-consciousness—all in parodic form. The month is October (at the end of a century too), the weather cold, the landscape grey and monotonous, the costumes drab. Harsh realities intrude—it is difficult to keep warm, the fire hard to ignite and keep going, the food primitive.[39]

What Hollington refers to in the beginning of the quotation is Grass's schoolboy attempt to write a story in which, as a young Nazi aspirant, he would glorify and romanticize Cassubian virtues. What Hollington subsequently emphasizes, with reference to the mature Grass, is the constant narratorial withdrawal from the temptation to sentimentalize and give in to nostalgia.

* * *

The rural countryside east of Danzig plays an important role in *Dog Years.* The beginning of the novel is set in the landscape of the Vistula flowing into the Baltic Sea. The Vistula is a symbol of the eternal flow of time; it is a stream from which yet untold stories may pour. In the words of Brauchsel: "What had long been forgotten rose to memory, floating on its back or stomach, with the help of the Vistula" (*DY,* 11). Hence, the Vistula emerges as a metaphor for history's elephantine memory. In Grass's work, history is always in motion, but without purpose, inner logic, or coherence (this is one reason for the oddly patterned microstructure of the novel). History is ultimately seen as chaos and catastrophe. The remembrance of a problematical past is determined by the way time as a creative filter discloses history as being replete with forgotten stories, stories endowed with a potential to persistently modify the very same history. As a consequence, history can no longer serve as a metaphysical point of anchorage, first, because it contains an immanent potential of "micropolitical" stories that undermine its own stability, and second, because it is not teleologically equipped with any ideological final point.

The beginning of *Dog Years* presents an image of the Vistula as a river that both gives and takes. On the one hand, it constantly throws up things that have been left behind in the dustbin of history; it hurls wreckage in front of the narrator's feet, objects just waiting to be unfolded and "told." Accordingly, Hollington alludes to "the river Vistula as an image of the course of history, a kind of preserving fluid in which concrete evidence of the reality of the past is gathered."[40] So, in the novel, history is a constant presence, or to be more precise, a presence of concrete objects, ruins, and wreckage in the Benjaminian sense. However, as opposed to Benjamin's angel of history, Grass never turns away from history; rather, he confronts it despite its brutality. Grass's mission is to rescue these objects from oblivion—in *Fünf Jahrzehnte* (Five Decades) he thus speaks of his "fixation on the objectedness [aufs Gegenständliche]."[41] On the other hand, history not only provides the narrator with objects and potential stories, but also has an enormous appetite; it swallows everything up. The engulfing power of history is explicitly evoked through the repetition of the word "took" nine times in relation to the Vistula on page 11 in the novel. In this way, nothing escapes history, everything is devoured by this monster, but at the same time history becomes a reservoir of objects and stories just waiting to be unfolded, and refolded into (if not orderly, then) meaningful patterns.

In *Dog Years* Grass thoroughly explores the Danzig area's history before 1900 for the first time, and he resumes this act of remembering the distant past in *The Flounder* (1977). In "Erinnerungslosigkeit" (Amnesia), Karl Heinz Bohrer criticizes German politicians, historians, and writers for their inability to remember the distant past. According to Bohrer, this leads to an unhealthy obsession with the years linked to the Third Reich:

> Without going further into these new accounts of historical epochs [. . .], which are marked by structural and causal clarities, one can nonetheless mention two main causes to the amnesia. First: German history is seen through the prehistory of the Third Empire. Second: A German history before Bismarck's founding of the Empire does actually not exist in this perspective—and what

is more: The concepts "German" and "German nation" become disqualified as historically obsolete.[42]

Bohrer may very well have a point, but in that case I see Grass as an exception to the rule. Grass never portrays historical periods with any structural or causal clarity; he does quite the opposite, always emphasizing the chaotic and absurd nature of history, and always trying to "portray the forgotten face of history" as it says in the Nobel Academy's statement. And although Grass's work is in general preoccupied with the history immediately preceding the Third Reich, he expands the historical horizon in both *Dog Years* and *The Flounder,* but also in *Too Far Afield,* which is deeply engaged with the notions of "German" and "German nation" before and around the time of Bismarck.

So, when Bohrer claims "that the present time of our epoch has become more and more broad, and therefore the past has become shorter," which means that "the good prevails, the evil is forbidden,"[43] it is only partly true when speaking of Grass, who irrefutably employs evil as a central motif. Undoubtedly, the present is expanded in Grass, but at the same time he extends the historical thread of the past—in fact, this extending of the past is what results in the broadening of our present. Merging the past and the present is precisely what Bohrer believes literature should do in the first place: "To poetic memory—memory is since the Greek Mnemosyne something like the basic definition of poetry—it is not about an objective invoking of past events, rather about the creation of an imaginative link between my present time and the past."[44] In my opinion, Grass uses imagination in his novels precisely to establish connections between present and past, since memory and amnesia are linked to the time-space configuration and to the "archaeological" discovery of cultural and ethnic heterogeneity.

However, let us take a closer look at how Grass actually engenders such a past, as well as at the implications this has for the territorial design of the novel. What I wish to show in the following is that Grass's archaeological rummaging of the past is a means by which to expand the present, to make it diverse and pluralistic—and now we are back to what Moretti calls the amplification of everyday life combined with the refraction of universal history. In the first book of *Dog Years,* Amsel informs the reader about Walter Matern's ancestors and describes how the Materns came to be millers: "August Matern in out-of-the-way Nickelswalde counted the Danish specie and two-thirds pieces, the quickly rising rubles, the Hamburg mark pieces, the Laubtalers and convention talers, the little bags of Dutch gulden and the newly issued Danzig paper money; he found himself nicely off and abandoned himself to the joys of reconstruction" (*DY,* 20–21). The territory of the Danzig region is shown here as playing host to a history of international encounters and transactions on its soil, being traversed as it was by Danish, Russian, Hamburgian, Dutch, and Danzig currencies. By digging into the past and showing us how the Danzig area was quite impure, Grass also causes a rupture and an expansion of (the reader's comprehension of) the present Danzig territory. He is, so to speak, trying to bring the multiple roots of the territory back to life by revitalizing them (through narration) in the present, which, for its own part, becomes multilayered.

This merging of past and present is best described as a technique of superimposition, a manifold exposure, or a tense configuration in which pasts and presents, myths, legends, and world history coexist in a complex constellation. It is a "Jetztzeit," a now-time, as Benjamin understands it; that is, a blasting of a monadic moment from history's continuum understood as homogeneous, empty time: "Where thinking suddenly comes to a stop in a constellation saturated with tensions, it gives that constellation a shock, by which thinking is crystallized as a monad."[45] The quoted passage above points to such a monadic crystallization in which the reader senses the tensions and potentialities of a given space-time.

Actually, Danzig was not the region's only city of plurality. The cities of the Hanseatic League, among them Kant's Königsberg, are other examples of Baltic cities dominated by Germans that were cosmopolitan in terms of commerce and population despite their small size. In fact, it could be argued that Kant's cosmopolitanism, like Grass's, springs from historical roots as well as from imaginative and ideological commitments. One of Grass's favorite authors, Theodor Fontane, captured the region's impurity as early as 1895. In *Effi Briest* the segregational processes of the area are exemplified by the separation of the Cassubians from the rest, just as the hybridity of the area is emphasized, as the area's inhabitants (apart from the Cassubians) are immigrants from many different parts of the world, all connected to the world largely through maritime trading routes.

Yet another way of amplifying the present by merging it with the past is Grass's etymological expeditions into the composite nature of certain place and proper names, in this case Harry's reflections on the etymological and historical roots of the names of Tulla and Osterwick:

> Duller, Tolle, Tullatsch, Thula or Dul, Tul, Thul. When the Pokriefkes were still living in Osterwick, they were tenants on Mosbrauch Hill near the lake, on the Konitz highway. From the middle of the fourteenth century to the time of Tulla's birth in 1927, Osterwick was written as follows: Ostirwig, Ostirwich, Osterwigh, Osterwig, Osterwyk. Ostrowit, Ostrowite, Osterwieck, Ostrowitte, Ostrôw. The Koshnavians said: Oustewitsch.

(*DY,* 133)

This passage shows a constellation of superimposed levels of time where myth and legend are interwoven with world history and the present. The narrow focus on a proper name and a place name contains a political dimension, implying the chaotic but nonetheless powerful mechanisms of world history. The passage underlines the plurality and transformative nature of the Grassian time-space dimension.

Regarding "narratives for a new belonging," Bromley points out that these "fictions engage with and renew the past, refiguring it as a contingent 'in-between' space, a space of innovation which interrupts the performance of the present which has cleansed, erased, expelled and buried difference."[46] Bromley's characterization applies perfectly to Grass by whom the past is reinvented as "a past charged with now-time,"[47] and thereby the present's stability and stabilizing effect are disturbed. His narrative emerges from a "technique of rupture" because "it makes impossible any return to ethnically closed and 'centred' original histories."[48] If history, and time as such, has a natural tendency to function palimpsestically—that is, to overwrite its own past layers with the new and present layers, thereby presenting itself as a homogenous continuum—Grass struggles against this palimpsestic process of history by way of bringing the overwritten layers back to life and situating them side by side with the present ones.

During the war years there is an expansion of the novelistic space in both novels, so that it now includes the entire European continent as an integral part and, at times, the entire world. In *The Tin Drum* we hear about Oskar visiting Stalingrad and Metz with Bebra's theater, but it is the episode featuring the company picnic at the Atlantic Ocean that best illustrates my argument. Their picnic basket includes caviar from Stalingrad and Dutch cacao, along with Danish butter and eggs, American canned biscuits, South African ginger marmalade, English corned beef, French mirabelle marmalade, and so forth. At first sight this is a remarkable example of a truly globalized picnic basket, representing a genuine image of universal brotherhood. However, the subtext of the whole scene is the war, an unsettling fact that seems to undermine the idyllic harmony that is otherwise suggested by the contents of the picnic basket. This is yet another example of ironic contrast, which is only strengthened by Grass's decision to stage the whole scene in the genre of the theater of the absurd.

The picnic scene is a perfect example of what Kundera calls a "terminal paradox," a concept that, according to him, can be said to epitomize the twentieth century in general. To Kundera, the modern era is characterized by the total victory of reason (Descartes), but it is actually pure irrationality (the force that only wills its own will, i.e., history) that has conquered the world nonetheless (as a result of there no longer being any recognizable universal systems of value to challenge this force). However, as a consequence of the illusory victory of universal reason, mankind has been cultivating the dream of a humanity that will one day achieve unity and eternal peace in spite of being divided into different nations and civilizations. And today, at last, the history of our planet reveals everything as inseparable, although it is, paradoxically, war, drifting and eternal, that realizes and guarantees this unity.

Allow me to develop Kundera's argument in greater detail so that we can return to Grass conceptually better equipped. In the novels of Kafka, Hasek, Musil, and Broch, history is a monstrous phenomenon that comes from the outside and no longer resembles adventure in any way: "it is impersonal, uncontrollable, incalculable, incomprehensible—and it is inescapable. This was the moment (just after the First World War) when the pleiad of great Central European novelists saw, felt, grasped the *terminal paradoxes* of the Modern Era."[49] According to Kundera, these novels show us how the meaning of existential categories (in Lukács's terms, the transcendental homes) is transformed under the condition of terminal paradoxes: What is "adventure" to K. if his liberty of action is illusory? What is "the future" if the intellectuals in *The Man Without Qualities* are not the least suspicious of the war that will change their lives the following day? What is a "crime" if Broch's Huguenau neither regrets nor remembers the murder he has committed? And, if the setting of the only great comic novel of the epoch (i.e., Hasek's *The Good Soldier Svejk*) is war, what has then happened to "comedy"? What is the distinction between the "private" and "public" sphere, if K., even when making love, can never escape the two observers from the castle? So, in Kafka the world has become a trap, and this idea is taken up by Grass, Kundera, and Rushdie.

Returning to Grass and the picnic, we might ask what has become of the idea of "universal brotherhood" when it seems possible for this ideal to be realized only in times of war? This is a clear-cut example of the clash between the (utopian) dream of unity and peace grounded in universal reason and the reality of a historical monster driven purely by irrational mechanisms. And in relation to some of the ideas developed earlier in this chapter, we might ask what has become of the idea of "love" when love letters include descriptions of concentration camps? What has happened to the concept of *Bildung* when it has to take place between the sheets of neglected petty bourgeois housewives (rather than among Wilhelm's countesses) and through a dwarf collaborating with the Third Reich (rather than in the traditional state institutions of school and church)? What has happened to "the novel" when apparently it must be narrated by a patient in a mental institution? And what has become of "individual freedom" when some major impersonal force (history) can just pick up Harry "with two fingers" and put him "into a life-size tank as an ammunition loader" (*DY*, 131)? What has happened to "the family" when a son no longer knows the identity of his father and even plays a role in the death of both his mother and his two possible fathers? In short, what has happened to what Lukács calls "the archetypal home": "love, the family, the state"?[50] The answer is that there are no longer any transcendental places that can be called home, and that the novel as a genre constantly contributes to and reflects the semantic transformations of these existential categories.

To return to Grass and the examples of hybrid space, let us turn our gaze on *Dog Years*. In *Dog Years* we hear about French prisoners of war now carrying blocks of ice in Danzig, and a bit further on in the novel, Harry describes how two Ukrainian workers at Liebenau's carpenter shop had to be replaced by two others: "there were plenty of them—and the first two, so we heard, were sent to Stutthof" (*DY*, 294). These are examples of an international element being integrated into the space of Danzig-Langfuhr, in this case alluding to the exploitation of immigrant workers that took place during the war. And in relation to Tulla and her mother, it says, "She and her mother wore underthings from all over Europe" (*DY*, 314–15). Once again, Europe is—tragicomically—brought into Danzig. Distant locations such as Paris, Belgrade, Salonika, Athens, Budapest, Vienna, and Copenhagen are evoked several times. At another point, Harry informs us about the weekly reviews in the cinemas linking Langfuhr to Europe: "All this and more could be seen not only in the two movie houses of the suburb of Langfuhr, but in Salonika as well" (*DY*, 341–15). All this indicates that no one can escape history; it involves everyone, especially during war when history is accentuated and everything is far more intensely interrelated. But in addition to this evocation of an international space and what seems to be a universal brotherhood, Grass concurrently emphasizes its subtext—that is, the war—which once again reveals Grass's technique of ironic contrast. In this case, Danzig's international atmosphere cannot be counted on the "positive" side, as it is brought about by the Nazi desire to dominate the world, a desire that also contained the explicit wish to eradicate and expel ethnic differences within the Reich.

The foregoing examples show an expansion of space in *Dog Years* and are thus indicative of a more complex spatial framework than just Danzig and the petty bourgeoisie. On the one hand, we come upon an outward spatial movement; for example, when we hear about the war unfolding around the globe, a war that both Walter Matern and Harry Liebenau participate in—here Danzig "explodes" into the world. On the other hand, we come upon an inward spatial movement; for example, when we hear about

Tulla's underwear from all over Europe—here the world "implodes" into Danzig, thus confirming Brode's idea of Danzig as a "Brennpunkt" (focus). The double mechanism of explosion and implosion (glocalization: the local dissipating into the global and the global permeating the local) is represented in one and the same place; namely, in the harbor of Danzig. The harbor, the sea, and the waterfront occupy a central topographic role in *The Danzig Trilogy* (as they do in *The Flounder* and *Crabwalk*). The harbor reinforces the international ambience of the city by connecting it to other cities and other "worlds," just as the harbor area itself is an international or cosmopolitan space where sailors from all over the world meet and collide. An example of this is the tavern where Herbert Truczinski works in a job that physically marks him with "international scars" and bruises from the fights he tries to prevent. Herbert's body thus belongs to the same category as the Vistula and Oskar's drum in symbolizing a reservoir of stories waiting to be unfolded. When Oskar taps his finger on one of Herbert's scars, Herbert tells him the story of how and from whom he got it.

The narrators of *The Tin Drum* and *Dog Years* all migrate to West Germany at some point during the novels, thereby making a final physical detachment from Danzig. The migration from Danzig contributes to the spatial expansion in the novel, in that quite a substantial part of the action now unfolds in the West. The migration is not just a migration in space but also in time and history—that is, from a childhood and adolescence spent in the world of National Socialism to an adulthood spent in the world of Western capitalism and the German "Wirtschaftswunder." It is a spatial, temporal, and indeed also a mental crossing of borders that has wide-ranging but different effects on the main characters, most of whom are struggling to adapt to their new environment and to the new historical epoch, the era after Nazism.

If the "classical" *Bildungsroman* (e.g., *Wilhelm Meister's Apprenticeship, Pride and Prejudice*) renounces universal history, as Moretti claims, it does so in order to ensure the protagonist's happiness and organic integration into society. Even though universal history is always seen from the viewpoint of everyday life, it becomes obvious in relation to Grass that it plays a far greater and more problematic role in Grass than it does in the classical *Bildungsroman*. *The Tin Drum* may be a "*Wilhelm Meister* auf Blech getrommelt" (drummed on tin), as Enzensberger once said, but it is just as much indebted to the picaresque novel, and to Grimmelshausen's baroque *The Adventurous Simplicissimus* (1668) in particular. In Grimmelshausen, the episodic structure mimes, as in *The Tin Drum*, the antiteleological and irregular thread of historical process. So, Grass rejects the optimistic principles and the progressive and coherent structure of the *Bildungsroman*;

instead, his work is influenced by existentialism in its belief in the individual's isolation in an absurd and contingent world in which progress is illusory: "History offers no comfort. It only hands out hard lessons. At the most, it can be read as absurd. Admittedly, it progresses, but progress is not its result. History never ends: we are situated in and not outside history."[51]

In Grass the heroes collide with history; they are never completely integrated into it. Being scarred by history, Oskar seeks to hide in the mental asylum in the hope that history cannot reach him there. And even if narrators like Pilenz, Amsel, Liebenau, and Matern never isolate themselves as radically as Oskar does, they still represent the impossibility of an unproblematic integration into society. Grass's novels thus confirm the basic form of Lukács's theory of the novel: problematic subject and contingent world, and an attempt at reconciliation that is deemed unsuccessful. Even though some of the narrators seem to get along well enough, their individual and collective writing project must be recognized as an attempt to come to terms with a problematic past. Because of this unresolved problem that keeps haunting them in what seems an eternal displacement into new challenges in Grass's ongoing discussion with the past, an organic integration into the present society also seems impossible. In short, to Grass, society is not worthy of the integration and approval of his heroes; instead, one must continue to criticize it, and that is exactly what he and his protagonists do—both in relation to the Nazi past and in relation to the capitalistic, neo-Biedermeier present. The narrators are profane redeemers of a society that is trying to forget the past, but to Grass, moving backward and retelling the past is the only way forward. This is why they remain skeptical toward postwar Germany: it tries to forget by metamorphosing itself into an idyllic past.

Linguistic Diarrhea

> We must be bilingual even in a single language, we must have a minor language inside our own language, we must create a minor use of our own language.
> —Gilles Deleuze and Claire Parnet, *Dialogues*

"The energy of his devices, the scale on which he works, are fantastic. He suggests an action painter wrestling, dancing across a huge canvas, then rolling himself in the paint in a final logic of design. The specific source of energy lies in the language."[52] These are the words of George Steiner, taken from a 1964 essay on *Dog Years* in which Steiner claims that Grass is the most inventive and brilliant writer to have emerged in Germany since 1945. The passage supports what I have previously said about Grass and about migration literature in general in regard to the important role of language, an importance that stems primarily from the fact that the migrant is situated between two languages that bequeath him a privileged double vision as well as an acute linguistic sensibility.

It is true that Grass has always been situated in the German language; hence, he has never been linguistically uprooted in the same way as Kundera, who has abandoned Czech in favor of French. Instead, during his childhood and adolescence, Grass was situated in the midst of several languages of which German was the major one, and this linguistic plurality marks his artistic profile. If one is to speak of a linguistic uprooting in the case of Grass, it would be in connection to the historical vantage point of 1945 and the change from Nazi-infected language to a new German language cleansed of the malevolent practices of 1933–45. In that sense Grass can be said to practice "a minor use" within his own language. With special reference to *Dog Years,* Steiner asserts that

> Grass plays on a verbal instrument of uncanny virtuosity. Long stretches of Baltic dialect alternate with parodies of Hitlerite jargon. Grass piles words into solemn gibberish or splinters them into unsuspected innuendo and obscenity. He has a compulsive taste for word-lists, for catalogues of rare or technical terms [. . .]. There are whole pages out of dictionaries of geology, agriculture, mechanical engineering, ballet. The language itself, with its powers of hysteria and secrecy, with its private parts and official countenance, becomes the main presence, the living core of this black fairy tale. [. . .] Grass has understood that no German writer after the holocaust could take the language at face value. It had been the parlance of hell. So he began tearing and melting; he poured words, dialects, phrases, clichés, slogans, puns, quotations, into the crucible. They came out in a hot lava. Grass's prose has a torrential, viscous energy; it is full of rubble and acrid shards. It scars and bruises the landscape into bizarre, eloquent forms. Often the language itself is the subject of his abrasive fantasy.[53]

Steiner's description is wonderful and quite accurate, and it correctly points to the complexity, hybridity, and vitality of Grass's language.

Early in *Dog Years,* the reader is confronted with a German dialect that is quite different from proper German. The narrator, Brauchsel, reflects explicitly on this divergence:

> In these parts stones are called *zellacken.* The Protestants say *zellacken,* the few Catholics *zellacken.* The rough Mennonites say *zellacken,* the refined ones *zellacken.* Even Amsel, who likes to be different, says *zellack* when he means a stone; and Senta goes for a stone when someone says: Senta, go get

a *zellack.* Kriwe says *zellacken,* Kornelius Kabrun, Beister, Folchert, August
Sponagel, and Frau von Ankum, the major's wife, all say *zellacken;* and
Pastor Daniel Kliewer from Pasewark says to his congregation, rough and
refined alike: "Then little David picked up a *zellack* and flung it at the giant
Goliath . . ." ["Da häd sech dä klaine David an Zellack jenomm ond häd
dem Tullatsch, dem Goliath . . ."] For a *zellack* is a handy little stone, the
size of a pigeon's egg.

(DY, 13–14)

This passage illustrates several features characteristic of Grass's work.
First, the language employed in the passage is a mixture of proper
German and a local dialect. Second, the language spoken by the locals is
a shared language, yet they constitute a heterogeneous assemblage of
Evangelists, Catholics, and Mennonites, high and low, fine and coarse.
Accordingly, language forms a local centripetal power that counteracts the
centrifugal power of the religious and cultural pluralism of the region.
Third, the hybridity of language and the opposition between major and
minor languages are both reflected on the level of discourse by the narratorial comments, as well as on the level of story by the direct speech of
the priest, the latter serving as an example of Steiner's Baltic dialect mentioned above.

The parody of the Hitlerite jargon, which Steiner also mentions as a
characteristic feature in *Dog Years,* is most evident in the passages in which
Hitler's dog Prinz escapes the German headquarters a few days before the
final defeat: "Attention everybody! Attention everybody! Führer's dog missing. Answers to the name of Prinz. Stud dog. Black German shepherd Prinz.
Connect me with Zossen. Attention everybody: the Führer's dog is missing"
(*DY,* 373–74). The parody relates to several things: First, combining a dog
with the activation of the entire war machinery and the urgency and seriousness with which this machinery carries out the orders is yet another
example of Grassian ironic contrast revealing the disproportion of the whole
scenario (the [un]importance of a dog and the massive machinery set in
motion in order to retrieve it). Second, the combination of the war machinery concentrating all its efforts on the search for a dog, on the one hand,
and the historical circumstances (i.e., the downfall of a whole society in
which people are starving, being raped, hanged, and shot), on the other, is
also an example of ironic contrast emphasizing the absurdity of a situation
in which dogs matter more than people. Finally, the parody also shows itself
on the level of syntax. Grass's use of exclamation marks, short sentences,
and repetitions emphasizes the overall militaristic quality of the Nazi language. This type of language is what many people thought had destroyed

the German language because of its incapacity to mediate and communicate the complexity of human experience. It reduces mankind to robots and machines carrying out (absurd) orders.

A few pages following this parody of Nazi language, we come upon another example of Hitlerite jargon, but this time it is combined with the much debated parody of Heideggerian language: "'The question of the dog is a metaphysical question, calling the entire German nation into question'—is followed by the famous Führerdeclaration: 'Berlin is still German. Vienna will be German. And never will the dog be negated'" (DY, 379). Besides criticizing the Heideggerian inclination toward metaphysics and its mystification of the German language, the passage quoted above also implies a critique of Heidegger's nationalistic thinking that conformed nicely with Nazi ideology. All in all, the passage is a Grassian attempt to reveal the emptiness and dangers inherent in metaphysical thinking and linguistic mystification. The absurdity of the world is here doubled, or even tripled, by the absurdity of metaphysics and the absurdity of a language deliberately perplexified.

But what about Grass's own language? Is it not itself an example of a deliberately perplexified language? Steiner even claims that language at times becomes the main protagonist in Grass's work. It is true that Grass's language is complex—it is indeed one of my main arguments that a complex language is one prerequisite, among others, for migration literature. Grass does not subscribe to a simplistic language, as his parody and critique of the Nazi discourse shows. "He knew the world and talked incoherent nonsense" (TD, 366), as he says in The Tin Drum as an indirect comment on the reductiveness of Nazi discourse. If Grass and Heidegger both agree that the world is complex and therefore requires a complex language to render it, their solutions or preferences point in opposite directions. Whereas Heidegger, at least according to Grass, espouses metaphysical speculations and esoteric concepts that actually support or even reinforce the German propensity for metaphysical idealism, Grass for his part opts for a language that is cleansed of metaphysical implications; instead, it owes its complexity to a baroque disposition that shows itself in an elaborately formal and magniloquent style in favor of the sensible and the concreteness of objects, people, smells, and idioms. It is also in this sense that Steiner's assertion about Grass's language being "the main presence" in his works should be read. The "presence effect"[54] in Grass is thus double: by virtue of its sheer physical quality, its vital energy, and its magniloquence, the reader is often overwhelmed by the presence of Grass's language, its materiality, and at the same time this language is referentially oriented toward concrete objects, bodies, smells, and so forth, elements that in themselves support the presence quality of Grass's work. Consequently, ideas and metaphysics are distrusted.

If we return to Steiner, how are we to read his remarks on Grass and *Dog Years?* Based on what I have quoted from his essay, he seems to applaud Grass and his use of the German language. But it was also Steiner who in the (in)famous essay "The Hollow Miracle" (1959) asked "whether the German language had survived the Hitler era, whether words poisoned by Goebbels and used to regulate and justify Belsen could ever again serve the needs of moral truth and poetic perception."[55] Steiner's much disputed comments were published just before the release of *The Tin Drum.* Did this novel and Grass's work in general provoke a change of opinion in Steiner? *The Tin Drum* was seen by many as a rebirth of German literature and people were led to believe that the German language had, in fact, risen from the ashes. However, Steiner is—in spite of what he writes about Grass's language in the passages quoted above—not so sure about this resurrection. Why is that? There are two sides to this question: one concerns German literature in general, and this is not something Steiner addresses in this specific essay; the other concerns Grass and *Dog Years* in particular.

First of all, Steiner's overall estimation of *Dog Years* is that it—regardless of its linguistic power—is a "baggy monster" that "tends to fall apart. What sticks in one's mind is the general statement of chaos and the brilliance of discrete episodes."[56] It is not that I disagree with Steiner's description, but instead of seeing the monstrosity, chaos, and discreteness as negative attributes, I tend to see them as positive, because the imperfection in many ways makes the novel much more interesting. This imperfection of *Dog Years* links the novel to Moretti's idea of the "modern epic" as a flawed masterpiece, flawed because the struggle to come up with formal-technical solutions to a new historical-epistemological situation inevitably ends unsuccessfully; but at the same time, the vainness of the attempt is revealing in regard to both the empirical historical situation of the novel and its formal history. While Steiner's first reason for believing that *Dog Years* does not represent the resurrection of German literature has to do with its monstrous and disparate form, his second reason has to do with the Grassian language. Despite his praise of its energy, Steiner believes that Grass's language often becomes the actual subject of the novel, and thereby fails to achieve moral truth. That Grass is, as Steiner remarks at one point, always too long, is, I suppose, a matter of personal preference; but I would argue that Grass considers linguistic diarrhea and formal monstrosity to be accurate and "truthful" descriptive techniques. To Grass they are necessary because "Every event casts its shadow" (*DY,* 521).

Return of the Storyteller

The telling of stories, the real telling, must have been before my time. I never heard anyone tell stories.

—R. M. Rilke, *The Notebooks of Malte Laurids Brigge*

In his famous 1936 essay "The Storyteller," Walter Benjamin expresses his belief that the art of storytelling is approaching its demise. It seems as if we no longer possess the ability to exchange experiences, which is due to the fact that the value of experience has decreased. How does Günter Grass fit into this picture? Grass's novels are characterized by their highly complex strategies of enunciation. By no means can the reader approach the texts with the solid categories of belief or disbelief, but only with "the fluid one of doubt."[57] However, Oskar Matzerath, Heini Pilenz, Eduard Amsel, Harry Liebenau, and Walter Matern are all storytellers, problematically so or not. In other words, in Grass's novels stories are incessantly narrated: in the trilogy, five narrators look back upon the prewar years, the war years, and the postwar years, and despite the fact that their experiences have supposedly plunged into bottomlessness, the five narrators nonetheless attempt to communicate their experiences to the reader.

In the same way that Auschwitz represents an experience that inevitably leads any aesthetic (lyrical) pretense of mimetic adequateness to an embellishment of the unrepresentable event, modernity, culminating with World War I, has, according to Benjamin, caused the impossibility of stories and storytelling. However, in spite of—or perhaps, rather because of—Auschwitz, someone had to carry on writing. And we might repeat: because of experience dropping into bottomlessness, this particular experience (the experience of the negativity of experience) must be rescued. But it is, of course, a "rescue" accomplished through other forms of expression and narrative modes than the ones Benjamin attaches to his concept of storytelling.

Benjamin sharply distinguishes the "story" from the "novel." To Benjamin, the story is characterized by a usefulness and a wisdom that the storyteller is able to pass on to the listener because he knows how to give practical advice or provide a moral. In short, he knows how to counsel: the storyteller knows how to tell a story in which the listener is able to sense the contours of a universal truth. Benjamin's idea of the novel does not include this specific potential of storytelling in that it no longer seems possible to communicate the kind of counseling that characterizes the story: "The earliest indication of a process whose end is the decline of storytelling is the rise of the novel at the beginning of modern times. [. . .] The art of storytelling is nearing its end because the epic side of truth—wisdom—is dying out. This is, however, a process that has been going on for a long time."[58]

Benjamin is, admittedly, partly right: any storyteller who attempts to counsel the reader today in a sincere, nonironic way would not be taken seriously, unless the storyteller were to act like a boomerang and, through a relativizing movement, immediately start to question his or her counsel. In Adorno's well-known essay from 1954 on the narrator, we come upon ideas quite similar to Benjamin's:

> He [the narrator] would be guilty of a lie: the lie of delivering himself over to the world with a love that presupposes that the world is meaningful; and he would end up with insufferable kitsch along the lines of a local-color commercialism [Heimatkunst]. [. . .] The identity of experience in the form of a life that is articulated and possesses internal continuity—and that life was the only thing that made the narrator's stance possible—has disintegrated. [. . .] A narrative that presented itself as though the narrator had mastered this kind of experience would rightly meet with impatience and skepticism on the part of its audience.[59]

Hence, Adorno seems to agree with Benjamin. If the storyteller of the past was characterized by the ability to guide the listener, thereby presupposing the continuity and meaningfulness of life, the contemporary storyteller's position seems to be impossible because of the general fragmentation of life. Nevertheless, Adorno provides us with the opening we need when he modifies Benjamin's complete separation of story and novel and actually grants the story a significant role in relation to the novel. Adorno thus claims that the role of the narrator in the contemporary novel is characterized by a paradox: "it is no longer possible to tell a story, but the form of the novel requires narration."[60] In fact, in Grass's novels the storytellers must narrate at any cost, and do this in a most rambling and fabulating manner, often with guilt as their driving force. Their counsel and advice, however, do not point toward any wisdom in the way Benjamin understands it, as certainty that is. Rather, the enunciatory strategies in Grass emphasize that his novels can be seen as examples of what Milan Kundera has called "the wisdom of uncertainty."[61]

On the one hand, Benjamin is right in proclaiming the end of the story; on the other hand, the story seems to survive, but in a different cloak. Thus, we have moved from the story as the wisdom of certainty to the novel as the wisdom of uncertainty. This uncertainty, however, is generated precisely through the novel's storytelling potential, what I have previously called the return of the narrative—a return, though, that combines old-fashioned storytelling with avant-garde elements. Another way to put it: the story transforms itself into a novel when the author is no longer satisfied with a simple story. Instead, he becomes an architect and starts constructing a building consisting of several story lines, episodes, descriptions, observations, and reflections. This new, complex form is a result of the heterogeneity and complexity of the material that confronts the author.

To Benjamin, the invention of print separated the novel from its original affiliation with oral storytelling. Hence, he does not acknowledge that the novel has been persistently inspired and informed by orality. Apart from the authors of concern here, just think of Rabelais, Cervantes, Sterne, Diderot, Conrad, Blixen, and García Márquez. As Peter Brooks has argued, the nineteenth-century novel appears to be "fully aware that it is a purely bookish phenomenon, dependent on the new industrial processes of printing and distribution."[62] However, the general "literacy" of the nineteenth-century novel is replaced by an "orality" in Grass's novels in which we come upon framed tales, tales embedded within one another and narrators addressing themselves to narratees and readers. Hence, the communicative act ("how" as opposed to "what"), what Roman Jakobson called the "phatic" and the "conative" functions of the text, is central in Grass's novels.

* * *

"Granted: I am an inmate of a mental hospital" (*TD*, 1). Thus reads the famous opening line in Grass's first novel. How are we supposed to respond to the advice and counsel put forward by a narrator who is locked away in a mental institution? With the very first sentence, Grass evidently discredits his narrator and thereby creates a fundamental ontological uncertainty in relation to the fictional universe. Consequently, form, truth, and value system are made uncertain by Oskar in the novel's opening line. Volker Neuhaus speaks in this regard of "the destruction of all-inclusive unities" and of a "reality smashed into atoms," phrases that remind us of Adorno's idea of the collapse of the identity of experience.[63] Accordingly, it thus seems that enunciation—and "Weltanschauung" (worldview) added to that—cannot be referred to a transcendental component capable of guaranteeing ideological certainty and coherence: "Grass is at pains to present a world of moral uncertainty in which no comforting constants exist," Keith Miles claims.[64] Just as Frédéric Moreau was not constructed to hide or reduce the fragmentation of the world, Oskar, in regard to both his narratorial authority and his general constitution as a character, embodies all the characteristics of a problematic and homeless individual. It goes without saying that Oskar is very important in an analysis of enunciation, as he is the sole medium through which the fictional universe is transmitted to the reader. Admittedly, at one point Bruno Münsterberg also gets to tell his side of the story, but it is still through Oskar's pen that Bruno's story is transmitted. However, the introduction of Bruno on the level of narration does contribute to undermining Oskar's credibility, as his version often contradicts Oskar's.

The Tin Drum consists of two levels of action and one level of narration. The first level of action takes place outside the asylum and takes the form of Oskar's autobiography unfolding from the story of the conception of Agnes in October 1899 until Oskar's arrest in Paris on his twenty-eighth birthday in September 1952. Oskar completes the writing of this story line on his thirtieth birthday in the beginning of September 1954. The second level of action takes place in the asylum and spans the period from the end of 1952, when Oskar decides to write his memoirs, until his thirtieth birthday. This level of story is written in the style of a diary, and the narrated events include the conversations with, and descriptions of, his visitors, Bruno, Klepp, Vittlar, and Maria.

The level of narration consists of the commentaries that Oskar, as a first-person narrator, makes on his own writing process; hence, it constitutes a level of metareflection. We find an example of this metafictional technique where the reader is invited into the novel's engine room at the beginning of the chapter "He Lies in Saspe." Here Oskar explicitly admits that he has not been entirely honest in the previous chapter:

> I have just reread the last paragraph. I am not too well satisfied, but Oskar's pen ought to be, for writing tersely and succinctly, it has managed [. . .] to exaggerate and mislead, if not to lie.
>
> Wishing to stick to the truth, I shall try to circumvent Oskar's pen and make a few corrections: in the first place, Jan's last hand [. . .] was not a grand hand, but a diamond hand without two; in the second place, Oskar, as he left the storeroom, picked up not only his new drum but also the old broken one [. . .]. Furthermore, there is a little omission that needs filling in: No sooner had Jan and I left the storeroom [. . .] than Oskar, concerned for his comfort and safety, made up to two Home Guards who struck him as good-natured, uncle-like souls, put on an imitation of pathetic sniveling, and pointed to Jan, his father, with accusing gestures which transformed the poor man into a villain who had dragged off an innocent child to the Polish Post Office to use him, with typically Polish inhumanity, as a buffer for enemy bullets.
>
> (*TD*, 228)

Worrying about truth and accuracy, Oskar, as a person, shows a rare moral side to himself. Oskar's confession of the exaggerations and white lies he had told in the previous chapter only reinforces the reader's assumption regarding the fragility of the novel's truth character. Even though Oskar comes clean and actually corrects his own (deliberate) mistakes, we are not convinced as readers that this is always his procedure. Oskar is too much part of the events he narrates for us not to notice the strong accentuations of his perspective.

Whereas the first two corrections (the card game and the used drum) are of lesser importance in regard to the overall truth character, the third confession and modification is more significant. Oskar's supplementary elaborations on the events leading up to his and Jan's capture may be considered as preliminary building blocks in the construction of the theme of guilt that distresses Oskar throughout the entire novel, primarily in relation to the deaths of his mother and two fathers. This way he refers to his own actions as "Judasschauspiel" and admits that he is ashamed of his past behavior. The previous chapter's account of Jan's death and Oskar's subsequent modification and explanation of the event thus become an exemplary image of the novel's migratory universe in which incessant deterritorializations of territories are instigated by a self-correcting, self-doubting, partial, and unreliable enunciation. Fictional micro-universes consisting of specific events, sentiments, opinions, values, and atmospheres are constructed only to be questioned, modified, corrected, and maybe even transformed into new micro-universes later on.

In a previous section, I have already mentioned the most important characteristics of enunciation in *The Tin Drum:* how the creation of a mobile, infantile, and detached perspective from below forms the cornerstone of the novel's enunciatory structure, just as it may be argued that Oskar's extraordinary perspective not only supports but also triggers the novel's "lines of flight." When Oskar meets Bebra for the first time, for instance, they discuss what social position to occupy as lilliputs. Bebra warns Oskar not to be content with a spectator's position in front of podiums; instead, the lilliputs ought to populate and conquer the podiums. Oskar remembers this advice during one of Maiwiese's recurring Sunday rallies of the Nazi Party, when he enters the open area from a different angle and sees the podium from behind: "Everyone who has ever taken a good look at a rostrum from behind will be immunized ipso facto against any magic practiced in any form whatsoever on rostrums. Pretty much the same applies to rear views of church altars; but that is another subject" (*TD*, 104). Because of his perspective from behind the scenes, Oskar is immunized against the particular Nazi art of seduction, as well as against any form of demagogical sorcery. The passage emblematically demonstrates the subversive power of Oskar's perspective: the capacity to break open the surfaces of the adult world from below; the capacity to see through any kind of hypocrisy; the capacity to expose the illusions that society rests upon; the capacity to profane anything sacred, clerical, or secular (Catholic or Nazi).

At the Maiwiese rally, Oskar cannot find a seat on the podium as Bebra had urged him to, and instead he finds himself a good spot under the podium. From his hiding place he transforms the official march music into a waltz and subsequently into a Charleston using his tin drum. As a consequence, the crowd of people—instead of supporting the symmetric perfection and martial order of the Nazi arrangement by submitting themselves uniformly to the march music and the propaganda speeches—starts to behave in an increasingly unrestrained and wild manner and ends up circulating through the streets of Danzig while dancing.

Oskar's ability to see what goes on behind the scenes means that his perspective functions like a Deleuzian simulacrum. Deleuze describes the simulacrum as a subversive power, surging up from the depths to shatter the false surfaces and resemblances. Simulacrum is not just a different perspective on the same world, and it is not simply a difference negating another concept in which the negation may be elevated to form a new concept bridging the opposition. Simulacrum is differential—that is, it creates a difference and a becoming, and as a result the world is deterritorialized:

> This simulacrum includes the differential point of view; and the observer becomes a part of the simulacrum itself, which is transformed and deformed by his point of view. In short, there is in the simulacrum a becoming-mad, or a becoming unlimited, [. . .] a becoming always other, a becoming subversive of the depths, able to evade the equal, the limit, the Same, or the Similar: always more and less at once, but never equal.[65]

Oskar represents precisely this "differential point of view"; he is a Dionysian machine and a symmetry-smasher, constantly unsettling the reader with his idiosyncratic, childish, and defamiliarizing descriptions of everyday events in the adult world. The reader experiences Oskar's delicate sensibility and his illusion-shattering perspective when he hides under the table and watches Agnes's and Jan's feet performing strange gymnastic exercises, or when the light goes out in the course of Oskar's birthday party and all the adults (except for grandmother Anna, Hedwig with the bovine gaze, and Greff the pederast) participate in a modern-day Sodom and Gomorrah. As with the simulacrum as it is defined by Deleuze, Oskar as an observer is indeed part of the story he tells, and this story is for its own part constantly modified and transformed through his extraordinary point of view. The limitlessness of Oskar's perspective as a simulacrum owes to the fact that the narrator, Oskar, functions as a demiurge whose point of view is incessantly on the move, subjective, self-questioning, and iconoclastic.

During the Crystal Night, Sigismund Markus, the Jewish supplier of tin drums, receives an unexpected visit from Nazis who demolish his toy shop, indicating the end of childhood innocence and play. When Oskar finds Sigismund dead in his office with an empty bottle by his side, his first thought is that Sigismund must have felt thirsty. Oskar's belief is a deautomatizing moment for the reader, as it effectively illustrates his productive misapprehension of the situation whose violent nature he has not understood because of his infantile naïvety. And yet the productive element is precisely due to the fact that Oskar's infantilism is not to be considered a weakness but rather a strength, as it is through this unique point of view mediating "a child's uninhibited, brutal directness of feeling"[66] that the events appear clear as crystal before the reader's eyes.

So, what Oskar believes is water, the reader knows is poison—but the actual content of the bottle is never explicitly revealed. This perspective of innocence and naïvety demonstrates the barbarity and absurdity of the world in the most effective manner. However, the novel never openly states such characteristics, because a direct description would not be adequate. Instead, Grass proves his originality through the creation of Oskar's inimitable point of view, which is capable of pinning down the unsayable, or what I previously referred to as the experience of the negativity of experience, more effectively than any explicit designation. Grass achieves this effect by subtly exploiting the gap between the historical consciousness of the reader and Oskar's naïve perception—that is, the ironic contrast between a contextual element and an intratextual strategy.

The ironic contrast between form and content is probably most apparent in the last chapter of Book One, "Faith, Hope, Love," a rewriting of Saint Paul's "First Epistle to the Corinthians" and its famous ending: "And now abideth faith, hope, charity, these three; but the greatest of these is charity" (13:13). The content of the chapter—that is, the contextual and historical background of the chapter—is the Crystal Night and its brutality. However, Grass employs different styles and techniques in a highly original manner to depict the events of this infamous night, which may seem completely out of place when taking the nature of events into consideration. Nonetheless, Grass succeeds artistically in his effort to invoke the horror of the night precisely because of the ironic contrast he creates between content and form. The reader is constantly unsettled as a result of a series of shocks caused by Grass's contrastive style of incongruity. Most notably, Grass recurrently employs the fairy-tale phrase "There was once . . ." The repetitive structure causes the events to force themselves upon the reader, who is overwhelmed by their persistent "presence." The repetitions, though, are accompanied by a strategy of variation that only increases the "unheimlichkeit" (unhomeliness) and forcefulness of the chapter, as it keeps introducing new atrocious material into the otherwise repetitive structure. Grass's technique, then, does not comply with Freud's idea of art as "the mild narcosis" that temporarily makes us forget the tormenting nature of life.[67] Rather, in Grass, art is—to use Adorno's words—a (formal) "mimesis of the hardened and alienated";[68] that is, it does not sedate its reader, but sharpens his or her sensibility toward life.

Why are enunciation and point of view so important? Because they are the final step toward a classification of Grass's work as migration literature. Rushdie asserted earlier that in Grass we come upon the migrant's viewpoint on the world, a viewpoint that is characterized by doubt, questioning, and skepticism, as well as by both deterritorialization and reterritorialization. The migrant, Rushdie says, does not accept the conventional images of the world presented by the mass media, politicians, and advertising agencies. Because of the triple rupture of reality (language, culture, place), the migrant has learned that "reality is an artefact, that it does not exist until it is made, and that, like any other artefact, it can be made well or badly, and that it can also, of course, be unmade."[69] Oskar exemplifies this as he dismantles the image of reality that most of us carry around with us (or at least most of the Germans in the late 1950s), only to reassemble it in a new and unexpected way. In his voluntary (spiritual) exile and because of his forced (geographical) migration, Oskar has attained the "privilege" of being able to see the world with fresh eyes just as he has achieved the necessary distance to reality to create a completely new and unique world. And for Oskar, exile is an experience of both painful suffering and liberating detachment.

Dog Years, which I will only briefly touch upon here, bears some similarity to *The Tin Drum* in terms of enunciation and composition. Both novels comprise three books dealing primarily with the prewar years, the war years, and the postwar years, respectively. *Dog Years,* however, is not narrated by a single person but by a consortium of three authors, Brauxel/Amsel (first book), Harry Liebenau (second book), and Walter Matern (third book), all of whom participate as characters in the novel (as was the case with Oskar). In this way Grass turns multiperspectivism into a constitutive principle in the formation of the fictional universe. Multiperspectivism is one reason why *Dog Years* may be seen as Grass's most complex novel in that Grass hereby achieves a triple image that reflects reality's fragmentary and contradictory nature. In my opinion, *Dog Years* is a masterpiece, but it may be formally flawed like the "modern epic" in which individual elements are formed in extreme contrast, thus making it difficult for the reader to reach any conclusive judgment about them.[70]

To bring this chapter to a conclusion, I want to return for a brief moment to Adorno's essay on the narrator in which he identifies two crucial transformations in the history of the novel that are related to the role of the narrator: one is the entry of reflection; the other, which is a consequence of the first, is the destruction of illusion:

> The traditional novel [. . .] can be compared to the three-walled stage of a bourgeois theater. This technique was one of illusion. The narrator raises a curtain: the reader is to take part in what occurs as though he were physically present. [. . .] There is a heavy taboo on reflection: it becomes the cardinal sin against objective purity. Today this taboo, along with the illusionary character of what is represented, is losing strength. [. . .] The new reflection takes a stand against the lie of representation, actually against the narrator himself, who tries, as an extra-alert commentator on events, to correct his unavoidable way of proceeding. *This destruction of form is inherent in the very meaning of form.*[71]

According to Adorno, the fictional universe is no longer allowed to uphold its illusionary effect. The reader is awakened from his or her slumber as a consequence of the narrator's self-reflectiveness that takes sides against "the lie of representation" and the narrator himself. The self-reflectiveness thus functions as little pin pricks puncturing the balloon of illusion at the same time that it keeps the story and the narrator in a perpetual process of self-correction. The reader has thus been led from the sundeck of the ship with its clear view of the world down into the engine room in which the very principles of constructing fictions are revealed. The reader can no longer assume an indifferent attitude and is forced out of his or her contemplative hiding place because of the "shocking" interferences. To Adorno, the creation of an aesthetic distance between reader and fictional universe and the annulment of any aesthetic distance between narrator and reader (the latter now finds himself in the engine room next to the narrator) are necessary in order to expose the superficiality and kitsch of what he calls "Heimatskunst" (patriotic art).

The element of intratextual self-reflection—legitimized by Lukács because the form of the novel is not supposed to hide the fragmentation of the world (irony as the self-correction of the abstract form), by Deleuze as it is a technique that reveals morphogenesis (becoming-form), and, finally, by Adorno as it functions as the crushing hammer stroke against the mirror of representation that the novelistic form demands in order to reach behind or below the surfaces—points to the novel's (nonlinear) ripening process and, furthermore, suggests a means of escape in relation to Benjamin's skeptical view of the genre.

CHAPTER 2

Milan Kundera

The exile knows that in a secular and contingent world, homes are always provisional. Borders and barriers, which enclose us within the safety of familiar territory, can also become prisons, and are often defended beyond reason or necessity. Exiles cross borders, break barriers of thought and experience.
—Edward Said, "Reflections on Exile"

Milan Kundera persistently attempts to uphold the barrier between private and public, between life and work. It is highly indicative that Kundera's "official biography," printed in the revised French editions of his works, reads thus: "Milan Kundera was born in Czechoslovakia. Since 1975 he has been living in France." This terseness is a result of his fervent belief that biography should be bracketed when reading a novel, and Kundera has repeatedly and explicitly defended himself against what he calls the "*biographical furor*" (*TB*, 266) of many readers. In addition to safeguarding his private sphere, Kundera also exercises strict control over his past publications, some of which have been downright erased from his official bibliography (Kundera disavows his Marxist literary output produced in the 1950s and 1960s), whereas others are constantly being edited by him.

However, out of this inclination to control both biography and bibliography, two problems of a seemingly paradoxical nature arise. First, how does the increasing presence of an "autobiographical" voice in Kundera's novels accord with his aversion to readings that legitimize themselves through the use of biographical data? Why does Kundera insist on the impermeable opposition between life and work while at the same time seeming to "pollute" his works with his biography? Arguably, the increasing presence of an "autobiographical" voice can, to a certain extent, be regarded as Kundera's attempt to control both the image of his past and his public self-image. Hence, the narrative voices in Kundera's novels are remarkable examples of *performative biografism.* Second, how do Kundera's erasure and modification of his past publications accord with his severe criticism of the attempts by totalitarian regimes to rewrite history by expunging unwanted elements? Kundera has apparently effectuated a "totalitarian" censorship in regard to his own history, and at the same time he condemns the efforts of censorship carried out by Communist historiography.

But is all this relevant? Why not simply accept the biography and bibliography sanctioned by Kundera himself? In general, it is because I believe that the experiences of exile and totalitarianism inform both the thematic and formal design of his novels. In "La francophobie, ça existe" (Francophobia Exists, 1993), Kundera thus seems to contradict himself (and to agree with my thesis) by claiming his emigration to be the key to understanding both his life and his work: "But midway through my life, my wife and I emigrated to France. This event is the most decisive in my entire life, it is the key to my life as well as to my work."[1] More specifically, it is relevant because Kundera's disavowal of elements of his own past, his attempt to blur his role as a leading Czech intellectual affiliated with Communism, and his self-stylization as a cosmopolitan, dissident writer are partially achieved *inside* his novels through the "autobiographical" voice he develops in his postemigration works.[2] In other words, Kundera is in need of a "controlling" voice in his fiction in order to create a specific image of himself, a self that would otherwise be all the more vulnerable to biographical scrutiny. So, let us have a look at Kundera's career, not in order to pry into his private affairs, but to take into critical account his biographical background.

Milan Kundera was born in Brno on April 1, 1929.[3] His family was highly cultured and middle-class. His father, Ludvík Kundera, was a pupil of the composer Leoš Janáček and an important Czech musicologist and pianist, the head of the Brno Musical Academy from 1948 to 1961. Kundera himself studied musicology in his youth, and his work is permeated with insights from the art of music, mainly pertaining to compositional strategies. In 1948 Kundera entered the ruling Czechoslovak Communist Party and began his studies in literature and aesthetics at Charles University in Prague, but he soon transferred to the Film Academy. In 1950 he was forced to interrupt his studies temporarily for political reasons and was expelled from the party for the first time. However, he was able to resume his studies shortly after that, even though he was not readmitted to the party until 1956. After his graduation in 1952, he was appointed lecturer in world literature at the Film Academy.

The German occupation of his beloved nation left a deep impact on Kundera. The close encounter with fascism and totalitarianism drove many young Czechs toward Marxism, among them the young Kundera. As for his literary career, Kundera's first book, a collection of lyrical poems called *Man, a Wide Garden,* was published in 1953, and in 1955 he published the long poem "The Last May." This was followed by the publication of another collection of poems, *Monologues,* in 1957. In 1962 Kundera published a play, *The Owners of the Keys,* which was very successfully staged at the National Theatre in Prague. These works can all be categorized as "Marxist literature," but some of them also transgress the dogmatic poetics of socialist realism. Moravian ethnicity is often used as a reaffirmation of the authenticity and value of national identity, themes that recur throughout Kundera's later work, although with great variations of perspective in what could be called an oscillation between a nostalgia toward an authentic, irrevocable past and a cynicism toward provincialism and nationalism.

On the Czech literary scene, Kundera's early works provoked much dispute and were regarded as major literary landmarks. Kundera was thus a household name in communist Czechoslovakia from the mid-1950s. He wrote for a number of literary magazines, and his articles were followed with great interest. His 1955 article "Arguing about Our Inheritance" defended the heritage of Czech and European avant-garde poetry, otherwise condemned as decadent by communist literary scholars. Nonetheless, Kundera sided with avant-garde poetry from a strictly communist point of view.

However, all the abovementioned early works have been disowned by Kundera. In an interview with Philip Roth in 1984, Kundera describes his life in the 1950s and 1960s as follows:

> Then they expelled me from University. I lived among workmen. At that time, I played the trumpet in a jazzband in small-town cabarets. [. . .] Then I wrote poetry. I painted. It was all nonsense. My first work which is worth while mentioning is a short story, written when I was thirty, the first story in the book *Laughable Loves.* This is when my life as a writer began. I had spent half of my life as a relatively unknown Czech intellectual.[4]

Kundera's account supports what I said earlier about his desire to eradicate his early work. In addition, Kundera's claim about being a relatively unknown Czech intellectual at the time seems to be a deliberate attempt to stylize himself as a dissident writer and to suppress his own leading role in Czech intellectual life, thereby obscuring his past affiliations with the Communist Party. As Milan Jungmann remarks, "The self-portrait is retouched so much that Kundera's true likeness is completely obliterated.

Everything *essential* to rendering his profile as the leading intellectual during the last decades of Czech history is concealed."[5]

However, Kundera was not merely an uncritical believer; he was also a liberalizing force and a rebel. At the Fourth Congress of the Czechoslovak writers in June 1967, Kundera thus gave a famous speech in which he called for more freedom for the Czech writers who felt enslaved by the authoritarian communist machinery. Among the themes of the speech were the issues of the revivification of the Czech language and the rescue of the Czech nation from extinction, both issues of persistent interest to Kundera. The year 1967 also saw the publication of *The Joke,* the novel he considers to be his first mature work. The following year, Kundera published *Laughable Loves,* a collection of short stories, some of which date back to the late 1950s.

Life Is Elsewhere came out in French in 1973. Kundera had begun writing the novel during the Prague Spring in 1968 and completed it in 1970 after his second and final banishment from the party. At this time Kundera witnessed his complete eradication from Czech cultural history as his books were removed from all libraries and bookshops, just as he lost his job as a professor. In *Life Is Elsewhere* Kundera indirectly confronts his communist past and frees himself from it by launching a scathing attack on lyricism, immaturity, youth, and narcissism.

The fact that Kundera no longer wrote with a Czech audience in mind made him simplify his language. This is true from *Life Is Elsewhere* onward. However, the earlier works belonging to his "official" bibliography (i.e., *The Joke* and *Laughable Loves*), have—in addition to being revised because of inaccurate first translations—also undergone radical changes in their linguistic appearance. Among other things, Kundera has removed all Czech diacritics (but only to replace them with new French ones), just as he has inserted short explanatory passages where the Western reader might otherwise find the text too "local" and too esoteric. This points to yet another paradox: Kundera constantly speaks up for the particular values related to Central European culture, but at the same time he "universalizes" his fiction by erasing the "regional" qualities that may have rooted it in its specific local environment. He can thus be said to attempt a blurring of the work's local inflection in order to make it more translocally mobile. Kundera's next novel, *The Farewell Party,* was published in French in 1976. Kundera completed it in Prague in 1972, and it was supposed to have been his last novel. It ends with one of the protagonists emigrating by car, thus anticipating Kundera's own decision to emigrate a couple of years later.

In 1975 Kundera and his wife, Vera, left Czechoslovakia for France, where he was invited to teach at the University of Rennes. Kundera has time and again declared that his emigration was liberating and that it brought him much relief: "In France, I have experienced the unforgettable feeling of being born again. After a six year break, I returned, timidly, to literature. My wife kept repeating to me: 'France is your second homeland.'"[6] Sometimes Kundera even denies being an emigrant: "I [. . .] have no hope whatever of returning. My stay in France is final, and, therefore, I am not an émigré. France is my only real homeland now. Nor do I feel uprooted. For a thousand years, Czechoslovakia was part of the West. Today, it is part of the empire to the east. I would feel a great deal more uprooted in Prague than in Paris."[7] The emigration was thus a defining moment for Kundera. Being already well-versed in French literature and culture, his firsthand experience of everyday life in the West has nevertheless endowed him with a "double vision" that has proved fruitful in his comparisons and contrastings of Eastern and Western Europe: "For a writer, the experience of living in a number of countries is an enormous boon. You can only understand the world if you see it from several sides," Kundera told Philip Roth in another interview in 1980.[8]

In 1979, Kundera published *The Book of Laughter and Forgetting,* a work that heralded a new stage in his career. Thematically, emigration and memory gain importance, and, formally, the novel is probably Kundera's most uncompromising attempt to create a "novel of variations" in which the thematic unity is the main principle, thus subordinating more traditional unifying elements such as the unity of action, character, plot, and milieu. The year before, Kundera and his wife moved to Paris, where he occupied a teaching post at the École des Hautes Études. After losing his Czech citizenship in 1979 (as a result of *The Book*), he obtained French citizenship in 1981. In Paris, Kundera completed the novel *The Unbearable Lightness of Being,* which was published in 1984.

Immortality, published in 1990, is the first novel by Kundera with no Czech characters. The following three novels, *Slowness* (1995), *Identity* (1997), and *Ignorance* (2000), mark yet a new stage in Kundera's career, primarily because they have all been written in French, but also because of their relative brevity. Kundera has also published three collections of essays, *The Art of the Novel* (1986), *Testaments Betrayed* (1993), and *The Curtain* (2005).

In the following, I will analyze the migratory experiences and exilic conditions of Kundera's protagonists and will then discuss the role of the nation in Kundera's fiction as well as nonfiction. Finally, I will analyze Kundera's compositional strategies and the role of the authorial narrator.

Heroes of Nonbelonging

The horns of an immigrant's dilemma, goring most severely exiles and intellectual émigrés, are either assimilation or an intransigent, sometimes curmudgeonly, espousal of marginality.

—Darko Suvin, "Displaced Persons"

In *Aesthetics: Lectures on Fine Art* (1835–1838), Hegel speaks of "the conflict between the poetry of the heart and the opposing prose of circumstances and the accidents of external situations" as the constitutive formal feature of the novel.[9] The novelistic enterprise is thus driven by the conflict between an individual yearning for meaning and completeness, on the one side, and a degraded and contingent world into which the individual is cast on the other. Hence, the relationship between hero and reality is problematic, and this is what prompts Hegel to refer to the novel as "the modern popular [*bürgerlichen*] epic"[10]—about eighty years later Lukács describes it as the epic of a world abandoned by God.

The conflictual tension makes the novel a story about the transformation of either the hero or the world. The organizing principles are those of quest, conquest, or inquest—that is, the narratological pattern resulting from an individual's desire for happiness, truth, love, glory, and so forth.[11] Consequently, the protagonist is usually active and struggling. Even though reconciliation or accomplishment seems unattainable, the hero continues to struggle as though his persistence will eventually provide him with the cryptogram capable of unlocking the gate that obstructs a converging communication between his own heart and outer reality. Just think of K.'s determination vis-à-vis the castle whose doors remain closed because he does not possess the key to their locks ("Schloß" means both castle and lock).

With regard to the heroes of the novel and their reactions to the prosaic reality, Hegel observes the following:

As individuals with their subjective ends of love, honour, and ambition, or with their ideals of world-reform, they stand opposed to this substantial order and the prose of actuality which puts difficulties in their way on all sides. Therefore, in this opposition, subjective wishes and demands are screwed up to immeasurable heights; for each man finds before him an enchanted and quite alien world which he must fight because it obstructs him and in its inflexible firmness does not give way to his passions but interposes as a hindrance the will of a father or an aunt and civil relationships, etc. [. . .] Now the thing is to breach this order of things, to change the world, to improve it, or at least in spite of it to carve out of it a heaven upon earth.[12]

The protagonists of Kundera's novels are also situated in the midst of a prosaic world full of obstacles. Yet, most of Kundera's protagonists are anti-Hegelian heroes: they rarely aspire to a better world, and when confronted with obstacles, they do not react impatiently by asserting their subjective desires in opposition to a world that oppresses them and against which they are determined to fight, because it offers resistance to their mental constitution (Franz, of course, is an exception, but he dies a farcical death precisely because of his "lyrical" aspirations for a better world). For Kundera's protagonists, it is neither about breaching the prosaic order of things, nor about changing the world or making it better, and it is certainly not about founding a piece of heaven on earth either. Rather, Kundera's protagonists, scarred by the irrational and impersonal forces of history, simply withdraw from the battleground and renounce the Hegelian premises by surrendering to the world: They are *heroes of nonbelonging*; they disappear, escaping through a side door.

Kundera may be said to incorporate a basic Hegelian/Lukácsian structure of conflict between problematic subject and contingent world in his novels, but his characters nonetheless offer a non-Hegelian reaction to the conflict—that of exilic withdrawal and absolute discord instead of an idealistic involvement and aspiration that are ultimately governed by teleological forces of progress. Exile is here to be understood as a *transcendental metaphysical condition*. The Kunderian novel also presents itself as a modification of Lukács's theory of the novel in which the protagonists are described as "seekers." To Lukács, the seeking hero is the actual objectification of the novel's "form-giving intention,"[13] which is characterized as "something in process of becoming." Nevertheless, Kundera's novel can still formally be said to be a process in Lukácsian (and Deleuzian) terms, but the processual form is not so much a result of the protagonist's seeking psychology as it is a result of the enunciatory strategies of variation and multiperspectivism and the fact that whatever uprootings the heroes experience, those are more a result of outer, impersonal, and contingent circumstances than a result of the individual's will to "seek" newness (or if will plays a part, it is a will to nonbelong).

In the "traditional" novel, the protagonist can be said to move blindfolded about in the world. At the end of the novel he regains his sight and usually sees his own disenchantment. The disenchantment has a punctual impact in the sense that it is related to a specific event (or chain of events) and occurs at the end of the novel. In Kundera this scheme is transformed, as disenchantment is no longer the conclusion of the hero's life; instead, it colors the hero's entire existence from beginning to end. In fact, disenchantment, or disillusionment is not even an appropriate word to apply to

Kundera's heroes, as it presupposes the presence of ideals and illusions that have failed.

It applies to Julien Sorel, Eugène de Rastignac, and Frédéric Moreau, to Rodion Raskolnikoff and Anna Karenina, to Effi Briest and Marcel, and even to Oskar Matzerath in his moments of vulnerability: they all wish to be integrated into society. But it equally applies to all of them that they realize their failures at the end of their journeys (Robinson Crusoe, Tom Jones, and Oliver Twist, on the other hand, are examples of desiring subjects who actually achieve integration and fulfillment). In Kundera, on the other hand, the condition of absolute nonbelonging constitutes the essence of the existence of several of the protagonists. This is especially true of Tamina, Sabina, Agnes, and Irena, but also of Tomas, Tereza, and Josef. Instead of seeking integration, they seek exit—in fact, they are to some extent peripheral from the very outset. It is as if they have learned the lesson of Kafka's K.: "What possibilities remain for a man in the world where the external determinants have become so overpowering that internal impulses no longer carry weight" (*AN*, 26)? However, some of the protagonists in Kundera's preemigration novels—for example, Ludvik and Jaromil—still bear the Hegelian mark of conflict and struggle, and they are both left disenchanted at the end. And Jakub in *The Farewell Party* is characterized by his past life of struggle, on the one hand, and by his future life in exile on the other. Accordingly, he embodies a transition in Kundera's novels from struggling to exilic protagonists. From *The Book of Laughter and Forgetting* and onward, it is as if the lives of the protagonists are lived beyond desire and adventure.

* * *

After her emigration to Switzerland, itself merely one component in a long series of escapes, Sabina is persuaded to attend a meeting where other Czech emigrants discuss whether they should have fought the Russians with arms or not. Sabina quickly realizes her mistake. She is among a group of involved people, and to her, involvement implies constant control, evaluation, and idealism: the questions of right or wrong lead to fascism in Sabina's eyes, whereas her gaze is purely aesthetic. Sabina thus deserts the meeting, just as she deserted her father and her country and will later desert Franz—she can even be said to constantly desert herself. To Kundera, the deserter is not necessarily a negative type, however: "the deserter is one who refuses to grant meaning to the battles of his contemporaries. Who refuses to see a tragic grandeur in massacres. Who is loath to participate as a clown in History's comedy. His vision of things is often lucid, very lucid, but it makes his position difficult to maintain: it loosens his solidarity with his people; it distances him from mankind" (*Cu,* 112). In Sabina's case, her complete detachment leads to both freedom and betrayal, one of the terminal paradoxes defining the "light" individuals in Kundera's novels: freedom, because she is without obligations to anyone and is therefore able to maintain her personal integrity, and betrayal, because in order to be completely free and autonomous, she must continually breach the immaterial, emotional bonds that she establishes with other people and places.

If flight (freedom *and* betrayal) is what essentially characterizes Sabina's life, she actually remains faithful to the bowler hat that she has inherited from her grandfather. However, if the bowler hat remains a constant as a physical object, it is nevertheless semantically unstable and "migratory":

> The bowler hat was a motif in the musical composition that was Sabina's life. It returned again and again, each time with a different meaning, and all the meanings flowed through the bowler hat like water through a riverbed [. . .]: each time the same object would give rise to a new meaning, though all former meanings would resonate (like an echo, like a parade of echoes) together with the new one. Each new experience would resound, each time enriching the harmony.
>
> (*ULB,* 86)

The bowler hat motif illustrates the oscillation between repetition and variation in Sabina's life. It constitutes what E. M. Forster has called a "rhythm"; that is, internal "stitchings" that make a novel cohere.[14] Hence, the bowler represents a counterweight to the otherwise unbearable lightness of Tomas's initial credo "Einmal ist keinmal" (Once doesn't count). It repeats itself and continues to be a river, although each repetition carries a new meaning. In addition, this newness is characterized by its accumulatory nature, which means that it always (virtually) contains its own past meanings. Kundera describes this by way of the musical analogy of the chord (as Bergson and Husserl did before him). The bowler symbolizes the musical composition of Sabina's life, on the one hand representing what holds her identity together by supplying the musical sheets that always remain musical sheets (the bowler as a physical object), on the other hand representing the lines of flight that deterritorialize her identity by supplying the ever-changing notes and chords that bear witness to flux and variations (the bowler as a semantic object).

Another motif that indicates a certain stability in Sabina's life is her kitsch—that is, "her image of home, all peace, quiet, and harmony, and ruled by a loving mother and wise father" (*ULB,* 252). Even though Sabina is the novel's most ferocious opponent to kitsch, and kitsch for Kundera means a "*categorical agreement with being* [. . .], a world in which shit is denied and everyone acts as though it did not exist" (*ULB*, 245, 246), Sabina cannot suppress her melancholic longing for a home and a family. The image of a harmonious home, however, makes itself felt only momentarily and only on rare occasions: "Sabina's path of betrayals would then continue elsewhere, and from the depths of her being, a silly mawkish song about two shining windows and the happy family living behind them would occasionally make its way into the unbearable lightness of being" (*ULB*, 253). Sabina, despite her personal song of kitsch, is basically a "light" individual who has defied the law of gravity as a true migrant. She is detached from all obligations and quests and, as François Ricard observes, "her existence is an endless emigration."[15] Her endless migration is due not to her seeking soul but to her desire to escape from a world in which people still believe that "to seek" may lead to reconciliation. Kundera, however, makes sure to emphasize the ambiguity of her endless migration, as lightness is partly desirable (as it amounts to freedom), partly unbearable (as it necessitates betrayal and, ultimately, meaninglessness). Sabina is therefore not the novel's true heroine, as she also embodies the negative side of lightness, betrayal. And what is more, her moments of kitsch indicate that her lightness is immanently contaminated by weight.

In *The Book of Laughter and Forgetting,* Tamina emigrates with her husband from Prague to a small town in Western Europe in 1969. Tamina and her husband are two further examples of exilic Kunderian heroes to whom the concept of struggle means little: "That first morning after their escape, when they woke up in a small hotel in the Alps and realized they were alone, cut off from the world which had been their entire life to that point, she felt liberated, relieved. They were in the mountains, mercifully alone. They were surrounded by unbelievable silence. For Tamina, it was an unexpected gift" (*BLF,* 96). Their detachment and solitude are emphasized as positive values. The scenario prefigures scenes from both *The Unbearable Lightness of Being* and *Immortality* in which Tereza (in the village with Tomas) and Agnes (alone or with her father in the mountains) enjoy peace and tranquility away from the noises and battles of the world.

In *Civilization and Its Discontents* (1929), Freud describes different strategies to cope with the sufferings stemming from relationships with other people or from the outer world that resemble the strategies of many of Kundera's protagonists: "Against the suffering which may come upon one from human relationships the readiest safeguard is voluntary isolation, keeping oneself aloof from other people. The happiness which can be achieved along this path [. . .] is the happiness of quietness. Against the dreaded external world one can only defend oneself by some kind of turn-ing away from it."[16] According to Freud, this leads to a hermit's life, an appropriate way to characterize Tamina's solitary existence in emigration. Shortly after their emigration, Tamina's husband dies and she experiences a sudden attack of nostalgia and homesickness. She considers returning to Prague, but back "home" everyone had betrayed her husband, and her return would therefore link her to their betrayal. Tamina attempts unsuc-cessfully to commit suicide. "When she awoke, she felt peaceful and quiet. She resolved to live in silence and for silence" (*BLF,* 97). Tranquility, peace, and stillness are also what attract Josef, Tereza, Tomas, and Agnes.

After her husband's death, Tamina's life has become oriented toward the past, as she has abandoned all hope of future happiness. In her solitude Tamina tries to build a platform of memories of her life with her husband on which she can continue to live. Their past correspondence becomes an important component in her "project," as Tamina believes that it may help her reconstruct their life together. Their notebooks and letters were left behind when they emigrated, and Tamina's mission is to retrieve them. This is an endeavor full of obstacles: a reluctant mother-in-law, a father who does not understand her, a state apparatus that controls everything passing over the state borders, an egocentric girlfriend, and a disdained "lover." This pattern may resemble the Hegelian idea of a conflict between a poetic heart and a prosaic world full of obstacles, but what differentiates Tamina from the typical Hegelian hero is the fact that her project is past-oriented rather than future-oriented. This means that all that really matters to her is the creation of an asylum of memories in which she can live all alone, cut off from the prosaic world. She is indeed a melancholic being.

The project is doomed to failure. Instead of building a platform of memories and continuity, forgetting and erasure become the dominant modes of Tamina's existence. Her anchor gradually comes loose from the world, and she slowly drifts away. One day she does not show up at work; she has disappeared out of a side door. In her longing for lightness and weightlessness, she travels to the children's island that represents the eternal, the paradisaical, the unbreachable circle, and stasis. These are Kunderian symbols of death, and for Tamina, the lightness she initially sought ends up becoming the heaviness by which she finally drowns.

As Ricard points out, Tamina, Jan, Jakub, Sabina, Agnes, Josef, and Irena all make up a significant group in Kundera's work: "Proscribed within or driven out of their country, these banished and exiled characters are most often solitary creatures as well, separate, without bonds. Whether they are unmarried, widowed, divorced, it is as if they had broken every contract with others and were living both cut off from and free of any community, withdrawn—rejected—in their single, private existence."[17] Tomas and Tereza, despite their emigration to Switzerland, do not entirely fit this description. First of all, they both return to Czechoslovakia because Tereza does not have the strength to live abroad. Second, they are (a rare Kunderian example of) a married couple who stays together until their deaths. Third, they maintain relationships with other people, although not with their families and former friends, but with their new village community.

However, Ricard is correct in describing the last part of *The Unbearable Lightness of Being*, the village chapter, as the most elaborated image of exilic existence in Kundera:

> The setting: an isolated, archaic village, where nature seems free of man's power; the characters' situation: Tomas a truck driver, Tereza a cowherd, both socially diminished, poor, and without a "mission" or plan; their solitude; the time they live in: shapeless, with no trajectory, become pure routine, pure repetition, infinite slowness: we are here in the absolute of exile. While the "Grand March" of history continues elsewhere, around Tomas and Tereza the world has completely vanished, along with its turbulences, mirages, and desires; what remains is only silence and repose.[18]

Ricard's characterization of Tomas and Tereza as being without any mission only emphasizes their non-Hegelian stature. Their lack of drive does not mean that their identities are stable, however. By portraying them through the opposites of lightness-weight and body-soul, what Kundera terms their existential DNA, and by constantly revealing the paradoxes inherent in these oppositional pairs, Kundera shows us the unstable, oscillatory, and metamorphic nature of their identities. In short, the key concepts (themes) that are essential to Kundera in order to characterize the protagonists are themselves constantly set in motion semantically as their paradoxical nature and relationship to other concepts are emphasized again and again. Because of these conceptual mutations and reversals (the idea's transcendental homelessness), the characters undergo migrations as their identities are closely bound up with and follow the concepts and ideas defining them.

One example is the libertine life that Tomas lives before he meets Tereza. Tomas here avoids any external imperatives and thus lives a life in lightness and freedom (to him positive values). When Tereza enters into Tomas's life carrying her heavy suitcase, she represents an enormous challenge to his meticulous libertinism. While Tomas manages to uphold the distinction between his erotic friendships and his relationship with Tereza in a physical sense, he struggles psychologically to keep up the distinction because of the feelings of jealousy and compassion, the trademarks of commitment, that

Tereza provokes in him. Tomas's compassion is an emotionally oppressive tie that challenges his ideals of noncommitment, and his jealousy is a paradox because of his ability to distinguish between eroticism and love. Whenever Tereza experiences anxiety, jealousy, happiness, or the peacefulness of their common sleep, Tomas feels the same emotions. This is why Tomas cannot but follow Tereza back to Prague when she decides to leave him in Zürich. At first, Tomas is thrilled to be on his own again. Initially he senses the smell of freedom and realizes that new adventures are waiting for him. But the feeling of lightness lasts for only two days. The thought of Tereza's miseries and her loneliness in Prague prevents him from enjoying his freedom. Tomas's situation in Zürich after Tereza's departure is an example of how the existential categories defining an individual suddenly reverse into their own opposites and thus catalyze an inner metamorphosis of the character. The freedom of Tomas's lightness suddenly becomes unbearable and oppressive as he realizes the emptiness of a life without Tereza. As Sabina remarks, the world of libertinism and the world of romanticism collide in Tomas, and he oscillates constantly between them, feeling home in neither of them, thus betraying both: "The meeting of two worlds. A double exposure. Showing through the outline of Tomas the libertine, incredibly, the face of a romantic lover. Or, the other way, through a Tristan, always thinking of his Tereza, I see the beautiful, betrayed world of the libertine" (*ULB*, 22).

Tomas, a true heir to Macbeth, to whom life was but a walking shadow signifying nothing, is convinced that life is transient and governed by coincidences. He cannot see any reason to pursue continuity, because the only constant in life is the inexperience of any individual. It is in this light that Tomas contemplates his meeting with Tereza, which was brought about by six coincidences. To Tomas, the love of his life is in no way governed by any "Es muss sein!" (It must be!), but rather by an "Es könnte auch anders sein" (It could also be otherwise). To Tomas and Sabina, betrayal is therefore only a confirmation of the fundamental absurdity of existence; it is their answer to life's evanescent and contingent nature. All of his life Tomas has thus run away from the oppressive weight of obligations and outer imperatives. He has guarded his erotic friendships in order to prove his freedom and the impermanence of existence. And yet, Tomas realizes that his meticulousness has actually turned his pursuit of freedom into a lifelong duty, an "Es muss sein!" as enslaving as all the other imperatives he has tried to avoid. He also comprehends that Tereza's sudden appearance was the only true accidental (nonimperative) event in his life: "She, born of six fortuities, she, the blossom sprung from the chief surgeon's sciatica, she, the reverse side of all his '*Es muss sein!*'—she was the only thing he cared for" (*ULB*, 216).

Tereza, like Tomas, is fully aware of the accidental nature of their first meeting. But contrary to Tomas's initial conviction, Tereza is excited about the fortuitous coordination of details (the cognac, Beethoven on the radio, the number six, the yellow bench), which only makes the meeting between a waitress and a customer even more beautiful and extraordinary. Tereza interprets the events as a predestined meeting between two persons who are meant for each other. Through Tomas, Tereza perceives the materialization of her highly idealized conception of love. And if it seems as if she casts her love upon Tomas too easily, it is because her idyllic and ideal idea of love implies her unconditional compliance. In this sense Tereza is a close relative of both Gelsomina (Giulietta Masina) in Federico Fellini's *La strada* (*The Road*) (1954) and Bess (Emily Watson) in Lars von Trier's *Breaking the Waves* (1996). Despite a definite inequality in their relationships with Tomas, Zampanò, and Jan, respectively, a strange paradox in each case causes the "weak" women to remain faithful, and thereby they exemplify a logic of reversal in which their apparent weakness is ultimately transformed into strength.[19]

If betrayal is the trademark of Tomas's lightness, vertigo is the trademark of Tereza's weight. Vertigo is the driving force behind her devotion to a man who constantly betrays her. Why does Tereza hold on to Tomas more tightly the more he betrays her? The answer provided in the novel is paradoxical because vertigo is not simply the fear of falling; it is also "the voice of the emptiness below us which tempts and lures us, it is the desire to fall, against which, terrified, we defend ourselves" (*ULB*, 58). Heights are thus paradoxically attractive to people suffering from vertigo.[20] Tereza stays with Tomas precisely because his infidelity makes her feel weaker—and thus her compliance and her longing to fall even stronger. Confronted with Tomas's strength and unlimited freedom, her weakness intoxicates her with dizziness and acquiescence.

Even when Tereza leaves Tomas in Zürich, she is not motivated so much by strength as by a craving for weakness. Tereza realizes that the strength and happiness she experienced in Prague during the first seven days of the Russian occupation were not rooted in her own personality. Instead they originated from a solidarity with the weak, which transforms weakness into an illusory strength. Far away from Prague, Tereza feels even more dependent on Tomas:

> Being in a foreign country means walking a tightrope high above the ground without the net afforded a person by the country where he has his family, colleagues, and friends, and where he can easily say what he has to say in a language he has known from childhood. In Prague she was dependent on Tomas only when it came to the heart; here she was dependent on him for everything.
>
> (*ULB*, 73)

Admittedly, it must have taken a lot of courage for Tereza to leave Tomas like that: "But when the strong were too weak to hurt the weak, the weak had to be strong enough to leave" (*ULB*, 74), it says in a passage that clearly shows the reversibility of the novel's key words. But what is the purpose? She does not leave Tomas in order to claim her independence; she leaves him in order to surrender herself to her own weakness among the weak. Tereza is not simply longing to fall because Tomas's freedom forces her up into vertiginous heights, however. Instead, we must insist that Tereza's vertigo is a fundamental attribute of her own paradoxical existence. She lives in a constant state of vertigo because she cannot be herself without Tomas (lightness), nor can she be herself through her complete devotion to Tomas (weight), but only through the endless oscillation between the two alternatives.

During the last two years of their lives, their relationship enters a new phase that seems more peaceful than hitherto. This is due neither to the fact that Tomas has abandoned his libertinism, nor to the fact that they have moved to the countryside, away from the tensions of the city. Kundera depicts rural life ambiguously: The apple trees that are mentioned may rightly be associated with Paradise, but at the same time they are crooked. In addition, the narrator makes it clear that a village under a communist regime does not resemble the ancient idyllic image of a village. Finally, it is emphasized that the brakes of the truck in which Tomas and Tereza are killed were in a very bad shape. One can read the last part not only as a parody of socialist realism, but also, arguably, as an intertextual reference with a parodic undertone to Levin's and Kitty's idyllic countryside happiness in Tolstoy's *Anna Karenina* (1875–77), one of Kundera's favorite novels—Tomas and Tereza's dog is actually named after Alexei Karenin. These are just a few examples of the counterweight to the romanticization of life in the countryside.

Doubtlessly, rural life helps their marriage and allows them to rediscover each other. But the true source behind the relative peace of their rediscovered relationship lies within themselves. The paradoxes are still there, but now Tomas and Tereza acknowledge them and thereby abandon them. Ricard:

> A particular feature of this idyll is that it is based neither on unawareness of conflicts nor on their resolution (real or supposed), but on capitulation. The conflicts are not denied, they are abandoned; and it is neither his innocence nor his strength that opens the doors of this idyll to the exiled person; it is only his refusal to fight, the exhaustion of all his innocence and strength. The idyll is granted him not as a victory, not as the return to a primordial paradise lost, and still less as the entry into a future utopia won by a hard-fought struggle, but rather as a cessation, a "last station" completely under the sign of forgetting, resignation, and fatigue.[21]

The importance of self-awareness is underlined in the last pages of the novel, which are devoted to Tereza's agonizing and self-searching retrospective on her love for Tomas and the tug-of-war that has kept them together for ten years: "We all have a tendency to consider strength the culprit and weakness the innocent victim. But now Tereza realized that in her case the opposite was true! [. . .] Her weakness was aggressive and kept forcing him to capitulate until eventually he lost his strength and was transformed into the rabbit in her arms" (ULB, 307). Tereza's thoughts reveal the interchangeability and interdependence of all their paradoxes: her weakness and his strength, her weight and his lightness, her vertigo and his freedom, her burdensome fidelity and his betrayals. Nevertheless, Tereza finds comfort or satisfaction in her acknowledgment of the vacillating character of these dualisms, a kind of happiness or joy that is in itself a paradox: "She was experiencing the same odd happiness and odd sadness as then. The sadness meant: we are at the last station. The happiness meant: we are together. The sadness was form, the happiness content. Happiness filled the space of sadness" (ULB, 310).

The novel's ending is ambivalent, trying to maintain a balance between kitsch and nonkitsch, sentimentality and nonsentimentality. On the one hand, it emphasizes the relative happiness of Tomas and Tereza; on the other hand, their happiness is counterweighted by Karenin's death, the constant insinuations that undermine the rural tranquility, and the reader's recognition of the absurdity of the way Tomas and Tereza end their lives, anticlimactically revealed halfway into the novel: "Their bodies had been crushed to a pulp. The police determined later that the brakes were in a disastrous condition" (ULB, 122). Accordingly, Tomas and Tereza seem to end their lives as heavy individuals; Tomas dies like Tristan rather than like Don Juan, as Sabina observes. According to Ricard, the close relationship between death and exile in this final part of the novel is also what counterweights the elements of idyllic kitsch: "mortality is not denied in it, but, on the contrary, fully accepted, and with it imperfection, transience, and corruption. It is, therefore, a prosaic, unillusioned idyll, whose walls are built of that 'categorical disagreement,' that absolute disavowal which frees the exile both from the world and from his destiny."[22]

Kundera's preoccupation with exile as understood here—that is, as an "absolute disavowal"—explains why he is bound to modify the Hegelian model. Instead of the adventure of a hero and a narratological pattern determined by action, quest, or conflict, the Kunderian novel is often populated by individuals who abandon the world before any conflict can arise, and this means that their existential situation is examined not through a single-stranded, chronological, and continuous plot in which their deeds determine who they are, but through certain key situations of an episodic character that are scrutinized from different perspectives and through several discursive modes.

The Modern Homecoming

Migration is a one-way trip. There's no "home" to go back to. There never was.

—Stuart Hall, "Minimal Selves"

Ignorance is a novel about two emigrants from Prague who emigrated after 1968: Irena, now living in Paris; Josef, in Denmark. Shortly after the fall of Communism in 1989, they meet by accident in a Paris airport, both en route to visit their "hometown." *Ignorance* deals with the problems of emigration and homecoming, the question of belonging, the role of memory, and the relationship between the nation, patriotism, and cosmopolitanism. The novel is a modern version of the *Odyssey*—a work that it explicitly refers to—in that it portrays the homecoming of its heroes. But by "modern" I also want to suggest that the Homerian idea of homecoming is challenged in *Ignorance*: the novel is not so much about the homecoming of its protagonists as it is about the impossibility of their homecoming.

The novel opens in a Parisian café and immediately introduces us to one of its major themes; namely, the "great return" to one's native country. Because of the democratic revolution taking place in Prague, Sylvie urges Irena to return "Home!" However, having spent the last twenty years in Paris, Irena no longer regards the Czech Republic as her home. Her entire life is in France: her lover, daughters, work, friends, and apartment. Sylvie, disappointed and confused by Irena's hesitations, says, "It will be your great return":

> Repeated, the words took on such power that, deep inside her, Irena saw them written out with capital initials: Great Return. She dropped her resistance: she was captivated by images suddenly welling up from books read long ago, from films, from her own memory, and maybe from her ancestral memory: the lost son home again with his aged mother; the man returning to his beloved from whom cruel destiny had torn him away; the family homestead we all carry about within us; the rediscovered trail still marked by the forgotten footprints of childhood; Odysseus sighting his island after years of wandering; the return, the return, the great magic of return.
>
> (*Ig*, 4–5)

The line of imagery that Sylvie's words evoke in the mind of Irena comprises some of the defining myths of the West: the idea of an original belonging, the idea of a natural desire to return home, and the belief in the possibility of a homecoming to the same home. These myths are ultimately undermined by Kundera's novel, however.

According to the narrator of *Ignorance*, Odysseus had to choose between an adventurous dolce vita away from home and a risky return to his beloved Ithaca: "Rather than ardent exploration of the unknown (adventure), he chose the apotheosis of the known (return). Rather than the infinite (for adventure never intends to finish), he chose the finite (for the return is a reconciliation with the finitude of life)" (*Ig*, 8). So, Odysseus is at one and the same time the greatest adventurer and the greatest nostalgic—but in the end he succumbs to nostalgia: "The dawn of ancient Greek culture brought the birth of the *Odyssey*, the founding epic of nostalgia" (*Ig*, 7).

Nostalgia, we are told, is made up of the Greek words *nostos* and *algos* and implies suffering caused by the inability to return or go back. The title of the novel is derived from this etymology in that the Spanish word for nostalgia is *añoranza*, which comes from the verb *añorar* (to feel nostalgia). The Spanish verb comes from the Catalan *enyorar*, which is derived from the Latin word *ignorare*: to be unaware of, not know, not experience; to lack or miss. Hence, one suffers because of one's ignorance of the well-being of one's family and friends and of one's ignorance of what is going on in one's native country. Odysseus could not bear this ignorance, which is why he decided to return to his beloved Ithaca. And for him, the homecoming was only initially and momentarily problematic:

> the Phaeacian seamen laid Odysseus [. . .] near an olive tree on Ithaca's shore, and then departed. [. . .] When he awoke, he could not tell where he was. Then Athena wiped the mist from his eyes and it was rapture; the rapture of the Great Return; the ecstasy of the known; the music that sets the air vibrating between earth and heaven; he saw the harbor he had known since childhood, the mountain overlooking it, and he fondled the old olive tree to confirm that it was still the same as it had been twenty years earlier.
>
> (*Ig*, 8–9)

The possibility of returning is due to the *logos* of the Greek world where transformations in the outside phenomenal world are regarded as mere appearances and false in relation to the true essences of eternal values and ideas. Odysseus actually recognizes the olive tree, not because its outward appearance is unchanged, but because its essence has never changed. Recognition is also the key word in relation to Penelope's acceptance of Odysseus. Accordingly, Odysseus's homecoming illustrates the copy's triumph over the simulacrum, a return *to* the same because the olive tree and

Ithaca as such have in essence remained the same, and a return *of* the same because Odysseus restores, with the help of his son Telemachos, the old order after killing the pretenders.

The case of Arnold Schoenberg provides the narrator with an alternative version of belonging, as Schoenberg's relationship with Germany was marked by detachment:

> In 1950, when Arnold Schoenberg had been in the United States for seventeen years, a journalist asked him a few treacherously innocent questions: Is it true that emigration causes artists to lose their creativity? That their inspiration withers when it no longer has the roots of their native land to nourish it?
>
> Imagine! Five years after the Holocaust! And an American journalist won't forgive Schoenberg his lack of attachment to that chunk of earth where, before his very eyes, the horror of horrors started! But it's a lost cause. Homer glorified nostalgia with a laurel wreath and thereby laid out a moral hierarchy of emotions. Penelope stands at its summit, very high above Calypso.
>
> (*Ig*, 9–10)[23]

According to Kundera, we in the West have historically sympathized with Penelope and her sufferings, whereas we have scorned Calypso and her tears. In other words, we hail nostalgia and homecoming and disregard adventure and the eternal drifting—and as the example of Schoenberg shows, we cannot forgive the person who does not feel attached to his native soil.[24]

For many years Irena used to look upon herself as a victim because her emigration was forced upon her from the outside, but at one point she realizes that this could be an illusion stemming from other people's views on the emigrant. She thus becomes aware of a liberating impulse in her forced emigration. However, while she once felt stigmatized as an exile because other people saw her as a victim, she now feels stigmatized because people expect her to want to return to Prague. The stigmatization also manifests itself in the Frenchmen's opposing views on Irena and Gustaf, her Swedish partner: Irena is looked upon as "*a young woman in pain, banished from her country*"; Gustaf, on the contrary, is regarded as "*a nice, very cosmopolitan Scandinavian who's already forgotten all about the place he comes from*" (*Ig*, 24).

Gustaf, too, joins the chorus of old romantics, taking it for granted that Irena wants to visit "her" Prague and maybe even live there part-time. He is left bewildered when she claims that Prague is not her city anymore, but at the same time he is himself unable to stand the idea of going back to Sweden, which he left voluntarily to escape a failed marriage. Kundera uses the paradox to criticize the idea of authenticity: "Both of them are pigeonholed, labeled, and they will be judged by how true they are to their labels (of course, that and that alone is what's emphatically called 'being true to oneself')" (*Ig*, 24). Irena *is* in fact true to herself, but does not act according to the stereotype of the exile, which is why she is looked upon with distrust and bemusement; Gustaf acts according to the stereotype of the cosmopolitan, and everybody finds his behavior natural and understandable.

When Irena visits Prague shortly after 1989, she is full of mixed emotions with regard to her reunion with her home city and old friends. During her meeting with her old friends at a bar, conversation proves difficult. Irena's former friends can neither accept that she has changed, nor understand that she has forgotten about so many things from the past. In addition, none of them shows the least interest in Irena's Parisian life; hence, she feels amputated in their company as if the last twenty years of her life had never existed. The reunion scene is an example of *incommensurable* subjective experiences (structurally similar to Sabina and Franz's vocabulary of misunderstood words). As a result of the failed communication, Irena is in fact an exile in her native city and among her Czech friends.

There is also an insurmountable divergence in the way that emigrant life is looked upon by the Czech women and by Irena herself. Those who stayed behind during the Communist years considered emigrant life abroad to be trouble free and life in Czechoslovakia hard, whereas Irena herself sees her life as an emigrant as being full of difficulties: "everybody thinks we left to get ourselves an easy life. They don't know how hard it is to carve out a little place for yourself in a foreign world" (*Ig*, 40).[25] What's more, people like Irena emigrated without any hope of ever seeing their native country again, something those who never left cannot understand: "*We did our best to drop anchor where we were*" (*Ig*, 40, my italics). Irena speaks here of a new kind of roots that are contingent and provisional; they are shaped by forced circumstances brought about by the irrational monster of history and lead to acquiescence. Irena is thus situated beyond the struggling Hegelian hero; she is nearer to stoicism than to Hegelian idealism.

Josef is faced with much the same difficulties as Irena. His conversation with his brother and sister-in-law proves difficult, as many of their perceptions of past events are incompatible: "He understood that there was nothing he could do about it; it was practically a law: People who see their lives as a shipwreck set out to hunt down the guilty parties. And Josef was doubly guilty: both as an adolescent who had spoken ill of God and as an adult who had emigrated" (*Ig*, 66). To the Czechs, Josef and Irena are guilty of betrayal for having left their home country, and this feeling is only reinforced by the sufferings endured by those who stayed behind "to face the enemy." Emigration is regarded as the easy solution. So, on the one hand the emigrants cannot expect any understanding from those who stayed behind, as they consider the emigrant a traitor, while on the other hand they are also stigmatized in their new country, where they are regarded as victims.

When Josef arrives in the Czech Republic, he first sets out to visit the cemetery where his mother is buried. But immediately upon reaching the small town, he realizes how much has changed. He cannot locate the cemetery and therefore asks a boy for help, but he fails to understand what the boy tells him: "It was the music of some unknown language" (*Ig*, 54). Josef neither speaks nor understands his own mother tongue. When he finally faces his mother's grave, he recognizes the names of quite a few other family members he did not know had died: "It was not their deaths that unsettled him [. . .], but the fact that he had not been sent any announcement. The Communist police kept watch on letters addressed to émigrés; had people been afraid to write him? He examined the dates: the two most recent were after 1989. So it was not out of caution that they didn't write. The truth was worse: he no longer existed for them" (*Ig*, 51). This passage reveals how the relationships between the emigrants and their families eventually ceased to exist. Hence, what is to be considered as natural is not an unbreakable bond between family members; on the contrary, it is the withering away of these bonds in much the same way as one's roots in the native soil gradually dry up.

One episode relating to Josef's homecoming presents itself as the exact opposite of the homecoming of Odysseus. Josef cannot recognize the landscape, because no Homerian olive tree reveals itself before his eyes: "During his absence, an invisible broom had swept across the landscape of his childhood, wiping away everything familiar; the encounter he had expected never took place" (*Ig*, 52). The moment of recognition never occurs; Josef is simply visiting an unrecognizable and strange country. And, as the narrator reflects, maybe this invisible brush that changes everything is not a new phenomenon; rather, it is to be regarded as an ever present, but accelerating phenomenon: "The gigantic invisible broom that transforms, disfigures, erases landscapes has been at the job for millennia now, but its movements, which used to be slow, just barely perceptible, have sped up so much that I wonder: Would an *Odyssey* even be conceivable today? Is the epic of the return still pertinent to our time?" (*Ig*, 54). The implicit answer to these questions—and also the novel's main idea—is that a fundamental transformation has taken place since antiquity, resulting in the impossibility of a Homerian return.

The epic of homecoming does not belong to our epoch, and we must abandon our belief in the possibility of a homecoming that does not take time and, with that, amnesia and difference into account. "The gigantic invisible broom" is nothing but time itself, which transforms and disfigures, wipes out and mutilates, but at the same time also invents and creates.[26] As the narrator tells us in relation to Josef's homecoming, "He had the sense he was coming back into the world as might a dead man emerging from his tomb after twenty years: touching the ground with a timid foot that's lost the habit of walking; barely recognizing the world he had lived in but continually stumbling over the leavings from his life" (*Ig,* 70). Josef is thus an inverted Odysseus in that he hardly recognizes his old world, and, furthermore, his bodily self has almost lost the habit of walking; Odysseus, on the contrary, recognizes the olive tree and the landscape as the same olive tree and the same landscape he had left twenty years before, and he does not experience any senso-motoric difficulties after Athena's godly intervention— his entire body feels at home immediately.

Yet another revealing example of the effacing and transforming work of time is Josef's reading of his old diary from his high school years: "He goes on reading and remembers nothing" (*Ig,* 72). This is not an example of a person's detachment from his family or from his native country; rather, it is an example of a person's detachment from himself. Josef completely fails to identify with his former self, whom he considers to be a total stranger.

The diary, the meeting with his brother and sister-in-law, his failure to understand his native language, and his experiences in front of his mother's grave and with the landscape as such, all these episodes emphasize the impossibility of a Homerian return, just as they point to Josef's general reluctance to return home in the first place: "he feels no affection for that dimly visible, feeble past; no desire to return; nothing but a slight reserve; detachment" (*Ig,* 74). This *detachment* of Josef's makes the narrator declare, "If I were a doctor, I would diagnose his condition thus: 'The patient is suffering from nostalgic insuffiency.'" He continues: "But Josef does not feel sick. He feels clearheaded. To his mind the nostalgic insufficiency proves the paltry value of his former life. So I revise my diagnosis: 'The patient is suffering from *masochistic distortion* of memory'" (*Ig,* 74, my italics). As mentioned already, the nature of time is deformation: it both erases and transforms. But why this masochism? In regard to Josef, it has something to do with his particular way of remembering: he only remembers situations that cause him to be dissatisfied with himself. But at the same time, there is a liberating element in Josef's masochistic memory: "such is the law of masochistic memory: as segments of their lives melt into oblivion, men slough off whatever they dislike, and feel lighter, freer" (*Ig,* 76). If a person remembered everything, he or she would carry around an unbearable weight. Because of memory's mechanism, which includes both remembrance and forgetting, this weight is usually tolerable.

Josef's diary contains the story of his relationship to a young girl, and even though he has forgotten almost everything from that period of his life, he still remembers fragments of his platonic love affair with this girl, who actually turns out to be Milada, the one woman with whom Irena can actually communicate in Prague. The point is that Josef remembers events in a wrong way, partly because he was already wrong in his perception of Milada's motives and their relationship back then, and partly because his memory fails to reconstruct the story correctly. Thus, Josef still believes that Milada's trip to the mountains with her school class was an excuse to meet a new boyfriend. As Milada's own version of the story in the novel shows, this was not the case at all. The consequence of this unreliable mechanism of memory is that every remembrance will never be anything but "the plausible plastered over the forgotten [une vraisemblable plaque sur de l'oublié]" (*Ig,* 126), a beautiful phrase expressing the *melancholy tone* that saturates the work of Kundera.[27]

The incommensurability of different interpretations of the same events is a typical trait in Kundera. This is what infuses his work with "modernity." In Kundera, every person is a modern monad—that is, characterized by a singular perspective on the world, a perspective that seldom converges with other persons' perspectives. In this way it seems as if intersubjectivity, to Kundera, does not exist in life, only in the novel.

Relationships in Kundera are often founded on asymmetrical pillars, partly because of his idea of man as a monad without any God to ensure a common ground between the monads. Sometimes the persons involved never realize this asymmetry, but the opposite can also be the case. The relationship between Josef and Irena is such an example, as Irena, toward the end of the novel, realizes how uneven her relationship with Josef has been since they met in the airport in Paris. When she sees him in the airport, she immediately recognizes him as the man who had flirted with her in a bar in Prague twenty years earlier. When she more or less offers herself to him in the airport, Josef is too embarrassed and too polite to admit to her that he cannot remember her. So if they seem to have a lot in common throughout the novel, especially because of their common experiences of emigration and homecoming, they are at the same time also very opposed to each other as the narrator explains in the following passage:

each of them retains two or three small scenes from the past, but each has his own; their recollections are not similar; they don't intersect; and even in terms of quantity they are not comparable: one person remembers the other more than he is remembered; first because memory capacity varies among individuals [. . .], but also [. . .] because they don't hold the same importance for each other. [. . .] From the very first moment their encounter was based on an unjust and revolting inequality.

(Ig, 126)

This passage provides us with an example of the incommensurability that Kundera almost considers a law between his characters. There is no longer any transcendent principle that can guarantee a certain semiotic convergence between individuals. This is also one of the reasons why the Kunderian protagonists are solitary, exilic, and nonbelonging. Even though Irena realizes their inequality when she meets Josef toward the end of the novel, the differences between their memories are not erased. Hence her moment of recognition at the end does not give her any hope for the future; all it does is cast an ironic light over her former beliefs.

The relationship between Irena and Josef is not exceptional in Kundera's work. It seems to be part of the human condition that inequalities, misunderstandings, and incompatibilities govern our relationships. This is also the case with Milada and Josef and with Irena and Gustaf: "Irena gave herself to him with all the weight of her life, whereas he wanted to live weightless" (*Ig*, 189). Irena and Gustaf (like Tereza and Tomas) enter the relationship with very different expectations, needs, and demands. The emphasis on difference can be ascribed to Kundera's antiromantic beliefs and, once again, his understanding of the subject as a modern monad. In that sense, his novels can also be said to be modern versions of Plato's *Symposium*: they are, on the one hand, very much occupied with the problems of love and relationships, but on the other hand, they never promise any wholeness, symmetry, or harmony. Aristophanes's idea that originally we were all whole and complete beings who were later cut into two halves and his belief that we are able to find our missing half and become whole again are outright rejected by Kundera, who insists on our unique individuality to which no perfect match exists.

*   *   *

As I mentioned at the beginning of this chapter, and as the analysis of the homecoming theme has implied, Bhabha's idea that "the shadow of the nation [still] falls on the condition of exile" also applies to Kundera.[28] Despite his personal experience of exile and migration, Kundera still believes that the concept of the nation has emotional and political validity, and he has always been highly sensitive toward the destinies of Europe's small nations in particular. Recently, in *The Curtain,* he stated thus: "Whether he is nationalist or cosmopolitan, rooted or uprooted, a European is profoundly conditioned by his relation to his homeland; the national problematic is probably more complex, more grave in Europe than elsewhere, but in any case it is different here" (*Cu,* 31).

However, to Kundera the existence of the modern nation is not a natural given; rather, it is the result of a deliberate choice. His famous speech held at the Fourth Congress of the Czechoslovak Writers' Union in June 1967—that is, fourteen months before the Russian-led invasion and at a time when the Prague Spring was only a few months away—already tells of a Kundera who is deeply concerned with the nation's role and with the "unobviousness" of the Czech nation's existence in particular:

> No nation has been on earth since the beginning of time and the very concept of nationhood is pretty recent. Despite that, most nations look upon their own existence as a self-evident destiny conferred by God, or by Nature, since time immemorial. Nations tend to think of their cultures and political systems, even their frontiers, as the work of Man, but they see their national existence as a transcendent fact, beyond all question. The somewhat cheerless and intermittent history of the Czech nation, which has passed through the very antechamber of death, gives us the strength to resist any such illusion. For there has never been anything self-evident about the existence of the Czech nation and one of its most distinctive traits, in fact, has been the *unobviousness* of that existence.[29]

This passage recalls Ernest Renan's celebrated 1882 lecture at the Sorbonne in which he emphasized the voluntariness underlying any nation's existence: "A nation's existence is, if you will pardon the metaphor, a daily plebiscite."[30] According to Kundera, any nation, and above all the small ones, is always followed by a question mark implicitly asking whether it will continue to exist as a nation or not. One question mark naturally leads to another: If one opts for the Czech nation's existence, as a group of Czech intellectuals—the so-called Revivalists—did in the nineteenth century, what legitimizes its existence? To the Revivalists the answer was its cultural production, above all its literature. However, to the Revivalists, and to Kundera who follows their ideas, the cultural artifacts should be measured not only in terms of their direct utility for the national project but also in terms of the criterion of "universal humanity," which is to say that they must belong to the world and to Europe as well.

Kundera locates this coexistence of the national and the universal in Goethe's concept of *Weltliteratur,* which entails a space of tolerance and diversity in which the work of art is not subject to any form of nationalistic project but is judged entirely by its aesthetic value. Moreover, Goethe's concept allows the cultures of the small nations to preserve their right to specificity, originality, and difference. The fact that the Revivalists' thoughts on the nation and its cultural creations were concurrent with Goethe's ideas on world literature only made Czech writers more aware of what was needed of them, says Kundera: a literature that would simultaneously contribute to the national project (by its specificity, i.e., what could only be expressed by this literature at this time and in this place) and possess the quality to play a part in world literature (through its proper value, i.e., its aesthetic/existential discoveries, which are its *raisons d'être* on the universal scale).

In his speech, Kundera situates the Czech nation and culture within the Greco-Roman and Judeo-Christian traditions of Europe. To Kundera, the intervention of Nazism and Stalinism in Czechoslovakia and Central Europe meant that Czech culture was severed from its European roots and that the Czech nation was permanently relegated to the cultural periphery of Europe. Kundera's speech is a reaction to this situation in that it optimistically attempts to instigate a new—or encourage the already ongoing—revival of Czech literature, language, and culture in general. As I said earlier, only fourteen months after the speech, the Russian tanks rolled into Prague and put an end to the emancipatory forces.

Because of the ongoing worldwide linguistic unification, Kundera saw the same crossroad situation for the Czech nation and its cultural values in 1967 as the Revivalists had in the nineteenth century. His present objective is unambiguous: "In such a situation a small nation can only protect its language and its individuality by the cultural standing of that language, by the uniqueness of the values it has created and which the world associates it with. [. . .] It is of paramount importance that our whole national community be fully aware of how vitally essential to us our culture and literature are."[31]

It is not too much of an exaggeration to characterize Kundera as a true patriot in 1967. However, it is out of such patriotism and deeply rooted national consciousness that Kundera's cosmopolitanism grows. And as Kwame Anthony Appiah argues in "Cosmopolitan Patriots," the two concepts are indeed compatible. Appiah thus speaks of a "rooted cosmopolitanism" and a "cosmopolitan patriotism," which he defines as a cosmopolitanism that enables you to always carry around your national roots. Appiah also claims that there is a difference between patriotism and cosmopolitanism on the one side and nationalism on the other: "Cosmopolitanism and patriotism, unlike nationalism, are both sentiments more than ideologies."[32] This is a useful distinction that can be applied in the case of Kundera, as his thoughts on the nation are based not on political ideologies but on sentiments rooted in language and in cultural and historical traditions.

Appiah's notion of cosmopolitanism involving patriotism also embodies a duality of local specificity and global universality that is relevant in a discussion of Kundera's position toward the nation. The actual national project, which has a limited geographical and temporal scope (the territory of Czechoslovakia and the revolutionary moment of 1948, as well as the accelerating optimism of the months leading up to the Prague Spring, which began in January 1968), is always contextualized by Kundera in a far greater geographical and historical tradition (Europe and its Greco-Roman and Judeo-Christian legacies). So Kundera defends *historical continuity* and criticizes the revolutionary strategy that tends to irrationally discard two thousand years of thought, a strategy that Kundera compares to the current state of *provincialism* that rules the minds of the Czech and Slovak people (and rulers), who live only in their immediate present without culture or awareness of historical continuity. However, Kundera not only criticizes the complete lack of historical consciousness and the revolutionary "ecstatic" mode (a being out of time), but also attacks the totalitarian and reactionary political trends that existed as counterforces to the progressive forces that ultimately led to the Prague Spring:

Any interference with freedom of thought and word, however discreet the mechanics and terminology of such censorship, is a scandal in this century, a chain entangling the limbs of our national literature as it tries to bound forward. [. . .] In our society it is counted a greater virtue to guard the frontiers than to cross them. The most transitory political and social considerations are used to justify all kinds of constraint on our intellectual liberty.[33]

Besides acknowledging his Enlightenment-inspired standpoint on the freedom of speech, opinion, and thought, Kundera also launches an assault on the subtle censorship politics of his country that constrain the public exchange of ideas and the cultural production in general.

It is important to underline the fact that Kundera does not conjure up an idea of the Czech nation as a continuous narrative of national progress; instead, he invokes his nation's *discontinuous* history, sometimes situated at "the antechamber of death," sometimes at the forefront of European cultural and political history: "The whole course of our nation's history, torn between democracy, fascist enslavement, Stalinism and socialism, and further complicated by its unique nationality problem, features every important issue that has made our twentieth century what it is."[34] The synecdochic significance of the Czech nation in relation to European history in the twentieth century is precisely what legitimizes its culture and its literature in particular, and this is the reason why the Kundera of 1967 pleads for his nation's continuous existence (provided that it can rise to the challenge of producing good cultural artifacts).

The Russian invasion in 1968 put a stop to the liberalizing forces that had dominated Czech society during the previous months. To Kundera, August 20, 1968, and the years that followed meant literally "to take a step from the modern period into the Middle Ages."[35] Some of his fears expressed in the 1967 speech had in fact materialized, and in 1983 he sums up the consequences in another famous essay, "Un occident kidnappé—ou la tragédie de l'Europe Centrale" (A West Kidnapped—or the Tragedy of Central Europe): "firstly, the opposition was crushed; secondly, the identity of the nation was undermined so that it could more easily be governed by the Russian civilization; thirdly, modernity (i.e., the epoch in which culture still represented the supreme values) was put to a violent end."[36] A new period resembling the Nazi occupation and Stalinist totalitarianism had begun. However, as one of history's strange paradoxes, Czech culture showed a remarkable survival instinct as it put up a fight against the oppressive forces.

Even though the 1967 speech is a reaction to a general atmosphere of growing oppression and censorship in the Czech society, optimism and a belief in "progress" nevertheless prevail. But in 1983, the Hegelian/Marxist-inspired perspective on history is replaced by a somewhat bleaker vision, due in part to the events in 1968:

> History, the goddess of Hegel and Marx, the incarnation of Reason which judges us and arbitrates us, it is the History of winners. But the peoples of Central Europe are not winners. They are inseparable from European History, they couldn't exist without her, but they merely represent the reverse of this History, its victims and outsiders. It is this disenchanted historical experience that is the source of the originality of their culture, their wisdom, their "non-serious spirit" which mocks glory's grandeur.[37]

The positive stance in 1967 toward worldwide integration, at the time counterweighted only by a carefully stated anxiety toward homogenization, is now replaced by a more direct concern for Europe's (small) nations and their vulnerability to the concentration of power.

Kundera strikes a balance between these gloomy visions of total unification on a global scale, on the one hand, and hopes for a blossoming diversity of national cultures on the other. It may be that cultural pessimism has gained the upper hand because of what Kundera considers to be the harsh realities of a homogenizing globalization, but this does not mean that he withdraws from formulating his ideal with regard to culture, literature, and the nation. This ideal is, as already indicated, Goethean, more specifically the Goethean idea of world literature—that is, a maximum of diversity on a minimum of space. According to Kundera, this condition existed in Central Europe at the beginning of the twentieth century, which saw the rise of such groundbreaking scientific and aesthetic achievements as psychoanalysis (Freud), the Prague School (Jakobson, Mukařovský), the dodecaphony (Schoenberg), the music of Bartók, and a new aesthetics of the novel (Kafka, Musil, Broch). Today, however, culture has lost its former value as a potential explanatory force in our contemporary society, in which the mass media have replaced literature, noise has replaced music, imagologists have replaced philosophers, and journalists have replaced authors.

Kundera's hope for a future of national and cultural diversity is closely tied to the novel as an art form: "in the modern world, abandoned by philosophy and splintered by hundreds of scientific specialties, the novel remains to us as the last observatory from which we can embrace human life as a whole" (*Cu*, 83). However, if the novel should perish, and Kundera believes this to be a possible scenario, it is not because it has exhausted its possibilities, but because the contemporary world of reductionism is no longer a world that corresponds to the antireductionism of the novel form.

A couple of questions beg for an answer: How does Kundera's defense of the Czech nation and its particularity (and thus its legitimacy)—secured by its culture and literature—accord with his choice to abandon the country, and especially its language (and thus its literature)? How does his anxiety about the advance of a few world languages and the subsequent restriction of the space for minor languages accord with his choice to write in French? Kundera's answer to these questions is *Ignorance,* and the novel seems to indicate that there is little agreement. Does this mean that Kundera has completely changed his views on the nation? Yes and no. As I stated earlier, Kundera believes that the nation still has emotional and political validity, but at the same time he believes that the nation is always dependent on people's choice. In Kundera's case, the twenty-five years in exile, from 1975 to the publication of *Ignorance* in 2000, have changed his relationship to his native country. Forced by circumstances and because of "the gigantic invisible broom that transforms, disfigures, erases," the Kundera of today in many ways feels more attached to his country of exile than to his native country. He has thus decided no longer personally to choose the Czech nation. This does not make the question of the nation obsolete in Kundera's work, but it implies a different attitude from the one he articulated in 1967, not toward the nation as such, but toward his native country. What is more, the experience of exile has also resulted in modifications in some of Kundera's former beliefs. His 1967 ideas regarding language, culture, people, and nation bear a resemblance to Romantic ideas as they were expressed in Johann Gottfried Herder's writings. But as his reaction to the Schoenberg case shows, Kundera no longer subscribes to this sense of belonging naturally and for all eternity to a language and a place.

However, as *Ignorance* also reminds us, the fate of the small nations is still very much on Kundera's mind, and the novel reflects many of the themes discussed above:

> To be willing to die for one's country: every nation has known that temptation to sacrifice. Indeed, the Czechs' adversaries also knew it: the Germans, the Russians. But those are large nations. Their patriotism is different: they are buoyed by their glory, their importance, their universal mission. The Czechs loved their country not because it was glorious but because it was unknown; not because it was big but because it was small and in constant danger. Their patriotism was an enormous compassion for their country. The Danes are like that too. Not by chance did Josef choose a small country for his emigration.
>
> (*Ig*, 140–41)

Being from Denmark, a small nation in Europe's northern regions, I can certainly understand Kundera's assertion about the particular patriotism exhibited by people who belong to small nations. The Danes are in fact very compassionate when it comes to their country. This is partly due to its considerable degree of "unobviousness," and this lack of self-evidence makes the Danish people constantly assert themselves as Danes, stress their Danishness, and express their (explicitly emphasized) national pride whenever a Danish pop group, writer, scientist, athlete, or athletic team achieves global recognition (which does not happen that often, I should say). So, I guess the question of nationality is always of greater concern when the nation is threatened or when it leads a life of anonymity.

However, in *Ignorance* Kundera suggests that the question of nationality may be on the wane among the younger generation, which has grown up in the aftermath of the Cold War and decolonization:

> He expected to hear a sarcastic response about worldwide capitalism homogenizing the planet, but N. was silent. Josef went on: "The Soviet empire collapsed because it could no longer hold down the nations that wanted their independence. But those nations—they're less independent than ever now. They can't choose their own economy or their own foreign policy or even their own advertising slogans."

"National independence has been an illusion for a long time now," said N.
"But if a country is not independent and doesn't even want to be, will anyone still be willing to die for it?"
"Being willing to die isn't what I want for my children."
"I'll put it another way: does anyone still love this country?"
N. slowed his steps: "Josef," he said, touched. "How could you ever have emigrated? You're a patriot!" Then, very seriously: "Dying for your country—that's all finished. Maybe for you time stopped during your emigration. But they—they don't think like you anymore."
"Who?"
N. tipped his head toward the upper floors of the house, as if to indicate his brood. "They're somewhere else."

(*Ig*, 155–56)

Without taking any unambiguous standpoints and without providing any unequivocal new definitions, the novel nevertheless pinpoints those existential problems and categories that are most affected by the processes of globalization. Through Josef, Kundera shows the enduring legitimacy of the national and the survival of patriotism in a so-called postnational world. Through N., Kundera shows a more pragmatic view, having abandoned the idealistic illusions of national sovereignty and accepted the homogenizing effects of global capitalism. Finally, the children of N. represent a new generation for whom the question of nationality means little at all. They simply seem to think beyond the nation.

However, in *Ignorance* the emotional legitimacy of the fatherland still occupies a central role in the narrator's consciousness, as when he recalls the events of 1968: "In August 1968 the Russian army had invaded the country; for a week the streets in all the cities howled with rage. The country had never been so thoroughly a homeland, or the Czechs so Czech" (*Ig*, 67). The reaction is typical: when something usually taken for granted is suddenly questioned and challenged, even undermined—in this case a nation's sovereignty and the freedom of a people—a collective will seems to erupt. Far from exemplifying a supranational utopia, this passage instead expresses the idea that the nation is still a political and emotional entity that cannot be disregarded, because, among other things, of the brevity of our lives: "For the very notion of homeland, with all its emotional power, is bound up with the relative brevity of our life, which allows us too little time to become attached to some other country, to other countries, to other languages" (*Ig*, 121). In fact, Kundera here delivers a counterargument to his own Schoenberg example and merely emphasizes the "incompleteness" of the novel's thematic issues.

The passage quoted above concerning the Czechs being real Czechs is the optimistic version of the events in 1968, however. In *The Unbearable Lightness of Being* we are told that the euphoria and the sense of solidarity among the Czech people during the first week of the occupation were replaced by acquiescence and a sense of vertigo, understood as a desire to fall, to feel weak, and to be among the weak. Besides, with regard to the many pictures and films that Tereza and many others had shot during the invasion, it turns out that what was to be understood as a desire to preserve a historical moment and allow the world to witness the cruelties—that is, an action of resistance—was in fact an action that undermined this very resistance: "Czech photographers and cameramen were acutely aware that they were the ones who could best do the only thing left to do: preserve the face of violence for the distant future [. . .] How naïve they had been, thinking they were risking their lives for their country when in fact they were helping the Russian police" (*ULB*, 65, 139). This is characteristic of Kundera: the purposes of human actions, when caught up in the irrational machinery of history, are turned into their own complete opposites.

Another example of human action that deviates from its initial intention, and that is also related to the theme of patriotism, is the tragicomic anecdote in *Ignorance* about the skeletons of the Icelandic poet Jónas Hallgrímsson and a Danish butcher. An Icelandic patriot saw it as his mission to take the skeleton of Hallgrímsson from Copenhagen, where Hallgrímsson was initially buried, back to Iceland, but tragicomically he ended up with the skeleton of a Danish butcher instead of those of the Icelandic national bard: "Therefore Hallgrimsson's bones still lie two thousand miles away from his Ithaca, in enemy soil, while the body of the Danish butcher, who although no poet was a patriot as well, still lies banished to a glacial island that never stirred him to anything but fear and repugnance" (*Ig*, 113).[38] It is no coincidence that this episode relates to a Romantic poet and to a small nation's attempt to wrestle its national "property" free from the claws of its oppressors (yes, the small nation of Denmark has in fact a long history of colonizing activities). However, while Kundera may well sympathize with the attempt, the overall intention underlying *Ignorance* is nevertheless to question the conventional meanings of concepts such as "home," "homecoming," "return," "native soil," "authenticity," "belonging," and "roots." There is of course a point to the way the skeleton story ends: it is an implicit critique of the idea of natural bonds to one's place of birth, and at the same time it is an attempt to formulate an alternative version of belonging. Irena has already provided us with this alternative version: "We did our best to drop anchor where we were."

The Art of Composition

For this our Determination we do not hold ourselves strictly bound to assign any Reason; it being abundantly sufficient that we have laid it down as a Rule necessary to be observed in all prosai-comi-epic Writing.

—Henry Fielding, *Tom Jones*

In *Aspects of the Novel* (1927), E. M. Forster claims, reluctantly though, that above all the novel tells a story: "That is the fundamental aspect without which it could not exist. That is the highest factor common to all novels. I wish that it was not so, that it could be something different—melody, or perception of the truth, not this low atavistic form."[39] In *Immortality* we come upon a passage that seems to indicate Kundera's agreement with Forster:

> I regret that almost all novels ever written are much too obedient to the rules of unity of action. What I mean to say is that at their core is one single chain of causally related acts and events. These novels are like a narrow street along which someone drives his character with a whip. Dramatic tension is the real curse of the novel, because it transforms everything, even the most beautiful pages, even the most surprising scenes and observations merely into steps leading to the final resolution, in which the meaning of everything that preceded it is concentrated. [. . .] A novel shouldn't be like a bicycle race but a feast of many courses.[40]

However, if this passage indicates that Kundera, like Forster, bemoans the story's dominion, it also suggests through the use of the word "almost" and the last sentence that he, in opposition to Forster, believes that literary history proves the novel's capacity to counteract the despotism of the story. In what follows, I will discuss different strategies of novelistic composition in literary history in order to situate Kundera within this history.

As the epigraph above indicates, in *Tom Jones* (1749) Henry Fielding proclaims his absolute sovereignty over the novel's composition and form; in fact, he even declines to label his work a novel. Fielding was writing during a period when the novel as a genre was still virtually free from conventional constraints. Consequently, the novelists of the eighteenth century regarded themselves not merely as inventors but also as legislators of their works. By invoking his right to formal freedom, Fielding is first and foremost refusing to reduce the novel to a causal chain of events (i.e., its story) that has, by and large, come to represent the essence of the novel, as Forster and Kundera testify to. In *Tom Jones* Fielding contrasts the novel's story line with his own narratorial reflections and metafictional comments, "these vacant Spaces of Time,"[41] which interrupt the story's progression. However, despite the infusion of these intruding digressions, the story line can still be said to provide compositional unity and, ultimately, chronological order in *Tom Jones*.

Forster's assertion seems even more problematic if we take Laurence Sterne's *Tristram Shandy* (1759–1767) into consideration. Kundera thus describes Sterne's novel as

> the first radical and total dethroning of "story." Whereas Fielding, so as not to suffocate in the long corridor of a causal chain of events, flung wide open the windows of digressions and episodes throughout, Sterne renounces story completely; his novel is just one big manifold digression, one long festival of episodes whose "unity"—deliberately fragile, comically fragile—is stitched together by only a few eccentric characters and their microscopic, laughably pointless actions.
>
> (*Cu*, 11)

It is, as Kundera argues, his demolition of the story that associates Sterne with some of the great novelists of the twentieth century, among them Robert Musil and Hermann Broch.

If Fielding and Sterne can be said to transform their readers into *listeners*, the readers of Flaubert and Tolstoy are transformed into *spectators*. Orality is replaced by literacy: the obtrusive and interfering narrative voices of Fielding and Sterne are replaced by the more discreet and "neutral" narrative voices of Flaubert and Tolstoy. In the nineteenth century, the novel's great era, the novel's capacity to captivate stems from its ability to visually evoke scenes, and, as a result, *verisimilitude* becomes the governing principle. Neither Fielding nor Sterne give verisimilitude much thought: Fielding offers no detailed descriptions of the historical background or of the characters' physical disposition; his episodic narration is focused primarily on those scenic fragments that are indispensable to the lucidity of the intrigue and the narratorial reflection. Sterne uses his narratorial digressions to enter the realm of nondrama and insignificance—that is, the realm of "microscopic, laughably pointless actions." In the descriptive novels of Flaubert and Tolstoy, the technique is to a large extent one of illusion. In Fielding and Sterne on the other hand, the narrative voices constantly shatter the illusion by leading the reader's attention away from the *effets du réel* (reality effects) and the causal events of the main story toward the narrator's metafictional comments and digressive reflections.

Kundera quite rightly observes that during the nineteenth century, the presence of *history* begins to make itself felt in every molecule of existence, and man apprehends, probably for the first time, that he will not die in the same world as the one in which he was born: "the clock of History began to toll the hour in loud tones, everywhere, even within novels whose time was immediately counted and dated. The shape of every little object [. . .] was stamped with its imminent disappearance (transformation). The era of descriptions began. (Description: compassion for the ephemeral; salvaging the perishable)" (*Cu,* 14). Kundera here sketches the historical circumstances that led to a transformation of novelistic form in authors such as Stendhal, Balzac, Dickens, Flaubert, Tolstoy, and, to some extent, Proust, all authors who belong to the era of description. Think for instance of the difference in descriptive accuracy and verisimilitude between Fielding's London and Balzac's Paris. In the latter, "every scene of the novel is stamped (be it only by the shape of a chair or the cut of a suit) by History which, now that it has emerged from the shadows, sculpts and re-sculpts the look of the world" (*Cu,* 14). What Kundera laments is that the poetics of description, illusion, and verisimilitude employed by the abovementioned authors in the period spanning from the 1830s to the 1920s seem to have obstructed the development of alternative novelistic forms. According to Kundera, the success of the descriptive novel in which the story makes up the architectural scaffold has consigned to oblivion the poetics of digression and nonseriousness of the novelists before the nineteenth century.

Kundera's own history of the novel consists of two halves: the first half includes authors such as Rabelais, Cervantes, Fielding, Sterne, and Diderot, all of whom digress, fabulate, improvise, insert metareflexive comments, and employ a nonserious tone; the second half includes authors such as Scott, Balzac, Dickens, Flaubert, Tolstoy, and Zola, all of whom adhere to the laws of verisimilitude, description, and illusion.[42] In the twentieth century, says Kundera, the originality of *each* of the two halves is appreciated, as many of the great authors of the twentieth century rediscover the formal innovations and existential discoveries of the fifteenth–eighteenth centuries without disregarding those of the nineteenth century.

As should be clear by now, Kundera disagrees with Forster's assertion that the story "is the highest factor common to all novels." Kundera may genuinely feel regret for the cruel destiny of the pre-nineteenth-century authors and their formal originality, but his insinuation regarding the inequality between the first and second half in terms of recognition and propagation is also used strategically to position himself as a true heir to Rabelais, Sterne, and Diderot. In other words, Kundera (despite his many recognitions of its aesthetic and existential discoveries) distances himself from the "traditional" nineteenth-century novel of verisimilitude dominated by a unilinear story, thereby claiming his own novels to be aesthetically original and affiliated with the "forgotten" poetics of the novel before 1800.

As concerns literary forerunners from his own century, Kundera specifically refers to Broch's *The Sleepwalkers* (1932) and Musil's *The Man Without Qualities* (1930–1942), novels that incorporate essayistic passages that interrupt the story's progression. To Kundera, Musil and Broch, together with Franz Kafka and Witold Gombrowicz, represent a similar aesthetic orientation:

> They were all *poets* of the novel, which is to say people impassioned by the form and by its newness; concerned for the intensity of each word, each phrase; seduced by the imagination as it tries to move beyond the borders of "realism"; but at the same time impervious to seduction by the *lyrical;* hostile to the transformation of the novel into personal confession; allergic to the ornamentalization of prose; entirely focused on the real world. They all of them conceived the novel to be a great *antilyrical poetry.*
>
> (*Cu*, 51)

To conceive of the novel in terms of its poetic capacity—that is, its ability to transgress realism understood as verisimilitude and the hegemony of the story—also recalls Federico Fellini, whom Kundera deeply admires. Fellini can be characterized as a cinematographic demolisher of the traditional story, most clearly demonstrated in *La dolce vita* (*The Sweet Life*) (1960) and *8½* (1963). With regard to *La dolce vita,* Fellini thus proclaims: "So I said: let's invent episodes, let's not worry for now about the logic or the narrative. We have to make a statue, break it, and recompose the pieces. Or better yet, try a decomposition in the manner of Picasso. The cinema is narrative in the nineteenth-century sense: now let's try to do something different."[43] Fellini's attempt to move the cinema away from the traditional nineteenth-century narrative (and away from the Italian neorealism of the late 1940s and early 1950s as well) leads him in the direction of "poetry." Instead of movies being chronologically structured as beginning-middle-end and governed by the causality of events, Fellini creates movies in which an image or a sequence of images gains autonomy on account of its *poetic density* and *visual quality* (but in contrast to the nineteenth-century novel, Fellini's visuality is not bound by verisimilitude). Hence they contribute to the movie's overall "message" without telling a story in the traditional sense of the word.

In Kundera, as in Picasso's abstract decomposition, in Musil's "thinking" novel, and in Fellini's poetic and episodic movies, the distinction between foreground and background is eliminated. Everything becomes foreground as every passage and every sequence of Kundera's novels is preoccupied neither with the creation of a vast background—as in, for example, Thomas Mann's *The Magic Mountain* (1924)—nor with "what-happened-next" or with motivating the action through psychological inspection, but rather with illuminating the existential theme of the novel through a variety of different genres and perspectives. Kvetoslav Chvatík calls this compositional technique "the permanent changes of the narrative's strategy and perspective."[44] Instead of a linear development of the plot, Kundera's use of different genres that all circle around the same existential problem creates a *multidimensional and contrapuntal space*. Linearity is thus replaced by a strategy of variation and sequential density. This compositional strategy is motivated in part by Kundera's belief that the novelistic plot does not exhaust the possibilities inherent in human identity.

In *The Joke*, Kundera's first novel, I would argue that the story is still a fundamental component of the Kunderian novel's architecture. However, the story is narrated from the point of view of each of the four protagonists in a manner quite similar to that of William Faulkner's *The Sound and the Fury* (1929). The four-part polyphonic construction means that the chrono-logical and linear development of the story is undermined and replaced by a contrapuntal space of nonlinearity and a-chronology, and as in *The Sound and the Fury* the interior monologues in *The Joke* are mediated through a stream of consciousness technique that results in an associative narrative structure rather than in a chronological rendering of the events. Furthermore, because the four perspectives on the story occasionally diverge, questions are raised about the general truth character of the story. The reader is able to more or less reconstruct the underlying story of the novel, but a certain ambiguity persists in regard to several episodes, as they are told in contrast-ing versions. And since there is no "superior" narrator among the four voices, it is difficult to determine which of the four voices can be trusted.

The polyphonic nature of the novel is achieved through the successful integration of the four voices among one another. Each person's monologue illuminates that individual, but also the other characters. This mutually "reflective" configuration demonstrates the coherence of the polyphonic structure. Furthermore, it can be argued that the four voices of *The Joke* are more fully integrated among one another than is the case in *The Sound and the Fury*. The latter is composed of four parts, each of which is narrated from the point of view of one of the protagonists (Benjy, Quentin, Jason, "Dilsey"); in this way the four parts stand beside one another and are relatively isolated, which naturally endows the last part/perspective with some sort of superior authority. However, the relative authority of the last part is not achieved solely by the fact that it is the conclusion of the novel. The fact that part 4 does not use the stream of consciousness technique applied in the first three parts (i.e., Benjy, Quentin, and Jason), but rather a more "objective" manner, through a third-person limited omniscient point of view (centering on Dilsey), suggests the authoritative status of part 4. *The Joke,* on the other hand, is composed of seven parts in which Ludvik's perspective dominates parts 1, 3, and 5; Helena's dominates part 2; Jaroslav's dominates part 4; and Kostka's dominates part 6. However, in part 7, the perspectives of Ludvik, Helena, and Jaroslav alternate. The alternation in part 7 between three voices ensures that no single perspective is endowed with a final authority as it could be argued is the case in *The Sound and the Fury.* Furthermore, in contrast to Faulkner's novel, the last part in *The Joke* does not deviate from the general narrative mode of subjective interior monologue; hence it remains on the same level of authority and "objectivity" as the preceding parts.

In spite of the nonlinear, a-chronological, and polyphonic structure of *The Joke,* the underlying story line still occupies a central role in the novel. The polyphony is a polyphony of perspectives on the *story* and the events that constitute it, and one of the reader's main tasks is to reconstruct what happened. In his second novel, *Life Is Elsewhere,* Kundera introduces the reflective and obtrusive narrator who contributes to the reduction in the story's hegemony, but only to abandon the technique again for a more objective third-person narrator in *The Farewell Party.* With *The Book of Laughter and Forgetting,* originally conceived as a follow-up to *Laughable Loves*—that is, as a collection of short stories—Kundera then launches a devastating attack on the tyranny of the story, an attack that is probably not surpassed in his later books, except perhaps in *Immortality.*

But what constitutes the unity of *The Book of Laughter and Forgetting*? Each of the seven parts in the book is based on different material and has different protagonists, except for parts 4 and 6 in which Tamina is the main character. Hence, it is not the unity of character or the unity of the story line that makes the novel cohere. As the narrator informs us,

> This entire book is a novel in the form of variations. The individual parts follow each other like individual stretches of a journey leading toward a theme, a thought, a single situation, the sense of which fades into the distance [dont la compréhension se perd pour moi dans l'immensité].
>
> It is a novel about Tamina, and whenever Tamina is absent, it is a novel for Tamina. She is its main character and main audience, and all the other stories are variations on her story and come together in her life as in a mirror.
>
> (*BLF,* 165–66)[45]

So, instead of a "traditional" novel in which each part contributes to the linear progression of the events that constitute the story—that is, depicting a causal chain of events—the parts in *The Book* are explorations of themes, thoughts, or existential situations, explorations that are drifting through various standpoints. In other words, every step taken by the narrator is not governed by the story's chronological progression from a natural beginning to a conclusive end. Rather, the narrator leads the reader deeper and deeper into the complexity of a theme or a situation. The reader's epistemological journey in *The Book of Laughter and Forgetting* is not about reaching the endpoint of a linear thread; it is about exploring "from diverse standpoints" (metafictional discourse, dream sequence, philosophical meditation, narratorial reflection, essay, historical excursion, story, etc.) the layers of meaning in a given existential situation and in the themes that define it. This situational structure is an aesthetic choice that is meant to formally answer the complexity and irreducibility of empirical reality, thereby rejecting the lure of the universal claims of any normative systems whatsoever.

Part 3 of *The Book of Laughter and Forgetting* ("The Angels") is an example of polyphony and the strategy of variation as the themes of angelic and demonic laughter, forgetting, repetition, the border, and the circle are examined and *refracted* through a variety of different discourses and viewpoints: (1) the anecdote about two female students and their levitation; (2) the autobiographical narration; (3) the critical essay on a feministic book; (4) the fable about the angel and the demon; and (5) the story about Éluard, who flies above Prague. What unites these otherwise disparate lines is the fact that they all explore the questions, What is an angel? What is a demon? What is laughter? Within each of the nine chapters, the five discourses frequently alternate, and this merely emphasizes the demolition of the traditional story line.

The compositional strategy of "migratory" explorations from diverse standpoints is precisely what makes Kundera's novels poetic: they are more metaphorical-paradigmatic than metonymical-syntagmatic in the Jakobsonian sense of the words—that is, they *decelerate time and open up a complex semantic space around a given situation*. In "Flaubert et la phrase" (Flaubert and the Sentence, 1968), Roland Barthes asserts that the author, when composing his work, has three types of corrections at his disposal—namely, the substitutive (paradigmatic), the elliptic (syntagmatic), and the catalytic (syntagmatic). If we transform Barthes's three types of corrections into three techniques of any finished novel, it is evident that Kundera's novels relate to all three types in a highly interesting fashion.

First of all, Kundera's novels are elliptically composed in regard to the story line, as the latter is made up of only the most important events and situations, whereas the unimportant elements (in regard to theme) of the story are simply left out. The story line is therefore an assemblage of dots more than it is an unbroken line: the many short chapters depicting brief scenes from diverse perspectives can be compared to a series of photographs or a discontinuous film that switches to slow motion in order to examine the key scenes in more detail (not descriptively speaking, but existentially). What ties the episodes together is not the logic of "what-happened-next," but a theme or a motif. Hence, Kundera exercises "censure" in that he syntagmatically condenses his work. Second, the elliptic technique does not, however, prevent Kundera from activating a catalytic component in his prose, but instead of being related to the story line, the expansive technique is related to the key situations and episodes that are constantly being perceived from new viewpoints: expansion in depth. And third, the vagabonding perspectives belong to the paradigmatic level in that they complement one another and thus act as substitutions for each other—but here the substitution does not imply that any former perspectives are erased. So, this is what variation signifies in Kundera: a given situation (syntagmatic censure) is seen from different perspectives that replace one another (paradigmatic substitution) without erasing one another (syntagmatic expansion).

So, Kundera renounces the unity of character and the coherence of the story. Even if the narrator posits Tamina as the heroine of *The Book of Laughter and Forgetting,* he cannot hide the fact that she participates in only two out of seven parts. Furthermore, the characters of the seven parts never meet, because the stories are mutually exclusive. Instead, *The Book* is a polyphonic montage of personal memories, philosophical essays, and a variety of stories; and the stories, instead of cohering through character, place, or action, cohere as variations on the same motifs and themes. The narrator opposes his own strategy of variation with that of a symphony. The latter, he says, is a musical epopee, as it is comparable to a journey that takes the listener through the infinity of the outer world, metonymically from one thing to the next. Variations are also comparable to a journey, but instead of leading the listener through an outer infinity, they draw him or her inward through the inner multiplicity hiding in each thing: "The variation form is the form of maximum concentration. It enables the composer to limit himself to the matter at hand, to go straight to the heart of it. The subject matter is a theme, which often consists of no more than sixteen measures. Beethoven goes as deeply into those sixteen measures as if he had gone down a mine to the bowels of the earth" (*BLF,* 164). In addition to Beethoven, Kundera also likens his own technique to that of Chopin's small compositions that are without a-thematical passages, and to Janacek, who allows a note to exist only if it contributes something essential: "My own imperative is 'Janacekian': to rid the novel of the automatism of novelistic technique, of novelistic verbalism; to make it dense" (*AN,* 73).

"We are all like Scheherazade's husband," says Forster, "in that we want to know what happens next. That is universal and that is why the backbone of a novel has to be a story."[46] However, the Kunderian narrator counteracts the atavism of the story and has parted with the weapon of suspense so essential to Scheherazade in order to conquer the reader by using means other than teasing him or her with "what-happens-next-ism." If Forster is right in claiming that every one of us is a potential Shahryar, then we are left with two choices when reading Kundera's novels: either we kill the Kunderian narrator and he becomes our victim number three thousand and one, or we must be willing to commit adultery to Scheherazade. I for my part belong to the ones who are ready for a little infidelity.

Return of the Authorial Narrator

> I realize that in undertaking the internal and architectonic analysis of a work [. . .], in setting aside biographical and psychological references, one has already called back into question the absolute character and founding role of the subject. Still, perhaps one must return to this question, not in order to re-establish the themes of an originating subject, but to grasp the subject's points of insertion, modes of functioning, and system of dependencies. [. . .] In short, it is a matter of depriving the subject (or its substitute) of its role as originator, and of analyzing the subject as a variable and complex function of discourse.
>
> —Michel Foucault, "What is an author?"

The roles of both narrator and author raise questions of great interest in the novels of Milan Kundera. First, Kundera's deliberate use of an extremely obtrusive narrative voice automatically calls attention to the role of the narrator and his degrees of authority and credibility. Second, the fact that the narrator frequently draws on material that is clearly autobiographical with reference to "Milan Kundera the author" and that he occasionally refers to himself as "Milan Kundera" apparently problematizes the post-structuralist idea of the author's death.

As to the question of the supposed death and the alleged return of the author, a question of a more principal-theoretical character, I will argue that Kundera's use of a narrator with autobiographical attributes does not necessarily contradict the fundamental purpose and assertions of Roland Barthes in his 1968 essay "The Death of the Author." As to the question of the narrator's authority, a question of a more practical-analytical character, I will argue that Kundera's novels strike a balance between dialogic and monologic tendencies—that is, at times the narratorial strategies endorse textual dynamism and openness; at times they contribute to textual closure and "objective" meaning.

At a first glance, the presence of an authorial narrator would seem to warrant a closure of the novels in terms of both theme and structure because of the narrator's authority and potential omniscience. However, as Mikhail M. Bakhtin remarks in *Problems of Dostoevsky's Poetics* (1929) with regard to the author's position in a polyphonic novel, this is not necessarily the case. The author can, in fact, administer his authority dialogically so as to continue to ensure polyphony: "The author of a polyphonic novel is not required to renounce himself or his own consciousness, but he must to an extraordinary extent broaden, deepen, and rearrange this consciousness [. . .] primarily in the sense of a special dialogic mode of communication with the autonomous consciousnesses of others."[47] Hence, the presence of an authorial narrator and consciousness is not opposed to polyphony if it manages to uphold a dialogic relationship with characters (and readers): "the new artistic position of the author with regard to the hero in Dostoevsky's polyphonic novel is a *fully realized and thoroughly consistent dialogic position*, one that affirms the independence, internal freedom, unfinalizability, and indeterminacy of the hero."[48] So, for us the principal analytical question is whether Kundera complies with Bakhtin's idea of dialogism, in relation to both character and reader.

In *The Death and Return of the Author* (1998), Seán Burke—partly following in the footsteps of Bakhtin, partly polemizing against Barthes—convincingly argues that the concept of the author is not necessarily opposed to the Barthesian "Text" that Barthes himself, in "From Work to Text" (1971), characterized by its paradoxicality, pluralism, and deconstruction of verisimilitude. On the one hand, Burke agrees with Barthes that the author should be denied his or her magisterial status, but, on the other hand, says Burke quite rightly, this does not mean that the concept of the author becomes completely superfluous.

The question is, however, whether Barthes himself really considers the author to be completely obsolete (as Burke seems to believe), or whether, as I would argue, he merely *redefines* the role of the author (in the same way as Foucault suggests a modification of the authorial role when he speaks of modes of function, points of insertion, and dependencies of the subject in the epigraph above). In "From Work to Text," Barthes actually acknowledges an authorial presence in the Text:

> It is not that the Author may not "come back" in the Text, in his text, but he then does so as a "guest." If he is a novelist, he is inscribed in the novel like one of his characters, figured in the carpet; no longer privileged,

paternal, aletheological, his inscription is ludic. He becomes, as it were, a paper-author: his life is no longer the origin of his fictions but a fiction contributing to his work; there is a reversion of the work on to the life (and no longer the contrary).[49]

According to Barthes, the author's role in the Text becomes *playful* in opposition to the more authoritative, privileged, and paternal role of the author in the traditional "work." As to the supposed opposition between life (fact) and work (fiction), Barthes asserts that an author's life can no longer be regarded as a privileged foundation of truth behind the work; instead, it becomes a fictionalized element on the same ontological level as the rest of the material in the work. What is more, in regard to temporality there is simultaneity between author and Text; they are both caught in a mutual process of becoming, whereas the temporal relationship between author and "work" is one of past and present, antecedent and descendant.[50]

If Burke may be said to simplify Barthes in that he fails to appreciate Barthes's actual admittance of authorial presence in the Text, Burke nevertheless develops some brilliant insights into the complex relationship between author, narrator, and text that are very useful for our discussion of these topics in relation to Kundera. As I have already insinuated, Burke's main purpose is to rethink the relationship between *bios* and *graphe* by reinstating the author in the text without this meaning that the text automatically becomes closed or equivalent to the author's intention: "Thus we can re-mobilise the autobiographical without lapsing once more into positivist or geneticist assumptions."[51]

With regard to the question of authorial intention, Burke proposes a way out of the critical deadlock that followed the publications of, on the one hand, Wimsatt and Beardsley's "The Intentional Fallacy" (1946), in which they claim that the author's intention is both unknowable and irrelevant, and, on the other hand, Knapp and Michaels's "Against Theory" (1982), in which they claim that the text means precisely what the author intends it to mean. Inspired by Jacques Derrida, Burke recommends a compromise between intentionalist and anti-intentionalist views in that he neither equates intention with the totality of textual effects, nor rejects the significance of intention as a factor in generating and shaping the text: "Intention is within signification, and as a powerful and necessary agency, but it does not command this space in the manner of an organizing *telos*, or transcendental subjectivity."[52]

Later in his book, Burke goes on to speak about "the redistribution of authorial subjectivity within a textual *mise en scène* which it does not command entirely."[53] This means that the author should be regarded as a shaping principle in discourse, but only as one principle among others. Burke thus allows for permeable borders between life and work; but he actually goes one step further by claiming that intratextual elements of authorial biography may downright contribute to the uncertainty and openness of the work:

> The entry of the author, and the author's biography into the text multi-determines the scene of its writing, dissolves any putative assumptions that an author's life does not belong with his work, or belongs to it only improperly. Reading biographically is not a neutralising, simplifying activity. So far from functioning as an ideal figure, from figuring as a function of Cartesian certitude, the author operates as a principle of uncertainty in the text, like the Heisenbergian scientist whose presence invariably disrupts the scientificity of the observation. [. . .] The processes of intention, influence and revision, the interfertility of life and work, autobiography and the autobiographical, author-functions, signature effects, the proper name in general, the authority and creativity of the critic, all these are points at which the question of the author exerts its pressure on the textual enclosure.[54]

According to Burke, authorial presence may well be compared to the presence of the Heisenbergian scientist, who is not a neutral observer of Cartesian certitude but rather an integral part of the "experiment." The question in our case is whether Kundera and his authorial narrator is a Cartesian or a Heisenbergian scientist. Or, to put the question in Bakhtinian terms: Does Kundera or his narrator monologically close or dialogically open the textual universe?

* * *

Having determined, with the help of Bakhtin, Barthes, and Burke, that authorial presence in principle does not automatically lead to monologism and closure, I will now move on to the more practical-analytical level to discuss the actual role of the narrator in Kundera's novels in order to determine their dialogic or monologic tendencies. Hana Pichova and Peter Bugge represent two, in many ways, opposing views on this question, the former arguing that Kundera's narrator ensures dialogism and openness, the latter arguing that the narrator contributes to both structural and thematic closure and unification.

Despite the potential omniscience resulting from his function as both "creator of characters and a director of the text," Pichova is of the opinion that the narrator in *The Unbearable Lightness of Being* "intentionally limits his powers to avoid subjugating his characters to the same totalitarian rule they try to escape on the thematic level," just as she argues that his "choice of narratological strategies and organization reflects his desire to create a textual world that in no way resembles the oppressive world he describes thematically."[55] So, in relation to both narrative form and the relationship between author/narrator and protagonists, Pichova affirms the polyphony and antitotalitarian quality of Kundera's novel. Bugge, on the other hand, claims that "Kundera's urge for control asserts itself not only with regard to biography, the definition of his œuvre, or the authorization of translations, but also in the narrative strategies employed in his fiction."[56] Bugge thus speaks of Kundera's "explanatory overkill," and he says he believes that Kundera's "urge to ensure that his work is understood correctly [. . .] may amount to a paradoxical distrust of the openness and irreducibility of the novel's message otherwise held high."[57] Whereas Pichova points to a deliberate narratorial softening of omniscience, Bugge sees a calculating control freak; and when Pichova talks of an open-ended narrative structure, Bugge speaks of a narratorial distrust in openness. In my opinion both Pichova's and Bugge's contributions represent valuable and accurate observations on the Kunderian narrator; the complementarity of their views actually mirrors the complementarity and paradoxical nature of the narrative strategies in Kundera.

It is true that the narrator at times offers the reader extensive explanations and interpretations in regard to character, situation, and theme. In *The Unbearable Lightness of Being*, for example, the narrator reflects on the relationship between human life, the novel, beauty, and coincidence and proclaims: "Without realizing it, the individual composes his life according to the laws of beauty even in times of greatest distress." And he continues: "It is wrong, then, to chide the novel for being fascinated by mysterious coincidences (like the meeting of Anna, Vronsky, the railway station, and death or the meeting of Beethoven, Tomas, Tereza, and the cognac), but it is right to chide man for being blind to such coincidences in his daily life. For he thereby deprives his life of a dimension of beauty" (*ULB*, 51–52). This passage shows a narrator who authoritatively offers his opinion on the constitution of human life and the novel and their relationship with chance and beauty. Furthermore, the narrator even blames those people (readers) who are unable to appreciate the beauty of chance. Kundera's novels offer many similar passages in which the narrator expresses himself in a rather unequivocal manner. Consequently, the reader's active participation in the creation of the novel's semantic universe is to a certain extent obstructed. Seán Burke regards such passages of authorial discourse as indispensable elements in an otherwise multidetermined, plural, and (potentially) chaotic text.[58]

Another technique often used by Kundera is having his narrator ask the reader a rhetorical question and then answer the question himself immediately afterwards. In relation to one of Tereza's many nightmares in which she, naked and alongside other naked women, marches around a pool, the narrator acts as our interpreter:

> But what was the meaning of the fact that Tomas shot at them, toppling one after another into the pool, dead?
> The women, overjoyed by their sameness, their lack of diversity, were, in fact, celebrating their imminent demise, which would render their sameness absolute. So Tomas's shots were merely the joyful climax to their morbid march. [. . .]
> But why was Tomas the one doing the shooting? And why was he out to shoot Tereza with the rest of them?
> Because he was the one who sent Tereza to join them. That was what the dream was meant to tell Tomas, what Tereza was unable to tell him herself. She had come to him to escape her mother's world, a world where all bodies were equal. She had come to him to make her body unique, irreplaceable. But he, too, had drawn an equal sign between her and the rest of them [. . .]. He had sent her back into the world she tried to escape, sent her to march naked with the other naked women.
>
> (*ULB*, 56–57)

This passage can easily be read as an example of what Bugge calls "explanatory overkill": the narrator posits himself as a Cartesian scientist rather than as a Heisenbergian one, in that he interprets the dream so as to remove any doubt of its meaning from the reader's mind.

One of Bugge's own examples is also taken from *The Unbearable Lightness of Being* in which, as he claims, the characters "are followed to the grave (with the exception of Sabina who doesn't want to be buried), and we are even offered explanations of the meaning of the text on their gravestones!"[59] What annoys Bugge in regard to the gravestone texts is not the simplicity and authoritative messages of the texts themselves. As he correctly asserts, the texts are of course deeply ironic, as they actually express the exact opposite of the novel's images of Franz and Tomas. Instead, Bugge claims that the narrator once again makes use of explanatory overkill by explaining this irony to the reader much too explicitly and obtrusively. I partly agree with Bugge, but I also tend to see more openness and ironic stance on the part of the narrator than he does. Let us examine the gravestone episodes more closely.

Both Tomas and Franz end up being completely betrayed by the text on their gravestones. It is Marie-Claude, Franz's wife, who chooses his epitaph and the text, "A RETURN AFTER LONG WANDERINGS," which is meant to imply that Franz, having abandoned her a few years earlier, realized at the end of his life that he belonged with her. In fact, in the days before he died, Franz himself came to a somewhat different conclusion: "He woke up in a hospital in Geneva. Marie-Claude was leaning over his bed. He wanted to tell her she had no right to be there. [. . .] He looked up at Marie-Claude with infinite hatred" (*ULB*, 271). However, he is unable to communicate with anything but his eyes, and Marie-Claude misunderstands the messages being conveyed by his eyes. In Marie-Claude's version, the scene thus means the exact opposite: "In his last days, when he was dying and had no need to lie, she was the only person he asked for. He couldn't talk, but how he'd thanked her with his eyes! He'd fixed his eyes on her and begged to be forgiven. And she forgave him" (*ULB*, 273).

Tomas's epitaph, "HE WANTED THE KINGDOM OF GOD ON EARTH," is chosen by his religious son whom Tomas has met only once or twice since divorcing his first wife many years ago. The religious content of the text stands in complete contrast to "the life and opinions" of Tomas. The gravestone episodes thus inscribe themselves into the themes of betrayal, misunderstanding, and kitsch, and they are not meant to be read as the narrator's final judgment on his characters. Instead, they are narrated from a narratorial position indicating a bittersweet, ironic critique of the way in which all of us are being transformed into kitschy posthumous one-liners: "Before we are forgotten, we will be turned into kitsch. Kitsch is the stopover between being and oblivion" (*ULB*, 274). Is this explanatory overkill? Well, in general we can say that what determines whether the narratorial discourse is monologic or dialogic is the degree of irony and playfulness versus explanatory overkill that permeates the text—and this is often very difficult to determine "objectively."

Pichova claims that the narrator has a double function in *The Unbearable Lightness of Being* that makes him potentially omniscient. The narrator's unmitigated transformation of fabula to sjuzet (story to discourse), which happens through the aesthetically motivated reorganization of the chronological and causal chain of events (the many prolepses, for example, often disclose events that would otherwise count as climaxes in a "traditional" plot and thus eliminate suspense), indicates his function as a supreme administrator and director of the textual material. Furthermore, the narrator's metafictional admittance that the characters "were born of a stimulating phrase or two or from a basic situation. Tomas was born of the saying *Einmal ist keinmal*. Tereza was born of the rumbling of a stomach" (*ULB*, 39) reveals his function as a creator of characters in much the same way as God created Adam. Accordingly, the narrator is bestowed with a potential omniscience not only with regard to the fabula, but also with regard to the inner thoughts of the characters.

However, as Pichova correctly points out, the narrator often withdraws deliberately from such an omniscient position, especially in relation to the characters. They preserve a sphere of privacy that neither narrator nor reader has access to. As one example reads: "I think that Sabina, too, felt the strange enchantment of the situation: her lover's wife standing oddly compliant and timorous before her" (*ULB*, 65). Here the narrator simply speculates and thus refrains from unequivocal declarations concerning the psychological or mental constitution of Sabina. At one point the narrator even admits that he has trouble understanding one of the characters, thereby implicitly inviting the reader to fill out the textual "Leerstelle" (blanks):

> Almost apologetically the editor said to Tereza, "Of course they're completely different from your pictures."
> "Not at all," said Tereza. "They're the same."
> Neither the editor nor the photographer understood her, and even I find it difficult to explain what she had in mind when she compared a nude beach to the Russian invasion.
>
> (*ULB*, 67)

My last example does not reveal a lack of psychological understanding, but rather a lack of physical presence: "If I were to make a record of all Sabina and Franz's conversations, I could compile a long lexicon of their misunderstandings. Let us be content, instead, with a short dictionary" (*ULB*, 87). Here the narrator shows a deliberate softening of his omniscience not only in relation to the characters but also in relation to the fabula: he remains (consciously) uninformed of some aspects of the story line involving Franz and Sabina.

What supports Pichova's argument about the structural and thematic openness of Kundera's novel, besides her own idea of the narrator's deliberate withdrawal from omniscience, is the fact that the narratorial discourse is only one discourse among others, as we have already seen in the previous section on compositional strategies. This means that the "track" in which the narrator proclaims his opinions should not be automatically regarded as the definitive authorial judgment, as it is not necessarily hierarchically privileged compared to the other tracks that contribute to the novels' totality. Remember what Barthes said: fragments of biography in the Text merely function as fictionalized elements alongside the rest of the "proper" fictional material.

The plurality and heterogeneity of tracks, the potentially antihierarchical relationship between them, and the a-chronological organization of the narrative structure in which coherence is founded on thematic topics rather than on the causality of "what-happened-next" turn Kundera's novels into rhizomes that Deleuze and Guattari characterize by their processual, anti-hierarchical structure and distinctive manner of linking heterogeneous elements. What is more, the rhizome functions as a network and is thus more horizontal than vertical, which is also true of Kundera's novels, primarily because of their polycentered structure consisting of virtually infinite possibilities for transversal connections and associations, intersecting lines and folds, and underground passages between the tracks or discourses that constitute the novel's multidimensional architecture. The Kunderian novel is not a thread, but a net; it is not a sexual intercourse entailing a rising curve of tension that leads to a conclusive ejaculation, but a plane of intensities made up of circles, links, leaps, crisscrossing threads—a *hyphos,* a *textura.*

Deleuze and Guattari's idea of the rhizome does not entail a completely chaotic and anarchic structure. The rhizome, primarily defined as a fluid work, also consists of "despotic formations" and "knots of arborescence."[60] As my analysis of the authorial narrator and my pointing out of several paradoxes in Kundera's work have shown, there are elements in his novels that counteract the purely fluid and chaotic. Above all there is the narratorial discourse that, at times, initiates rather solid despotic formations because of its moralizing, controlling, and judgmental conduct. In this way it may be argued that there are certain discrepancies between theme and form in Kundera's novels, as they are thematically concerned with the protagonists' freedom from totalitarian constraints while at the same time they occasionally exercise a "formal totalitarianism."

CHAPTER 3

Salman Rushdie

The migrant's sense of being rootless, of living between worlds, between a lost past and a non-integrated present, is perhaps the most fitting metaphor of this (post)modern condition.

—Iain Chambers, *Migrancy, Culture, Identity*

In *Step Across This Line,* Salman Rushdie admits to a shift in attitude toward the question of belonging: "There was always a tug-of-war in me between 'there' and 'here,' the pull of roots and of the road. In that struggle of insiders and outsiders, I used to feel simultaneously on both sides. Now I've come down on the side of those who by preference, nature, or circumstance simply do not belong. This unbelonging—I think of it as *disorientation,* loss of the East—is my artistic country now" (*SATL,* 266). Due to statements like this, Rushdie has come to epitomize the migrant writer par excellence. In his essays he frequently proclaims migration to be the defining concept of the twentieth century, in regard to both sociology broadly speaking, and literary history in particular, where it proves important as a thematic and formal stratagem. However, Rushdie's own biography of "unbelonging," his preference for route over root, which has taken him from India to England to Pakistan to England to the United States, but also from a public life into a life in hiding, is another reason for the epitomization.[1]

Salman Rushdie was born in Bombay on June 19, 1947, only two months before India's independence on the stroke of midnight between August 14 and 15. Rushdie's father came from Delhi and was a businessman, but he had a degree in law from Cambridge University. Rushdie's mother worked as a teacher and was from Aligarh in northern India. The family was affluent and Muslim and, in addition to a house in Bombay—Windsor Villa—they owned real estate in northern India. Although the Rushdies were a Europeanized and secular-progressive family, suspicion was thrown on them after 1947 because they, being Muslim, did not emigrate to Pakistan.

At thirteen Rushdie was sent to England to attend the exclusive boarding school Rugby. His first genuine migration thrilled him and, with reference to one of his favorite movies, he has claimed that "it felt as exciting as any voyage beyond the rainbows."[2] His stay at Rugby turned out to be a rough time, though, as he was the target of racist abuse. Rushdie, who considered himself British, suddenly felt like a pariah: "I remember very bad moments when I felt very depressed, but it did get better as I got older. I never had any friends at school [. . .]: when I left school I consciously determined never to see any of those people ever again,[. . .] I just wiped them out. I did decide to be cleverer than them—which wasn't difficult—and Rugby did have brilliant teachers."[3] It also seems that Rushdie felt content at Rugby at times. Hence, he won the Queen's Medal for History, and he was subsequently offered a scholarship to both Balliol College, Oxford, and King's College, Cambridge. However, in 1965 Rushdie was tired of England and wanted to return home.

But where was home? In Bombay his father's business was in ruins, and being a Muslim in India became increasingly hard. For Rushdie, the partition of India ultimately took away his country and hometown. After a brief spell in England, his family emigrated to Karachi, Pakistan, in 1964. Rushdie's father had sold the family's house in Bombay, and this deeply affected Rushdie. His beloved Bombay and India no longer figured as an alternative choice of home; now it was either Pakistan or England. More than ever Rushdie felt the disorientation that was later to become a permanent theme in his fiction.

In October 1965 Rushdie began his studies of history at King's College, Cambridge. The ensuing three years, with the Vietnam War, sex, drugs, and rock 'n' roll, made a great impact on Rushdie, who fell for the whole '60s package:

> In those days everybody had better things to do than read. There was the music and there were the movies and there was also, don't forget, the world to change. Like many of my contemporaries I spent my student years under the spell of Buñuel, Godard, Ray, Wajda, Welles, Bergman, Kurosawa, Jancsó, Antonioni, Dylan, Lennon, Jagger, Laing, Marcuse, and, inevitably, the two-headed fellow known to Grass readers as Marxengels.[4]

Rushdie went to the movies five times a week and also developed an interest in the occult. It was also at Cambridge that the satanic verses episode in the history of Islam caught his attention, just as he cultivated his interest in acting.

In 1968, having completed his studies at Cambridge, Rushdie returned to Karachi, his new "home" in Pakistan. He took a job in television, but before long he felt constrained by the power of censorship and decided to leave for London to pursue his acting/writing career. Rushdie began his first (unpublished) novel in a house in Fulham that he shared with his sister Sameen and some friends from Cambridge. Through a friend Rushdie became acquainted with advertising copywriting, and he got a job at a small agency. In 1971 the manuscript for "The Book of the Pir" was complete, but it was turned down everywhere.

Rushdie did not give up his dream of becoming a novelist, and in 1975 his first novel, the science-fiction novel *Grimus*, was published by Victor Gollancz. In 1976, Rushdie moved to Kentish Town in northern London. Here he experienced the grievances of minorities firsthand; he got involved in a project whose purpose was to provide jobs to immigrants from Bangladesh, and through this job he became aware of an England that had forgotten all about tolerance. At the same time, he began writing his second novel, which was to be more rooted in personal experiences. The experiment was called "Madame Rama," and its main character bore a certain likeness to Indira Gandhi. Yet, to Rushdie's great astonishment, the novel was rejected. Subsequently, the manuscript became an inspirational source for *Midnight's Children* (1981), Rushdie's artistic and commercial breakthrough. It is a novel about India in the period between 1919 and 1978 and is narrated by one of the country's midnight children. The novel was awarded the Booker Prize, and it later won the prize for being the best Booker Prize winner in the first twenty-five years of the institution's history.

Shame was published in 1983 and was also nominated for the Booker Prize. In *Shame* Rushdie has moved the location from India to Pakistan, and he depicts the brutality of male political power, the repression of women, and the culture of shame. By now Rushdie was a coveted speaker all over the world, and in 1984 he traveled around Australia with Bruce Chatwin, who was collecting material for *The Songlines* (1987). Rushdie's association with the intellectual left wing grew stronger in those years. He was often seen in the company of Margaret Drabble and Harold Pinter, and in 1986 he was invited to Nicaragua by the Sandinista Association of Cultural Workers, with whom he sympathized. In January 1987 Rushdie published a book about his Nicaraguan experiences, *The Jaguar Smile*.

In 1987 Rushdie had been on a trip to India with the purpose of shooting *The Riddle of Midnight,* a movie about the midnight children—that is, the generation that was born in 1947. To Rushdie, India turned out to be a country one could no longer place any great faith in, as it was marked by violent clashes between Muslims and Hindus. *The Satanic Verses,* a novel about two Indian emigrants and their oscillations between Bombay and London and between faith and doubt, was released on September 26, 1988. Five months later, on February 14, 1989, Iran's Ayatollah Khomeini issued a fatwa encouraging all Muslims to kill Rushdie and his translators and editors. The following day Rushdie was offered protection by the Special Branch and went into hiding.[5]

The fairy tale *Haroun and the Sea of Stories* (1990) is about a boy's confusion about his parents' breakup, but it is also about censure and the importance of telling stories. *Imaginary Homelands,* a collection of essays from 1981 to 1991, was released in 1991. Among other things, it contains a closing section on Rushdie's own perspective on the Rushdie affair. "The Wizard of Oz," published in 1992, is an essay in which Rushdie pays tribute to the movie that originally motivated him to write. Before the publication of *The Moor's Last Sigh* in 1995, the collection of short stories *East, West* came out in 1994.

In *The Ground Beneath Her Feet* (1999), Rushdie supplements the Indian and English territories with the American territory. The novel deals with the role of celebrity and rock music in a globalized world. In 2000 Rushdie moved to New York, and he also visited India for the first time since 1987. On September 4, 2001, exactly one week before 9/11, Rushdie published his eighth novel, *Fury,* which takes place primarily in New York. *Step Across This Line,* a collection of nonfictional writings from 1992 to 2002, was published in 2002. Rushdie's most recent publication is *Shalimar the Clown,* a novel published in 2005 that deals with the extraterritoriality of both international diplomacy and terrorism.

Rushdie may epitomize the migrant writer par excellence with all its potential for reinventing the world and the subject of human identity, but the Rushdie affair also places him in a position in which he seems to personify the flip side of globalization—that is, the clash of civilizations, the increasing gap between cultures, and the proliferation of fundamentalism.

Heroes of Disorientation

As long as the old European order prevails, there will indeed be problems. But it won't last. As the ancient Greeks knew, all is flux. We shall come. [. . .] Several hundred thousand are already on their way. Not all of them will make it. But still others are packing their bags. Regard me, if you please, as a forerunner or billeting officer of the future world society, in which the egocentric worries of your compatriots will be lost.

—Günter Grass, *The Call of the Toad*

"Who what are we?" The question of what it means to be human has been one of the driving forces in the history of the novel. The (modern) novel arose at a moment when the individual's identity and position in the world were no longer self-evident. Traditionally, birthplace, language, family, and culture have been regarded as the most important coordinates in the constitution of human identity. However, as we saw with Josef and Irena in Kundera's *Ignorance,* their emigration eventually exiled them from their native country, their mother tongue, their families, and their original culture. Being disrupted from (some of) these "archetypal homes," the migrant is forced to discover new ways of being human and thus personifies a potential for expanding the territory of human identity. Yet, the disruption of place, language, family, and culture experienced by the migrant does not necessarily make these dwellings obsolete; rather, it leads to their *renegotiation* and suggests the necessity for *alternative* coordinates by which a human being can be defined.

In the age of the transcendental homelessness of the idea, human bewilderment is not merely a question of proportion (of too much or too little insight, home, family, faith, etc.); rather, it is the result of a complete and irreversible deterritorialization of the primary dwellings. What is more, knowledge is not a question of recognition, of simply removing a veil of obscurity (as did Athena when she lifted the veil that obscured Odysseus's vision). Knowledge is not a question of disclosing an eternal, but hidden reality (e.g., the timeless idea of Ithaca); instead, it is to be understood as a *production* taking place *in the moment:* "We have invented the productivity of the spirit: that is why the primeval images have irrevocably lost their objective self-evidence for us, and our thinking follows the endless path of an approximation that is never fully accomplished," says Lukács.[6] In an age in which the primary dwellings no longer present themselves as given, Rushdie explicitly installs this kind of "productivity of the spirit"—only he calls it *imagination*—as a constitutive element in the production of human identity. Our essence, no longer self-evident and thus problematical, has to be produced. Our identity has become a *postulate.* And because the migrant has been disrupted from the traditional coordinates that could have territorialized him or her in an otherwise deterritoralized world, he or she comes to personify the condition of transcendental homelessness.

Birthplace, mother tongue, family (defined as ties of blood), and social norms are usually thought of as genealogical trees. They are defined by a temporality of origins—that is, their lines of descent date back to the moment when the individual is born (and even further back). Consequently, the development of an individual is thought of as a progression determined by the parallel and continuous evolution of these four lines from their points of origin. However, a renegotiation of the coordinates entails their transformation from genealogical trees with fixed points of origin (i.e., essentialized meanings) into lines functioning by way of a-parallel communications—lines that scramble the genealogical trees. This involves the subject opening up to the molecules of the world: "Things—even people—have a way of leaking into each other [. . .] like flavours when you cook" (*MC*, 38), as Saleem says in *Midnight's Children*. Accordingly, transversalism replaces genealogy understood as fixed points of origin and parallel evolution; the rhizomatic network replaces the tree. In what follows, I will elaborate on this dichotomy by analyzing migrant identity and the metaphors ascribed to it in Rushdie's novels.

In *Midnight's Children* the narrator and protagonist, Saleem Sinai, emphasizes the complexity of human identity when he suggests that the individual is an intricately knitted network situated in an even larger network: "Who what am I? My answer: I am the sum total of everything that went before me, of all I have been seen done, of everything done-to-me. I am everyone everything whose being-in-the-world affected was affected by mine. I am anything that happens after I've gone which would not have happened if I had not come. [. . .] to understand me, you'll have to swallow a world" (*MC*, 383). This passage reveals an inspiration from modern chaos theory and its idea of everything being connected to everything. The fluttering of a butterfly's wings in China setting off a tornado in the United States implies a horizontal, a-parallel transversalism in which vertical, parallel evolution means little.

Rushdie's reformulation of human identity clearly points to an *encyclopedic* ambition that finds its most telling expression in the concept of elephantiasis.[7] "Elephantiasis" is Rushdie's metaphor for an encyclopedic aesthetic that attempts to incorporate life in its totality, and, as such, elephantiasis relates to human identity, life in general, and novelistic form. To suffer from elephantiasis, as Saleem does, can be life threatening, however. The end of the novel confirms this as Saleem dies. Writing the novel has required very demanding physical as well as mental efforts on the part of Saleem, causing the progressive fracturing of his body and its eventual dissolution. Hence, there is a reciprocal proportionality between the novel and its narrator: the closer the novel gets to its completion, the closer Saleem gets to his annihilation. The procedure illustrates how life is transformed into art and how identity is *produced* as an artwork.

Before his personal disintegration, Saleem attempts to produce a meaningful personal identity, mainly through the correspondences he creates between his personal story, his family's story, and the history of the Indian subcontinent. However, these attempts at *fusion*—that is, the metaphorical attempts to bring together what at a first glance might seem to be disparate elements into a meaningful whole—are accompanied by the forces of *fission* that the novel also employs. As I will argue in the following, fusion (metaphor) and fission (metonymy) are two complementary textual strategies in the production of identity, and it is exactly this complementarity that constitutes the novel's encyclopedic impulse.

The framework that prevents the baroque structure of *Midnight's Children* from falling apart is constituted by Saleem's repeatedly evoked parallels between himself and India. Above all, these parallels are legitimized by the fact that Saleem is born at the stroke of midnight at the exact moment that India gains its independence. This mirror structure means that Saleem functions as a prism for all of India. One prismatic element is family genealogy, traditionally one of man's defining dwellings. Throughout the entire first book of *Midnight's Children*, Saleem meticulously outlines his own family tree. To a great extent genealogy determines what and who Saleem is, and since Saleem is not even born until the second book, he is actually rooting himself before being born. The drawing of family trees is a commonly used technique to stabilize and root a person, not only in the realism of the nineteenth century, but also in the antique epopee, the Icelandic sagas, the medieval novel of chivalry, and so forth. The tree is thought of as an explanatory model that is capable of capturing the true essence of a person, just as it legitimizes and ensures a person's social position. If bewilderment does exist, it is simply a matter of returning to one's authentic position by recovering it from behind a false surface. However, in *Midnight's Children* the genealogical structure so carefully outlined by Saleem throughout the first book is completely subverted when he discloses that instead of being the true son of Amina and Ahmed, he is in fact a simulacrum in the genealogies of the Aziz and the Sinai families.

The disclosure obviously destabilizes Saleem's identity. More importantly, however, this destabilization is not followed by a restabilization when Saleem's genuine genealogy is eventually revealed, partly because Saleem's new pedigree in itself testifies to his inherent impurity, partly because lineage as an explanatory model is both renegotiated as a transversal coordinate and supplemented with a multitude of other models characterized by their transversal nature. Rushdie's genealogical inspiration stems from Dickens, among others, although Rushdie at the same time radically transforms the Dickensonian genealogical model. In Dickens the family tree functions as an ultimate frame of explanation and as a stabilizer of the novel's social hierarchies. Having endured so much misery, Oliver Twist finally discovers his proper and reputable position on the social ladder toward the end of the novel when a lot of entanglements are unraveled and his true identity/genealogy is revealed.

In Dickens there is often a movement from suffering, injustice, and disorder, caused by the absence of genealogy (or the presence of a false genealogy), to a state of happiness, justice, and order, caused, in contrast, by the legitimizing role of genealogy. Quite the opposite is at work in *Midnight's Children,* where the movement is, arguably, one from order to chaos (or from "traditional" order to new "order") and where genealogy does not occupy a legitimizing and stabilizing role. The discovery of Saleem's true pedigree does not transplant him into a stable position within his new pedigree; instead, the disclosure of the illusory genealogy causes family trees to be renegotiated and supplemented with other frames of explanation. "Family: an overrated idea" (*MC,* 396), Saleem concludes late in the novel.

But what do I mean when I say that genealogy is renegotiated and supplemented with other explanatory models? When Saleem's ayah confesses to the swapping of the babies, the family gradually acknowledges that ties of blood count less than past experiences: "when we eventually discovered the crime of Mary Pereira, we all found that it *made no difference!* I was still their son: they remained my parents. In a kind of collective failure of imagination, we learned that we simply could not think our way out of our pasts" (*MC,* 118). Hence, love is not dependent on ties of blood; rather, it seems to thrive in a common experience of lived life. Accordingly, identity is not produced through genealogical trees understood as vertical, parallel lines with fixed points of origin; instead, it is produced in horizontal, transversal communications that disturb the parallel evolution of tree structures.

However, family as understood by a traditional temporality of origin must not only yield to a renegotiated concept of family, but also be supplemented by an alternative coordinate; namely, the macrocosmic forces of history: "In fact, all over the new India, the dream we all shared, children were being born who were only partially the offspring of their parents—the children of midnight were also the children *of the time:* fathered, you understand, by history" (*MC,* 118). Hence, Saleem represents Rushdie's attempt to wrench human identity away from a narrow family framework, as he is open to transversal lines of communication such as the history and politics of the Indian subcontinent and the collective sphere of friends and midnight children. As Martine Hennard Dutheil puts it, "the vertical, linear, genealogical familial logic gives way to a wide, intricate and changing network of multiple relationships which open up the familial unit to the outside and the other: the old family tree is felled and transformed into the leaves upon which the transformative action of writing can take place."[8]

Midnight's Children opens with an episode in 1915 when Saleem's grandfather Aadam Aziz has just returned from his medical studies in Heidelberg, Germany. But if Aadam is not Saleem's grandfather, what makes the episode so important that Saleem chooses it for the novel's opening? If Rushdie discards ties of blood as the most important coordinate of human identity, what *correspondences* does the episode imply between Aadam's and Saleem's identities? Saleem and Aadam are both characterized by an inner void because they no longer consider religion capable of answering life's ultimate questions. So, on his return from Heidelberg, Aadam finds himself positioned *between* Muslim faith and Western science: "But it was no good, he was caught in a strange middle ground, trapped between belief and disbelief, [. . .] knocked forever into that middle place, unable to worship a God in whose existence he could not wholly disbelieve. Permanent alteration: a hole" (*MC*, 12). The hole caused by the absence of religion is not a void, but a space filled with doubt. It is a metaphor for the desire that constantly plugs man into an outside and catalyzes identity's continual flux and branching out. Aadam is therefore not a disintegrated person; instead, his identity bifurcates as a network. He has not been forced into an exclusive either-or, but is gifted with an inclusive both-and: on the one hand, he is unable to worship God; on the other, he cannot wholly disbelieve his existence. Throughout his life, Aadam thus remains a half-and-halfer, and this is precisely the characteristic that Saleem "inherits" from him. However, the inheritance is not so much an a priori characteristic passed on genealogically from Aadam to Saleem as it is an effect of Saleem's extraordinary talent for *imagining* correspondences that are useful in the production of identity. Imagination becomes the medicine with which the migrant can cure the detrimental effects of disorientation.

The important role of imagination with regard to genealogy and personal identity shows when Saleem "invents" several fictive parents. Throughout his life, Saleem has longed for fictional ancestors, and his lineage thus includes his biological mother, Vanita; his foster mother, Amina; his ayah, Mary Pereira; his aunt, Pia Aziz; his biological father, William Methwold; Vanita's husband, Wee Willie Winkie; his foster father, Ahmed Sinai; Amina's first husband, Nadir Khan; the snake expert, Dr Schaapsteker; his uncle, Zulfikar; and finally the magician, Picture Singh.[9] This network of multiple rootings in England, France, India, and Pakistan, but also in Christianity, Hinduism, and Islam, points to Saleem's hybrid identity.

If Saleem and India function as reflections of each other, Bombay may be regarded as an interface between the individual and the nation: "Our Bombay: it looks like a hand but it's really a mouth, always open, always hungry, swallowing food and talent from everywhere else in India" (*MC*, 125–26). Here, Bombay is regarded as a microcosmic magnet that attracts elements from the great macrocosmic India. The final step on the way toward the encyclopedic incorporation of the whole world is completed through parallels to events in the Aziz family: "Far away the Great War moved from crisis to crisis, while in the cobwebbed house Doctor Aziz was also engaged in a total war against his sectioned patient's inexhaustible complaints" (*MC*, 25). Again and again the novel employs these *metaphorical connections* based on similarities between Saleem, his family, Bombay, India, the subcontinent, and the world.

Another fact that indicates Saleem's representative role in regard to the Indian nation is his ability to function as a "center" of consciousness for the thousand and one midnight children. This magical talent underlines Saleem's multicentred identity and further implies his *synecdochical* relationship to India.[10] As a rhetorical figure, the synecdoche reduces complexity and points to a reciprocal relationship between a microcosm and a macrocosm. Saleem's telepathic talents and his pluralistic parental heritage result in a transgression of being just "any one person"; instead, he can be considered a Leibnizian monad who, potentially, has the whole world present within itself. At one point in the novel, Saleem in fact compares his own condition as a fetus to an encyclopedia, thereby underlining the mutual dependency between *bíos* (identity) and *gráphos* (writing): "What had been (at the beginning) no bigger than a full stop had expanded into a comma, a word, a sentence, a paragraph, a chapter; now it was bursting into more complex developments, becoming, one might say, a book—perhaps an encyclopaedia—even a whole language" (*MC*, 100). Identity produced through writing points yet again to an alternative way of describing the individual: not defined by vertical lines of descent, but rather by imaginative creativity.

However, this *centripetal* tendency in the novel, which sustains the stability of Saleem (and the novel) as a circular form, is counterweighted by *centrifugal* forces that disrupt the circle drawn around his identity (and around the novel's universe). I have already mentioned the personal fission that Saleem undergoes at the end of the novel. This dissolution is just one fission in a whole line of fissions, including the splits between India and England, Pakistan and India, and Bangladesh and Pakistan. Two additional examples of fissions: the midnight children's attempt to form a strong and unbreakable circle must be abandoned because disagreements evolve in the community; and the harmony in the ghetto is shattered by internal disputing fractions. The latter example prompts Saleem to state that "our ancient national gift for fissiparousness had found new outlets" (*MC*, 399). There is a constant rhythm between moments when "the modes of connection still seemed to function" and moments when "the connections between my life and the nation's have broken for good and all" (*MC*, 287, 395).

The centrifugal impulse with regard to the novel's identity politics also shows at the level of syntax. At one point in the novel, the hybridity and processuality of the subject are emphasized as Saleem describes himself as "Snotnose, Stainface, Sniffer, Baldy, Piece-of-the-moon" (*MC,* 118). This technique is metonymic in a double sense: as concerns identity, Saleem describes himself through a line of metonymies; with regard to style, the text amasses elements asyndetically without uniting them. Saleem is not just described as a fragmentary individual; the description itself is fragmentary.

Rushdie's fondness for linking several words in bunches with the help of hyphens or by amassing a long line of nouns, adjectives, or verbs asyndetically bears a close resemblance to the list or the catalogue. According to Moretti, the list is a typical encyclopedic device in the modern epic, as the hyperbolic dimension of the list reveals the intention to embrace the whole universe: on the one hand, the list seems complete; on the other hand, it implicitly suggests its own eternal continuation. And one might ask: Is there any actual difference between these two modes? Complete is only what is incomplete. This is also the Lukácsian formula for *irony* in regard to novelistic form.

As opposed to the attempts at fusion that function centripetally and point to the stability of framing, the attempts at fission function centrifugally and point to a breaking of frames. By means of correspondences, the attempts at fusion result in a *punctual manifestation of meaning,* a sort of contraction of the semantic field of possibilities of identity where meaning reveals itself in flashes. The following passage refers to the question of national identity, but Saleem's assertion about a national longing for form equally applies to the question of personal identity as the two are, as we have seen, intertwined: "As a people, we are obsessed with correspondences. Similarities between this and that, between apparently unconnected things, make us clap our hands delightedly when we find them out. It is a sort of national longing for form—or perhaps simply an expression of our deep belief that forms lie hidden within reality; that meaning reveals itself only in flashes" (*MC,* 300). The attempts at fission, on the contrary, result in an eternal sliding or overload of the meaning of identity, or perhaps more accurately, in a semantic monstrosity. In that sense, the metonymic mode produces a migratory dynamism in the novelistic universe; its function is inclusive and distributive; it keeps a field of possibilities open in that it proceeds by way of conjunction, whether this is presupposed, as in the asyndeta, or explicated by an "and." The encyclopedic identity, the elephantiasis, proposed by *Midnight's Children* is thus produced by *vibrating resonances* created by metaphors and synecdoches, on the one hand, and by *dynamical processes* created by metonymies and fragments on the other.

The most radical example of Rushdie's production of cross-pollinated identities in *Midnight's Children* is found in the famous chapter that takes place in the Sundarban jungle. Here everything seeps into everything else, and the border between subject and object is more or less liquefied: "In the turbid, miasmic state of mind which the jungle induced, they prepared their first meal, a combination of nipa-fruits and mashed earthworms, which inflicted on them all a diarrhoea so violent that they forced themselves to examine the excrement in case their intestines had fallen out in the mess" (*MC*, 362). Here, identity and its transformations are produced through molecular miasmas causing intensified oscillations between man and world. The image of excrement and intestines indicates that the border between subject and object can no longer be upheld in a Cartesian manner. Human consciousness and identity do not precede space, nor are they preceded by space; instead, they are produced by space, which, for its own part, is produced by them.

In the Sundarban, Saleem's identity assumes a schizophrenic nature in that he, among other things, goes through a becoming-dog, a becoming-transparent, and a becoming-jungle. The condition of transparency is the ultimate form of interaction between subject and object, and it is in this condition that the body is most open to the world's inscription. The chapter thus shows Saleem undergoing a becoming-world as Deleuze and Guattari understand it: "We *are* not *in* the world, we *become with* the world; we become by contemplating it. Everything is vision, becoming. We become universes. Becoming animal, plant, molecular, becoming zero."[11] Throughout the novel, and in the Sundarban chapter in particular, Saleem seeks to become or is forced into a "body without organs"—that is, an identity brought back to a state of pure virtuality, a kind of zero degree. According to Deleuze and Guattari, the body is not defined primarily by its organs and their functions, but by the effects of which it is capable. It may be that the "body without organs" sounds like a utopian state of being, but in many ways it is comparable to the embryonic life conditions that exist before the body is rooted. It is thus a genuine attempt to open up the possibilities of the human body toward new intensities. Saleem's comparing his fetal self to an encyclopedia is such an attempt to return identity to the state in which it is most open to alternative evolutions and definitions. Besides, as I have said previously, the encyclopedia metaphor underlines the emphasis on imagination and human creativity in the production of identity.

In the Sundarban jungle, Saleem embodies precisely such conditions of life that are distinctive of embryonic life—that is, conditions that are beyond the limits of genus, species, order, or class.[12] He is an embryo, but as he is not shielded by a uterus, he is entirely exposed to the a-parallel communications of the world. He is "abraded," as it says evocatively of the migrant's condition in V. S. Naipaul's *The Enigma of Arrival* (1987).[13] Accordingly, Saleem is in a state of pure virtuality, a rootless state in which the body has not yet developed its organs and its practical functionality— that is, its habits. The Sundarban chapter is an emblematic example of Rushdie's anti-genealogical identity politics, and it illustrates his desire to discover alternative ways to describe human identity. Saleem's embryonic state not only positions him beyond species and class, but also, if we recall the opening lines of this section renegotiates or even undermines the role of birthplace, language, family, and culture.

*   *   *

In *Shame* we come across a number of narratorial reflections on migration as a metaphor for the human condition. At one point, the semiautobiographical narrator thus proclaims:

> I have a theory that the resentment we *mohajirs* [migrants] engender have something to do with our conquest of the force of gravity. We have performed the act of which all men anciently dream, the thing for which they envy the birds; that is to say, we have flown.
>
> I am comparing gravity with belonging. [. . .] We know the force of gravity, but not its origins; and to explain why we become attached to our birthplaces we pretend that we are trees and speak of roots. Look under your feet. You will not find gnarled growths sprouting through the soles. Roots, I sometimes think, are a conservative myth, designed to keep us in our places.
>
> The anti-myths of gravity and of belonging bear the same name: flight. *Migration, n., moving, for instance in flight, from one place to another.* To fly and to flee: both are ways of seeking freedom.
>
> (*Sh*, 85–86)

Rushdie here emphasizes the horizontal flight of birds and migrants as opposed to the vertical forces of gravity and roots. He sees migrant identity as rhizomatic—that is, as a network of multiple *knots* and *threads* that interconnect and proliferate through air; not as a tree, but as moss or grass.

Identity as rhizome does not imply complete rootlessness, though, and emotional attachment to one's place of birth can indeed be part of the rhizomatic identity. In addition, it is not merely the roots of a stabilized past that determine us, the roots of the inconclusive, open-ended future also reach out and touch us, thus bearing witness to our ever-present unrealized potential. What the rhizome nevertheless entails, if not exactly a severing of the roots that connect you with your place of birth, is an addendum of these roots with a variety of other roots: "I don't think that migration, the process of being uprooted, necessarily leads to rootlessness. What it can lead to is a kind of multiple rooting. It's not the traditional identity crisis of not knowing where you come from. The problem is that you come from too many places. The problems are of excess rather than of absence," says Rushdie.[14] What is more, the vertical genealogy is supplemented with, or even replaced by, horizontal roots or threads that are constantly being affected and modified by transversal communications. The ability to fly—that is, the ability to deterritorialize oneself geographically (but also through imagination)—endows the migrant with a dimension of freedom, says Rushdie. But what does Rushdie mean by freedom? I would argue that freedom can only be understood as relational—that is, as freedom *from* something. In this light, the migrant's freedom is a freedom from being defined solely by place of birth and does not imply that the migrant is free per se. The migrant may propose alternative ways of being human, but the same ways of course threaten to become oppressive or reductive categories themselves.

The narrator of *Shame* describes the migrant condition as an oscillation between hopefulness and emptiness and explains in regard to the latter: "we have come unstuck from more than land. We have floated upwards from history, from memory, from Time" (*Sh*, 86–87). Accordingly, the narrator does not support complete rootlessness unreservedly, but clearly points to the ambivalence of the migrant situation. For the migrant, with no firm ground beneath his or her feet, worlds of opportunity may uncover themselves, resulting in optimistic hopefulness; but at the same time, the migrant, due to the conquest of gravity, has become severed from history, time, and memory. As we saw in Kundera, this complete unattachment may result in meaninglessness; the lightness may become unbearable. This is also why Rushdie admits, "And to come back to the 'roots' idea, I should say that I haven't managed to shake myself free of it completely" (*Sh*, 87–88).

In "Imaginary Homelands" Rushdie concludes the following with regard to migrant identity:

> Our identity is at once plural and partial. Sometimes we feel that we straddle two cultures; at other times, that we fall *between* two stools. But however ambiguous and shifting this ground may be, it is not an infertile territory for a writer to occupy. If literature is in part the business of finding new angles at which to enter reality, then once again our distance, our long geographical perspective, may provide us with such angles.
>
> (*IH*, 15)

Just as the rhizome in Deleuze and Guattari's theory cannot be conceived without a tree (the rhizome and the tree never appear as pure forms; rather, the rhizome arborizes and the tree rhizomatizes), migration is never conceived by Rushdie without (a longing for) roots of some kind. However, to Rushdie the potential reductionism of roots and borders must inevitably be challenged because, as he says, "In our deepest natures, we are frontier-crossing beings" (*SATL*, 350). This is as close as we get to an explicitly expressed "subjectology" in Rushdie.

*　*　*

So, Rushdie does not see the question of identity as being one of either rooted or rootless; to him it is a matter of planting the self in several places. In *The Satanic Verses* this idea is illustrated through the fate of the two protagonists, with Saladin being the one who ends up accepting his chimeric identity of multiple roots and therefore surviving, and Gibreel being the one who fails to accept his identity's plural nature and to root himself in reality and therefore ends his life tragically. In the following, I will concentrate on the metamorphoses of the two migrant protagonists in *The Satanic Verses,* the first main characters in Rushdie's *œuvre* to migrate to Europe and, accordingly, to illustrate the words in this chapter's epigraph.

Saladin and Gibreel are both characterized by a split. In Saladin's case it is caused by a *national* disorientation; in Gibreel's case by a *religious* disorientation. In Rushdie's own words:

> *The Satanic Verses* is the story of two painfully divided selves. In the case of one, Saladin Chamcha, the division is secular and societal: he is torn, to put it plainly, between Bombay and London, between East and West. For the other, Gibreel Farishta, the division is spiritual, a rift in the soul. He has lost his faith and is strung out between his immense need to believe and his new inability to do so. The novel is "about" their quest for wholeness.
>
> (*IH,* 397)

The in-betweenness of these double frames outlined by Rushdie—in the one case, India-England; in the other, belief-doubt—points to a new global space consisting of discontinuous historical realities, something that characterizes migration literature and cultural globality in general.

In Gibreel's case, metamorphosis is set off at the moment he, reluctantly and bewildered, realizes that he no longer needs Allah: "On that day of metamorphosis the illness changed and his recovery began. And to prove to himself the nonexistence of God, he now stood in the dining-hall of the city's most famous hotel, with pigs falling out of his face" (*SV,* 30). The scene contains another key moment in Gibreel's life as he catches sight of Alleluia Cone. Consequently, Allie replaces Allah.

Gibreel's religious doubt becomes a catalyst for the "dream" tracks about Mahound, the Imam, and Ayesha (the novel's B- and C-lines). Furthermore, these "dream" tracks are shaped by Gibreel's experiences in the film industry and by the self-understanding his mother has helped engender, first, by naming him Ismail Najmuddin (Ismail: the child involved in the sacrifice of Ibrahim; Najmuddin: star of the faith) and, second, by calling him *farishta* (angel in Urdu). Added to this, Gibreel used to pour himself into books in frustration with his lack of success with the female sex:

> To get his mind off the subject of love and desire, he studied, becoming an omnivorous autodidact, devouring the metamorphic myths of Greece and Rome, the avatars of Jupiter, the boy who became a flower, the spider-woman, Circe, everything; and the theosophy of Annie Besant, and unified field theory, and the incident of the Satanic Verses in the early career of the Prophet, and the politics of Muhammad's harem after his return to Mecca in triumph; and the surrealism of the newspapers, in which butterflies could fly into young girl's mouths.
>
> (*SV*, 23–24)

Accordingly, his loss of faith, his conquest of Allie, his profession as an actor embodying several Indian gods, his names and, finally, his familiarity with the old metamorphic myths and the story of the satanic verses are all elements that contribute to his disoriented and, ultimately, schizophrenic identity.

In Saladin's case the division and subsequent disorientation begin the day he stumbles on a wallet with English banknotes and his authoritarian father takes it away from him: "from that moment he became desperate to leave, to escape, to place oceans, between the great man and himself" (*SV*, 36–37). Whereas Gibreel's metamorphosis is uncalled for, Saladin's metamorphosis is more willed. The divide between Indianness and Englishness represents a conscious resolve to escape his roots and become "a goodandproper Englishman" (*SV*, 43). When Saladin is sent to boarding school in England, he endures a trying period with bullying and isolation, but "these exclusions only increased his determination, and that was when he began to act, to find masks that these fellows would recognize, paleface masks, clown-masks, until he fooled them into thinking he was *okay*, he was *people-like-us*" (*SV*, 43). Saladin thus invents various identities, alternating between them and in that way producing an identity shaped as discontinuous leaps. In contrast, Gibreel's identities coexist and seem more continuous. At this point in the novel, Saladin seems to represent Lucretius's theory on metamorphosis (metamorphosis implies a complete death of the old in order for the new to be born; hence metamorphosis is freedom from the essence of the self), while Gibreel represents Ovid's theory (like wax, metamorphosis implies only a change on the surface of the soul; the essential identity is thus preserved under identity's otherwise protean forms).

When Saladin visits his family in Bombay after his stay at the boarding school, his transformation into an English gentleman is at an advanced stage, and his bitterness toward his father and everything Indian is steadily growing. At the same time, his mother passes away, an event that merely exposes the fragile relationship between father and son. After graduating from university, Saladin settles in London and goes on the stage. Returning to Bombay during a tour, he experiences several intense confrontations with his past, which causes his present mask of Englishness to crack. The past resurfaces in, for instance, Saladin's speech, which up until now has manifested itself as the Queen's English, but gives way to his old Urdu-English idiom on the flight back to London. When a stewardess wakes him from a slumber to offer him drinks, Saladin semiconsciously mumbles: "'Achha, means what?' [. . .]. 'Alcoholic beverage or what?' And, when the stewardess reassured him, whatever you wish, sir, all beverages are gratis, he heard, once again, his traitor voice: 'so, okay, bibi, give one whiskysoda only'" (*SV,* 34). The nature of metamorphosis and the condition of disorientation are here staged through the materiality of language in that Saladin's idiom reveals a hybridity of Indian-Urdu-English, of past-present, and of self-control-capitulation. Above all, it is Saladin's friend Zeeny who sees through his project and criticizes his attempt to escape the past: "You know what you are, I'll tell you. A deserter is what, more English than, your Angrez accent wrapped around you like a flag, and don't think it's so perfect, it slips, baba, like a false moustache" (*SV,* 53).[15]

When Saladin visits his father, he feels overpowered by the past once again. The *necessity* of the metamorphosis of identity, a necessity caused by the transversalism of a *contingent* encounter with an outside, for example the childhood home, questions Saladin's invention of masks independent of past experiences. This explains why Saladin is off-balance, and increasingly so, when he is faced with the scenario his father inhabits with the old servant couple, Vallabh and Kasturba. As it transpires, Changez maintains respect toward his late wife Nasreen, Saladin's mother, on the one hand, by preserving the house exactly the way it was when she died, and, on the other hand, by having Kasturba dress in Nasreen's old saris and perform the role of the lady of the house in every conceivable way. The perversity of this arrangement stirs Saladin's irreconcilable anger at his father, causing him once again to break up their relationship. Hence, Saladin boards the plane to London with highly complex motives and feelings: the once repressed past reimposes itself, but at the same time this uncontrollable pressure prompts Saladin to cut the anchor chain permanently, the perverse scenario in his childhood home merely underpinning the necessity of this decision.

So, Gibreel and Saladin both suffer from painful splits of a sacred and a profane nature, and these internal splits have consolidated themselves as the determining factors of their identities. Onboard the plane, Saladin's split reveals itself in the contrast between (Indian) superstition and (English) rationality as a nightmare he has just had about hijacking starts to become real—this blurring of ontological boundaries is, by the way, an example of the novel's migratory form. In the thrall of his internal division and clinging to English virtues, such as common sense and rational explanations, or simply by repressing the connection between his dream and reality, Saladin tries to dismiss the increasingly forceful indications that the figments of his imagination are materializing around him. As for Gibreel, the serial dreams about Mahound, the Imam, and Ayesha begin to haunt him during the 111-day hijacking.

When the uncompromising Tavleen pulls the string and blows up the plane, one of these threshold situations between the old and the new is set off: a destruction containing a construction. Gibreel hovers in an inter-mezzo between a waking and a dreaming state; a schizophrenic process has begun, the course of which is directed by doubt, religion, and love. Saladin floats in an intermezzo between India and England, between the past and the present, at one and the same time fervently intent on flight and help-lessly deadlocked by remnants of memory squeezing his superficial skin.

The opening of the novel introduces the reader to the theme of meta-morphosis and mutation. The time is New Year's Day, or thereabouts, a symbol of the transition from the old to the new, like the midnight hour in *Midnight's Children*. The place is the airspace above England: "Out of thin air: a big bang, followed by falling stars. A universal beginning, *a miniature echo of the birth of time* . . . the jumbo jet *Bostan,* Flight AI-420, blew apart without any warning, high above the great, rotting, beautiful, snow-white, illuminated city, Mahagonny, Babylon, Alphaville" (*SV,* 4).

In this transient, illusory airspace, properties are transferred between our two heroes "Gibreelsaladin Farishtachamcha" as they begin their "angelicdevilish fall," while at the same time a number of new properties are conferred to them: "there was a fluidity, an indistinctness, at the edges of them" (*SV,* 8). In this metamorphic zone, which recalls the Sundarban chronotope, the boundaries of Saladin's and Gibreel's bodies become permeable and liquid, as they are intensely receptive to molecular microforces deterritorializing the once solid organism by discharging new lines of flight.

The cause of their metamorphoses is ambiguous. The text catalogues various frames of explanation, primarily through intertextual references: *The theory of evolution* is suggested through a comparison with the Big Bang and an allusion to Lamarck. In addition, a *religious interpretation* is proposed, as the name of the plane, Bostan, is the name of one of the gardens of Paradise in the Koran. Hence, the fall may be read as a secularized parallel to the story in the Koran about Iblis's expulsion from Heaven (Sûra 15, verses 31–36) or the story in the Bible about Satan's banishment from Heaven. A third explanation centers on *airspace* as a symbol of the migrant's conquest of gravity, Saladin and Gibreel's fall reflecting the movement and hybridization of the migrant in an intensified sense. Finally, the novel reflects a notion of the *borderlessness of the imagination,* stated as "anything becomes possible" (*SV,* 5). The imperative behind this reflection is one of pushing art to the limits of the thinkable in order to create new understandings of existence. As Kundera asserts, "A novel examines not reality but existence. And existence is not what has occurred, existence is the realm of human possibilities, everything that man can become, everything he's capable of."[16]

Similarly, there is a connection between the "dream" tracks and the novel's metamorphosing quality that points to the possibility of a *psychological interpretation* of the nature of the metamorphosis. The psychological interpretation has been deployed in the defense of Rushdie. The argument is that the blasphemous sections are only dreams. However, this is a highly problematic argument, as it presupposes that the novel's ontological levels can be clearly separated. In fact, the composition of *The Satanic Verses* is of such a complex nature that it is often impossible to maintain a clear distinction between "dream" and "reality" as elements from one track occasionally migrate into the other tracks. One example of elements from the "dream" tracks showing up in the "real" world is when Gibreel suddenly starts quoting passages from the Koran in Arabic, a language he does not speak. In addition, because the relationship between the chapters in terms of time is often unspecified, it becomes difficult, if not impossible, to uphold a clear distinction between what is real and what is dream. So, the psychological analysis that defends Rushdie is problematic, first, because it does not take the complexity of the novel's composition into consideration and, second, because it excludes the other possible reasons behind the metamorphoses. It is certainly one of the main formal characteristics of *The Satanic Verses* that it stages a multiplicity of explanatory frames, not only in regard to the causes of metamorphosis, but also in regard to almost every phenomenon it addresses. This multiplicity contributes to the novel's dynamic and migratory form.

Gibreel and Saladin miraculously survive the fall and land on the English coast, where Rosa Diamond invites them to stay in her house. They have been reborn and find themselves in a kind of virginal state, characteristic of the migrant position: "Then nothing existed. He was in a void, and if he were to survive he would have to construct everything from scratch, would have to invent the ground beneath his feet before he could take a step" (*SV,* 132). By now their bodily transformations are at an advanced stage: "around the edges of Gibreel Farishta's head, as he stood with his back to the dawn, it seemed to Rosa Diamond that she discerned a faint, but distinctly golden, *glow.* And were those bumps, at Chamcha's temples, under his sodden and still-in-place bowler hat? And, and, and" (*SV,* 133). The last line in this quotation is interesting, as it reminds us of Deleuze and Guattari's characterization of rhizomatic literature as an "and-literature." In this case, "And, and, and" indicates the continuous proliferation of the metamorphoses of our two main characters.

Saladin is arrested and endures a terrible ordeal of police violence, racism, and painful metamorphoses. Subsequently, after the policemen have recognized their mistake of arresting a respectable British citizen, he is admitted to a hospital where monstrous creatures are admitted. The patients all suffer because of Western orientalism: "They have the power of description, and we succumb to the pictures they construct" (*SV,* 168). To the patients in the hospital, the colonial gaze has become the defining element in their self-understanding and self-image. However, the patients escape and thereby project a collective line of flight that deterritorializes the colonizers' previous monopoly of power. In this way, the patients stage an iconoclastic event that problematizes the demonization of the immigrant. Instead of being objects acted upon, they become transforming subjects: "To migrate is certainly to lose language and home, to be defined by others, to become invisible or, even worse, a target; it is to experience deep changes and wrenches in the soul. But the migrant is not simply transformed by his act; he also transforms his new world. Migrants may well become mutants, but it is out of such hybridization that newness can emerge" (*IH,* 210). The performative agency of the migrant is explicitly suggested in the novel when the migrant is likened to sperm cells.

After his escape from the hospital, Saladin calls on his wife, Pamela Lovelace (clearly a Richardsonian simulacrum). Saladin's marriage to Pamela is characterized by two lines of flight crossing each other, as both of them wanted to escape their backgrounds by marrying their opposites. Fleeing his Indian past, Saladin saw Pamela as the incarnation of the English upper-class life that he aspired to be part of, whereas Pamela, in her effort to snub the aristocracy, threw herself into the arms of the dark Indian with the outlandish customs and the exotic name.

While Saladin is dismissed from his own home by Pamela, Gibreel is on his way to London, which he perceives as an evasive city. In his schizophrenic state as the archangel Gibreel, he has come to save London but encounters only superficiality and fictions. His dreams are beginning to take control of his personality: "Even the serial visions have migrated now; they know the city better than he. And in the aftermath of Rosa and Rekha the dream-worlds of his archangelic other self begin to seem as tangible as the shifting realities he inhabits while he's awake" (*SV,* 205). The serial visions invoked in the passage refer to the "dream" tracks (the B- and C-line), and, as it says, these visions are migrating into conditions more real than "reality," which clearly indicates the constant blurring of ontological borders in the novel.

Saladin regains human form after a violent fit of rage in the Hot Wax Club. After a period of severe pain as a result of his ceaseless metamorphoses, it is suggested that all Saladin's transformations are a consequence of his self-denial: "*humanized*—is there any option to conclude?—by the fearsome concentration of his hate" (*SV,* 294). Saladin is pleased to have regained his old bodily self, but he soon comes to realize that moral categories are internal matters rather than external and eternally determined truths. This also means that the entire process of his metamorphosis into a goat is an integral part of him: "What Saladin Chamcha understood that day was that he had been living in a state of phoney peace, that the change in him was irreversible" (*SV,* 418). As he is once again confronted with Gibreel later in the novel, evil flares up in him in the form of vindictiveness, but this time his hatred is aimed at an object whereby he retains his human shape.

Gibreel, on the other hand, oscillates between exhausting spells of drifting, during which his schizophrenia spurs him on as the rescuing archangel, and periods of recovery in Allie's embrace: "'The craziness is in here and it drives me wild to think it could get out any minute, right now, and *he* would be in charge again.' He had begun to characterize his 'possessed,' 'angel' self as another person: in the Beckettian formula, *Not I. He.* His very own Mr Hyde. Allie attempted to argue against such descriptions. 'It isn't *he,* it's you, and when you're well, it won't be you any more'" (*SV,* 340). Unlike Saladin, Gibreel fails to acknowledge that he comprises both good and evil.

A significant cause of Gibreel's illness is his jealous mind, and Saladin exploits this to drive him mad. Saladin starts calling Allie and Gibreel, pretending by means of his thousand and one voices to be Allie's endless number of (nonexisting) lovers. Hence, the motif of the satanic verses figuring in the B-line is repeated, but also altered, as it unfolds as a drama of love and revenge instead of arising out of a religious discourse. In both cases, though, it is a drama of purity versus impurity. As a consequence of Saladin's satanic verses, Allie leaves Gibreel. When Gibreel learns that Saladin is behind the verses, he plays the role of the rescuing archangel, saving Saladin from the apocalyptic flames in the Shaandaar Café. However, Gibreel is not cured by his act of mercy, but continues to be locked in a pathological dead-end, which finally drives him to kill both S. S. Sisodia and Allie, whereupon he seeks out Saladin and commits suicide.

Saladin, on the other hand, seems well on the way to becoming a "whole" person, and the episode in the Shaandaar Café, where he is rescued by the victim of his own smear campaign, helps him in this process. When Saladin decided to break definitively with his past earlier in the novel, he asked his father to chop down the walnut tree that had been planted in the family garden on the occasion of his birth. The felling of the tree symbolized Saladin's desire to escape from home, and he has been tormented by this symbol throughout the novel. However, one day when he is watching a TV program featuring a chimera, a grafted tree, he starts hoping for cohesion: "There it palpably was, a chimera with roots, firmly planted in and growing vigorously out of a piece of English earth: a tree, he thought, capable of taking the metaphoric place of the one his father had chopped down in a distant garden in another, incompatible world. If such a tree were possible, then so was he; he, too, could cohere, send down roots, survive" (*SV*, 406). The chimera represents Saladin's acceptance of both his English and Indian identities, of identity as a network of roots in preference to complete rootlessness or entrenched rootedness. Tellingly, the walnut tree, symbolizing gravity and rootedness, is replaced by Saladin's own chimera, symbolizing air-bred roots and threads and the potentiality of flight.

In my opinion, D. C. R. A. Goonetilleke misunderstands the significance of the chimera in the novel when he says that Rushdie "entertains a doubt and worry regarding hybridity [. . .]. Saladin, in the end, turns his back on it. Otto turns his back *via* suicide."[17] As I see it, Saladin is not turning his back on chimeric hybridity, because he comes to terms with his Indian roots without discarding his English experiences. And if Otto Cone commits suicide, it is precisely because his life, which develops as one prolonged rejection of his own roots, accords badly with his ideal intentions of devoting himself to the chimera and hybridity. It is also Goonetilleke who, in relation to Saladin, speaks of "a return to his original identity," just as he believes that Saladin has "found himself" and that he "completes his process of regeneration."[18] Saladin does not return to his original self; instead, he accepts his Indian roots and his past by combining them with his English roots and the present; to Rushdie, returning is always a matter of reinscription or redescription—that is, a matter of translation as a survival strategy. Goonetilleke's idea of regression also accords badly with Saladin's former insight into the irreversible nature of metamorphosis. Finally, his idea of Saladin completing his rebirth is also wrong, as completion is an illusory thing in Rushdie's universe. The novel's ending suggests openness, not completion.

In a long passage the narrator explicitly reflects on the difference between the novel's two main characters:

Should we even say that these are two fundamentally different *types* of self? Might we not agree that Gibreel, for all his stage-name and performances; and in spite of born-again slogans, new beginnings, metamorphoses;—has wished to remain, to a large degree, *continuous*—that is, joined to and arising from his past; that, in point of fact, he fears above all things the altered states in which his dreams leak into, and overwhelm, his waking self, making him that angelic Gibreel he has no desire to be;—so that his is still a self which, for our present purposes, we may describe as "true" ... whereas Saladin Chamcha is a creature of *selected* discontinuities, a *willing* re-invention; his *preferred* revolt against history being what makes him, in our chosen idiom, "false"? And might we then not go on to say that it is this falsity of self that makes possible in Chamcha a worse and deeper falsity—call this "evil"—and that this is the truth, the door, that was opened in him by his fall?—While Gibreel, to follow the logic of our established terminology, is to be considered "good" by virtue of *wishing to remain*, for all his vicissitudes, at bottom an untranslated man.

(*SV,* 427)

However, the narrator immediately modifies the luring simplicity of the above: "Such distinctions, resting as they must on an idea of the self as being (ideally) homogeneous, nonhybrid, 'pure'—an utterly fantastic notion!—cannot, must not, suffice" (*SV,* 427). Who says that truth is to remain the same and that to change is a matter of deceit? Thus, what seems to be crystallizing here as the novel's overall politics of identity is an affirmation of human identity as heterogeneous and complementary, as impure and hybrid, not without roots, but with roots planted in several places.

Saladin experiences a kind of emancipation or redemption because he comes to understand his hybrid nature and acknowledge his past. His insight is triggered by episodes such as the fire in the Shaandaar Café and the wedding between Mishal Sufyan and Hanif Johnson, but the actual conversion happens when he receives a letter informing him of his father's imminent death: "Only a few days ago that *back home* would have rung false. But now his father was dying and old emotions were sending tentacles out to grasp him" (*SV,* 514). The last part of the novel is written with love and reconciliation as the guiding principles, but it is also toward the close of the novel that Gibreel dramatically kills himself. Yet, for Saladin's part a positive conversion seems to take place as he recovers a "non-completed wholeness": "Although he kept it quiet, however, Saladin felt hourly closer to many old, rejected selves, many alternative Saladins—or rather Salahuddins—which had split off from himself as he made his various life choices, but which had apparently continued to exist, perhaps in the parallel universes of quantum theory" (*SV,* 523). As Bhabha correctly asserts,

Saladin lands somewhere between Lucretius and Ovid: "there is no resolution to it because the two conditions are ambivalently enjoined in the 'survival' of migrant life. [. . .] From somewhere between Ovid and Lucretius, or between gastronomic and demographic pluralisms, he confounds nativist and supremacist ascriptions of national(ist) identities."[19]

Toward the end of the novel, Saladin regains the ability to love: he falls in love with Zeeny, he can now forgive his father, and, finally, it becomes possible for him to receive his father's and Zeeny's love and forgiveness in return. The novel's ending depicts a path that is opening for Saladin and Zeeny and that promises a new and better place, but Saladin partly rejects the pulling power of fairy tales to rely on the tangible and real situation with Zeeny by his side. Deciding to have his childhood home torn down, Saladin picks up the thread from the opening quotation of the novel: in order for the new to be born, the old has to die. The novel has produced many interpretations of this idea, however. May parts of the old order be allowed to survive? Or does the old have to die completely? Rushdie has given us examples of both.

Language Deterritorialized

> One's always writing to bring something to life, to free life from where it's trapped, to trace lines of flight.
>
> —Gilles Deleuze, *Negotiations*

The deterritorialization of language means that forms of expression and language systems are set in motion and forced out of balance. In Rushdie's case, the English language is forced out of balance as Rushdie's status as both an outsider and an insider provides him with an essential and prolific double vision. He functions as a "difference within" in relation to both the English and Indian languages. By leaking the cadences of the subcontinent, especially Urdu, into English, Rushdie deterritorializes English as an imperial, unitarian language.

According to Rushdie, language is the most important instrument in the construction of reality, and because the English language carries an immanent metaphysics of power ("coca-colonisation") that contributes to the fortification of imperial dominance over the former colonies, it is of paramount importance that English be deterritorialized from its margins: "those peoples who were once colonized by the language are now rapidly remaking it, domesticating it, becoming more and more relaxed about the way they use it—assisted by the English language's enormous flexibility and size, they are carving out large territories for themselves within its frontiers" (*IH*, 64). So, as "the Empire writes back to the centre with a vengeance," the territory of the English language is expanded—that is, it is deterritorialized from within. In addition, the process of conquering English, of domesticating and territorializing it (the territorialization of English by "foreign" voices entails a deterritorialization of "proper" English), may ultimately lead to the freedom of those initially dominated by it, says Rushdie: "Those of us who do use English do so in spite of our ambiguity towards it, or perhaps because of that, perhaps because we can find in that linguistic struggle a reflection of other struggles taking place in the real world, struggles between the cultures within ourselves and the influences at work upon our societies. To conquer English may be to complete the process of making ourselves free" (*IH*, 17).

In Rushdie's novels, deterritorialization (that is, liberation by way of mapping new linguistic and "wordly" territories)—happens through collisions between Indian and English and through a deliberate attempt to exploit the immanent flexibility of English itself—by dismantling it, by challenging the parts contaminated with an imperial metaphysics of power and by putting it back together—in order to prompt its constant spilling over its own borders.

In their book on Kafka, Deleuze and Guattari urge us to follow Kafka's example and always strive to be strangers in our own language. Besides exercising a kind of bilingualism and a minority use within our own language, we should also make our language stutter, say Deleuze and Parnet in another book:

> We must pass through [*passer par*] dualisms because they are in language, it's not a question of getting rid of them, but we must fight against language, invent stammering, not in order to get back to a prelinguistic pseudo-reality, but to trace a vocal or written line which will make language flow between these dualisms, and which will define a minority usage of language, an inherent variation as Labov says.[20]

One is a stranger in one's language when one causes the language to move, for instance by tracing lines in between the (inescapable) dualisms as referred to above, but also by exploiting the polylingual nature of language: "To make use of the polylingualism of one's own language, to make a minor or intensive use of it, to oppose the oppressed quality of this language to its oppressive quality, to find points of nonculture or under-development, linguistic Third World zones by which a language can escape, an animal enters into things, an assemblage comes into play."[21] Rushdie typically moves about in linguistically heterogeneous localities, such as Bombay,

London, and New York. As a result, his novels orchestrate a heteroglossia in which countless types of discourse collide, contaminating official or imperial English. Furthermore, "points of nonculture" are deliberately strived for as the *semantic* codes of language are played down and supplemented with a *material intensity* producing "presence effects."

According to Deleuze and Guattari, the German spoken in Prague in Kafka's time was subject to deterritorialization. In a conversation with Günter Grass, Rushdie expresses a similar idea in connection with the postwar German writers: "The practitioners of 'rubble literature' [. . .] took upon themselves the Herculean task of reinventing the German language, of tearing it apart, ripping out the poisoned parts, and putting it back together" (*IH,* 279). Likewise, it may be argued that migrants in the United States from the West Indies, Philippines, South East Asia, Mexico, and other Spanish-speaking countries, together with the Afro-Americans, have been deterritorializing American English for decades. However, English has always been attacked by linguistic "war-machines" such as Gaelic English or Irish English.[22]

In *The Satanic Verses* we find an example of linguistic deterritorialization in connection with S. S. Sisodia, whose stuttering (the name itself stutters!) unintentionally produces startling collisions between elements that are usually kept apart. Sisodia, speaking to Saladin: "The top gogo goddess is absolutely Lakshmi" (*SV,* 512). Sisodia's articulation creates an encounter between gogo-girls and the goddess Lakshmi, Rushdie thus producing a metamorphosis through the materiality of language (sound, rhythm) and its sociality (context), which in this case circumvents the experience of the character, or superimposes it so to speak. My point is that metamorphosis is not merely a process related to human identity; it can be attributed to the novel's form and its materiality (language) as well. Sisodia also asks Saladin, "What lie lie line are you in?" (*SV,* 512). Here the concepts of "lying" and "profession" are brought together—unintentionally by Sisodia, but intentionally and very subtly by the narrator as an allusion to Saladin's deceitful and dishonest activities (his job, his identity, his satanic verses). Once again linguistic creativity is produced through the sound and sociality of language rather than through the experience of the character. As Dutheil remarks, "The 'migratory' rhetoric of Rushdie's novels tampers with the English language from a position 'between two worlds.' It displaces commonplaces and reinscribes familiar metaphors away from home, thereby infusing them with new life and fresh meaning."[23]

The first Sisodia example plots the theme of profanity versus sacredness, whereas the theme of deceit versus honesty is projected in the latter, and both examples serve as a variation or refraction within the overall thematic structure of the novel. However, the examples also show that it is insufficient for any interpretation of the novel to base itself solely on an analysis of the experience of the characters; in order to draw a qualified picture of the novel's *overall aesthetic form,* it is necessary to include the material level of sound and rhythm, since the meaning produced on this level escapes the experience of the characters, as the examples above show. Form and rhetoric "backstab" the characters, so to speak.

Minor literature attempts to disturb the innocence and transparency of official language. It attempts to invoke the "presence effect" of language. This means that language is not to be understood solely in a metaphysical dimension in which it carries a meaning that has to be unearthed. Rather, "meaning effects," which of course cannot (and should not) be completely suppressed, are supplemented by "presence effects" created by the materiality of language—that is, rhyme, rhythm, alliterations, typography, and so forth. Language ceases to function exclusively via a conjoining mechanism ("as"), which means that focus is moved from a meaning-making relation of similarity to an intensity-producing, replenishing relation of difference. Language use in minor literature follows the a-signifying, intensive lines outlined by sounds and smells, by light and tactility, by the free shapes of imagination, and by elements from dreams or nightmares. Here the point is to escape the straightjacket of meaning by means of the flux that is produced by a yet formless matter—by materiality before it is coded. But sounds (e.g., Jamila Singer's song), smells (e.g., the smell of grasshopper-green chutney leading Saleem on the track of his childhood in a Proustian moment), tactility (e.g., the almost physical encroachment of the Sundarban jungle), and elements of nightmares (e.g., the nightmare of the green-black widow) are of course conveyed through language. However, the idiosyncratic use of language that escapes doxa manages to create these exceptional conditions through the internal tensions of language and by way of exploiting the materiality of language.[24] What Rushdie repeatedly seeks to invoke can be characterized as a "being" that refers to "the things of the world independently of (or prior to) their interpretation and their structuring through any network of historically or culturally specific concepts."[25] Experiencing the "things" of the world in their preconceptual "thingness" calls for a language that does not solidify our sensual impressions but, on the contrary, stutters and traces lines in between dualisms (solidifications). Such a language retrieves the kind of intensity that characterizes "being" understood as a condition before forms become solid forms.

By referring to the border zones of a language and its paradoxical intrinsic possibilities, minor literature escapes a mere representative use of language that would otherwise preserve the world in a locked position and block human becoming. In a 1982 interview with Jean-Pierre Durix, Rushdie speaks of the syntactical-technical sides of his own distinctive use of language, admitting his indebtedness to G. V. Desai's *All About H. Hatterr*:

> it showed me that it was possible to break up the language and put it back together in a different way. To talk about minor details, one thing it showed me was the importance of punctuating badly. In order to allow different kinds of speech rhythms or different kinds of linguistic rhythms to occur in the book, I found I had to punctuate it in a very peculiar way, to destroy the natural rhythms of the English language; I had to use dashes too much, keep exclaiming, putting in three dots, sometimes three dots followed by semi-colons followed by three dashes . . . That sort of thing just seemed to help dislocate the English and let other things into it.[26]

Dislocating the English language and opening it up so other things (apart from conventional meanings) can leak into it . . . What other things? Well, "things" actually, substances, intensities, affects, sensations, and lines of flight. In the interview with Haffenden, Rushdie speaks of the Sundarban chapter's language as having a different *texture* compared to the language in the other chapters.[27] The difference in texture, I will argue, has to do precisely with the intensity and "presence effect" of the chapter's unusual language—that is, a language occupied more with materiality and surfaces than with meaning and depths. It is a writing that liberates life from its imprisonment in solidified forms (of content).

DissemiNation

> The nation fills the void left in the uprooting of communities and kin, and turns that loss into the language of metaphor.
>   —Homi K. Bhabha, *The Location of Culture*

Writing, says Rushdie in "Notes on Writing and the Nation," is a kind of mapping: "the cartography of the imagination" (*SATL*, 60). In this sense Rushdie seems to verify Benedict Anderson's idea of the close relationship between the novel and the nation understood as an "imagined community." This is underlined when he claims in regard to *Midnight's Children* that "however highly fabulated parts of the novel were, the whole was deeply rooted in the real life of the characters and the nation" (*SATL*, 72). On the other hand, Margaret Cohen argues that the novel "is a constitutively international genre across its history."[28] First, the novel is characterized by its cosmopolitan thematics: novels have always been populated with nomadic heroes whose adventures unfold in an "international" space, even in the prehistory of the form with the travels of Odysseus and the adventurers of Hellenistic romance. Second, the migrating/migratory poetics of the novel make it difficult, not to say impossible, to "incarcerate" the novel in literary histories that are organized nationally. The novel by its very nature resists being confined in a national literary tradition, not only because of its thematics, but also owing to its form, says Cohen: "Returning to the early modern genesis of the form, the poetic story is one of cross-cultural and supranational transit, translation, and appropriation."[29]

Throughout the history of criticism, the institutional organization of literary studies has nonetheless been dominated by a powerful tradition in which the novel is subsumed under the study of nationally based literary formations. Accordingly, one of the most fruitful articulations of the national focus, characteristic of the 1980s and 1990s in particular, was a consideration of the novel's role in "founding" the nation as an imagined community. However, as Cohen points out, even though images of the nation at certain historical moments may have been offered on the level of the novel's content, national identification has never been an issue on the level of the novel's form. Although the nineteenth century was the era of modern cultural nationalism, novelists actually used a single poetics—that is, historical realism—to construct narratives of the modern nation in Germany, France, Spain, Russia, and the United Kingdom. There were of course local variants of historical realism, but it is remarkable that the novels most occupied with imagining the nation all used a transnational literary currency.

What Cohen problematizes is the tradition that considers the novel primarily in a national context. On the level of content, the novel's history (and prehistory) reveals a predominantly cosmopolitan thematics through its itinerant heroes, and if the novel occasionally engages in the task of narrating the nation, its form nonetheless remains translated, cross-cultural, and supranational. In addition to Cohen's argument about the double internationalism of the novel (cosmopolitan thematics, supranational form), we might add a third component: the migrant author. The increasing number of migrant novelists belonging to several countries (or to none at all) merely accentuates the novel's "frontierlessness" and transgressive potentials in terms of both thematics and form. At the same time, though, we must insist that the migrant author's experience of national uprooting also results in a thematic focus on the nation's role. The nation is not an obsolete phenomenon, but it is narrated and imagined in new hybrid and antinativist ways, as we shall see in what follows.

Rushdie recognizes this oscillation between acknowledging the nation as a source of inspiration and concrete material, on the one hand, and admitting that the nation's borders are always already surpassed, on the other. He thus speaks of the escalating *permeability* of the nation's borders in an age of migration: "Is the nation a closed system? In this internationalized moment, can any system remain closed? Nationalism is that 'revolt against history' that seeks to close what cannot any longer be closed. To fence in what should be frontierless. Good writing assumes a frontierless nation. Writers who serve frontiers have become border guards" (*SATL*, 61).

The ambiguity of the nation's role in contemporary writing takes center stage in Homi Bhabha's seminal essay "DissemiNation." Notwithstanding the fact that the migrant is the archetypical figure of our age, and despite what many critics often seem to believe, Bhabha never dismisses the nation as a phenomenon that has been superseded. The Western nation, he says, is

> an obscure and ubiquitous form of living the *locality* of culture. [. . .] a form of living that is more complex than "community"; more symbolic than "society"; more connotative than "country"; less patriotic than *patrie*; more rhetorical than the reason of State; more mythological than ideology; less homogeneous than hegemony; less centred than the citizen; more collective than "the subject"; more psychic than civility.[30]

With this idea of nationness as a predominantly cultural, rhetorical, and symbolic construction (but no less "real" for that matter), partly inspired by, partly opposed to Anderson's idea of the imagined community, Bhabha wants to direct our attention to the *representation* of the nation as a *temporal process*.

In his attempt to articulate the complex strategies of cultural and national identification, Bhabha first of all seeks to problematize the idea of a people, a nation, or a national culture as a holistic cultural entity—and this is why he problematizes Anderson's focus on (a synchronic) "meanwhile," that is, his idea of the nation's development in an empty, homogeneous time. To Bhabha, the contemporaneity of a national present is always disturbed by the distracting presence of another temporality.[31] The split between the two temporalities in the narration of the nation is "a split between the continuist, accumulative temporality of the pedagogical, and the repetitious, recursive strategy of the performative." Hence, the nation's double-writing is the result of a process of splitting between two discourses: a nationalist, centripetal pedagogy and a migrant, centrifugal performativity. On the one hand, the people are signified "as an a priori historical presence, a pedagogical object"; on the other hand, the people are constructed "in the performance of narrative, its enunciatory 'present' marked in the repetition and pulsation of the national sign."[32] The people and the nation can thus be seen as an articulation *produced* in the ambivalent movement between the discourses of pedagogy and performativity (or fusion and fission).

The pedagogical operates with a prefigurative self-generating nation in-itself, on the one side, and with extrinsic other nations, on the other, both characterized by a temporality of origins, whereas the performative intro-duces a temporality of the in-between: it obscures the border between inside and outside by installing differences within. Bhabha's performative thus disturbs what might be described as Goethe's and Kundera's ideas of rela-tively homogeneous nations coexisting in an international space of cultural diversity. According to Bhabha, the performativity of the migrant splits the nation *within* itself through its evocation of nonsynchronous simultaneities such as minority discourses of minorities and the heterogeneous histories of contending peoples.

If a certain (Romantic) essentialism can be detected in Kundera's idea of a nation, at least in the early Kundera, the migrant counternarratives of the nation persistently invoke and erase the nation's totalizing borders, thereby disrupting those ideological strategies through which imagined communities are essentialized. As we saw, Kundera more or less turned the Czech territory into a homogeneous tradition and the Czechs into one people, admittedly a tradition and a oneness that was occasionally disturbed by the external inter-ventions of totalitarian regimes, but these regimes were themselves seen as essentialized cultural formations—formations completely in contrast to the *essence* of the Czech people and its affiliation with a Western European history of ideas. However, in regard to national essentialism, Bhabha points out "how easily the boundary that secures the cohesive limits of the Western nation may imperceptibly turn into a contentious *internal* liminality providing a place from which to speak both of, and as, the minority, the exilic, the marginal and the emergent."[33] Actually, it could be argued that Kundera in the late 1960s and early 1970s came to embody this sort of minority voice within his own country as a result of the Russian invasion, but that does not refute my argu-ment about Kundera's more or less essentializing idea on national identity.

Considering Rushdie, it is obvious that *Midnight's Children* exemplifies the close bond between the novel and the nation. Several passages in the novel point to the relevance of Anderson's concept of the imagined com-munity. On the one hand, Anderson claims that the nation is primarily a discursive phenomenon and that it is made up of immaterial elements such as myths, emotions, and symbols. On the other hand, this imagined quality does not mean that the nation is not a real and concrete phenomenon; rather, it means that the nation is not characterized by a natural and eternal essence; it is dependent on the people's will and their ability to collectively imagine the nation and believe in the myths surrounding it.

To Anderson, the "reality effect" of the myths is more important than their "truth effect," or as it says in *Midnight's Children*, "Sometimes legends make reality, and become more useful than the facts. [. . .] What's real and what's true aren't necessarily the same" (*MC*, 47, 79). The willingness to believe in the (new) myths of the (new) nation is underlined in a passage describing the atmosphere in the hours before Independence:

> the city was poised, with a new myth glinting in the corners of its eyes. August in Bombay: a month of festivals, the month of Krishna's birthday and Coconut Day; and this year—fourteen hours to go, thirteen, twelve—there was an extra festival on the calendar, a new myth to celebrate, because a nation which had never previously existed was about to win its freedom, catapulting us into a world which, although it had five thousand years of history, although it had invented the game of chess and traded with Middle Kingdom Egypt, was nevertheless quite imaginary; into a mythical land, a country which would never exist except by the efforts of a phenomenal collective will—except in a dream we all agreed to dream; it was a mass fantasy shared in varying degrees by Bengali and Punjabi, Madrasi and Jat, and would periodically need the sanctification and renewal which can only be provided by rituals of blood. India, the new myth—a collective fiction in which anything was possible, a fable rivalled only by the two other mighty fantasies: money and God.
>
> (*MC*, 112)

This passage shows how calendar time and the temporality of synchronic "meanwhile" support national unification. The national contemporaneity is emphasized through the evocation of Bombay alongside Bengal, Punjab, Madras, and Jat and through the mentioning of Krishna's birthday and Coconut Day alongside Independence Day. However, there is another temporality of differences that disturbs the unifying tendencies of the contemporary national history, and this temporality is actually present in the very constellations just mentioned. It is explicitly stated that the five localities share the same mass fantasy "in varying degrees," which indicates a difference within Indian national consciousness, and in relation to Coconut Day and Krishna, they do not merely function as contemporary reenforcers of national unity through the gatherings of people; they also point to different historical traditions within the nation. Hence, simultaneity as transversal cross-time and temporal coincidence coexists with simultaneity as "now-time" and simultaneity-along-time.

Furthermore, despite the continent's long and glorious past, Rushdie emphasizes more than once the imaginary and myth-like quality of the new nation. It rests on porous pillars because it depends on the will of the people, but also because *internally* India is a multiplicity of cultures, languages, and religions. As we have already seen in the section on disoriented heroes,

Rushdie employs the narrative strategies of fusion and fission, the first indicating a national longing for *form* brought about stylistically through metaphorical and synecdochical correspondences, the latter indicating a national gift for *dispersion* brought about stylistically through metonymical and fragmentary processes. Another point of interest in the passage is Rushdie's recognition that India as a nation has something to do with freedom; the nation is actually seen as the vehicle through which freedom from the former oppressor can materialize. This is important because it challenges those who view Rushdie as a postnationalist. Finally, when Rushdie admits that the nation will occasionally need to be sanctified anew and that this will happen through the usual rituals of blood, he hints at internal national differences. Accordingly, the new unity is the bearer of both freedom and new suppressive powers. What gains the upper hand is difficult to say: the chapters on Indira Gandhi's Emergency tell a story of violence, nationalism, sectarianism, and oppression, but, despite the fact that Saleem seems to undergo a fission, the end of the novel suggests brighter prospects for the new generation and India as such.

In *The Satanic Verses* we enter into the heart of the Empire in the company of two characters from the Empire's margin. If we witnessed the birth of a new nation in the periphery of the old Empire in *Midnight's Children,* we witness a radical transformation of the old central nation and its historiography in *The Satanic Verses.* "The trouble with the Engenglish is that their hiss hiss history happened overseas, so they dodo don't know what it means" (*SV,* 343), claims S. S. Sisodia in a famous passage. As mentioned already, Rushdie compares the airborne migrants to spermatozoa waiting to be spilled over England thereby fertilizing the country in new and hybrid ways. The image hints at the migrant's performative powers that enable him or her to disturb the centripetal pedagogy of nationalist history. However, it is not merely because of the sheer presence of physical otherness within the Empire's center that the migrant transforms contemporary society; the transformation also occurs at a historiographical level, since the migrant embodies a historical experience that is foreign to the nationalist historiography, but part of it, nonetheless, as its shadow side.

The novel not only stages the double-writing of pedagogy and performativity through its migrant characters, but also through Rosa Diamond, an archetypal English woman, who is a representative for the English homeland, but with her colonial experiences in Argentina during her youth, she also exposes the blind spots of English history. A millennium of English history is inscribed on the fragile and translucent body of Rosa, but in addition to making her feel solid and rooted in English history, it also makes her crack: "Constructed from the well-worn pedagogies and pedigrees of national unity [. . .] and, at the same time, patched and fractured in the incommensurable perplexity of the nation's living," Bhabha remarks.[34]

When Gibreel dresses in the clothes of Rosa's dead husband, the ex-colonial landowner Sir Henry Diamond, he turns into a double exposure of Henry and Martin de la Cruz, Rosa's former "native" lover from the time when she and Henry lived in Argentina. Through this double appearance, Gibreel merely intensifies the split that haunts Rosa, a split between a continuist national history and a performative narration in which the blind spots cannot be suppressed. Hence, in connection with Rosa Diamond, we witness "the emergence of a hybrid national narrative that turns the nostalgic past into the disruptive 'anterior' and displaces the historical present—opens it up to other histories and incommensurable narrative subjects."[35]

As to Gibreel, he *is* the English history that happened elsewhere. Both he and Saladin come to haunt the center and destabilize the nationalist gaze: "Gibreel's returning gaze crosses out the synchronous history of England, the essentialist memories of William the Conqueror and the Battle of Hastings. [. . .] he is the mote in the eye of history, its blind spot that will not let the nationalist gaze settle centrally."[36] Through Gibreel and Saladin, Rushdie stages the avenging repetition of the migrant who returns to estrange the holism of national history. As a result, the frontiers of the Western nation are deterritorialized as the (primarily) metropolitan central space of the Western nations is supplemented with a postcolonial space. The Western metropolis is not simply a palimpsest; it is also a double exposure, a spatial configuration that reveals a simultaneity of past and present, of fullness and perplexity, of outside and inside, and of pedagogy and performativity.

Rhizomatic Forms

> Form is a crucial issue because these texts are often working against autho-rised and authorising paradigms. They are multi-lingual, polyvocal and vari-focal, inter-textual and multi-accented; the relationship between dominant and subaltern is destabilised.
>
> —Roger Bromley, *Narratives for a New Belonging*

In this section I will look into the compositional and enunciatory aspects of *Midnight's Children* and *The Satanic Verses* in order to determine their possible contribution to the novels' migratory poetics. I will argue that the novels in their very structure are migratory—that is, fluid, wandering, transgressive, and multicentered narratives.

The composition of *Midnight's Children* oscillates between stringency and anarchy. The novel consists of three books, but also of three enuncia-tory levels: a first story line depicting Saleem's family history as it develops in the years between 1915 and 1978, a second story line depicting Saleem's writing process, and a third level, which is the level of narration—that is, a level composed of metafictional comments that interrupt the progression of the two story lines. As concerns stringency, the novel's outer form can be characterized as a symmetrical 1-2-1 composition: the first book consists of eight chapters that unfold over 112 pages and narrate nine years; the second book consists of fifteen chapters that unfold over 224 pages and narrate eighteen years; the third book consists of seven chapters that unfold over 118 pages and narrate eight years. In addition, the novel has a relatively steady rhythm, as the length of the chapters is more or less even. What is more, the symmetry is underlined by the fact that Saleem's birth occupies the center of the narrated time. Hence, the novel's scaffold seems like a carefully devised piece of structural engineering that holds the novel's multitude of interlaced stories together.

On the other hand, if we include the level of the second story line and the level of narration in our analysis, the symmetry, the steady rhythm, and the immediate order begin to take a different shape and, at times, even splinter. The manner in which Saleem tells his stories is characterized by digressions and the fabrication of connections across time and space, breaking the linear progression of the main story. As a consequence, the steady rhythm in the length of the chapters is replaced by a rhythm that persistently varies between the main story and its substories. As a consequence of Rushdie's "aesthetics of elephantiasis," millions of stories are all waiting to be told, and Saleem does not always manage to hold them back or tell them at the right moment relative to their chronology. Saleem's slips of tongue provide the reader with premonitions of future events, and we are often told explicitly what will happen, but not when and how it will happen. In addition to the many anticipations of events (prolepsis), Saleem also uses the reverse technique, analepsis or resumé, where the foregoing events are summarized, assisting the reader in keeping stock of the novel's multitude of stories. The metafictive passages Saleem inserts between the stories he tells also infuse more nuance into the rhythm. In this way the novel shifts between past and present, between the narrated events on the two levels of story and the metareflective passages on the level of the narration.

The novel assumes the quality of an erotic machine of seduction where narrator and listener enter into a complementary, dialogical partnership. As Nancy Batty points out, the novel's rhythm is determined by the tension between Padma's "what-happened-nextism" and Saleem's "carefully poised balance between concealment and disclosure."[37] Uma Parameswaran argues that the role of Padma is comparable to that of the chorus of a Greek tragedy, as they are both constantly present on stage without prompting any action.[38] This is only partly correct: it is true that Padma is the ear Saleem needs and thus, on the one hand, a passive listener, but at the same time she functions as an *active co-designer* of Saleem's narrative.

Batty observes that Saleem's use of prolepsis and analepsis resembles the episodic structure we know from film-trailers and resumés of TV series. The rhythm is characterized by a shifting between a summarizing synopsis and an anticipatory "sensationalism," and both techniques represent Saleem's invitation to the reader to participate in the enunciatory setup of the novel. Both prolepsis and analepsis contribute to the creation of order—in small "clusters"—in the otherwise chaotic texture of the novel. Accordingly, *Midnight's Children* demonstrates a formal complexity as its composition reveals a microstructural chaotic multiplicity of open-ended stories and a macrostructural stringency and symmetry.

The most recurrent principle of composition in *Midnight's Children* is the correspondence between Saleem and India, between story and history, and between microcosm and macrocosm. However, the analogy does not have a "natural" foundation; rather, it is legitimized by the contingency of the simultaneous births of Saleem and India and represents Saleem's subjective and intellectual will to establish order in chaos. Hence, events in India's history are persistently connected to events in Saleem's story, through which public and private spaces are brought into interaction. Saleem enumerates four modes of connection between family and nation, between the individual and history: (1) active-literal, (2) passive-metaphorical, (3) active-metaphorical, and (4) passive-literal. The active-literal mode represents Saleem's direct influence on history; for example when he collides with a group of demonstrators on his bicycle and, as a result, causes a subsequent outbreak of riots. The passive-metaphorical mode represents the influence of larger socio-political movements on Saleem's life; for example, the connection between India's much too fast growth into "adulthood" and Saleem's own much too fast growth. The active-metaphorical mode represents incidents in Saleem's life that are indirectly connected to events in history; for example, the mutilation of Saleem is seen as a metaphor for India's condition. Finally, the passive-literal mode is the direct influence of history on Saleem's story; for example, how the freezing of Ahmed's financial means by the state and the blasting of a water reservoir have immediate significance for Saleem's family. The two metaphorical modes represent Saleem's subjective will to establish meaningful patterns (fusion) in an otherwise chaotic reality (fission). Through the transversal connections he imagines between history and story, Saleem tries to harmonize transindividual forces and the life of the individual. However, as mentioned in the previous sections, the connection between individual, nation, and narration is always of a porous nature.

The most important leitmotif in the novel is the perforated sheet, as it recurs among all three generations of Saleem's family. Apart from being a metaphor for Saleem's metonymic and fragmentary narrative technique, the perforated sheet is also a metaphor for the metonymic nature of mankind's epistemological condition (as exemplified by Aadam, Amina, and Jamila), as we are destined to perceive the world in fragments.

Saleem's point of view in the novel is not stable, and this, I would argue, contributes to the novel's overall migratory poetics. Saleem writes down his story in 1978, which provides him with a temporal distance to his material and his previous self. For this reason Saleem also shifts between "I" and "he." Saleem as narrator is both present and absent in the narrated events, and he shifts between empathy and distance in relation to his past self. He is dramatized, which is to say that he actively participates in the events of the story. Furthermore, he is present on the level of both story (in the autobiography and in the frame story) and discourse (the level of narration). It is through Saleem that the story is served to us, and in this way his consciousness becomes the central medium for generating the novel's universe.

Saleem moves plastically between several different positions: at times he knows "more than," at other times he knows "as much as," and, finally, sometimes he knows "less than" what the situation on the level of events and characters logically allows. When Saleem is confronted with his mother's "black mango" from the vista of the laundry basket and is subsequently transformed into a telepathic communication center, he is given access to information that characters do not usually have. But in this case Saleem's position is not necessarily elevated above the situation of events, as the miraculous situation in itself provides him with unusual insights—and as readers we are asked to acknowledge the miraculousness of the fictional universe. Therefore, Saleem knows only as much as the internal logic of the novel's universe allows him to know, a logic determined by his ability to roam through other people's minds.

Obviously, the narrated time before Saleem's birth is problematic in regard to narratorial authority. When Saleem tells his grandfather's story, he is placed outside the natural reach of his own perception: "I've been sniffing out the atmosphere in my grandfather's house in those days after the death of India's humming hope" (*MC*, 52). Here Saleem explains his knowledge with his olfactory super-skills, but the explanation only succeeds in convincing us in a metaphorical sense. The narrative position in this case contains more information than is logically possible for Saleem to know. Often the point of view is simultaneous with the events before the birth of the narrator, and at times we are given perspectives from within the minds of the characters. Hence, Saleem functions not only as a neutral, passive observer and an active agent in the novel, but also as a *creator* of the novel's universe and of the story that is being told. Like Oskar, Saleem is a demiurge.

A "knowing-more" may also be at issue when it comes to the time distance between the main character, Saleem, and the narrator, Saleem. The narrator's retrospection equips him with a natural overview and an intellectual surplus in the processing of his material. With his retrospective knowledge, the narrator can withdraw from the story line and comment on events from an elevated position. The narrator's "knowing-more" obtained through a distance in time is tied to the level of events, and hence there is nothing "unnatural" about the position.

The same may be argued in cases when the time distance results in a limited point of view and causes a shortage of information. In such cases the narrator does not have access to certain parts of the story line: "but the curtain descends again, so I cannot be sure" (*MC,* 87), Saleem admits at one point when memory fails him. Saleem's most important instrument in the creation of his biography is his memory, but often this instrument proves to be unreliable. The limited point of view is not necessarily a product of the whims of memory, however. Even if memory works, Saleem may find himself excluded from the surrounding world or from the people around him: "I must leave the question-marks hanging, unanswered" (*MC,* 428) is the conclusion he often reaches. Saleem's dependency on other people's evidence is another way of establishing a point of view. In such cases, the narrator is subjected to the categories of time and space in the novel's universe, which limits his narrative position. Our access to parts of the universe thus depends on secondary narrators.

As has already been noted, memory is Saleem's most important instrument in the reconstruction of his life story. But memory is a porous mainstay that, in addition to being capricious, is useless in the reconstruction of the periods that precede Saleem's birth. Secondary narrators may remedy this problem, but Rushdie's primary solution is to grant the narrator a creative and innovative role in reconstructing the family story. In addition to his being a reflective and dramatized narrator, Saleem is also a self-conscious narrator. He interrupts the scenic (mimetic) and panoramic (diegetic) modes of narration, relating to the narrated story, with metareflective passages, relating to the act of narration and the actual construction of the biography. Here is an example of the narrator's reflection on his own working method: "'I told you the truth,' I say yet again, 'Memory's truth, because memory has its own special kind. It selects, eliminates, alters, exaggerates, minimizes, glorifies, and vilifies also; but in the end it creates its own reality, its heterogeneous but usually coherent version of events; and no sane human being ever trusts someone else's version more than his own'"

(*MC,* 211). Besides being a reflection on Saleem's working method by describing memory as an important tool in his creative process, this passage is also a reflection on the ontology of memory that is vested with its own logic of truth. Consequently, Saleem is unreliable as a narrator.

However, as the metareflective level of narration may be said to superimpose the two levels of story line in such a way that Saleem as narrator is fully aware of and open about his own unreliability, Rushdie's narrative technique is different from that of, for instance, Henry James. The narrator in James is also unreliable, but this unreliability is not discussed explicitly as it is in Rushdie: "I remain conscious that errors have already been made, and that, as my decay accelerates (my writing speed is having trouble keeping up), the risk of unreliability grows" (*MC,* 270). Both writers, however, seem to recognize unreliability as the individual's epistemological condition in a world without God: "Reality is built on our prejudices, misconceptions, and ignorance as well as on our perceptiveness and knowledge. The reading of Saleem's unreliable narration might be, I believed, a useful analogy for the way in which we all, every day, attempt to 'read' the world" (*IH,* 25), says Rushdie. Yet, in James there is an attempt to keep up a mimetic–realistic illusion that is completely ripped open in Rushdie by passages such as this one: "I must interrupt myself. I wasn't going to today, because Padma has started getting irritated whenever my narration becomes self-conscious, whenever, like an incompetent puppeteer, I reveal the hands holding the strings" (*MC,* 65).

Saleem's conscious unreliability—his reliable unreliability—and the fact that he is a dramatized narrator, and, as a result, does not have the same distance from his material that a nondramatized narrator's "objective eye" would have (e.g., the narrator in Flaubert's *Madame Bovary*), contribute to the novel's "fictionality" because it is explicitly acknowledged on the level of narration that the story lines, particularly the first one, are marked by being unreliable, provisional, limited, and constructed.

So, to what extent does the novel correspond to a rhizomatic and migratory construction? The novel is composed as a tapestry of interwoven and antihierarchical stories. The chronology, admittedly a significant component in the novel's basic story line, is disrupted by the digressive technique of the narrator who not only initiates other stories but also inserts reflections and metafictive passages, providing the narration with a leaping character. In fact, according to Rushdie, "the digressions are almost the point of the book."[39] By deconstructing the traditional hierarchy between main story and substories, *Midnight's Children* establishes a flat structure where the stories are interlaced with one another as in a network of grass roots.

The dominant antilinear or multilinear mode of narration relativizes concepts like beginning, middle, and end. The rhizome is precisely characterized as an intermezzo—that is, something that is persistently situated in the middle. There is a great deal of contingency in the novel's opening scene, as we learn that Aadam is not Saleem's grandfather. Furthermore, the opening lines of the novel, in which Saleem attempts to describe his moment of birth, are interrupted, thereby emphasizing the contingency of any natural beginning of a novel. The novel's ending seems equally contingent as Saleem explicitly indicates: "An infinity of new endings clusters around my head" (*MC,* 444).[40] The symmetrical scaffold of the novel thus turns out to be contingent, but at the same time, the stringent form is an outcome of the necessary deletions of material that the narrator must make in a world where everything leaks into everything else. The thirty chapters of the novel and the stories they tell may, to a certain extent, be said to be replaceable and thus interchangeable. The episodic structure causes the novel to be an open structure with several different entryways, and the element of contingency produces proliferating connections between the stories rather than a preexisting hierarchy. *Midnight's Children* resembles *The Tin Drum* in this respect: they are both episodic, and in contrast to the episodic structure in Kundera, which is elliptically condensed and vertically oriented toward the in-depth exploration of a given theme, the episodic structure in *Midnight's Children* and *The Tin Drum* is primarily horizontally oriented in that it metonymically proliferates as explorations in width of the character's interactions with the surrounding world. Action and character still function as unifying elements in Rushdie and Grass, whereas it is theme that unifies in Kundera.

The idea of the novel's overall rhizomatic structure is supported by the fact that identity is understood as a network of roots rather than as one deeply anchored tap root. With the status of identity as flux through a-parallel (r)evolutions, a clearer picture of the aesthetics in *Midnight's Children* emerges: the novel is a rhizome, an a-centered system in which the center (Saleem as both character and narrator) is in constant movement and equipped with a complicated and pluralistic genealogy.

* * *

How does one map a novel that constantly disperses into new forms? *The Satanic Verses* is not merely a novel that internally transgresses geopolitical borders; it also challenges boundaries of genre, monolingualism, and national character, just as it involves fundamental changes in narrative modes. Its substance is the desert sand with its shifting dunes and plumes of sand blowing from their peaks: "Soft mountains, uncompleted journeys, the impermanence of tents" (*SV,* 370).[41] However, as was the case with

Midnight's Children, The Satanic Verses counteracts the seemingly chaotic and fluid microstructure with a more systematic macrostructure.

Milan Kundera has characterized the composition of *The Satanic Verses* as a musical rondo.[42] The distinctive characteristic of a rondo is a recurring main theme interspersed with a number of subthemes. The novel consists of three story lines: (A) the story of Gibreel and Saladin, two contemporary Indians who oscillate between Bombay and London; (B) the story of Mahound and the conception of the Koran; and (C) the story of Ayesha and the villagers' pilgrimage to Mecca, supplemented by the story of the Imam in exile in Paris. Quantitatively, the A-line takes up five-sevenths of the novel's space, whereas each of the B- and C-lines takes up one-seventh. As Kundera notes, the nine parts of the novel and their respective lengths are dispensed in the following way: A(85)-B(36)-A(74)-C(36)-A(114)-B(36)-A(73)-C(35)-A(37). The outer form plays a part in furnishing the otherwise effervescent novel with a rhythmic precision on the macrostructural level.

So, the novel's center of gravity is composed of the A-line about Gibreel and Saladin, but as Kundera makes clear, it is within the B- and C-lines that "the *aesthetic wager*" of the novel is concentrated as they

> enable Rushdie to get at the fundamental problem of all novels (that of an individual's, a character's, identity) in a new way that goes beyond the conventions of the psychological novel: Chamcha's and Farishta's personalities cannot be apprehended through a detailed description of their states of mind; their mystery lies in the cohabitation in their psyches of two civilizations, the Indian and the European; it lies in their roots, from which they have been torn but which, nevertheless, remain alive in them.[43]

Kundera's analysis of the compositional strategy points to the fact that Rushdie sees human identity as inseparably connected with macropolitical forces such as history, nation, and religion. The two minor lines are not mere appendixes, present but useless; rather, they are crucial components in the novel because they formally articulate new ways to understand an individual.

Rushdie himself has said that he used "an idea of construction which was mosaic rather than linear, so that I would take a number of stories which were fitted together in a mosaic pattern rather than a straightforward linear pattern."[44] This quote reflects how important composition is to Rushdie: the formation of a mosaic through an amalgamation of heterogeneous elements has more significance than the linear drive of the individual lines. The heterogeneity of the novel, its persistent stepping across lines of genre, of story, of dream and reality, of language, of religion, of nationality, and so forth, is what makes it formally migratory: "And I thought that, well, if you're going to write a novel about transformation, then the novel itself should also be *metamorphic in form,* so it should constantly change."[45] These could have been Lukács's words.

On the one hand, the mode of narration in *The Satanic Verses* is more traditional than in Rushdie's previous novels; on the other hand, it is also more complex. Narration is predominantly restricted to third-person descriptions, and the metafictional breaches of illusion, which are abundant in *Midnight's Children, Shame,* and *The Ground Beneath Her Feet,* have been toned down (as in *Shalimar the Clown*). Likewise, the superior, self-conscious handling of the plot through prolepsis and analepsis that characterized the earlier novels is almost absent. In contrast, we are now presented with an elusive narrator who refuses to identify himself unequivocally. The narrator reveals himself a few times in the course of the novel, but his identity ultimately remains obscure.

The following tirade of questions results from the novel's breakneck opening when the reader meets Gibreel and Saladin frantically plummeting from 29,002 feet: "How does newness come into the world? How is it born? Of what fusions, translations, conjoinings is it made? How does it survive, extreme and dangerous as it is?" (*SV,* 8). Here the *engaged* narrator rolls out a condensed catalogue of the themes of the novel: newness, survival, birth, and death. Yet, the questions remain suspended in midair, to some extent at least. But then again, the narrator does make a concession that gives us a clue to his position and character:

> I know the truth, obviously. I watched the whole thing. As to omnipresence and -potence, I'm making no claims at present, but I can manage this much, I hope. Chamcha willed it and Farishta did what was willed.
>> Which was the miracle worker?
>> Of what type—angelic, satanic—was Farishta's song?
>> Who am I?
>> Let's put it this way: who has the best tunes?
>
> (*SV,* 10)

Is the narrator satanic, angelic, or no more than human? In connection with the opening scene, the narrator claims to know the answer to the questions asked; and in regard to the ambiguity of his status as satanic or angelic, the last question in the passage indicates that we are dealing with a satanic narrator, insofar as the Devil is said to have the best tunes.

In one of Gibreel's dreams, in which he is haunted by agonizing doubt, he suddenly sees a man sitting on his bed: "He saw, sitting on the bed, a man of about the same age as himself, of medium height, fairly heavily built, with salt-and-pepper beard cropped close to the line of jaw. What struck him most was that the apparition was balding, seemed to suffer from dandruff and wore glasses. This was not the Almighty he had expected" (*SV*, 318). The description clearly draws on the traditional icon of God, but at the same time it is a parody, as the man on his bed is suffering from dandruff, a receding hairline, and impaired vision. Is this Ooparvala, the man from "upstairs," or Neechayvala, the man from "downstairs"? Or is this Rushdie himself?

Still, the text does not provide us with any clear-cut answers; on the contrary, the man on the bed throws a tantrum in response to Gibreel's doubt, refusing to explain his status: "'We are not obliged to explain Our nature to you,' the dressing-down continued. 'Whether We be multiform, plural, representing the union-by-hybridization of such opposites as *Oopar* and *Neechay*, or whether We be pure, stark, extreme, will not be resolved here'" (*SV*, 319). The appearance of this figure intensifies the complexity of the novel's enunciation, as this figure is evidently not the actual narrator. Within the passage there is a cue through which the actual narrator reveals himself as someone other than the figure on the bed ("the dressing-down continued" is not stated by the man on the bed). Yet this figure clearly believes himself to be the novel's narrator: "Don't think I haven't wanted to butt in; I have, plenty of times. And once, it's true, I did. I sat on Alleluia Cone's bed and spoke to the superstar, Gibreel. *Ooparvala or Neechayvala,* he wanted to know, and I didn't enlighten him" (*SV,* 408–409). In my view we are dealing with an inconsistency between the two passages above: the first passage unequivocally contains a narrator who is not identical to the figure on the bed, and the second passage indicates that the man on the bed is the narrator. But is it important to make this distinction? Perhaps it just supports the idea of a schizoid narrator who hides behind numerous masks.

Hence, the narrator remains elusive, and it is not a static opposition between belief and unbelief that defines Rushdie's universe: "Question: What is the opposite of faith? Not disbelief. Too final, certain, closed. Itself a kind of belief. Doubt" (*SV,* 92). The logic of exclusion (*either* faith *or* disbelief) is replaced by a logic of inclusion, in which the narrator may be said to assume a status of being *both* angelic *and* satanic—or perhaps rather a human status, as an implicit allegory of the role of the writer. Thus, the pivotal point of the novel's enunciation is doubt, *human doubt,* which endows the narrator and the novel's universe in general with a schizophrenic nature, explicitly accentuated through the following leitmotif that recurs several times throughout the novel: "Once upon a time—*it was and it was not so,* as the old stories used to say, *it happened and it never did*—maybe, then, or maybe not" (*SV,* 35). In a universe such as this, notions such as true and false lose their significance as the story carries its own form of truth—that is to say a truth of possibilities, limitedness, and provisionality.

So far, my examination of the narrator's status has determined him to be both satanic and angelic, or perhaps simply human. What do I mean by this? Can we not reach a more precise characterization? We have to think beyond the traditional connotations of God and Satan as conveyed to us by the Bible and the Koran. It is necessary to anthropomorphize the divine and the satanic in much the same way as Deleuze has done with his idea of simulacrum. The narrator in *The Satanic Verses* is a simulacrum, I will argue. A simulacrum contains both something satanic and something divine. In modernity, says Deleuze, man ceases to resemble God without ceasing to be an image of God. In an optical system like that, man is furnished with a grain of divinity, which is precisely expressed in the unique perspective that characterizes man as a *monad*. On the other hand, man as a monad is also characterized as a *nomad* whose unique perspective is a differential one, and thus man becomes a producer of difference, and it is precisely the satanic part of man, a part that will always preclude any unifying perspective, which will allow diversity to disrupt closed systems of classification. So, there is a flicker of (Romantic) divinity in the work of art as a unique creation (the monadic perspective), but the angelic element never gets to represent anything preexisting, a divine hierarchy or system, because of the simultaneous presence of the demonic, differential, and nomadic perspective.

The Satanic Verses opens with an epigraph from Daniel Defoe's *The History of the Devil*, and Martine Hennard Dutheil calls attention to the alteration Rushdie performs in relation to the original: in Defoe Satan is portrayed as a migrant, whereas in Rushdie the migrant is portrayed as satanic. Accordingly, and as mentioned above, we need a redefinition of concepts like the satanic and the divine. Perhaps we should characterize the narrator as a *migrant* rather than in terms of satanic and angelic. The migrant, like the simulacrum and the nomad, represents the difference within. Rushdie himself acknowledges the idea of the narrator as a migrant: "If *The Satanic Verses* is anything, it is a migrant's-eye view of the world. It is written from the very experience of uprooting, disjuncture and metamorphosis (slow or rapid, painful or pleasurable) that is the migrant condition, and from which, I believe, can be derived a metaphor for all humanity" (*IH,* 394).

As we have seen so far, the narrator's discourse shows engagement, through among other things the many questions addressed to the reader and through the narrator's occasional physical presence in the story, but the novel also makes use of a more neutrally observing camera-eye. Nicholas Rombes has analyzed the novel's facets of filmic narration, and he also points out the dichotomy in the novel between an engaged narrative voice and a disinterested camera description. In addition, Rombes notes how the novel is inspired by film in regard to language, point of view, and narrative technique.

The filmic *vocabulary* is, for example, used to introduce and dispatch characters as if we were dealing with the stage directions or instructions in a screenplay: "Exit Pimple, weeping, censored, a scrap on a cutting-room floor" (*SV,* 13). The novel contains numerous mise-en-abyme scenarios like these in which representations are enfolded within other representations. In this case, the description of a film shooting, a vocabulary is moved from one discursive frame (i.e., the filmic) to another (i.e., the novelistic). Pimple is not only literally censored out of the movie, but also figuratively censored out of the novel. In relation to the movie, she is to be perceived literally as a useless strip of film tossed on the table in the cutting room, but in a figurative sense she may be understood in the same way in relation to the novel. By transferring the vocabulary of film into the discourse of the novel, Rushdie establishes what Arjun Appadurai, with regard to the globalized mass media and mass migration, calls "the transformation of everyday discourse,"[46] and, along with that, a transformation of the sensibility and epistemological apparatus of the subject.

In addition, the filmic strategy is employed by Rushdie to create unusual *perspectives* on the novel's universes, as for instance in Gibreel's dreams where we come across several reflections on possible angles:

> Gibreel: the dreamer, whose point of view is sometimes that of the camera and at other moments, spectator. When he's a camera the pee oh vee is always on the move, he hates static shots, so he's floating up on a high crane looking down at the foreshortened figures of the actors, or he's swooping down to stand invisibly between them, turning slowly on his heel to achieve a three-hundred-and-sixty-degree pan, or maybe he'll try a dolly shot, tracking along beside Baal and Abu Simbel as they walk, or hand-held with the help of a steadicam he'll probe the secrets of the Grandee's bedchamber.
>
> (*SV,* 108)

Perspectives like these cause the universe to be rather flat, as the description and the view are subject to a camera's two-dimensionality. The eye of the camera is destined to describe surfaces, whereas the discourse of the committed narrator is three-dimensional in its projection of character and universe. In line with this, Nicholas Rombes notes:

> unlike "normal vision," the photographed image is presented on a plane in which the foreground and background tend to gravitate toward each other, reducing three-dimensional images to two-dimensional ones. [. . .] Yet the image is distorted even further, beyond flatness, as the aerial vantage point tends to reduce parts to whole. If anything, these "high shots" reveal the relativism of perspective—what we're shown from up close becomes something else from an aerial view.[47]

Thus, the camera introduces a form of *relativism* in the creation of the fictive universe. However, according to Rombes, it is not simply that this technique indicates a flatness in the perception of events; this flatness becomes one of Rushdie's themes in describing the fictive universe on several levels: the political, the ethical, and the artistic. In view of this, the novel is not only postmodern on the level of story (what does it say?), but also on the level of discourse (how does it say it?).

Moreover, the film medium affects the novel's *narrative techniques*. Rushdie uses montage or crosscutting, for example. In *Midnight's Children* there is an example of crosscutting in which four lines alternate:

1. Doctor Aadam Aziz and Tai in the boat on their way to Ghani and Naseem
2. Aadam conversing with his mother
3. Ghani at home waiting for Aadam
4. Saleem in a state of enunciation in front of his desk in the pickle factory

Each line, recurring several times in the course of four pages (pp. 18–21), is introduced with three ellipses points [. . .], indicating that the scene continues from where we left it last time. In addition, the lines are connected in time by the word "while," indicating the simultaneity between some of these lines. Crosscutting as a literary technique, along with its resulting structure of simultaneity, dates back to modern classics such as John Dos Passos's *Manhattan Transfer* (1925) and Alfred Döblin's *Berlin Alexanderplatz* (1929), which was written during the first decades of movie making and was very much inspired by its new narrative possibilities.

The crosscutting technique underscores the narrator's control over his material, and at the same time it also makes the universe more dynamic for the reader. The alternations between the four lines in *Midnight's Children* are one way to satisfy Saleem's inclusive desire to incorporate the entire world, as the technique can be described as a deceleration of time that brings virtuality into play through the opening of new spaces. The jumping from one story line to another slows down the progress of narrated time and instead expands the novel's spatial universe. Simultaneity calls attention to the possibilities in a given space and simply emphasizes the schizophrenic nature of subjectivity in an eternally displacing and expanding movement. However, in contrast to Franz Biberkopf, Saleem seems capable of handling this modern space of possibility in a constructive way.

As to *The Satanic Verses* and film, I agree with Rombes when he argues that "Rushdie not only uses film language and technique to imbue the novel with the 'feel' of cinema and to shape the novel narratologically, but to raise episte-mological questions as well."[48] The epistemological problem is present as a reflection of the status and constitution of the point of view. As we have seen, the novel's narrator shows a persistent interest in the story and the characters. The motives behind this interest may be satanic, and they may be divine—in any case the narrator's discourse is informed by a *singular* alertness.

But what about the constitution of the camera-eye? According to Rombes, the camera does not succeed in capturing the situational circum-stances and intentions behind the captured facts. It is not interested in meaning and truth, but simply in recording facts. I believe that Rombes's observation is only partially correct. If we take a look at the scene in which the riots in Brickhall have placed the police and the media on full alert, we encounter a few implicit reflections on the meaning-generating and inten-tional method of the camera:

> This is what a television camera sees: less gifted than the human eye, its night vision is limited to what klieg lights will show. A helicopter hovers over the nightclub, urinating light in long golden streams; the camera understands this image. The machine of state bearing down upon its enemies. —And now there's a camera in the sky; a news editor somewhere has sanctioned the cost of aerial photography [. . .]. The noise of the rotor blades drowns the noise of the crowd. In this respect, again, video recording equipment is less sensi-tive than, in this case, the human ear.
> – Cut. — [. . .] The reporter speaks gravely; petrolbombs plasticbullets poli-ceinjuries watercannon looting, confining himself, of course, to facts. But the camera sees what he does not say. A camera is a thing easily broken or purloined; its fragility makes it fastidious. A camera requires law, order, the thin blue line. Seeking to preserve itself, it remains behind the shielding wall, observing the shadow-lands from afar, and of course from above: that is, it chooses sides.
>
> (SV, 454–55)

Rombes seems to think that the novel, via the camera, may realize the Jamesian and Lubbockian ideal of pure *showing*. But, as the passage above shows, the camera cannot be reduced to a neutrally registering eye only: the camera is biased, it is operated by a person, and there are financial consid-erations behind every news shot.

The camera may not be as skilled as the human eye, and therefore it may often have only a limited point of view, but the opposite may also be true: in certain situations the camera may take in what the human eye does not, causing the two modes of perspective to complement each other.

Moreover, at a later point in the text, the image of the camera is endowed with opinion: "The camera observes the wax models with distaste" (*SV,* 455). In this way the intentionality of news images is accentuated: they can never sever themselves from ideology, because the frame will always contain an inside and an outside, and the frame-setting will inevitably lead to the establishment of its own individual center of enunciation and ideology. Rushdie critically reflects on the news coverage of the race riots in Brickhall, where the state machine is in collusion with the news machine through financial, social, and ideological power relations. The bashful "of course," inserted in connection with the otherwise strictly "factual" discourse of the news reporter, represents a micropolitical, ironic subversion of the reporter's sincerity and objectivity.

The oscillation between the engaged narrator and the partially neutral filmic description helps the reader maintain a critical stance relative to the novel's methods of representation, as it involves a reflection on the manipulative strategies of discourse. In this respect, Rushdie seems to agree with Appadurai's considerations on the role of the mass media in the development of the modern subject's position between acquiescence and agency. Appadurai believes that the mass media are not necessarily guilty of a general dumbing down and idleness: "There is a growing evidence that the consumption of the mass media throughout the world often provokes resistance, irony, selectivity, and, in general, *agency.*"[49] Through its complex orchestration of a schizophrenic and migratory enunciation, in which filmic inspiration plays a major role, the novel can be said to fine-tune and update our epistemological apparatus and thus prepare us for global modernity with its hybrid and cross-cultural formations of subjectivity and its unstable and liquid images of the world.

To conclude: *The Satanic Verses* is the epitome of rhizome. It is a schizo-novel constantly migrating. Composition and enunciation render any kind of centralization of types of discourse, narrative voices, and stories impossible. The novel is antihierarchical and antigenealogical, as any form of origin proves to be a construction and therefore open to re-interpretation. Ontological complementarity and ambiguity are generated primarily by allowing the three lines to leak into one another via metamorphoses and echoes, making dream and reality indistinguishable. The question of identity also supports the overall rhizomatic character of the novel, in that identity is portrayed as heterogeneous and complementary, as processual and decentered, and as hybrid and impure.

CHAPTER 4

Jan Kjærstad

The journey creates us. We become the frontiers we cross. [. . .] The frontier is an elusive line, visible and invisible, physical and metaphorical, amoral and moral. [. . .] To cross a frontier is to be transformed.
— Salman Rushdie, *Step Across This Line*

When I first began to conceive of this project on the role of migration in post–World War II European literature, I wanted to include an author from my own part of the world—that is, Scandinavia. However, it soon became clear to me that the literatures of Denmark, Norway, and Sweden were not exactly teeming with migrant authors, and the few names that could be categorized as such were household names neither on the world market nor even among their respective national readerships.

In her article "Migrant or Multicultural Literature in the Nordic Countries" (2005), Ingeborg Kongslien offers the reader an overview of migrant authors in Denmark, Norway, Sweden, and Finland and begins her article by asserting: "The Nordic literary landscape has seen a number of new names with somewhat unfamiliar design emerge during the last three or four decades of the previous century. Immigrants and second generation representatives have since around 1970 increasingly published poems, short stories, and novels in the Scandinavian languages, and with that, expanded the national literatures with new themes, settings, and fields of reference." Furthermore, Kongslien goes on to claim that these migrant writers have become part of "the general literary discourse and are about to challenge the established national canon."[1] In her concluding remarks, she not only repeats her idea about the migrant authors' challenge of the literary canon but also speaks of their expansion of this canon.

Kongslien is correct in her claim that Scandinavia has witnessed a rise in the number of "new names with somewhat unfamiliar design" within its national literatures, but in my opinion she exaggerates the actual impact of these names. The Scandinavian literatures have not been greatly affected by the Scandinavian migrant writers mentioned by Kongslien in terms of "new themes, settings, and fields of reference." What is more, the names on Kongslien's list have not really had any profound bearings on either the general literary discourse or the national canon, just as they have not obtained any extensive public readership.

However, there are national differences (as Kongslien also points out) in regard to both the date of the emergence of migrant authors and their actual impact on the national literary consciousness. Not surprisingly, Sweden was the first Scandinavian country to open the gates of its literary republic to migrant literature; it happened around 1970. In the case of Norway, it was around the mid-1980s, and in Denmark, the late 1980s to the early 1990s. In terms of impact, Sweden can also be said to surpass its two neighbors, primarily because of the relative commercial success and general recognition of Theodor Kallifatides, who came to Sweden from Greece in 1964 and published his first "Swedish" novel, *Utlänningar (Foreigners)*, in 1970. Three Iranian women authors with migrant background have joined Kallifatides in the category of migrant writers—namely, the novelists Fateme Behros and Azar Mahloujian and the poet Jila Mossaed. Finally, the Nigerian immigrant Cletus Nelson Nwadike and the Kurdish immigrant Mehmed Uzun must be mentioned, too.

In Norway the emergence of migrant literature dates back to 1986, when Khalid Hussain published his novel *Pakkis*. In 1996 Nasim Karim published *IZZAT. For ærens skyld (Honor. For the Sake of Honor)*. In addition, Michael Konupek, originally from Prague, has written a number of works dealing with the themes of exile and acculturation. Finally, He Dong, from China, and Jamshed Masroor, from India, should be mentioned. In Denmark, Milena Rudez, from Bosnia-Herzegovina, published a bilingual collection of poetry in 2002, *Den blinde rejsende fra Sarajevo (The Blind Traveller From Sarajevo)*. The two most well-known migrant writers in Denmark, however, are the Kurd Adil Erdem and the Chilean Rubén Palma, both of whom have published migrant literature in a variety of genres. However, neither of them can be said to play a major role in the discourse of the literary establishment.

In her conclusion, Kongslien remarks that to single out migrant literature is "to draw attention to its existence because that is not always sufficiently done so."[2] The passage reveals an ultimately self-undermining, prescriptive strategy that supplements Kongslien's otherwise descriptive and evaluating strategy (consisting of outlining the number of migrant authors and assessing the impact of migrant literature in Scandinavia). Throughout her article,

Kongslien claims that migrant literature in Scandinavia has become part of the established literary discourse and that it has not merely challenged but also expanded the national literary canon. However, by asserting that we need to draw attention to this kind of literature precisely because it has not garnered much attention to date, Kongslien actually admits that Scandinavian migrant literature has, in most cases, been collecting dust on the shelves of bookshops and libraries instead of challenging/expanding the canon and being part of the national literary discourse.

Within the past five years, though, Scandinavia has, in fact, witnessed an emergence of migrant literature that has (finally) succeeded in obtaining both a wide readership and, in particular, the attention of the media and the publishing houses. The most prominent example is the second-generation immigrant Jonas Hassen Khemiri, from Sweden, who has published two commercially successful and critically acclaimed novels, *Ett öga rött* (*An Eye Red*, 2003) and *Montecore: en unik tiger* (*Montecore: A Unique Tiger*, 2006).

In Denmark, especially after the infamous Muhammad cartoons were published in the Danish newspaper *Jyllandsposten* in 2006, prompting riots throughout the Muslim world, the media and publishers have been eager to lure the so-called "new voices" out of their hiding places. In response to the continuous literary silence of the Danish immigrants and their descendants, Gyldendal (by far the largest publishing house in Denmark) and *Berlingske Tidende* (one of the major newspapers) arranged a competition in which they solicited poems and short texts written by people living in Denmark but who were of non-Danish ethnic background. Their motive (besides sensing a new commercial avenue) was to call forth a more exact picture of Denmark, which has been a homogeneous nation-state for more than a thousand years, but is now in the process of becoming multiethnic and intercultural. Fourteen of the best contributions have been collected in an anthology, *Nye stemmer* (*New Voices*, 2006).

So, to return to my initial desire to include a Scandinavian author in my project: When I first began to conceive this project about eight years ago, the landscape of Scandinavian literature did not offer an abundance of migrant writers, at least none with the combination of migrant experience *and* global recognition that applies to Grass, Kundera, and Rushdie. However, when reading Jan Kjærstad's trilogy, it became clear to me that he could be the, admittedly unconventional, Scandinavian example that I was in search of, because I immediately saw some thematic and formal affiliations with what I usually considered to be migrant literature. Using Kjærstad as an example would thus accord with my general aim, which was to outline the distinctiveness of migrant literature and point to its important role in literary history, as well as its transformative powers in regard to the organization of literary studies and literary historiography. At the same time, Kjærstad would add some new and (to some people at least) slightly provocative dimensions to my project in that he is not a traditional migrant. However, very recent works by scholars such as Roy Sommer (2001), Azade Seyhan (2001), Leslie Adelson (2005), and Rebecca Walkowitz (2006) have supported my proposed conceptual shift from "migrant literature" to "migration literature," as well as my initial intuition about the explanatory power of a broadened concept of "migration."

Born in Oslo in 1953 and still a resident of the capital of Norway, Jan Kjærstad is not a "true" migrant. However, as already indicated, his ambitious and celebrated trilogy about the life of the fictional Norwegian TV producer Jonas Wergeland, *The Seducer* (1993), *The Conqueror* (1996), and *Oppdageren* (*The Discoverer,* 1999),[3] has a lot in common with migrant literature as it has been characterized in the previous chapters. As to his background, Kjærstad had actually been living in Zimbabwe for two years when he decided to write the trilogy, and the geographical and mental distance from his native country was a decisive prerequisite for his daring to undertake the task (as it was for both Grass and Rushdie). It is therefore reasonable to assume that a kind of double vision and spatial distance is encountered in the trilogy's epistemological design.

However, my intention is not to claim that Kjærstad's personal experience of living in Africa (as a result of his wife's transfer by the Red Cross) is identical to the experiences of Grass, Kundera, and Rushdie, who were forced to leave their native countries and cities of birth. Rather, my aim is to show that Kjærstad's trilogy can be read as a "symptom" of an age in which migration has more or less become the condition of humanity (like it or not) and in which the nation-state is undergoing considerable transformations. In other words, "traditional" migrant literature written by migrants (this generalization should of course be taken with all kinds of precautions)—combined with the globalizing forces in contemporary society—has made an immense impact on literature in general. Hence, literature written by nonmigrants can in some cases be likened to migrant literature in terms of both form and theme.

In the following, I will focus on four topics in the trilogy—narrator, nation, human identity, and novelistic form—in order to outline more precisely in what way Kjærstad's trilogy can be likened to migrant literature. As to enunciatory strategies, Kjærstad offers an interesting and subtle solution to the problem of narrating in an age of modernity by constructing a narratorial oscillation between transcendent perspectives from without or above and immanent perspectives from within or below. This stylistic dynamic is supplemented in one of the books by his use of an actual migrant narrator who offers an outlandish, exoticizing gaze upon the all too familiar and provincial Norway. The question of national identity is of paramount importance to Kjærstad, who uses the trilogy to criticize the Norwegian tendency toward isolationism. The national image that Kjærstad's evokes has both descriptive and prescriptive qualities. On the one hand, he unearths layers of international interdependency in the national self-image that have been obscured by the nation's desire to remain pure and untouched by foreign impulses. On the other hand, Kjærstad not only depicts how Norway, despite its efforts to avoid the global whirlwinds, inevitably is and has been entangled in the world, but he also explicitly urges Norway and the Norwegian people to involve themselves in global matters, be it politics, economics, or art. Finally, in Kjærstad we come upon an ambitious attempt to create a novelistic form that offers the reader a new image of what it means to be a human being. In doing so, Kjærstad challenges concepts such as chronology and causality of actions and replaces the "traditional" novel's temporal orientation with a focus on spatiality and a causality of correspondences and associations. This means that concepts such as field, network, and rhizome occupy center stage in Kjærstad's poetics.

Narratorial Oscillations

In post-independence literature [. . .] the cosmopolitan rootlessness which developed in urban pockets at the time of early twentieth-century modernism has in a sense "gone global."
—Elleke Boehmer, *Colonial and Postcolonial Literature*

One of the reasons for the artistic and commercial success of Kjærstad's trilogy is its subtle play on the role and identity of its five narrators. The multiperspectivism in the trilogy implicitly problematizes the status and position of the narrator in general. It may be that the condition of modernity can be characterized *abstractly* as problematical subject and contingent world, but the *concrete* ways in which this relationship is shaped in literature actually changes throughout modernity. Consider for example Émile Zola's opening lines in *Germinal* (1885): "Over the open plain, beneath a starless sky as dark and thick as ink, a man walked alone along the highway from Marchiennes to Montsou, a straight paved road ten kilometers in length, intersecting the beetroot-fields."[4] Étienne Lantier may be a problematical subject, and the French world during the Second Empire may have been contingent, but Zola never questions the fact that Étienne and the world are "narratable." Zola's narrator is unproblematically positioned *outside* the fictional universe and *above* the reader as a narrator-god, and as readers, we occupy the role of spectator.

With Proust, Joyce, and Woolf, it is still possible to narrate. However, the fictional universe is now no longer narrated from outside and from above, but from *within*. The "narrateur-dieu" (narrator-god) is replaced by an immanent "narrateur-zéro" who is situated *in* the fictional universe and its contingent flow of events.[5] The authors of modernism come to the conclusion that no outside exists from which a story can be narrated, but at the same time, narrative still requires a position from whence a story can be told. Technically, modernists such as Joyce and Woolf employ the stream of consciousness, which is a way of transmitting the narrator's inner thoughts, partly set off by outside stimuli. The stream of consciousness can be characterized as a one-to-one stream: what comes in, comes out. In the French *nouveau roman,* if we move a little forward in time, the inner thoughts of the narrator are replaced by the camera's paratactic accumulation of events and details. However, the camera is not a transcendent outside, as one might think, but still a perspective immanent to the fictional universe; think of Robbe-Grillet's *Jealousy* (1957). The consequence of the stream of consciousness and the camera's (supposedly) disinterested registration of events is, ultimately, *the end of narrative*: narrative's catch-22 is that it requires a privileged outside, but this position can never be truly accurate. In other words, narrative demands a narrator who no longer seems to exist.

Kjærstad's trilogy offers one possible solution to this dilemma, and a remarkable one indeed. It does so without renouncing either the indispensable transcendent, outside position, or the inevitable immanence of "truth." The staging of multiperspectivism is brought to its full potential only when all three books of the trilogy are considered simultaneously—that is, if we somehow disregard the *movement* from one book's singular perspective to the next book's singular perspective. However, the fact that the books were published with a distance of three years between them makes it possible for Kjærstad to operate (shamelessly) with an almost uncontested, old fashioned "narrateur-dieu" in the first book. The narratorial position in *The Seducer* allows Kjærstad to establish and uphold a "classic" narrative situation that more or less ignores the epistemological problems usually associated with such an old-fashioned enunciatory construction: "I am capable of taking the broader view, of seeing Norway from above, with all the necessary detachment" (*Se,* 63), the narrator proclaims. *The Seducer* never reveals the identity of its narrator, but it is intimated on several occasions that it is God himself who narrates Jonas's life. The most famous example pointing toward this is the following authorial interruption:

> I ought to have introduced myself, I know, but I am very much afraid that this would only lead to misunderstanding. For some, this tale would thus be

lent too much authority; it would lose all credibility in the eyes of others. My own popularity is, after all, plummeting, and—this much I can say—I am now so much *persona non grata* that a lot of people have declared me to be dead. I must, therefore, choose my words with care. I am who I am.

(*Se,* 62)

Besides alluding to Nietzsche and the death of God, the passage also plays on the dichotomy between God's authority (to believers) and his unreliability (to nonbelievers). It is the quote's last sentence, though, which points most explicitly to the godly identity of the narrator as it repeats the words of God in Exodus 3:14: "I AM THAT I AM."

It is not until the publication of *The Conqueror* three years later—a publication that the reader of *The Seducer* is not led to expect—that the narratorial position in the predecessor is relativized. The second book's new perspective on Jonas Wergeland's life challenges the version in the first book, as its perspective is more or less contrary to the perspective in *The Seducer.* As was the case in the first book, the identity of the second book's narrator is not revealed, but numerous examples point to the Devil as the narrator. However, it is not merely by staging a new perspective of Jonas's life that *The Conqueror* casts doubt on the authority of the version promoted by *The Seducer. The Conqueror* also transforms the (by and large) omniscient "narrateur-dieu" of *The Seducer* into an immanently situated personality by revealing that the book is a hagiography on Jonas Wergeland written by a woman in love with him. Her name is Kamala Varma, an Indian woman now living in Norway. *The Seducer,* we come to realize, is thus written by a migrant who offers a foreign (Indian) voice to a local, homogenous (Norwegian) material.

The narratorial situation in *The Conqueror* is both similar to and different from that in *The Seducer.* It is similar because the narrator is apparently once again omniscient. However, the Olympian position of the first book's narrator is transformed into a dramatized authorial partnership between a seemingly privileged narrator (with devilish traits in both a mental and physical sense) and a history professor (epitomizing professional "objectiveness"), the latter being responsible for writing down the mysterious stranger's tales. The partnership and the frame story situated in the tower (the professor's office) make the narratorial position more closely connected with the fictional universe than was the case in the first book's more Olympian perspective. In addition, the fact that the second book reveals the identity of the first book's narrator suggests to the reader that the same procedure can be expected in the third book.

The same movement does actually happen in *The Discoverer* as the storyteller's identity in *The Conqueror* is revealed and thus transformed from omniscient authority to situated personality. The narrator is revealed as Rakel, Jonas's sister. However, the disclosure of Kamala Varma and Rakel does not completely erase the positions of "narrateur-dieu" and "narrateur-diable," even though it converts their transcendent positions into immanent ones: they are no longer positioned outside, but inside the fictional universe, and both of them have dubious motives.

The Discoverer does not initially reveal the identity of its own multiple narrators. It begins in a transcendent mode, but over the course of the book, the narrators are personalized as the reader realizes that six of the chapters are narrated by Kristin, Jonas's daughter, whereas the two remaining chapters are narrated by the protagonist himself. The enunciatory complexity is emphasized by the fact that Kristin's chapters are partially based on a manuscript written by Jonas (when he was in prison) that he allowed Kristin to read (a manuscript he subsequently chose to burn). In this sense Kristin's chapters repeat the subtle blending of two voices, which characterizes the enunciation in *The Conqueror*.

Whereas Rushdie in *The Satanic Verses* stages a dialectics between satanic and angelic perspectives within one single work and within one single narrator, and furthermore makes the two discourses indistinguishable, Kjærstad makes them discernible and provides each with its own book. In this way he gets away with employing an old-fashioned "narrateur-dieu"/"narrateur-diable" who is allowed a certain degree of sovereignty before being disavowed (three years later).

Changing the focus a little to the inside-outside dialectics, a similar thing can be said to distinguish Kjærstad's trilogy from *The Tin Drum* and *Midnight's Children*. In the latter two, the dialectics between outside and inside perspectives is staged between narrator (outside) and hero (inside) within each novel. But as the narrator and the hero in both novels are the same person, Oskar and Saleem, respectively, the same radical "positional purity" that we get in Kjærstad is never achieved. The outside positions of Oskar and Saleem as narrators are made relative *immediately*, as they are simultaneously caught up in the fictional universes as heroes. Because of the trilogy's internal "migration" of narratorial positions and enunciatory constructions (the movement from a first "outside" to a second "outside" that transforms the first "outside" to an "inside" and then from the second "outside" to a third "outside" that transforms the second "outside" and its own "outside" into "insides"), Kjærstad offers a subtle resolution to the problem of narrative positions in an age in which stories no longer merely tell themselves. The stories are traditional, and they are traditionally narrated *in the moment,* but the overall narrative form and enunciatory construction are experimental.

It is tempting to read *The Discoverer* as a novel that ultimately provides answers to the many enigmas put forward in the two first books. After all, in *The Discoverer* Jonas Wergeland finally offers his own version of the events surrounding the death of Margrete, his wife. It may be that the preceding narratorial positions have been transformed from transcendent, "objective," and outside perspectives to immanent, "subjective," and inside perspectives, but their insights nevertheless remain significant contributions to the network of life threads that constitutes the biographies of Jonas Wergeland. Jonas's own version cannot be anything but a supplement to the other versions, as he is as much caught up in the events and as much governed by personal motives as the other narrators are. He is himself a "narrateur-zéro."[6]

In regard to enunciation and narratorial constructions, the trilogy ends up without one definite center; instead, it has many centers, making it practically impossible for the reader to "finalize" the work. We are left with the building blocks, but not with the building's master plan. However, the progressive undermining of the narratorial positions does not mean that we end up with nothing. On the contrary, by refusing one single authority on Jonas's life, the trilogy proposes a multiplicity of meanings, correspondences, and possibilities by admitting to the autonomy and relevance of the multiple narratorial positions. This is not the same as arguing that the truth is relative; rather, as Deleuze (and Kyndrup) remarks, it implies that relativity is true. The bottom line is not a line, but a proliferating rhizome of intricate relations that possess the potential to link up in new ways. Kyndrup concludes:

> In an almost paradoxical pragmatization of the dilemma, the literary artwork nevertheless becomes a place of truth, or, perhaps more accurately: a becoming-truth. The work creates a passage between the hermetic immanence of existence and the possibility of a pragmatic, earthly transcendence. A passage that we could call "paramodern" in the sense that it, on the one side, acknowledges and accepts the limitless earthliness in the condition of the Modern: There is no "outside." But, on the other side, that it can demonstrate that this immanence comprises the possibility of creating oneself from the "outside" through fiction, that is, to establish a kind of transcendence from below or to raise a metaphysics from there.[7]

It is in the *oscillation* between transcendent and immanent positions that truth can be found—not as a stable entity, but as a constant becoming of new perspectives and stories. What is important here is that each new perspective or story is not merely an addition to the existing ones; rather, a new perspective or story actually changes the nature of the entire landscape of preceding stories/perspectives. This function corresponds to the Deleuzian idea of the simulacrum—that is, a differential point of view with the power of *nachträglich* (subsequent) transformation.

As already mentioned, the migrant can be said to give a foreign voice to a local material, on the one hand, and to make a foreign material locally familiar, on the other. Kjærstad persistently makes use of this structure in the trilogy. The narrator of *The Seducer,* Kamala Varma, is a migrant who has previously published a critical anthropological study on Norway in which she labeled the country a mere appendix on a global scale. As a foreigner she has a valuable cultural distance to Norway that enables her to soften an otherwise solidified and homogeneous local material.

Kjærstad is not a migrant, but he makes use of literature's imaginative freedom to construct a migrant perspective in *The Seducer.* Rakel, the narrator of *The Conqueror,* is an atypical Norwegian who is deeply influenced by the *Arabian Nights* and Albert Schweitzer. She no longer lives in Norway but travels the world in her big truck as a Red Cross employee. She has thus chosen the nomadic life. Whereas Kamala Varma embodies the foreigner becoming native, Rakel embodies the native becoming foreigner. Rakel's devouring of the *Arabian Nights* during her teenage years clearly leaves its stamp on the narrative form and technique of *The Conqueror.* Like the first book, the second is distinguished by its oral nature and digressive structure, and Rakel explicitly tells the professor that she, as did Scheherazade, narrates in order to save a life. In *The Discoverer,* Kristin represents the new generation that combines the principles of the old media (e.g., television, classical music, and books) with the possibilities inherent in the new media (e.g., the World Wide Web, virtual reality, and digital music). She is not so much a foreign voice as she is a new globalized voice embracing the new potentials for translocal mobility and cultural encounters in a hitherto nationalistic-isolationistic Norway.

These "foreign" migrant and globalized positions are of course constructed, and they are constructed by a nonmigrant author. But this is irrelevant. Instead, the significant question is, Does it work? My answer would be, Yes it does, because Kjærstad manages to create perspectives similar to the perspectives characteristic of migrant literature—that is, perspectives situated *between* cultures and endowed with a performative foreignness that deterritorializes and "smoothes" the national, "striated" territory. In addition to this concrete use of foreign perspectives on a local material, Kjærstad has also—on a more abstract-formal level—created a highly original enunciatory structure that "migrates" between transcendent and immanent positions, thus accentuating the perspectival mobility in the trilogy.

Norway Glocalized

Things are more confused now. A scratchy recording of the Norwegian national anthem blares out from a loudspeaker at the Sailor's Home on the bluff above the channel. The container ship being greeted flies a Bahamian flag of convenience. It was built by Koreans working long hours in the giant shipyards of Ulsan. The underpaid and the understaffed crew could be Salvadorean or Filipino. Only the Captain hears a familiar melody.

—Alan Sekula, *Fish Story*

"Norway's nationalist nostalgia cannot drown out the babel on the bluff" is Bhabha's comment on the above-cited epigraph.[8] It could easily have been Kjærstad's too. The contemporary challenge posed by the babel to nationalist nostalgia has provoked Kjærstad to ask the following questions, which can be regarded as driving forces behind his literary project: How does one make the (in Kjærstad's opinion) isolationistic Norwegian people realize that Norway's greatness and the greatness of its most famous personalities are and always have been deeply dependent on the world outside the borders of Norway? How does one narrate the modern nation, knowing that the traditional nationalist discourse (Bhabha's "pedagogical") is unable to embrace the cultural, linguistic, and religious heterogeneity and diversity of the modern nation?

The "realistic" novel of the nineteenth century is by and large a nationalist narrative. In the age of imperial ambitions, which is also the age of nationalism, the novel is, admittedly, concerned with depicting cross-cultural encounters. But more often than not, it uses these encounters to essentialize images of the glorious nation and contrast them with other nations/cultures. If one can speak of multiculturalism in regard to the novel in the nineteenth century, it is a multiculturalism structured by a parallelism of monocultures. Furthermore, the ending of the realistic novel typically transforms the work into a unified whole. The causality dominating the realistic novel implies that a filtration takes place between what is absolutely necessary to the (nationalist) plot and what is meaningless or irrelevant. Life's contingencies, dark corners, and absurdities are sorted out for the sake of shaping a well-balanced organism. The pedagogical suppresses the performativity of the different, the strange, and the abnormal.

Kjærstad's trilogy is, formally speaking, very different from the so-called realistic novel of the nineteenth century. The latter operates with a traditional causality—that is, a progressive causality that supports the creation of a homogeneous, imagined community by excluding anything irrelevant to the formative logic of "what-happened-next." The novel as organic, well-balanced unity reflects the nation as organic, well-balanced unity. In contrast, Kjærstad liberates each event from what would otherwise be its fixed position in a traditional causal, chronological plot sequence in order to open it up to alternative connections and meanings. He emphasizes the complexity and "fullness" of each situation at the expense of the succession of events (as Kundera does). The realistic novel's causality of "what-happened-next" is replaced by new principles of connection: those of *correspondence* and *association*. As a result, the focus on a central story line characteristic of the realistic novel is replaced by a multiplicity of "autonomous" episodes and stories that are organized paratactically. It is the alternative "causality" governed by the principles of correspondence and association that structurally produces the trilogy's *virtual* dimension (its "meanwhile"), in which meanings that are not determined by a traditional causality can become actualized. Such a compositional strategy endows Kjærstad with an extreme degree of artistic freedom with regard to material, just as it invites the reader to participate in the task of linking the episodes in meaningful patterns: "Life stories arranged as a field, with holes and openings, will allow greater possibilities for the 'unlikely' and the contingent, the irrational and irregular, for the inconsistent, even the crazy, in life," says Kjærstad.[9] With regard to narrating the nation, the composition of autonomous episodes separated by large blank spaces thus makes it possible to bring all sorts of forgotten, repressed, or alternative stories back from obscurity.

The trilogy strikes a balance between ruthless criticism and unreserved praise of Norway. It can be argued that the first two books of the trilogy are, for the most part, critical of the Norwegian nation and merely present through their postmodern structure a fragmented image of a heterogeneous modern nation, whereas *The Discoverer* offers a more positive image of the nation and also formally functions as a sort of *Bildungsroman*—in regard to both protagonist and nation—that assembles the diversity into a coherent whole. However, one must be cautious about proclaiming the unifying potentials of *The Discoverer* just as it would be wrong to disregard the many positive images of Norway in *The Seducer* and *The Conqueror*.

Jonas's ambitious project, the TV serial *Thinking Big*, which portrays twenty-three famous Norwegians, is to be regarded as his attempt at "overcoming the Norwegian rock-face, that massive hurdle denoted by lack of imagination and pettiness and an unwillingness to think big" (*Se*, 9). This statement obviously testifies to the dimension of criticism in *The Seducer*, but at the same time both *The Seducer* and *The Conqueror* consist of quite a few chapters devoted to the depiction of the brilliance of each of the programs' protagonists (as well as Jonas's creative brilliance), be it Fridtjof Nansen, Trygve Lie, Liv Ullmann, Niels Henrik Abel, Sigrid Undset, or Gro Harlem Brundtland. These chapters actually function in the same way that the TV programs are said to function: they are a tribute to Norway, and at the same time they make the reader/spectator realize what the country is capable of. So on the one hand, Norway is criticized as a nation of spectators slumbering in their "stressless" chairs; but, on the other hand, the trilogy continually points out that the history of Norway has proven the country capable of producing unique individuals who have left deep impacts on the world.

In addition to criticizing Norway for its politics of isolationism, *The Seducer* and *The Conqueror* also offer tributes to Norway through the ekphrastic chapters on *Thinking Big*. Jonas's TV serial thus represents both a pedagogical and a performative dimension. Jonas seeks to teach his countrymen about their nation, but the teaching is oriented toward the hidden layers of both past and present. What characterizes Jonas's portrayals is his insistence on finding a *different angle* that will enable him to capture the essence of each of the protagonists. The will to discover an alternative angle results from Jonas's desire to challenge the ossified, official national image of the famous person, on the one hand, and to show that the exceptional talent of the protagonist is unthinkable without his or her experiences outside Norway, on the other.

In *The Discoverer*, the frame story is set on Sognefjorden aboard *Voyager*, the ship known in the first books as *Norge* and owned by Gabriel Sand. The name shift is highly indicative of the direction in which the trilogy as a whole wishes to take its reader (and its country): the ship never cut its moorings when it was called *Norge*, but as *Voyager* it sets sail and leaves the safe haven. Norway should cut its moorings, too, and become a voyager.

Aboard *Voyager* are, apart from Jonas, Kristin and her group of fellow cartographers. Their mission is to create a map of Sognefjorden in a geographical, historical, and mental sense and convert the map into an Internet portal. In the passages describing Sognefjorden and the group's cartographic efforts, *The Discoverer* may be said to offer an almost idyllic image of Norway. Not to be forgotten, though, are the many passages in the book condemning "Festung Norwegen" (Fortress Norway) and its anxiety toward anything unfamiliar or foreign. Harastølen, a former asylum for refugees, is thus called "a monument of our brutal attitude towards the non-Norwegian" (*Di,* 67). Confronted with this godforsaken place, Jonas begins a confused mix of eulogy and elegy in relation to Norway's recent development:

> And he came to the conclusion that it had gone too fast. This was the reason for our becoming so insensitive, so intolerant, so brutally rejecting, characterized by an almost panicking collective narrow-mindedness that merely allowed us to see what we wanted to see, and which, in a misunderstood

battle to secure goods for ourselves, made us lose sight of the demand for common human decency.

(*Di,* 67)

The mission aboard *Voyager* is meant as a counterweight (in the same way that *Thinking Big* is) to this image of Norway. It is meant to educate the Norwegian people and to show them what a fantastic country Norway is—but fantastic for reasons that are the direct opposite of those the majority of Norwegians (according to Kjærstad) believe it to be fantastic. In contrast to "Festung Norwegen," the mapping of Sognefjorden shows that every single locality in Norway is connected to every other locality, globally speaking. Instead of vertical roots isolating a place, we are shown how each place sends out local horizontal threads and how these in turn are touched by global horizontal threads. Hence, the territorial dimension of the trilogy is made up of what we could call singularities of space characterized by, on the one side, a considerable *specificity of locality,* and, on the other side, a *large degree of globality.* As is the case in *The Discoverer, The Conqueror* also underlines this by means of the frame story's spatial setting, in that the professor lives on Snarøya, near Oslo, where his office is situated in a tower connected to his house: "From my desk I can watch the planes landing and taking off at Fornebu Airport, on the south-western section of the runway, as well as the boats sailing up and down the coastline of the Nesodden peninsula. It's an inspiring vista: it makes me feel as though I am at a junction, that I am sitting in a control tower from which I have a complete overview" (*Co,* 59). Hence, every single place in the trilogy is to be regarded as a crossroads, not as a fortress.

The Internet portal in *The Discoverer* portrays modern Norway as an ever-changing nation subjected to influx from the outside. Furthermore, the Internet media emphasize the interactive and always incomplete dimension of nation building. Finally, the crew aboard *Voyager* bears witness to the nation's hybridity. Toward the end of the novel, *Voyager* leaves Sognefjorden in order to follow the planetary currents of the great oceans: "We saw how the old life boat turned westward, how they set the sails—mainsail, foresail, jib—so that *Voyager* suddenly, in this distance, appeared to be a timeless vessel. It was a beautiful vision. And a beautiful thought. A Norwegian, a half-American, a Korean, and an Indian. And all of them Norwegian. On its way toward Utvær. A Wide Left, I thought. A new Norway" (*Di,* 516). The ship thus represents a new glocalized Norway: "A perfect, mobile base" (*Di,* 62).

The glocalization of Norway is also staged in another manner. Throughout the trilogy, Norwegian place names are linked with foreign places as a result of shared qualities. At one point, Grorud is compared to Eastern Europe and the Soviet Union because of the grayness and general tristesse they both invoke in Jonas: "In his memory he was in Moscow, in reality he approached the Grorud shopping mall" (*Di*, 12). However, the grayness of Grorud-Moscow is counterweighted by the exceptionality of the Moscow Subway, which reminds Jonas of the City Hall in Oslo. Other connections are Snertingdal-Samarkand, Grorud-Provence, Hemingland-Africa, Bank of Norway-Karlsbad, Grorud-Jerevan, Alna-The Nile, The Rosenberg Forest-Transylvania, and Østfold-Jebel Musa. The motto behind these transversal communications is, "you can find any place in the world in Norway if you look hard enough" (*Co*, 338). The trilogy quite literally teems with both foreign and local place names. In this sense the trilogy contracts the international space at the same time that it expands the national space. Glocalization thus means that the local is a convolution of the global and the global is an evolution of the local.

Kaleidoscopic Form and Human Identity

There always remains an unrealized surplus of humanness.
—Mikhail M. Bakhtin, "Epic and Novel"

The trilogy comprises three biographical books about Jonas Wergeland. Every biography's attempt to portray the life of its protagonist entails the question of how the pieces of the protagonist's life fit together. This question constitutes an explicit leitmotif in *The Seducer* and an implicit one in *The Conqueror* and *The Discoverer*. However, the biographical narrative's orientation toward the question of how the pieces of a life fit together necessarily involves the question of how the novel's parts, the narrative building blocks, themselves fit together. Another way of asking how Jonas Wergeland's life coheres is thus to ask how each of the three books cohere. The question of (biographical) novelistic form is thus intrinsically related to the question of human identity.

Different metaphors throughout the trilogy indicate possible answers to the following questions: Do the pieces of a life cohere as a circle with its tangent? As a wheel with its spokes? As a dragon with its twisting patterns? Or as a fjord with its many ramifications of smaller inlets? Common to these metaphors is their rejection of the straight line and its connotations of one-dimensionality, chronological sequence, and temporal progression ($a \rightarrow b \rightarrow c \dots$). The metaphors propose spatial images of human identity and novelistic form instead of temporal ones. Jonas's life, therefore, cannot be regarded as an "effect" of time understood in mechanistic terms. In the trilogy, time is not represented as a continuum; rather, it boils down to monadic moments blasted out of the otherwise homogeneous continuum of history. These moments are not related to one another as beads on a string, but are to be considered as components in a multidimensional space.[10] Temporal progression is replaced by spatial universe, and project (space is here understood as something preordained that one inhabits) is replaced by process (space is here "born"; i.e., constituted, at the same time as the subject who interacts with it). Kjærstad says,

> The novel has a long tradition that seeks to organize a life through time, that is, time is the coherent principle in the sequence of stories. I ask: Is it possible to describe the same life through place, space, as the organizing factor? In this question there is also, implicitly, another point: By moving focus away from time towards space, causality is emphasized in a new way, and we see the possibility of alternative causes.[11]

Therefore, what at first seems like a fragmentation with regard to both novelistic form and human identity proves to be a new way of cohering, a new *connectivity* grounded in spatiality instead of temporality. Kjærstad evokes the concept of "field" taken from physics in order to describe this type of novel as a force field of stories. It is structured as a network of relations where the stories interact in all directions.

Another way to describe how each book of the trilogy coheres and how Jonas's life coheres is by using an analogy to the universe, with its stars and planets symbolizing the stories about Jonas. First, the stars and planets of the universe are precisely spread out in a *multidimensional space*. Second, each star and each planet is *interrelated* in different degrees as they all act upon one another through gravitational forces; despite varying distances between them, they are all *contiguous* to one another. Third, the field or system may be regarded as a totality, but it is a totality that is transforming: the universe is constantly *expanding;* old stars burn out and new ones arise; new planets are discovered. The universe analogy accords well with what Kjærstad says in the following:

> Nevertheless, I believe that a form taking shape as a field can be created by moving, so to speak, the building blocks of the text, in our case the stories, a bit away from each other, creating inbetween white spaces or openings, at the same time as time is abandoned as the coherent principle of the sequence. Thereby we have dissolved the traditional causality. The stories are now organized in a network [. . .] in which the elements create a multiplicity of connections and influence each other reciprocally.[12]

In the image of the universe, the planets and stars (the stories) are also positioned far from one another, but they are still exerting influence on one another. The universe of the trilogy is a field of forces that work on one another. Besides pointing to the instability of such a "system," the fact that the stories are positioned at a greater distance relative to one another means that the reader is asked to participate in the creation of the connections between the stories.

Finally, the notion of Jonas (and each of the books) as a universe emphasizes his structural *polycentrism*. It may be that *The Seducer* toys with the idea of *one* center in Jonas's life, but the point is that his life consists of many potential centers: "Important things happen all the time. And so this day too, like the others I have described, can be regarded as being the center of Jonas Wergeland's life. All days are, in a way, holy days" (*Co*, 367). The centers themselves are constantly on the move, as they are influenced each time a new story is added or each time someone attempts to put the stories together in new ways.

Human identity understood as a field, as a multidimensional space of interrelated stories, is a renunciation of man as a purely biological machine. Not that Kjærstad rejects the tremendous insights that the discovery of the human genome brings about (he is generally very much influenced and very fascinated by the latest discoveries in science), but it questions the sometimes too simplistic determinism inherent in DNA-inspired biological thinking. "Christ, Jonas, we're talking out-and-out reductionism. An attempt at utter simplification. Downright materialism. A one hundred percent mechanical view of life. A totally passé bit of Newtonian logic when you come down right to it" (*Se*, 418), says Axel Stranger on behalf of Kjærstad. According to Axel, DNA cannot explain Life; that is, life is understood not only as biology but also as the experiences that make a person into a human being and cause him or her to change. To Axel, the stories we hear or read are at least as important as the molecules that constitute us as biological creatures. The stories settle in us and make up an alternative DNA structure, but as we constantly absorb new stories and renegotiate the old ones, this specific type of DNA structure is constantly modified. Consequently, the question "What is a human being?" is replaced by a question of greater relevance: "What is a human being capable of becoming?" Kjærstad and Jonas both set out to discover what human potentialities are as yet not realized.

Supported by the structure of the novels, this idea of *becoming* (as opposed to *being*) is a governing principle in relation to the trilogy's attempt to describe the life of Jonas Wergeland. Jonas's actual experiences of migration, or rather nomadism, are constitutive elements in this conception of human identity as incessantly mutating. It is emphasized many times in the trilogy that Jonas is a nomad. Globally, he explores most of the world; nationally, he explores most of Norway; and locally, he explores most of the Grorud-Oslo area.

Two things are important. First, Jonas's many physical-geographical explorations are always assisted by his extraordinary imaginative powers. As a result, the explorative missions in the local area can have immense effects on Jonas: "of all Jonas Wergeland's more or less epic journeys, of all his, to varying extents, hazardous voyages of discovery, there was one which never palled, which stood as the most heroic, gruelling, groundbreaking and, not least, perilous, journey he had ever embarked upon: a journey to the interior of Østfold" (*Se*, 11). The transgressive elements in the journey to Østfold are not only conditioned by his well-developed sensibility and imagination, but also by the specific conception of space in the trilogy: "that every country contains the whole world. And that the whole world contains something of Norway" (*Se*, 18). The extreme consequence of this powerful combination of imagination (children, especially, are endowed with the capacity to occupy and live the whole of history and geography in the *here and now*) and spatial virtuality and interrelatedness is that Jonas can travel *on the spot*. According to Deleuze and Guattari, this is precisely what characterizes the true nomads: "*they do not move*. They are nomads by dint of not moving, not migrating, of holding a smooth space that they refuse to leave, that they leave only in order to conquer and die. Voyage in place: that is the name of all intensities, even if they also develop in extension. To think is to voyage."[13] What distinguishes the different types of travel, say Deleuze and Guattari, is neither the objective quality of the place, the measurable quantity of the movement, nor something purely spiritual. Rather, it is the mode of spatialization, the manner in which one occupies space. The nomad and the child are gifted with the power to smooth the spaces they occupy—that is, they are capable of stripping away the layers of conventions that obscure the semantic and experiential potentialities of a given space. Jonas's explorations, especially with Nefertiti and Bo Wang Lee, are obvious examples of a renegotiation of space in the trilogy. It is never a question of space being subsumed to time: space is not simply providing the milieu in which personal projects are realized through time. Instead, Jonas and his friends are open to the influences and potentialities of space: they invite space to work upon them, and therefore space and self are born at the same time in a chiastic exchange.

Second, Jonas's explorations are not always to be regarded as travels entailing transgressions of his personality. Recurrently, we are told that Jonas did not travel in order to escape home but, on the contrary, in order to come home: "Why did Jonas Wergeland travel? His travels had something to do with memory, with visiting places that were part of him but which he could not recall. Jonas Wergeland always set off on a journey with a suspicion that he was, in fact, going home" (*Co*, 82). So, Jonas does not travel in order to become another in the strict sense; instead, he travels in order to become what he already (virtually) is. The travels activate something already immanently present within him, a potential that has not yet been realized, as in a pencil's graphite that immanently possesses the potential to become a diamond. It is the same thing that happens when the famous Norwegians portrayed in *Thinking Big* travel: abroad they are subjected to the right pressure and are transformed into diamonds. Rather than transgressions, we can speak of expansions, like a universe that expands. The expansions catapult Jonas into new epistemological and emotional dimensions.

As has already been hinted at, it is not only the physical travels that expand Jonas. His sexual encounters with women are characterized as having a dimension other than the mere sexual. Instead of being a seducer in a traditional sense, Jonas is rather the one seduced when it comes to women. What happens during the erotic séance is that the unique talents (mathematical, musical, architectural, hunting, sailing, athletic, etc.) of the well-chosen women are transferred to Jonas: "So Jonas Wergeland's women did not just make love to him, they activated, they transformed the stories within him. A story that had been lying there for ages, like boring black graphite, suddenly stood revealed as a scintillating diamond" (*Co*, 393). This exceptional receptivity of his also shows in circumstances of a less pleasurable nature. The traumatic episode in which he witnesses the gang rape of Laila Mer Agurk (Laila More Cucumber) and the episode in which Jonas himself is raped by Gabriel Sand both produce crucial, positive changes in him. What Gabriel activates in Jonas through his atrocious action is a special intuitive talent that, among other things, enables Jonas to discern which women will take him into new dimensions and expand him. The same happens when he witnesses Margrete's trance in which she monotonously bangs her head against the wall. Instead of intervening straight away, Jonas observes her uncanny action and something happens inside him: he enters into a zone of contact with a new dimension. He is expanded.

The last thing I wish to mention regarding identity is its hybrid constitution in the trilogy. Jonas's family is clearly constructed in order to show the heterogeneity and hybridity that are potentially, as well as actually, present in Norway.[14] Jonas's name is loaded with connotations: the Biblical Jonas who "seduced" the people of Nineveh; the Norwegian platonic-romantic nationalist poet Henrik A. Wergeland, who became a symbol of the fight to celebrate the constitution on May 17, later to become the Norwegian National Day (which exemplifies Kjærstad's qualms about Norwegian nationalism, as May 17 is celebrated rather fanatically each year by many

Norwegians); and finally, his last name, Hansen, indicates that he is just an ordinary person, typical of the Social Democratic Norwegian welfare state of the 1950s and 1960s. As already mentioned, Rakel is inspired by Oriental love poetry and philosophy, and she becomes a truck driver for the Red Cross; in addition, her name points to Judaism. Daniel, Jonas's brother, represents not only Communism but also theology in that he becomes a priest; his name also refers to the Bible. The father is a Hansen, which is a very common name, but beneath the surface exists an exceptionally talented pianist whose Bach performances not only heal Jonas but also impress the Bach expert, Albert Schweitzer. The mother is a factory worker, but at the same time she is endowed with an extraordinary intelligence and wisdom. What is more, the parents practice the teachings of the *Kama Sutra*. Finally, Jonas's younger brother, "Buddha," has Down's syndrome and thus symbolizes the genetic deviation from the ordinary. What follows from this is that Jonas (and the Wergeland Hansen family in general) embodies the Norwegian mediocrity, but at the same time he possesses the performative ambivalence that grants him the potential to be unique. He achieves a balance between nationalist triviality and glocal eminence.

Epilegomena: Literary Studies and the Canon

This may well be, for comparative literary history, the next step in choosing its future tasks and justifications: to acknowledge the relativity of all systems within the perpetual motion of the world system, but also to highlight creatively particular past and/or present commonalities that at a given moment, within the present discourse of one or several cultures, light up and make sense together.

—Eva Kushner, *The Living Prism*

This book has dealt with four post–World War II authors using migration as its vantage point. I have argued that the twentieth century witnessed an increase in the number of migrant authors, especially after World War II. The rise of Nazi Germany in the 1930s resulted in waves of migrants, on the one hand those German Jews trying to escape racial persecution; on the other hand those Germans migrating outward as the borders of the Reich expanded. In 1945, the collapse of the Third Reich inverted the formerly outbound migration to an inbound movement as many thousands of Germans living in the newly conquered territories of the Third Reich, among them the young Günter Grass, were driven back across the old borders. The rise of Communism in Eastern Europe, in Czechoslovakia partly a postwar answer to the fascist oppression of the Nazis, was another cause of mass migrations and political exilations. One of its victims was Milan Kundera, initially a member of the Communist Party, who left his Czech homeland in 1975 after being publicly banned from libraries and bookshops, as well as from any future professional positions. Finally, not only does Salman Rushdie exemplify how decolonization accentuated the post–World War II epoch as an age of (voluntary) migration, but his writing also testifies to the drastic changes in the relationship between the former colonizer and the former colonized as the old dualisms of center/periphery and home/abroad were abandoned or renegotiated.

In terms of aesthetics and thematics, the accumulation of migrant authors has caused immense transformations in twentieth-century literary history. Because of their position *between* cultures, nations, and languages—discursive "forms" that used to function as unproblematical categorizations and signs of homogeneity—migrant authors have made significant contributions to both the formal innovative and historical descriptive aspects of literature. In this book we have seen how Grass, Kundera, Rushdie, and Kjærstad have enriched the history of the novel with memorable narrative voices and complex enunciatory constructions, be it as foreignness of voice or of vagabonding perspectives, which contribute to the in-between dynamics and processual aesthetics of the migration novel. Furthermore, in the novels of Grass and Rushdie, the impurity of language typical of migrant authors is present on the level of story as national languages and idioms are mixed; in Kundera and Kjærstad, on the other hand, language as heteroglossia is contemplated rather than practiced—that is, the dialogic nature of language is here present on the level of discourse. In terms of narrative form, especially *Dog Years, The Satanic Verses, The Book of Laughter and Forgetting,* and the Wergeland trilogy can be characterized as highly successful and demanding novels, first, because they challenge the way in which novels traditionally cohere and, second, because of their general formal inconclusiveness. With regard to thematics, the book has shown the authors' fascination with the archaeologies of personal, national, and cultural identity. The rewriting and revision of these identities are typically issues of great significance to migrants as a result of their uprooting and national and cultural doubleness.

As we have seen, the significant impact of migrant literature on literary history is not simply traceable as a shift in the balance between the number of migrant authors and nonmigrant authors within literary history. The impact of migrant authors also exerts itself on nonmigrant authors whose works are heavily influenced formally and thematically by the works of the former, as exemplified here by Jan Kjærstad. In addition, the world's globalizing forces contribute to the transformation of the works by nonmigrant authors in the direction of migration literature because the general tendencies in contemporary society seem to suggest that migration, mobility, and a greater interrelatedness between the global and the local have increasingly become humanity's fundamental condition. In this book, Kjærstad has been used with the precise purpose of illustrating this close relationship between globalization, migration, and literary history.

Grass, Kundera, and Rushdie are marked by the experiences of totalitarianism and persecution, whether it be Nazi, Communist, Islamic fundamentalism, or Indian sectarianism. However, despite the common denominator of totalitarianism, their artistic "temperaments" are different; this is partly due to their distinct experiences with totalitarianism, partly due to their specific contextual backgrounds and, finally, a consequence of their historical position. Cultural pessimism in the tradition of European master-thinkers such as Nietzsche, Spengler, and Heidegger characterizes the work of Kundera. To Kundera, history is stupidity incarnate and is a trap from which man cannot escape. His experience with Communism has made him aware of the permeable boundaries between the public and the private spheres, the former no longer capable of representing anything but standardization, surveillance, and imagology, the latter representing either an individual uniqueness being invaded by the public space or a postmodern compulsion to express its banalities in public. Although Kundera sees great potential in the new literatures from the Southern hemisphere, because of, among other things, their local specificity, formal experiments, and universal value, he nonetheless seems to believe that cultural standards are inevitably decreasing worldwide, mainly because Western capitalism erases cultural diversity and instigates the demise of traditional forms of high culture such as classical music and philosophy. Kundera's position clearly stems from his background, raised as he was in a family in which high culture, classical music in particular, played a significant role.

If Grass in comparison to Kundera seems slightly less concerned about the future of humanity and the novel, it may be because Nazism (and his personal involvement with Nazism) functions as a moral and cultural nadir that must be answered to. Personal guilt, then, becomes Grass's driving force in an artistic endeavor characterized by a paradoxical "rhythm" entailing, on the one hand, a constant (and almost masochistic) looking back into history's atrocities in order to keep the wound of European history open, and, on the other hand, a compulsory move forward and away from the haunting cruelties. "As long as stories keep coming, [. . .] no hell can take us in." That seems an appropriate motto for Grass's work, on the one side indicating an awareness and potential presence of hell; on the other side showing a belief in storytelling's capacity to hold hell at bay and rescue humanity.

Compared to Grass and Kundera, Rushdie seems to a far greater degree to be the offspring of contemporary globalization with its constant challenge to the former purities of nations and people. Although very similar in terms of narrative techniques, Grass and Rushdie differ in terms of "temperament." Rushdie's work is influenced by his experiences in Bombay as a multicultural, -linguistic, -ethnic, and -religious metropolis, and as a financial center symbolizing modern India as well. Grass's Danzig may be said to hold similar characteristics of impurity, but the guilt that keeps haunting Grass's novels is neither theme nor driving force in Rushdie. However, the starting point for Rushdie is, to a certain extent, also a coming to terms with the past, mainly the loss of Bombay and India. But as his novels clearly indicate, and as he has repeatedly stated, he considers the loss (of one country) and the subsequent gain (of another) as a fertile ground for an author to occupy. Not blind to "the sorrows of estrangement" and to the flip side of the increased permeability of borders under globalization (e.g., terrorism), he relishes the opportunities that perpetual movement, multiple rootings, and disorientation bring about. In opposition to Kundera, he is not so worried by the present state of things—for example, the demise of traditional forms of "high" culture or the role of English as a global language. Whereas Kundera detests the proliferation of the language of advertising within the spheres of everyday language, Rushdie's work thrives on the creative, poetic, and everyday aspects of the one-liners of advertising language, just as his books are influenced by the "low" culture of comics and B-movies.

Kjærstad is very similar to Rushdie in regard to his stance toward contemporary globalization. His trilogy is a tribute to the possibilities of renegotiating personal, national, and cultural identities brought about by the contraction of global space into local space and the expansion of local space into global space. In an impressive imaginative tour de force, Kjærstad "drags" Norway into a contact zone with the world, allowing him to disclose the impurities and ambivalences inherent in an otherwise isolationist nation and people. His project is both descriptive and prescriptive: he unearths hidden layers in the official image of the nation, but he also urges his fellow countrymen to abandon their isolationism and embrace the globalized world in which everything is connected to everything else. Kjærstad's trilogy is a eulogy to mankind and an attempt to unveil what he sees as unrealized potential in man.

*　*　*

Before ending this book I wish to touch upon a few questions concerning the role and method of comparative literature and literary studies in general. In 2006 the American Comparative Literature Association (ACLA) published *Comparative Literature in an Age of Globalization,* their 2004 report on the state of the discipline. In his contribution, David Damrosch discusses the relationship between what he calls hypercanon, countercanon, and shadow canon (a tripartition replacing the old two-tiered model of "major authors" and "minor authors"), and he urges us to "resist the hegemony of the hypercanon." Instead of writing yet another article that compares James Joyce and Marcel Proust, we should compare Joyce to Rabindranath Tagore, Clarice Lispector, and/or Higuchi Ichiyo, thereby drawing "new lines of comparison across the persisting divisions between the hypercanon and the countercanon of world literature."[1]

Reading Damrosch's essay made me ask myself: What is it exactly that I have been doing throughout this book? Günter Grass and Milan Kundera are certainly hypercanonical writers, and Salman Rushdie, initially a countercanonical writer, is now part of what Damrosch labels the "new, postcolonial hypercanon." However, could it not be argued that both Grass and Kundera were also countercanonical writers when they wrote *The Tin Drum, Dog Years, The Joke,* and *The Book of Laughter and Forgetting*? Grass's first novel shook the very foundations of the German literary canon and changed it forever; *Dog Years* has never been hypercanonized but remains, I would argue, a sort of countercanonical work within a hypercanonized author's *œuvre,* primarily as a result of its monstrous form (but maybe also because of the hypercanonical status of its "twin brother"). As with Grass's *The Tin Drum,* Kundera's first novel, *The Joke,* changed the literary landscape in Czechoslovakia, on the one hand because of its polyphonic form and stream of consciousness technique, on the other hand because of its critique of Marxist politics and its erasure of the Czech nation's folkloristic traditions. *The Book of Laughter and Forgetting,* like *Dog Years,* has never been hypercanonized (as, e.g., *The Unbearable Lightness of Being*) and thus remains a countercanonical work, probably due to its relentless "attack" on the novel's traditional markers of unity, such as character and action.

The examples of Grass, Kundera, and Rushdie point to a general tendency in the mechanisms of canonization: you start out being countercanonical before becoming hypercanonized. In a way, then, I have been doing what Damrosch advises us not to do; that is, I have chosen to compare three hypercanonical male writers, and in so doing I have merely consolidated their "market share by adding value from the postcanonical trends"[2] such as transnationalism and postcolonialism. On the other hand, Grass, Kundera, and Rushdie are, as I have argued, characterized by an ambiguous canonical status that positions them somewhere in between the hypercanon and the countercanon or, rather, in both at the same time. However, even if we were to admit their unequivocal hypercanonical status (which is, after all, not an unreasonable categorization), Damrosch actually acknowledges that hypercanonization is a "fact of life" and consequently recommends that we take advantage of this fact as a means to attract students into our classrooms. There is also good pedagogical reasoning in this, Damrosch continues, "because writers enter the hypercanon only when they really are exciting to read and talk about in a wide variety of contexts."[3] So instead of always asking, How can we resist the star system? a question that seems to me to be a sort of knee-jerk reaction (of political correctness) in these so-called postcanonical times, we also might want to ask, Do we want to resist it at all?

But where does Kjærstad fit into Damrosch's tripartition of hyper- counter-, and minor canonical writers? From a Scandinavian perspective, Kjærstad is hypercanonical with countercanonical traits (he is, for example, much more celebrated in Denmark than in his native Norway, partly as a result of his constant critique of Norwegian parochialism and isolationism, I believe), but from a global perspective he is rather countercanonical with the potential to become hypercanonical.[4] In other words, Kjærstad is my Ichiyo or Lispector. Consequently, and to my great relief, I seem to have acted as a well-behaved scholar in accordance with Damrosch's recommendations after all.

In fact, and let me make this clear, I do sympathize with Damrosch's prescriptions for comparatists in a globalized world, a world in which literary departments are still trying to come to terms with a literary world system that is no longer an exclusive club for male writers from the West, on the one hand, and in which authors are increasingly belonging to two or more nations on the other. Both these realities, the expansion of the canon and the extraterritoriality of the writers, simply challenge the way we have done things in the past. However, and this is the reason I was only partly joking, I am always suspicious when people try to lay down rules and tell other people what they should do and how they should do it.

This is why I like Richard Rorty's contribution to the ACLA report so much. Here, Rorty is advocating a laissez-faire attitude and warns against any kind of dogmatism:

> As I see it, both comparative literature and philosophy departments should be places in which students receive plenty of suggestions about what sorts of books they might like to read, and are then left free to follow their noses. Members of these departments should not worry about the nature of their discipline or about what makes it distinctive. [. . .] Nor should they speculate about whether to be a "true comparatist" one needs to know the literature of at least one non-European language as well as a few European ones. They should not fuss about what "a sound preparation" in their field consists in. They should just worry about finding intellectually curious students to admit to graduate study and about how to help such students satisfy their curiosity.[5]

Yes. Curiosity, together with intuition, is indeed the fundamental attribute required of a literary scholar or a student of literature. Let us encourage any kind of conjunction our students come up with, whether purely hypercanonical, purely countercanonical, purely minor canonical, or any given mixture between them, as long as the creatively highlighted commonalities "light up and make sense together" (Kushner), as long as we sense that curiosity and intuition are driving forces, and, finally, as long as we make sure that our students are aware of the mechanisms of canonization and of the globalization of the canon.

This flexibility in terms of disciplinary boundaries and method also means that I am a strong advocate of the mutual dependence between comparative literature departments and national literature departments. We do things differently, but we also do many things in similar ways, at least when we are doing good research. We just do these things with different degrees of commitment, I think. Those working in national literatures may be more vertically focused—that is, oriented toward the "trunks" of national literary history, national linguistics, national culture, and national history in general, whereas the comparatist may be more horizontally focused—that is, oriented toward inter- or transnational continuities and discontinuities in terms of thematics, aesthetics, and poetics. According to Moretti, we have trees *and* waves, national literatures *and* world literature: "the universe is the same, the literatures are the same, we just look at them from a different viewpoint; and you become a comparatist for a very simple reason: *because you are convinced that that viewpoint is better.*"[6] While I believe in the complementarity of the two viewpoints, I would like to stress, though, that it seems to me that comparative literature is better geared to analyze, reflect upon, and theorize about literature in a world of increased migration and mobility. In a way, the whole foundation of national literature departments—that is, "the national"—is currently undergoing profound transformations. However, two points are important in this regard: first, "the national" lives on and will continue to do so; second, the national literature departments are already catching up with the new order of immanent national interculturalism.

So, nothing good ever comes out of trying to define the essence of an academic discipline, because they simply do not possess such essences, Rorty claims. Referring to Daniel Dennett, Rorty instead argues that comparative literature and other academic disciplines are like selves in that they are best thought of as "centers of narrative gravity." That is, they are constantly renegotiating their self-image through a rewriting of their own histories, and what used to be central sooner or later moves to the periphery, and vice versa. In light of this, let the following statement by Rorty conclude this book and serve as motto for the future spirit of literary studies: "We should rejoice in the mutability and fashion-proneness of academic disciplines, for the only alternative is decadent scholasticism."[7]

Notes

Prolegomena

1. See Walkowitz, "The Location of Literature," p. 533.
2. Adelson, *The Turkish Turn in Contemporary German Literature*, p. 23.
3. See Madsen, "World Literature and World Thoughts," p. 58. I am drawing on Madsen's thoughts on Auerbach further down the text as well.
4. Lukács, *Entwicklungsgeschichte des modernen Dramas*, p. 10, 12. Translation is mine.
5. Lukács, "Zur Theorie der Literaturgeschichte," p. 32. Translation is mine.
6. Moretti, "The Soul and the Harpy," p. 11.
7. Lukács, *The Theory of the Novel*, p. 72–73.
8. Moretti, *Modern Epic*, p. 6.
9. Moretti, "The Soul and the Harpy," p. 9.
10. Steiner, *Extraterritorial*, p. 11.
11. Moretti, *Modern Epic*, p. 6.
12. Moretti, *Graphs, Maps, Trees*, p. 57.
13. Ibid., p. 64.
14. Seyhan, *Writing Outside the Nation*, p. 9.
15. Said, *Culture and Imperialism*, p. 337.
16. See Rushdie, "Günter Grass," p. 277.
17. See Said, "Reflexions on Exile," p. 174.
18. Prendergast, "The World Republic of Letters," p. 23.
19. Levin, "Literature and Exile," p. 62.
20. Brandes, *The Emigrant Literature*, p. vii.
21. Levin, "Literature and Exile," p. 62.
22. Auerbach, "Philology and *Weltliteratur*," p. 17.
23. Said, *Culture and Imperialism*, p. 386.
24. Bhabha, *The Location of Culture*, p. 5.
25. Ibid., p. 12.
26. Damrosch, *What is World Literature?* p. 283. On the concept of *Weltliteratur*, see also Prendergast (ed.), *Debating World Literature;* Moretti, "Conjectures on World Literature" and *Graphs, Maps, Trees;* and Thomsen's forthcoming *Mapping World Literature: International Canonization and Transnational Literatures.*
27. Cooppan, "World Literature and Global Theory," p. 33. The shaping force of the local in world literature and migration literature is precisely what makes

them differ from what we could term "global literature," that is, a literature constructed on McDonald's restaurants, airport transit halls, Starbuck cafés, and Hilton hotels.

28. See Said, *Culture and Imperialism*, p. 82.
29. Chambers, *Migrancy, Culture, Identity*, p. 5.
30. Sommer, *Fictions of Migration*, p. 6. Translation is mine.
31. Walkowitz, "The Location of Literature," p 534.
32. Bauman, *Globalization*, p. 1–2, my italics.
33. See Deleuze and Guattari, "Rhizome," p. 25.
34. Lukács, *The Theory of the Novel*, p. 121.
35. Ibid., p. 78.
36. Ibid., p. 39, 60.
37. Bergson, *Creative Evolution*, p. 11.
38. Lukács, *The Theory of the Novel*, p. 121.
39. Ibid., p. 124.
40. Ibid., p. 122.
41. Deleuze, *Proust and Signs*, p. 163.
42. Lukács, *The Theory of the Novel*, p. 76.
43. Moretti, *Modern Epic*, p. 214.
44. Bergson, *Creative Evolution*, p. 318–319.
45. See Deleuze, "Bergson's Conception of Difference," p. 40.
46. Bergson, *Creative Evolution*, p. 51.
47. Bergson, *Time and Free Will*, p. 134.
48. Lukács, *The Theory of the Novel*, p. 60.
49. Deleuze, *Logic of Sense*, p. 174.
50. Deleuze and Guattari, "Rhizome," p. 25.
51. Ibid., p. 21.

Chapter 1

1. Grass, "Speech to a Young Voter Who Feels Tempted to Vote for the N.P.D.," p. 55–56.
2. Michael Hollington and Hanspeter Brode both recognize the connection between Grass's experience of proper migration, his unconventional educational trajectory, and his intellectual and artistic flexibility and mobility. Hollington: "The most important thing about this stage of Grass's development seems to be that he did not resume the normal middle-class educational progression from *Abitur* to university; instead, he became nomadic, working first as a farmhand in the Rhineland, then in a potash mine near Hildesheim, then as a stonemason's apprentice in Düsseldorf," *Grass. The Writer in a Pluralist Society*, p. 7. Brode: "In Grass is thus united an absence of inherited constraints of thought with intellectual mobility, both a result of the petty bourgeois start conditions," *Grass*, p. 12. This and subsequent translations of Brode are mine.
3. Grass, "Shame and Disgrace," p. 32, 34. The English translation overlooks the adjective "unveränderlich" (irrevocable), which Grass uses in relation to the

reasons for the war. The feeling of irrevocability is important, as it explains Grass's rather pragmatic view of his own uprooting and loss of hometown.

4. Grass, "Short Speech by a Rootless Cosmopolitan," p. 7.
5. Grass, "Speech to a Young Voter," p. 58.
6. Rushdie, "Günter Grass," p. 279.
7. Adorno, *Minima moralia,* p. 87.
8. Rushdie, "Günter Grass," p. 280.
9. Adorno, "Cultural Criticism and Society," p. 34. In fact, Adorno reasserts, reflects upon, and modifies his initial statement in later texts such as "Engagement," *Negative Dialectics,* "Die Kunst und die Künste" and "Zur Dialektik von Heiterkeit."
10. Grass, "Writing after Auschwitz," p. 99.
11. Ibid., p. 104–105.
12. Ibid., p. 102.
13. Grass, "*The Tin Drum* in Retrospect or The Author as Dubious Witness," p. 26.
14. Ibid., p. 27.
15. Said, "Reflections on Exile," p. 173.
16. Hollington, *Günter Grass,* p. 45.
17. Said, "Reflections on Exile," p. 182.
18. Ibid., p. 183.
19. Alter, *Rogue's Progress. Studies in the Picaresque Novel,* p. 84.
20. Reddick, The 'Danzig Trilogy' of Günter Grass, p. 58.
21. Ibid., p. 65.
22. Ibid., p. 218.
23. Hollington, *Günter Grass,* p. 78–79.
24. Reddick, The 'Danzig Trilogy' of Günter Grass, p. 203.
25. Bhabha, *The Location of Culture,* p. 218.
26. Brode, *Günter Grass,* p. 59, 62.
27. Moretti, *The Way of the World,* p. 35.
28. Brode, *Günter Grass,* p. 62.
29. Hollington, *Günter Grass,* p. 2, 3.
30. Ibid., p. 54.
31. Cunliffe, "Aspects of the Absurd in Günter Grass," p. 95.
32. Reddick, The 'Danzig Trilogy' of Günter Grass, p. 16.
33. Neuhaus, *Günter Grass,* p. 20. This and subsequent translations of Neuhaus are mine.
34. Croft, "Günter Grass' *Katz und Maus,*" p. 121.
35. Brode, *Günter Grass,* p. 22f.
36. Steiner, "The Hollow Miracle," p. 100.
37. Bromley, *Narratives For a New Belonging,* p. 100.
38. Hollington, *Günter Grass,* p. 5.
39. Ibid., p. 36.
40. Ibid., p. 68.
41. Grass, *Fünf Jahrzehnte,* p. 15. Translation is mine.

42. Bohrer, "Erinnerungslosigkeit," p. 18–19. This and subsequent translations of Bohrer are mine.
43. Ibid., p. 21.
44. Ibid., p. 11–12.
45. Benjamin, "On the Concept of History," p. 396.
46. Bromley, *Narratives For a New Belonging*, p. 7.
47. Benjamin, "On the Concept of History," p. 395.
48. Bromley, *Narratives For a New Belonging*, p. 97.
49. Kundera, *The Art of the Novel*, p. 11–12.
50. Lukács, *The Theory of the Novel*, p. 33.
51. Grass, *Dokumente zur politische Wirkung*, p. 225. My translation. Michael Hollington also remarks: "The concept of history as 'absurd process' has a good deal in common with Sartre's 'contingency,' and indeed the problems of the individual characters in *Dog Years* in coming to terms with their place in history are expressed in existentialist terms. Grass calls the protagonists of Döblin's novels 'heroes against absurdity;' the characters of *Dog Years* search for an 'authentic' identity in the midst of a radically diseased historical process," *Günter Grass*, p. 75.
52. Steiner, "The Nerve of Günter Grass," p. 34.
53. Ibid., p. 34–35.
54. Hans Ulrich Gumbrecht: "'production of presence' points to all kinds of events and processes in which the impact that 'present' objects have on human bodies is being initiated or intensified," *Production of Presence: What Meaning Cannot Convey*, p. xiii. Gumbrecht also speaks of the presence effect as a violence that forces itself upon us and characterizes it as "experiencing the things of the world in their preconceptual thingness," p. 118.
55. The quote is taken from George Steiner, "The Nerve of Günter Grass," p. 35, in which Steiner comments on his 1959 essay.
56. Steiner, "The Nerve of Günter Grass," p. 33.
57. Reddick, *The 'Danzig Trilogy' of Günter Grass*, p. 82–83.
58. Benjamin, "The Storyteller," p. 146.
59. Adorno, "The Position of the Narrator in the Contemporary Novel," p. 30–31.
60. Ibid., p. 30.
61. Kundera, *The Art of the Novel*, p. 7.
62. Brooks, "The Storyteller," p. 76. It must be mentioned, though, that Brooks's purpose actually is to explore the survival of the oral tradition in the literary culture of the nineteenth century: "I find it significant that the work of Balzac, the first novelist to be fully aware of the new conditions of an industrializing and commodified literature, very often stages situations of oral communication where the exchange and transmission of narrative is at issue," p. 78–79.
63. Neuhaus, *Günter Grass*, p. 6, 11.
64. Miles, *Günter Grass*, p. 140.
65. Deleuze, "The Simulacrum and Ancient Philosophy," p. 258.
66. Steiner, "The Nerve of Günter Grass," p. 33.
67. Freud, *Civilization and its Discontents*, p. 81.

68. Adorno, *Aesthetic Theory*, p. 21.
69. Rushdie, "Günter Grass," p. 280.
70. Reddick: "Interestingly enough, Grass has said that he is more attached to *Dog Years* than to any of his other prose works—but for the very reason that it did not quite come off ('es ist oft misslungen'), and because it is the 'least rounded' ('das unfertigste') of his books," *The 'Danzig Trilogy' of Günter Grass*, p. 269.
71. Adorno, "The Position of the Narrator," p. 33–35, my italics.

Chapter 2

1. Kundera, "La francophobie, ça existe," p. 249. This and subsequent translations of this text are mine.
2. I thank Peter Bugge for directing my attention to this connection between narrative voice, emigration, and stylization of one's public image. See Bugge, "Clementis's Hat; or, Is Kundera a Palimpsest?"
3. As to Kundera's biography, I am indebted to Jan Čulík, http://www2.arts.gla. ac.uk/Slavonic/Kundera.htm
4. "In Defense of Intimacy," Milan Kundera interviewed by Philip Roth, p. 49ff.
5. Jungmann, "Kunderian Paradoxes," p. 121.
6. Kundera, "La francophobie, ça existe," p. 251.
7. Carlisle, "A Talk With Milan Kundera," p. 72. Kundera's view on exile as liberating is repeated by Joseph Brodsky in his "The Condition We Call Exile": "The truth of the matter is that from a tyranny one can be exiled only to a democracy. For good old exile ain't what it used to be. It isn't leaving civilized Rome for savage Sarmatia anymore [. . .]. No, as a rule what takes place is a transition from a political and economic backwater to an industrially advanced society with the latest word on individual liberty on its lips. And it must be added that perhaps taking this route is for an exiled writer, in many ways, like going home—because he gets closer to the seat of the ideals which inspired him all along," pp. 23–24.
8. "The Most Original Book of the Season," Milan Kundera interviewed by Philip Roth, p. 7.
9. Hegel, *Aesthetics*, vol. 2, p. 1092.
10. Ibid.
11. See Ricard, *Agnès's Final Afternoon*, p. 10. I am in general indebted to Ricard's book which is very much concerned with the theme of exile in Kundera.
12. Hegel, *Aesthetics*, vol. 1, p. 593.
13. Lukács, *The Theory of the Novel*, p. 60.
14. Forster, *Aspects of the Novel*, p. 148–149.
15. Ricard, *Agnès's Final Afternoon*, p. 196.
16. Freud, *Civilization and Its Discontents*, p. 77.
17. Ricard, *Agnès's Final Afternoon*, p. 73–74.
18. Ibid., p. 198.

19. As Fellini himself has stated in *Fellini on Fellini:* "in the midst of it all, there is always—and especially in the films with Giulietta—a little creature who wants to give love and who lives for love," p. 52.

20. The famous cinematographic example is of course Alfred Hitchcock's *Vertigo* (1958). At the end of the movie, Madeleine/Judy (Kim Novak) is uncannily seduced by the bell tower of the San Juan Bautista Mission from which she ultimately jumps.

21. Ricard, *Agnès's Final Afternoon,* p. 199.

22. Ibid., p. 200–201.

23. Kundera's example with Schoenberg bears certain similarities to Grass's refusal of nostalgia as a legitimate feeling in his depictions of the past brutalities of the Danzig area (e.g., in the case of Stutthof).

24. One can, of course, always find examples of the opposite in the Occidental tradition, and early ones, too. In Sophocles's *Oedipus at Colonus* (406/401 BC), Oedipus, at the end of his life and after many years of wandering, refuses to accept the invitation to return to Thebes to be buried in his native soil, preferring instead to be buried at Colonus, just outside of Athens. Another example is Shakespeare's *Coriolanus* (1605–10) in which the protagonist at one point, after being banished by his native city of Rome, exclaims: "I banish you! [. . .] There is a world elsewhere!" *Coriolanus,* III, 3. Coriolanus's belief in the existence of a world elsewhere corresponds, as we shall see in what follows, to the experiences of Irena and Josef, thereby revealing an early example of an alternative belonging.

25. Compare Kundera's anti-idealist "carve out a little place for yourself in a foreign world" with Hegel's idealist "carve out of it a heaven upon earth."

26. In *The Curtain* Kundera remarks, "man is separated from the past (even from the past only a few seconds old) by two forces that go instantly to work and cooperate: the force of forgetting (which erases) and the force of memory (which transforms)," p. 148.

27. The Kunderian melancholy makes one think of another Central European migrant author, namely W. G. Sebald and his *The Emigrants* (1992) and *Austerlitz* (2001), where melancholy and memory play important roles. However, it is not only the melancholic mood that is shared by Sebald and Kundera. Another common trait is the structure of their novels which combines heterogeneous discourses such as (pseudo) autobiographical passages, digressions on architecture and music, civilization critique, and excursions of a historical-historiographical character.

28. Bhabha, *The Location of Culture,* p. 141.

29. Kundera, "Speech made at the Fourth Congress," p. 168–169.

30. Renan, "What is a nation?" p. 19.

31. Kundera, "Speech made at the Fourth Congress," p. 172–173.

32. Appiah, "Cosmopolitan Patriots," p. 91–92. It is a similar thought that Cheah promotes in "The Cosmopolitical—Today," although he uses the concept of nationalism in the way Appiah uses patriotism, when he says: "In the initial moment of its historical emergence, nationalism is a *popular* movement distinct from the state it seeks to transform in its own image. Thus, before the nation

finds its state, before the tightening of the hyphen between nation and state that official nationalism consummates, the ideals of cosmopolitanism and European nationalism in its early stirrings are almost indistinguishable," p. 25.

33. Kundera, "Speech made at the Fourth Congress," p. 174–175.

34. Ibid., p. 176.

35. Ibid., p. 176. In *The Curtain* Kundera recalls the days after the invasion and discloses that he found it very difficult under such circumstances to relate to the Czech Revivalists' patriotism and their desire to create a Czech nation: "Separated as I was from that period by only three or four generations, I was surprised by my inability to put myself in my ancestor's skin, to re-create in imagination the concrete situation they had experienced. [. . .] I wasn't even sure that, a century earlier, I would have chosen to be Czech," pp. 156–57. Kundera's statement may seem rather strange if we take into account his enthusiasm in his 1967 speech for the Revivalist idea of a Czech nation. The statement may therefore be read as an example of Kundera's manipulation with his past position toward the Communist regime, which was probably less clarified at the time than he seems to want to admit.

36. Ibid., "Un occident kidnappé—ou la tragédie de l'Europe Centrale," p. 20. This and subsequent translations of this text are mine.

37. Ibid., p. 15.

38. In Grass's *The Call of the Toad* (1992), Alexander and Alexandra establish a company whose primary purpose is to make it possible for emigrants to be buried in their native soil. The company turns out to be a massive success as a result of the migrants' overwhelming and Odyssean desire for homecoming. However, the novel ends with the death of the two protagonists in a car accident in Italy where they are subsequently buried, far from their native soil. And as the narrator laconically states at the end of the novel, "They are lying well there. There let them lie," p. 248. In Grass, too, human actions are indeed alienated from their initial intentions, and like Kundera, he problematizes the idea of our natural belonging to our place of birth.

39. Forster, *Aspects of the Novel*, p. 40.

40. Kundera, *Immortality*, p. 266.

41. Fielding, *Tom Jones*, III, 1, p. 77.

42. Kundera's categorization may of course be contested. To mention just two very different examples, think of Thackeray's *Vanity Fair* (1847–48) and Melville's *Mardi* (1849).

43. Kezich, *Il dolce cinema*, p. 25. Translation is mine.

44. Chvatík, *Le monde romanesque de Milan Kundera*, p. 23. Translation is mine.

45. As is clear from the quotation, "sense" and "distance" are somewhat misleadingly used to translate the French words "compréhension" (understanding) and "immensité" (immensity).

46. Forster, *Aspects of the Novel*, p. 41.

47. Bakhtin, *Problems of Dostoevsky's Poetics*, p. 68.

48. Ibid., p. 63.

49. Barthes, "From Work to Text," p. 161.

50. In "The Death of the Author," Barthes thus states: "The Author, when believed in, is always conceived of as the past of his own book: book and author stand automatically on a single line divided into a *before* and an *after*. The Author is thought to *nourish* the book, which is to say that he exists before it, thinks, suffers, lives for it, is in the same relation of antecedence to his work as a father to his child. In complete contrast, the modern scriptor is born simultaneously with the text, is in no way equipped with a being preceding or exceeding the writing, is not the subject with the book as predicate; there is no other time than that of the enunciation and every text is eternally written *here and now*," p. 145.
51. Burke, *The Death and Return of the Author,* p. 126.
52. Ibid., p. 140.
53. Ibid., p. 184.
54. Ibid., p. 190–191.
55. Pichova, "The Narrator in Milan Kundera's *The Unbearable Lightness of Being,*" p. 217.
56. Bugge, "Clementis's Hat; or, Is Kundera a Palimpsest?" p. 2.
57. Ibid., p. 8.
58. See Burke, *The Death and Return of the Author,* p. 109.
59. Bugge, "Clementis's Hat; or, Is Kundera a Palimpsest?" p. 8.
60. Deleuze and Guattari, "Rhizome," p. 20.

Chapter 3

1. In what follows on Rushdie's biography I am indebted to Ian Hamilton's "The First Life of Salman Rushdie."
2. Hamilton, "The First Life of Salman Rushdie," p. 93.
3. Haffenden, "Salman Rushdie," p. 32–33.
4. Hamilton, "The First Life of Salman Rushdie," p. 96.
5. Ian Hamilton's article deals with Rushdie's life before the fatwa and ends here. There is no corresponding article on Rushdie's life after the fatwa. Here one has to look through the miscellaneous interviews with Rushdie since 1989 and "Messages From the Plague Years," the second part of *Step Across This Line,* which comprises letters, papers, and articles written by Rushdie in the years after the fatwa.
6. Lukács, *The Theory of the Novel,* p. 33–34.
7. "Encyclopedia" is formed by the Greek words *enkyklios paideia,* which means "circular instruction." Encyclopedic literature is here understood as a genre that attempts to enclose or encircle all knowledge. The genre is discussed in Edward Mendelson's two 1976 articles, "*Gravity's* Encyclopedia" and "Encyclopedic Narrative: From Dante to Pynchon." However, Northrop Frye had already spoken about an encyclopedic form in literary history in the four lectures he gave at Princeton in 1954 (the lectures that form the foundations of *Anatomy of Criticism* published in 1957), and in Franco Moretti's *Modern Epic* (1992/1996) the encyclopedic is also mentioned as a constitutive element.

8. Dutheil, *Origin and Originality in Rushdie's Fiction*, p. 2–3.

9. The theme of the polyglot and performative character of genealogy also applies to Rushdie himself: "it is perhaps one of the more pleasant freedoms of the literary migrant to be able to choose his parents. My own—selected half consciously, half not—include Gogol, Cervantes, Kafka, Melville, Machado de Assis; a polyglot family tree, against which I measure myself, and to which I would be honoured to belong," *Imaginary Homelands*, p. 20. And in the interview with John Haffenden, "Salman Rushdie," nationality as a defining coordinate is actually rejected: "I don't define myself by nationality—my passport doesn't tell me who I am. I define myself by friends, political affinity, groupings I feel at home in . . . and of course writing. I enjoy having access to three different countries, and I don't see that I need to choose," p. 56.

10. In "Encyclopedic Narrative: From Dante to Pynchon," Edward Mendelson argues that the synecdoche is an essential device in encyclopedic narratives: "Encyclopedic narratives all attempt to render the full range of knowledge and beliefs of a national culture [. . .]. Because they are products of an era in which the world's knowledge is vastly greater than any one person can encompass, they necessarily make extensive use of synecdoche," p. 1269.

11. Deleuze and Guattari, *What Is Philosophy?* p. 169.

12. See Pearson, *Germinal Life*, p. 94.

13. Naipaul, *The Enigma of Arrival*, p. 174.

14. Reder (ed.), *Conversations with Salman Rushdie*, p. ix. Reder quotes an interview from *The New York Times Book Review*, November 13, 1983, made by Michael Kaufmann, "Author From 3 Countries."

15. Compare the concept of "deserter" with Kundera's earlier reflections. In addition, there are obvious parallels between Saladin and Walter Matern's identity of masks in *Dog Years*.

16. Kundera, *The Art of the Novel*, p. 43.

17. Goonetilleke, *Salman Rushdie*, p. 82.

18. *Ibid.*, p. 90–91.

19. Bhabha, *The Location of Culture*, p. 224, 228.

20. Deleuze and Parnet, *Dialogues*, p. 34.

21. Deleuze and Guattari, *Kafka. Towards a Minor Literature*, p. 27.

22. See Deleuze and Parnet, *Dialogues*, p. 58.

23. Dutheil, *Origin and Originality in Rushdie's Fiction*, p. xxii.

24. In "From Work to Text" Roland Barthes says about the reader of the Text: "what he perceives is multiple, irreducible, coming from a disconnected, heterogeneous variety of substances and perspectives: lights, colours, vegetation, heat, air, slender explosions of noises, scant cries of birds, children's voices from over on the other side, passages, gestures, clothes of inhabitants near or far away. All these incidents are half identifiable: they come from codes which are known but their combination is unique, founds the stroll in a difference repeatable only as difference," p. 159.

25. Gumbrecht, *Production of Presence*, p. 70.

26. Durix, "Salman Rushdie: Interview," p. 10.
27. See Haffenden, "Salman Rushdie," p. 37.
28. Cohen, "Travelling Genres," p. 481. The following is inspired by Cohen's arguments.
29. Ibid., p. 481.
30. Bhabha, *The Location of Culture*, p. 140.
31. Both Anderson and Bhabha draw on Benjamin's "The Storyteller" and "On the Concept of History." Anderson stresses Benjamin's idea of the traditional storyteller and his idea of homogeneous, empty time in which simultaneity is "transverse, cross-time, marked not by prefiguring and fulfilment, but by temporal coincidence, and measured by clock and calendar," *Imagined Communities*, p. 24. Bhabha, on the other hand, focuses on Benjamin's idea of "now-time," that is, the simultaneity of past and future in an instantaneous present (the blasting of a monadic moment from the homogeneous continuum of history that renews the past instead of merely recalling it, thereby innovating and interrupting the present), and his idea of the modern storyteller who is doomed to manoeuvre in-between incommensurabilities instead of working with organic and well-balanced wholes: "Here, as the pedagogies of life and will contest the perplexed histories of the living people, their cultures of survival and resistance, Benjamin introduces a non-synchronous, incommensurable gap in the midst of storytelling," *The Location of Culture*, p. 161. Another way to put it: Anderson underlines the centripetal forces, whereas Bhabha underlines the centrifugal forces of narratives of the nation.
32. Homi K. Bhabha, *The Location of Culture*, p. 145, 147.
33. Ibid., p. 149.
34. Ibid., p. 167.
35. Ibid.
36. Ibid., p. 168.
37. Batty, "The Art of Suspense," p. 56.
38. See Parameswaran, *The Perforated Sheet*, p. 8.
39. Durix, "Salman Rushdie: Interview," p. 13.
40. This is also what Lukács means when he speaks of the novelistic form's lack of "a true-born organic relationship": "The consequence of this, from the compositional point of view, is that, although the characters and their actions possess the infinity of authentic epic literature, their structure is essentially different from that of the epic. The structural difference in which this fundamentally conceptual pseudo-organic nature of the material of the novel finds expression is the difference between something that is homogeneously organic and stable and something that is heterogeneously contingent and discrete. Because of this contingent nature, the relatively independent parts are more independent, more self-contained than those of the epic and must therefore, if they are not to destroy the whole, be inserted into it by means which transcend their mere presence. In contrast to the epic, they must have a strict compositional and architectural significance," *The Theory of the Novel*, p. 76. What Lukács says, among other things, is that the composition of a novel no longer shapes itself

naturally according to an existing material as in the epic. On the contrary, composition has now become the designing principle itself, the task of which it is to master an unmanageable chaotic material, cognizant of the fact that it will always remain a contingent frame or a convention.

41. In Rushdie's own words: "*The Satanic Verses* celebrates hybridity, impurity, intermingling, the transformation that comes of new and unexpected combinations of human beings, cultures, ideas, politics, movies, songs. It rejoices in mongrelization and fears the absolutism of the Pure. *Mélange,* hotchpotch, a bit of this and a bit of that is *how newness enters the world.* It is the great possibility that mass migration gives the world, and I have tried to embrace it. *The Satanic Verses* is for change-by-fusion, change-by-conjoining. It is a love-song to our mongrel selves." *Imaginary Homelands,* p. 394.

42. See Kundera, *Testaments Betrayed,* p. 21.

43. Ibid., p. 22.

44. Ball, "An Interview with Salman Rushdie," p. 102.

45. Ibid., my italics.

46. Appadurai, *Modernity at Large,* p. 3.

47. Rombes, "*The Satanic Verses* as a Cinematic Narrative," p. 49.

48. Ibid., p. 50–51.

49. Appadurai, *Modernity at Large,* p. 7.

Chapter 4

1. Kongslien, "Migrant or Multicultural Literature in the Nordic Countries," p. 34–35.

2. Ibid., p. 43.

3. At the time this book was being written, only the two first volumes of the trilogy had been translated into English. Quotations from *Oppdageren* in the present study are translated by me, and I will henceforth be referring to it as *The Discoverer* (Di).

4. Zola, *Germinal,* p. 1.

5. See Kyndrup's "Udenfor, indeni. Et passageværk," p. 166, from which the following is inspired.

6. In *Menneskets nett* Kjærstad remarks: "Seemingly autobiographical passages are always a dubious source to biographical truth," p. 26.

7. Kyndrup, "Udenfor, indeni. Et passageværk," p. 168. Translation is mine.

8. Bhabha, *Location of Culture,* p. 8.

9. Kjærstad, *Menneskets felt,* p. 192. This and subsequent translations of this book are mine.

10. In "Den demiurgiske romanhelt" Frederik Tygstrup says: "In *The Seducer* the temporal progression is dissolved and frozen in an achronological sequence consisting of flakes of time whose interrelationships are more important than the progression of time," p. 26. Translation is mine.

11. Kjærstad, *Menneskets felt,* p. 190.

12. Ibid., p. 191.
13. Deleuze and Guattari, *A Thousand Plateaus,* p. 482. Deleuze and Guattari actually make an important distinction between the nomad and the migrant. However, they understand the migrant as someone whose itinerary is temporary and delineates a movement from two fixed points of departure and arrival, respectively. This is not the way migration has been understood throughout this book. Instead, migration has been used as a concept capable of embracing both the migrant and the nomad as Deleuze and Guattari understand them—that is, as both a temporary movement (with fixed points of arrival and departure) and as a perpetual movement (whose point of departure and point of arrival are subject to constant mutations, just a the itinerary itself changes its direction all the time). In regard to the last sentence of the quotation, "To think is to voyage," it is worth remembering the passages in *The Discoverer* devoted to Jonas's extraordinary capacity to handle several disparate lines of thought simultaneously and to discover unexpected correspondences between them. Jonas realizes that he achieves the best results when skipping, which can be precisely regarded as an intensive form of travel on the spot.
14. See Riis , "Fra postkolonialisme til postnationalisme," p. 190–191.

Epilegomena

1. David Damrosch, "World Literature in a Postcanonical, Hypercanonical Age," pp. 50, 53. Hypercanonical writers are the authors formerly categorized as major authors who have survived and maybe even gained from globalization's expansion or remodeling of the Western canon into a world canon (e.g., William Wordsworth); the shadow canon is populated by the former minor authors who have not survived this remodeling (e.g., William Hazlitt); finally, the countercanon is composed of the subaltern and "contestatory" writers in "minor" languages or in "minor" literatures within "major" languages (e.g., Felicia Hemans).
2. Ibid., p. 45.
3. Ibid., p. 50.
4. Arcadia Books has contributed to the potential hypercanonization of Kjærstad by paratextual means, such as a glowing praise from Paul Auster on the cover of *The Seducer.*
5. Richard Rorty, "Looking Back at 'Literary Theory,'" p. 65f.
6. Franco Moretti, "Conjectures on World Literature," p. 68.
7. Richard Rorty, "Looking Back at 'Literary Theory,'" p. 66.

Bibliography

General

Adelson, Leslie A. *The Turkish Turn in Contemporary German Literature: Toward a New Critical Grammar of Migration.* New York: Palgrave Macmillan, 2005.

Adorno, Theodor W. *Aesthetic Theory* (1970). London: Athlone, 2002.

———. "Cultural Criticism and Society" (1949). In *Prisms.* London: Spearman, 1967.

———. *Minima Moralia: Reflections on a Damaged Life* (1951). London: Verso, 2005.

———. "The Position of the Narrator in the Contemporary Novel" (1954). In *Notes to Literature.* Vol. 1. New York: Columbia University Press, 1991.

Alter, Robert. *Rogue's Progress: Studies in the Picaresque Novel.* Cambridge, MA: Harvard University Press, 1965.

Anderson, Benedict. *Imagined Communities: Reflections on the Origin and Spread of Nationalism* (1983). London: Verso, 1991.

Appadurai, Arjun. *Modernity at Large: Cultural Dimensions in Globalization.* Minneapolis: University of Minnesota Press, 1996.

Appiah, Kwame Anthony. "Cosmopolitan Patriots." In Cheah and Robbins, *Cosmopolitics.*

Apter, Emily. *The Translation Zone: A New Comparative Literature.* Princeton and Oxford: Princeton University Press, 2006.

Arnold, Heinz Ludwig, ed. *Text + Kritik.* 5th reprint. Munich, 1978.

Auerbach, Erich. "Philology and Weltliteratur" (1951). *The Centennial Review* 13 (1969).

Bakhtin, M. M. *The Dialogic Imagination* (1981). Austin: University of Texas Press, 1994.

———. "Epic and Novel." In *The Dialogic Imagination.*

———. *Problems of Dostoevsky's Poetics* (1929). Minnesota: University of Minnesota Press, 1984; 1993.

Barthes, Roland. "The Death of the Author" (1967–1968). In *Image, Music, Text.* London: Fontana, 1977.

———. "From Work to Text" (1971). In *Image, Music, Text.*

———. "L'effet du réel" (1968). In *Œuvres complètes (1966–1973).* Vol. 2. Paris: Éditions de Seuil, 1994.

———. "La phrase du Flaubert" (1968). In *Œuvres complètes.* Vol. 2.

Bassnett, Susan. *Comparative Literature: A Critical Introduction.* Oxford: Blackwell, 1993.

———. *Translation Studies* (1987). London: Routledge, 2002.

Bauman, Zygmunt. *Globalization: The Human Consequences.* Cambridge: Polity Press, 1998.

Benjamin, Walter. "On the Concept of History" (1940). In *Selected Writings.* Vol. 4, 1938–40. Cambridge and London: Belknap Press of Harvard University Press, 2003.

———. "The Storyteller" (1936). In *Selected Writings.* Vol. 3, 1935–38. Cambridge and London: Belknap Press of Harvard University Press, 2002.

Bergson, Henri. *Creative Evolution* (1907). London: Macmillan, 1911; 1960.

———. *Time and Free Will: An Essay on the Immediate Data of Consciousness* (1889). London: George Allen and Unwin, 1910.

Bernheimer, Charles, ed. *Comparative Literature in the Age of Multiculturalism.* Baltimore, MD: Johns Hopkins University Press, 1995.

Bhabha, Homi K. "Introduction: Narrating the Nation." In Bhabha, *Nation and Narration.*

———. *The Location of Culture.* London: Routledge, 1994.

Bhabha, Homi K., ed. *Nation and Narration.* London: Routledge, 1990.

Boehmer, Elleke. *Colonial & Postcolonial Literature: Migrant Metaphors.* Oxford: Oxford University Press, 1995.

Bohrer, Karl Heinz. "Erinnerungslosigkeit" (2001). In *Ekstasen der Zeit.* Munich: Hanser, 2003.

Brandes, Georg. *The Emigrant Literature* (1867). In *Main Currents in Nineteenth Century Literature.* Vol. 1. London: William Heinemann, 1901.

Brodsky, Joseph. "The Condition We Call Exile, or Acorns Aweigh." In *On Grief and Reason: Essays.* New York: Farrar Straus Giroux, 1995.

Bromley, Roger. *Narratives For a New Belonging: Diasporic Cultural Fictions.* Edinburgh: Edinburgh University Press, 2001.

Brooks, Peter. "The Storyteller." In *Psychoanalysis and Storytelling.* Oxford: Blackwell, 1994.

Casanova, Pascale. *La république mondiale des lettres.* Paris: Éditions de Seuil, 1999.

Castles, Stephen and Mark J. Miller. *The Age of Migration* (1983). London: Macmillan, 1998.

Chambers, Iain. *Migrancy, Culture, Identity.* London: Routledge, 1994.

Cheah, Pheng. "The Cosmopolitical—Today." In Cheah and Robbins, *Cosmopolitics.*

———. *Spectral Nationality: Passages of Freedom from Kant to Postcolonial Literatures of Liberation.* New York: Columbia University Press, 2003.

Cheah, Pheng and Bruce Robbins, eds. *Cosmopolitics: Thinking and Feeling Beyond the Nation.* Minnesota: University of Minnesota Press, 1998.

Cohen, Margaret. "Travelling Genres." *New Literary History* 34, no. 3 (2003).

Cooppan, Vilashini. "World Literature and Global Theory: Comparative Literature for the New Millennium." *Symploke* 9, no. 1–2 (2001).

Damrosch, David. *What is World Literature?* Princeton, NJ: Princeton University Press, 2003.

———. "World Literature in a Postcanonical, Hypercanonical Age." In Saussy, *Comparative Literature in an Age of Globalization.*

Deleuze, Gilles. "Bergson, 1859–1941." In *Desert Islands and Other Texts, 1953–1974.* Cambridge and London: MIT Press, 2004.

———. *Bergsonism* (1966). New York: Zone Books, 1991.

———. "Bergson's Conception of Difference." In *Desert Islands.*

———. *Logic of Sense* (1969). London: Athlone, 1990.

———. *Negotiations: 1972–1990.* New York: Columbia University Press, 1995.

———. *Proust and Signs* (1964; 1973). London: Athlone, 2000.

———. "The Simulacrum and Ancient Philosophy" (1968). In *Logic of Sense.*

Deleuze, Gilles and Claire Parnet. *Dialogues.* London: Athlone, 1987.

Deleuze, Gilles and Félix Guattari. *Kafka: Toward a Minor Literature* (1975). Minnesota: University of Minnesota Press, 1986.

———. "Rhizome." In *A Thousand Plateaus.*

———. *A Thousand Plateaus* (1980). Minnesota: University of Minnesota Press, 1987.

———. *What is Philosophy?* (1995). London: Verso, 1995.

Doody, Margaret Anne. *The True Story of the Novel* (1986). New Brunswick, NJ: Rutgers University Press, 1997.

Eco, Umberto. "The Poetics of the Open Work." In *The Open Work.* Cambridge, MA: Harvard University Press, 1989.

Faulkner, William. *The Sound and the Fury* (1929). London and New York: W. W. Norton, 1987.

Fellini, Federico. *Fellini on Fellini.* London: Methuen, 1976.

Fielding, Henry. *The History of Tom Jones, a Foundling* (1749). New York: W. W. Norton, 1973; 1995.

Flaubert, Gustave. *The Dictionary of Received Ideas.* London: Penguin, 1994.

———. *Sentimental Education* (1869). London: Penguin, 2004.

Fontane, Theodor. *Effi Briest* (1895). In *Sämtliche Werke.* Vol. 7. Munich: Nymphenburger Verlagshandlung, 1959–75.

Forster, E.M. *Aspects of the Novel* (1927). London: Penguin, 2005.

Foucault, Michel. "What is an Author?" In *Language, Counter-Memory, Practice.* London: Blackwell, 1977.

Freud, Sigmund. *Civilization and Its Discontents* (1929). In *Complete Psychological Works: Standard Edition.* Vol. 21. London: Hogarth, 1978–81.

Gumbrecht, Hans Ulrich. *Production of Presence: What Meaning Cannot Convey.* Palo Alto, CA: Stanford University Press, 2003.

Gurr, Andrew. *Writers in Exile: The Identity of Home in Modern Literature.* Sussex: Harvester, 1981.

Hall, Stuart. "Minimal Selves." In *Identity: The Real Me,* ICA Document 6, 1988.

Hegel, G.W.F. *Aesthetics: Lectures on Fine Art.* Vols. 1–2. Oxford: Clarendon, 1998.

Hutcheon, Linda. *A Poetics of Postmodernism.* London: Routledge, 1988.

Iser, Wolfgang. *The Implied Reader: Patterns of Communication in Prose Fiction from Bunyan to Beckett* (1972). Baltimore, MD: Johns Hopkins University Press, 1974.

Kezich, Tullio. *Il dolce cinema*. Milan: Bompiani, 1978.

King, Bruce, ed. *1948–2000: The Internationalization of English Literature*. In *The Oxford English Literary History*. Vol. 13. Oxford: Oxford University Press, 2004.

Kongslien, Ingeborg. "Migrant or Multicultural Literature in the Nordic Countries." In *Nordic Voices*, edited by Jenny F. Grønn. Oslo: Nordbok, 2005.

Kushner, Eva. *The Living Prism: Itineraries in Comparative Literature*. Montréal and Ithaca: McGill-Queen's University Press, 2001.

Levin, Harry. "Literature and Exile" (1959). In *Refractions: Essays in Comparative Literature*. New York: Oxford University Press, 1966.

Lukács, Georg. *Entwicklungsgeschichte des modernen Dramas* (1911). In *Werke*. Vol. 15. Darmstadt und Neuwied: Luchterhand, 1981.

———. *The Theory of the Novel* (1916–1920). London: Merlin, 1971.

———. "Zur Theorie der Literaturgeschichte" (1910). In Arnold, *Text + Kritik*, 1973, no. 39–40.

Madsen, Peter. "World Literature and World Thoughts." In Prendergast, *Debating World Literature*.

Mann, Thomas. *The Magic Mountain* (1924). New York: A. A. Knopf, 2005.

McHale, Brian. *Postmodernist Fiction* (1987). London: Routledge, 1996.

Moretti, Franco. "Conjectures on World Literature." *New Left Review* 1 (2000).

———. *Graphs, Maps, Trees: Abstract Models for a Literary History*. London: Verso, 2005.

———. *Modern Epic: The World-System from Goethe to García Marquez*. London: Verso, 1996.

———. "The Soul and the Harpy: Reflections on the Aims and Methods of Literary Historiography." In *Signs Taken for Wonders: On the Sociology of Literary Forms*. London: Verso, 1983.

———. *The Way of the World: The Bildungsroman in European Culture* (1987). London: Verso, 2000.

Naipaul, V.S. *The Enigma of Arrival*. New York: Alfred A. Knopf, 1987.

Nietzsche, Friedrich. *Briefwechsel. 1.2. September 1864–April 1869*. Berlin: Walter de Gruyter, 1975.

Pavel, Thomas. *La pensée du roman*. Paris: Gallimard, 2003.

Prendergast, Christopher, ed. *Debating World Literature*. London: Verso, 2004.

———. "Introduction." In Prendergast, *Debating World Literature*.

———. "The World Republic of Letters." In Prendergast, *Debating World Literature*.

Proust, Marcel. *In Search of Lost Time I–VI* (1913–27). London: Penguin, 2003.

Renan, Ernest. "What is a Nation?" (1882). In Bhabha, *Nation and Narration*.

Rilke, R.M. *The Notebooks of Malte Laurids Brigge* (1910). New York: W. W. Norton, 1992.

Rorty, Richard. "Looking Back at 'Literary Theory.'" In Saussy, *Comparative Literature in an Age of Globalization*.

Said, Edward. *Culture and Imperialism*. London: Vintage, 1993.

———. "Reflections on Exile" (1984). In *Reflections on Exile and Other Essays*. Cambridge, MA: Harvard University Press, 2002.

———. *The World, the Text, and the Critic.* Cambridge, MA: Harvard University Press, 1983.

Sartre, Jean-Paul. *The Reprieve.* London: Vintage, 1992.

Saussy, Haun, ed. *Comparative Literature in an Age of Globalization.* Baltimore, MD: Johns Hopkins University Press, 2006.

Sebald, W.G. *Austerlitz* (2001). London: Penguin, 2002.

———. *The Emigrants* (1992). London: Vintage, 2002.

Seyhan, Azade. *Writing Outside the Nation.* Princeton and Oxford: Princeton University Press, 2001.

Shakespeare, William. *Coriolanus* (1605–10). London and New York: Methuen, 1987.

Sophocles. *Oedipus at Colonus* (401–406 BC). Cambridge and London: Harvard University Press, 1994; 1998.

Sommer, Roy. *Fictions of Migration. Ein Beitrag zur Theorie und Gattungstypologie des zeitgenössischen interkulturellen Romans in Großbritannien.* Trier: Wissenschaftlicher Verlag Trier, 2001.

Spivak, Gayatri Chakravorty. *Death of a Discipline.* New York: Columbia University Press, 2003.

Steiner, George. *Extraterritorial* (1971). London: Faber and Faber, 1972.

Stevenson, Randall, ed. *1960–2000: The Last of England?* In *The Oxford English Literary History.* Vol. 12. Oxford: Oxford University Press, 2004.

Suvin, Darko. "Displaced Persons." *New Left Review* 31 (2005).

Thomsen, Mads Rosendahl. *Mapping World Literature: International Canonization and Transnational Literatures.* London: Continuum, 2008.

Tolstoy, Leo. *Anna Karenina* (1875–77). London: Penguin, 2003.

Walkowitz, Rebecca L. "The Location of Literature: The Transnational Book and the Migrant Writer." *Contemporary Literature* 47, no. 4. (2006).

Waugh, Patricia. *Metafiction.* London: Routledge, 1984.

Zola, Émile. *Germinal* (1885). Montana: Kessinger, 2005.

By Günter Grass

Beim Häuten der Zwiebel. Göttingen: Steidl, 2006.

The Call of the Toad (1992). New York: Harcourt Brace Jovanovich, 1992.

Cat and Mouse (1961). San Diego, CA: Harcourt Brace, 1963.

Crabwalk (2002). London: Faber and Faber, 2003.

Der Bürger und seine Stimme: Reden, Aufsätze, Kommentare. Darmstadt: Luchterhand, 1974.

Dog Years (1963). New York: Harcourt, Brace & World, 1965.

The Flounder (1977). New York: Harcourt Brace Jovanovich, 1978.

"Fortsetzung folgt . . ." Göttingen: Steidl, 1999.

From the Diary of a Snail (1972). New York: Harcourt Brace Jovanovich, 1973.

Fünf Jahrzehnte: Ein Werkstattsbericht. Frankfurt a.M.: Verlag Buchhändler-Vereinigung, 2001.

My Century (1999). New York: Harcourt Brace, 1999.

On Writing and Politics, 1967–1983. London: Penguin, 1987.
"Shame and Disgrace" (1989). In *Two States One Nation?*
"Short Speech by a Rootless Cosmopolitan." In *Speak Out!*
Speak Out! Speeches, Open Letters, Commentaries. London: Secker & Warburg, 1969.
"Speech to a Young Voter Who Feels Tempted to Vote for the N.P.D." (1966). In
    Speak Out!
The Tin Drum (1959). London: Secker & Warburg, 1962.
"*The Tin Drum* in Retrospect or The Author as Dubious Witness" (1973). In *On
    Writing and Politics.*
Too Far Afield (1995). London: Faber and Faber, 2000.
Two States One Nation? San Diego, CA: Harcourt Brace Jovanovich, 1990.
"Writing after Auschwitz" (1990). In *Two States One Nation?*

On Günter Grass

Arnold, Heinz Ludwig. "Gespräche mit Günter Grass." I. Berlin, November 28,
    1970, II. Göttingen, September 14, 1977. In Arnold, *Text + Kritik.*
———, ed. *Text + Kritik,* 1;1a, 5th reprint, 1978.
Arnold, Heinz Ludwig and Franz Josef Görtz, eds. *Dokumente zur politische
    Wirkung.* Munich: Richard Boorberg Verlag, 1971.
Brode, Hanspeter. *Günter Grass.* Munich: C. H. Beck, 1979.
Croft, Helen. "Günter Grass's *Katz und Maus.*" In O'Neill, *Critical Essays on Günter
    Grass.*
Cunliffe, W. G. "Aspects of the Absurd in Günter Grass." In O'Neill, *Critical Essays
    on Günter Grass.*
Frank, Søren. "Territories and Histories. Transgressive 'Space Travels' and 'Time
    Travels' in Grass's *Dog Years.*" *Quest* 2 (2006).
Hollington, Michael. *Günter Grass: The Writer in a Pluralist Society.* London: Marion
    Boyars, 1980.
Just, Georg. *Darstellung und Appell in der "Blechtrommel" von Günter Grass.
    Darstellungsästhetik versus Wirkungsästhetik.* Frankfurt a.M.: Athenäum Verlag,
    1972.
Keele, Alan F. *Understanding Günter Grass.* Columbia: University of South Carolina
    Press, 1988.
Loschütz, Gert. *Von Buch zu Buch—Günter Grass in der Kritik. Eine Dokumentation.*
    Berlin: Luchterhand, 1968.
Madsen, Peter. "Vidnesbyrd fra neden—*Bliktrommen.*" In *Kultur og Klasse* 95 (2003).
Miles, Keith. *Günter Grass,* London: Vision, 1975.
Neuhaus, Volker. *Günter Grass.* 2nd rev. ed. Stuttgart: Metzler, 1993.
O'Neill, Patrick, ed. *Critical Essays on Günter Grass.* Boston: G.K. Hall, 1987.
———. "Introduction." In O'Neill, *Critical Essays on Günter Grass.*
Preece, Julian. *The Life and Works of Günter Grass: Literature, History, Politics.*
    Basingstoke: Palgrave Macmillan, 2001.

Reddick, John. *The 'Danzig Trilogy' of Günter Grass*. New York: Harcourt Brace Jovanovich, 1975.

Reich-Ranicki, Marcel. *Günter Grass. Aufsätze*. Frankfurt a.m.: Fischer, 1994.

Richter, Frank-Raymund. *Die Zerschlagene Wirklichkeit. Überlegungen zur Form der Danzig-Trilogie von Günter Grass*. Bonn: Bouvier Verlag Herbert Grundmann, 1977.

——. *Günter Grass. Die Vergangenheitsbewältigung in der Danzig-Trilogie*. Bonn: Bouvier Verlag Herbert Grundmann, 1979.

Rushdie, Salman. "Günter Grass" (1984). In *Imaginary Homelands: Essays and Criticism 1981–91*. London: Granta Books, 1991.

Steiner, George. "The Hollow Miracle" (1959). In *Language and Silence*. New York: Atheneum, 1967.

——. "The Nerve of Günter Grass" (1964). In O'Neill, *Critical Essays on Günter Grass*.

Weber, Alexander. *Günter Grass's Use of Baroque Literature*. London: Maney and Son, 1995.

Wormweg, Heinrich. *Günter Grass*. Hamburg: Rowohlt Taschenbuch Verlag, 2002.

Ziolkowski, Theodore. "Günter Grass's Century." *World Literature Today* 74, no.1 (2000).

Øhrgaard, Per. *Fortsættelse følger . . . Et essay om Günter Grass*. Copenhagen: Gyldendal, 2002.

By Milan Kundera

The Art of the Novel (1986). London: Faber and Faber, 1988.

The Book of Laughter and Forgetting (1979). London: Faber and Faber, 1982.

The Curtain (2005). London: Faber and Faber, 2007.

The Farewell Party (1976). New York: Knopf, 1976.

"La francophobie, ca existe," *Le Monde*, September 24, 1993. Cited from Chvatík, *Le monde romanesque de Milan Kundera*.

Identity (1997). London: Faber and Faber, 1998.

Ignorance (2000). London: Faber and Faber, 2002.

Immortality (1988). London: Faber and Faber, 1991.

The Joke (1967). London: Faber and Faber, 1983.

Laughable Loves (1968; 1981). New York: Knopf, 1974.

Life is Elsewhere (1973). New York: Knopf, 1974.

"Un Occident kidnappé—ou la tragédie de l'Europe centrale". *Le Débat* 27 (1983).

"Le pari de la littérature tchèque." *Liberté* 135 (1981).

Slowness (1995). London: Faber and Faber, 1997.

"Speech made at the Fourth Congress of the Czechoslovak Writers' Union June 27–29, 1967." In *Writers Against Rulers,* edited by Dušan Hamšík. New York: Random House, 1971.

Testaments Betrayed: An Essay in Nine Parts (1993). London: Faber and Faber, 1995.

The Unbearable Lightness of Being (1984). London: Faber and Faber, 1999.

On Milan Kundera

Aji, Aron, ed. *Milan Kundera and the Art of Fiction: Critical Essays*. New York and London: Garland Publishing, 1992.

Bugge, Peter. "Clementis's Hat; or, Is Kundera a Palimpsest?" *Kosmas* 16, no. 2 (2003).

Caldwell, Ann Stewart. "The Intrusive Narrative Voice of Milan Kundera." *Review of Contemporary Fiction* 9, no. 2 (1989).

Carlisle, Olga. "A Talk With Milan Kundera." *New York Times*, May 19, 1985.

Chvatík, Květoslav. *Le monde romanesque de Milan Kundera*. Paris: Gallimard, 2005.

Čulík, Jan. http://www2.arts.gla.ac.uk/Slavonic/Kundera.htm.

Jungman, Milan. "Kunderian Paradoxes." In Aji, *Milan Kundera and the Art of Fiction: Critical Essays*.

Kimball, Roger. "The Ambiguities of Milan Kundera." *The New Criterion* 4, no. 5 (1986).

Lodge, David. "Milan Kundera and the Idea of the Author in Modern Criticism." *Critical Quarterly* 26, nos. 1/2 (1984).

O'Brien, John. "Milan Kundera: Meaning, Play, and the Role of the Author." *Critique: Studies in Contemporary Fiction* 34, no. 1 (1992).

Petro, Peter, ed. *Critical Essays on Milan Kundera*. New York: G.K. Hall, 1999.

Pichova, Hana. "The Narrator in Milan Kundera's *The Unbearable Lightness of Being*." *The Slavic and East European Journal* 36, no. 2 (1992).

Ricard, François. *Agnès's Final Afternoon: An Essay on the Work of Milan Kundera*. London: Faber and Faber, 2003.

Roth, Philip. "In Defense of Intimacy." *London Times Magazine*, May 20, 1984.

———. "The Most Original Book of the Season." *New York Times Book Review*, November 30, 1980.

Scarpetta, Guy. "Kundera's Quartet (On *The Unbearable Lightness of Being*)." *Salmagundi* 73 (1987).

Straus, Nina Pelikan. "Erasing History and Deconstructing the Text: Milan Kundera's *The Book of Laughter and Forgetting*." *Critique* 28, no. 2 (1987).

Wawrzycka, Jolanta W. "Betrayal as a Flight from Kitsch in *The Unbearable Lightness of Being*." In Aji, *Milan Kundera and the Art of Fiction*.

By Salman Rushdie

East, West (1994). London: Jonathan Cape, 1994.

Fury (2001). London: Jonathan Cape, 2001.

Grimus (1975). London: Vintage, 1996.

The Ground Beneath Her Feet (1999). New York: Henry Holt, 1999.

Haroun and the Sea of Stories (1990). London: Granta Books, 1991.

Imaginary Homelands: Essays and Criticism 1981–91 (1991). London: Granta Books, 1992.

The Jaguar Smile: A Nicaraguan Journey (1987). London: Picador, 1997.

Midnight's Children (1981). London: Vintage, 1995.

The Moor's Last Sigh (1995). London: Vintage, 1994.

The Satanic Verses (1988). New York: Viking, 1989.

Shalimar the Clown (2005). London: Jonathan Cape, 2005.

Shame (1983). London: Vintage, 1995.

Step Across This Line: Collected Nonfiction 1992–2002 (2002). New York: Random House, 2002.

The Wizard of Oz (1992). London: British Film Institute, 1998.

On Salman Rushdie

Bader, Rudolf. "Indian Tin Drum." *International Fiction Review* 11, no. 2 (1984).

Ball, John Clement. "An Interview with Salman Rushdie" (1988). In Reder, *Conversations with Salman Rushdie.*

Batty, Nancy E. "The Art of Suspense: Rushdie's 1001 (Mid-)Nights." *ARIEL* 18, no. 3 (1987).

Birch, David. "Postmodernist Chutneys." *Textual Practice* 5, no. 1 (1991).

Brennan, Timothy. *Salman Rushdie and the Third World.* London: Macmillan, 1989.

Cundy, Catherine. *Salman Rushdie.* Manchester: Manchester University Press, 1996.

Durix, Jean-Pierre. "Magic Realism in *Midnight's Children.*" *Commonwealth* 8, no. 1 (1985).

———. "Salman Rushdie: Interview" (1982). In Reder, *Conversations with Salman Rushdie.*

Dutheil de la Rochère, M.H. *Origin and Originality in Rushdie's Fiction.* Frankfurt a.M.: Peter Lang, 1999.

Finney, Brian. "Demonizing Discourse in Salman Rushdie's *The Satanic Verses.*" *ARIEL* 29, no. 3 (1998).

Fletcher, M.D., ed. *Reading Rushdie: Perspectives on the Fiction of Salman Rushdie.* Amsterdam: Rodopi, 1994.

Frank, Søren. "Medier, migration og narration. Salman Rushdie og den moderne subjektivitet." *Apparatur* 13 (2006).

———. "Pas og migration. Salman Rushdie og den transnationale identitet." In *Paskultur,* edited by Jesper Gulddal and Mette Mortensen. Copenhagen: Informations Forlag, 2004.

———. "Saleems elefantiasis. Rushdies *Midnight's Children* som encyklopædisk projekt." *Passage* 47 (2003).

———. *Salman Rushdies kartografi.* Odense: University Press of Southern Denmark, 2003.

Gonzalez, Madelena. *Fiction after the Fatwa: Salman Rushdie and the Charm of Catastrophe.* Amsterdam and New York: Rodopi, 2004.

Goonetilleke, D.C.R.A. *Salman Rushdie.* London: Macmillan, 1998.

Grant, Damien. *Salman Rushdie.* Plymouth: Northcote House, 1999.

Grass, Günter and Salman Rushdie. "Fictions Are Lies That Tell the Truth: Salman Rushdie and Günter Grass: In Conversation" (1985). In Reder, *Conversations with Salman Rushdie.*

Haffenden, John. "Salmen Rushdie" (1983). In Reder, *Conversations with Salman Rushdie.*

Hamilton, Ian. "The First Life of Salman Rushdie." *New Yorker*, December 25–January 1, 1995–96.

Harrison, James. *Salman Rushdie*. New York: Twayne Publishers, 1992.

Jussawalla, Feroza. "Beyond Indianness: The Stylistic Concerns of *Midnight's Children*." *Journal of Indian Writing in English* 12, no. 2 (1984).

Kerr, David. "Migration and the Human Spirit in Salman Rushdie's *The Satanic Verses*." *Commonwealth Review* 2, no. 1/2 (1990–1991).

King, Bruce. "Who Wrote *The Satanic Verses?*" *World Literature Today* 63, no. 3 (1989).

Kirpal, V., ed. *The New Indian Novel in English: A Study of the 1980s*. New Delhi, 1990.

Kortenaar, Neil Ten. "*Midnight's Children* and the Allegory of History." *ARIEL* 26, no. 2 (1995).

Krishnaswamy, Revathi. "Mythologies of Migrancy: Postcolonialism, Postmodernism and the Politics of (Dis)Location." *ARIEL* 26, no. 1 (1995).

Kuortti, Joel. *Fictions to Live In: Narration as an Argument for Fiction in Salman Rushdie's Novels*. Frankfurt a.M.: Peter Lang, 1998.

Lipscomb, David. "Caught in a Strange Middle Ground: Contesting History in Salman Rushdie's *Midnight's Children*." *Diaspora* 1, no. 2 (1991).

Malak, Amin. "Reading the Crisis: The Polemics of Salman Rushdie's *The Satanic Verses*." *ARIEL* 20, no. 4 (1989).

McCabe et al. "Interview: Salman Rushdie Talks to the London Consortium About *The Satanic Verses*." *Critical Quarterly* 38, no. 1 (1996).

Merivale, Patricia. "Saleem Fathered By Oskar: *Midnight's Children*, Magic Realism, and *The Tin Drum*." In *Magical Realism: Theory, History, Community*, edited by Lois P. Zamora and Wendy B. Faris. Durham, NC: Duke University Press, 1995.

Naik, M.K. "A Life of Fragments: The Fate of Identity in *Midnight's Children*." *Indian Literary Review* 3, no. 3 (1985).

Parameswaran, Uma. *The Perforated Sheet: Essays on Salman Rushdie's Art*. Madras: Affiliated East-West Press, 1988.

Pathak, R.S. "History and the Individual in the Novels of Rushdie." *Commonwealth Review* 1, no. 2 (1990).

———. "Identity Crisis in the Novels of Salman Rushdie." *Language Forum* 18, no. 1/2 (1992).

Petersson, Margareta. *Unending Metamorphoses. Myth, Satire and Religion in Salman Rushdie's Novels*. Lund: Lund University Press, 1996.

Rao, M. Madhusudhana. "Quest For Identity: A Study of the Narrative in Rushdie's *Midnight's Children*." *Literary Criterion* 25, no. 4 (1990).

Reder, Michael R., ed. *Conversations with Salman Rushdie*. Jackson, MS: University Press of Mississippi, 2000.

Rombes, Nicholas D., Jr. "*The Satanic Verses* as a Cinematic Narrative." *Literature/Film Quarterly* 21, no. 1 (1993).

Sage, Vic. "The 'God-Shaped Hole': Salman Rushdie and the Myth of Origins." *Hungarian Studies in English* 22 (1991).

Sanga, Jaina C. *Salman Rushdie's Postcolonial Metaphors—Migration, Translation, Hybridity, Blasphemy, and Globalization.* Westport, CT: Greenwood, 2001.

Spivak, Gayatri C. "Reading *The Satanic Verses.*" In *What is an author?* edited by Maurice Biriotti and Nicola Miller. Manchester: Manchester University Press, 1993.

Srivastava, Aruna. "*The Empire Writes Back*: Language and History in *Shame* and *Midnight's Children.*" *ARIEL* 20, no. 4 (1989).

Suter, Davis W. "Of the Devil's Party: The Marriage of Heaven and Hell in *Satanic Verses.*" *South Asian Review* 16, no. 13 (1992).

Taneja, G.R. and R.K. Dhawan, eds. *The Novels of Salman Rushdie.* New Delhi: Indian Society for Commonwealth Studies, 1992.

By Jan Kjærstad

The Conqueror (1996). New York: Arcadia Books, 2006.

Menneskets felt. Oslo: Aschehoug, 1997.

Menneskets matrise. Oslo: Aschehoug, 1989.

Menneskets nett. Oslo: Aschehoug, 2004.

Oppdageren (The Discoverer). Oslo: Aschehoug, 1999.

The Seducer (1993). New York: Arcadia Books, 2003.

On Jan Kjærstad

Kyndrup, Morten. "Udenfor, indeni. Et passageværk. Om Jan Kjærstads romantrilogi." *Passage* 50 (2004).

Markussen, Bjarne. *Romanens optikk: komposisjon og persepsjon i Jan Kjærstads* Rand og Svein Jarvolls En australiareise. Kristiansand: Høyskoleforlaget, 2003.

Mogensen, Tine Engel. *Den gode historie.* Odense: University Press of Southern Denmark, 2002.

———. "Mellem himmel og helvede. Om stemmer i Jan Kjærstads *Forføreren* og *Erobreren.*" *Edda* 4 (1998).

Riis, Signe Vestergaard. "Fra postkolonialisme til postnationalisme. Jan Kjærstads *Oppdageren* som gendigtet nationalfortælling." *Spring* 22 (2004).

Tygstrup, Frederik. "Den demiurgiske romanhelt. Nogle bemærkninger til Jan Kjærstads *Forføreren.*" *Kritik* 111 (1994).

Index